THE WONDERFUL COUNTRY

THE
WONDERFUL
COUNTRY

A *NOVEL BY* TOM LEA

WITH DRAWINGS BY THE AUTHOR

LITTLE, BROWN AND COMPANY
BOSTON

To the memory of
my mother and father
who lived at the pass

"Oh, how I wish I had the power
to describe the wonderful country
as I saw it then."

Texas Ranger JAMES B. GILLETT

CONTENTS

PART ONE

CHAPTER I

An hour before daylight the wind came up and swept along the floor of the desert, moving the sand, changing the shapes of the hummocks under the dark mesquite. It blew across the bare mesas, over the summit stones of the mountains, down to a desert river flowing south through a pass where hills pitched steep to the edges of the narrowed water. Below the pass, the wind followed the stream into a valley where it found the houses of a lonely town sleeping by trees and plowed fields.

Hidden and small, four separate companies of travelers rode that morning before sunrise toward the lonely town. Unknown to each other, discovered only by the wind, they rode converging from the four compass points of the wide circling dark.

North, the wind struck a blow at the backs of three men hunched on the seats of an open buckboard headed south along the trees by the river. The wind bit at the hands of the driver holding the lines, of the man holding the rifle across his knees, of the man peering into the darkness by the mail sacks and the baggage.

West, on a long slope to the river, the wind puffed a sting of grit against the lips of six mounted cavalrymen and an officer escorting a mule-drawn ambulance headed east. The wind flapped at the fastenings on the wagon curtains; behind the canvas it brushed the face of a frightened woman alone on the jolting seat in the dark.

East, the wind stirred the dagger points of the stiff-rooted soap-weed, clacking seeds in the pods dry on the brittle stalks. It blew powdery dust on an armed convoy of seven horsemen and two loaded frontier wagons headed west. The wind caught a tink of harness rings and a jingle of spur rowels in a multiple scuff of hooves, and lost them in the brush nearer the river.

South, in the twisting ruts of a road among hills and high mounded dunes, the wind cut against the moving shape of a massive high-wheeled Mexican cart. A driver with a pole walked beside the long double file of yoked oxen that brought the cart lumbering in the darkness. Two horsemen rode guarding the cart, headed north.

CHAPTER II

DIEGO CASAS, who knew the road and led the way, tightened rein and waited for the other horseman who came following the cart as rear guard.

"From here you could see the pass," Casas said. He was hoarse from the cold and the long silence. "Our animals feel the river."

Martin Brady did not answer. It was too windy and too early yet to talk. And it was necessary to be alert. He looked into the darkness and listened.

Casas spoke again, turning in his saddle, "Thanks to God —" With his chin he indicated the morning star. "El Lucero, the bringer of the light."

Martin Brady saw it. After daylight, so near the garrison, they would not expect Apaches. Until then they would.

"A long night," Casas offered. It cheered him to say something.

From far off in the noise of the wind they heard a thin howl. The horsemen stopped. The howl quavered and broke into high wobbly-toned yelps.

"Authentic. Serenade to Lucero," Casas said. He paused. "We have music but no Indians, eh Martín?"

"Not yet." The wind blew grit on his teeth when he opened his mouth.

From low beneath the morning star a luminous faint pallor climbed the sky. It marked a line in the east, then reached slowly around the circuit of all the horizon, bringing the first gray shapes to the build of the dark earth, adding detail moment by moment in the dim developing light.

The peon Pablo walking by the oxen called out to the horsemen, "There it is!" He pointed ahead with his driving pole, beyond the shelving hills, up the shadowy valley.

Martin Brady looked north and saw the pass for the first time.

Diego Casas pointed. "The butt end of that mountain, to the right of the pass — the town of Puerto is at the foot of it, where we take the ore. On the other side of the Río Bravo. The town Del Norte is on this side."

The peon Pablo had driven oxen there before. He made another motion with his pole, and showed his teeth. "The limits of Mexico," he said, partly to himself. "Far north." He felt well about it. "Very far from Valdepeñas. — Heh!" he said to the oxen, using the pole.

Martin Brady's horse smelled the river and danced sideward chafing, checked to the plod of the oxen by the light reining from Martin Brady's hand.

"The horse Lágrimas, he wants to see gringos," Diego grinned.

Martin Brady was not sure that he wanted to see gringos himself. Today, he would see them, finally. All the way north, twenty-six days with the oxen and the heavy ore — and long before that — he had thought about it, about being again on the other side of the river. He had thought about it for years. When the *patrón* had told him to take the ore north, he wanted to go. He wanted to see what it would be like. Now he was almost there.

The wind blew harder, as if the approach of the sun were a

signal. The sky in the east turned amber above the coppery dust clouded along the sunrise horizon. It grew ruddy and then red-edged as the high sky paled and darkness left the windswept hills, the speckled flats, the twisting line of the valley. The lighted tops of the mountains were pink in the first reaching rays before the sun itself came climbing fiery in the east. Then blue shadows sprang slanting far and thin from the wheels of the cart and the hooves moving along the windy slope high in the first yellow sunlight. Ahead, the bell tower of the church at Del Norte stood small and white, over the tops of the brown trees.

The sky tanned with thicker dust in the growing wind. The view shortened; the sun showed like a round burning hole in the haze. Martin Brady, with mud at the corners of his eyes, rode holding his horse to a jumpy walk, trying to see into the wind, into the grit beyond the river.

He counted the fourteen years since the night he was the scared boy leaving the country. Fourteen years in Mexico, more than half his life. There had been a long time when that night haunted him; he swam the river in his dreams, getting away, and waked up afraid. It came to him now, here at that river.

He looked over at his companion Diego Casas, thinking of the debt he owed Diego's father, old Mateo, who hid him that night. Who took him with the wagons to Valdepeñas, fed him, helped him, taught him, long ago. The old man was proud of him. "This kid Martín used his father's pistol on his father's killer," Mateo Casas boasted.

They won't remember it on the other side now, of course they won't, Martin Brady thought. It was too long ago, too far down the river. They won't remember Martin Brady from Kingdom Prairie, Missouri. They will take him for a Mexican. He guessed he was a Mexican. Not really. He discovered himself guessing it in English and he suddenly felt self-conscious about crossing the river, today. He pulled his horse toward Diego's.

"Dieguito, you can tell me now. Did we bring it to the pass?"

"I will tell you, boy. We brought it. I hope the water is low in the river. This load of rock won't swim. Anyway, our first thing is to go get the Señor Sterner from the other side. With the arrangements. With the coyote tune, at the customs house."

"I know that. Listen, Diego, what class of man is this Sterner?"

"He has the talents of his race. He will unload the cart and fill it with things of high price from his warehouse over there. Then back we go, to Don Cipriano. Before that, Martín, *yee*, we taste a cup and feel some little fleshes! They say it has a flavor in the North."

After the long desert they were near the trees. The road down the last sandy slope led them by the first mud hut on the edge of the settlements hidden in the dusty haze ahead. A shaggy dog with yellow eyes ran out barking. It came snarling toward Pablo, who picked up a rock and hurled it. Martin Brady's horse shied. The dog ran hurt, yelping into the brush.

"Ssss-s," Pablo hissed. "You won't bite now."

A wild gust bearing sharp-grained sand hit them, and Martin Brady pulled the sombrero tighter to his head. In the Mexican boots, in the Mexican stirrups, he moved his numbed toes. His feet felt the swollen sticky way they felt when they had been too long in leather. He looked down at his frayed jacket and the greasy dust caked on the hardened edges of the wrinkles in his worn Mexican breeches. With the back of his hand he brushed at the grainy wire stubble on his chin, and felt the scales on his cracked lips. He was not exactly a sweetheart going to fiestas.

At least he would find out what they thought of him on the other side of the river. And damned to what they thought. He took a hitch at the cartridge belt strapped around his belly, and turned his mind to his business coming into town.

CHAPTER III

MAJOR
Starke Colton stopped his horse and waited for the ambulance.
Thick dust blew forward from the trotting hooves of the mules
and he turned out away from it, then spurred in alongside the
wagon. He pulled the yellow neckerchief down from over his
mouth.

"Ellen!" he called.

There was no response from inside the curtained wagon. He leaned over and slapped the canvas, calling louder.

His wife's gloved hand unfastened the forward edge of the curtain by the rear seat and he saw her veiled face in the crack where the canvas flapped loose.

"It's only a little way now," Colton raised his voice in the wind. "Just wanted to see how you are. You all right?"

Ellen Colton nodded. She was not all right, but a nod seemed the easiest way to deal with her husband's absurdity about it.

"You want to roll up a curtain, so you can see? We're coming into the pass. The post is built right below the gap. How about some light on the subject?"

"If you like," she said. "I thought this terrible dust — "

"Driver!" the major commanded, "stop the wagon. Let's give Mrs. Colton some air. Roll up the curtain."

The troopers of the escort halted ahead while the driver and the major rolled up the ambulance curtains on the river side of the road.

"Some breeze, for a country that's not fastened down," Colton said to his wife, cheerfully, he hoped.

Ellen Colton looked out at her husband's red face and dusty mustache. Narrowing her eyes at the glare beyond him, she saw the sandy river bottom and the slope of the barren hill on the other side of the brown trickle of water, and the weeds bent in the wind. She did not trust herself to say anything.

"And some river, to have such a big name, Rio Grande," Colton added. "A regiment of horse could drink it dry, eh Williams?"

Williams, the driver, thought it could, sir.

When the mules started, the major rode again alongside the wagon, by the opened curtains. He tried to speak so that Williams would not hear.

"A little while longer, Ellen, and everything will be fine. I hope you are all right. You better primp now to meet the garrison." He smiled at her and put spurs to his horse.

She watched his back as he cantered forward rejoining the troopers. To follow him, she thought. To this dreadful place, oh Ellen Henderson Colton, you have followed that back of his in that uniform, to this dreadful place.

She ached in all her body, from the bruising wagon, and she felt utterly used, from trembling in the darkness. Now in the light her terror was gone, changed to raw-edged longing. She wanted only to be safe and to be clean again.

She wanted to be at Fort Jefflin. Whatever that might be, it was the blessed earth of a United States military reservation, where Ellen Colton expected some familiar things, some security, some order, in this wild, horrid, unknown place.

The hills closed in suddenly steep against the river and the road, and the travelers moved through the pass with the wind howling along its high, bare, sunlit sides. Around a turn and a last jut of hill, the valley opened out.

Colton saw his post in the distance down the river. There was the white staff flying the colors, a dim small oblong, against the mountains of Mexico. The gaunt sides of two barracks rose above the half-hidden roofs of the few buildings around what he judged was parade ground, where the wind was lifting haze streamers of sand high into the sky. He saw a corner of a stable, and the yellow shape of a great pile of hay.

As they came trotting along the road by the fence of the reservation, the sentry on duty by the guardhouse at the gate saw the wagon and its escort. Colton could not hear in the wind at that distance, but he knew what the sentry shouted; he watched the guard turn out. He saw the dressed line standing at the Carry; when he rode up, the sergeant of the guard called, "Present, *Arms!*" and Colton saluted.

The sergeant was a powerful black man wearing the crossed sabers of the Tenth Cavalry. "Order, *Arms!*" he said.

"Thank you, Sergeant. Dismiss the guard," Colton said. "Then show me to the adjutant's."

"Arms, *Port;* Break Ranks, *March,*" the sergeant barked. His Negro troopers filed toward the guardroom with their carbines, back to their interrupted card games and naps, while the sergeant stood stiffly at attention. The major's eyes were no longer upon him; Colton saw an officer riding toward the gate at a gallop. At twenty paces the officer reined and dismounted. He came forward saluting.

"Major Colton? Lieutenant Scanlon, officer of the day. We have been expecting you, sir. Welcome to Jefflin!"

"Thank you, Mr. Scanlon." Colton dismounted and shook the lieutenant's hand. "Hold these mounts," he said to the sergeant. He turned again to Scanlon.

"I would like to present you to Mrs. Colton, in the Dougherty wagon, Lieutenant, and then show her to quarters. She is tired, as you can imagine."

"I can certainly imagine it, Major. You have any trouble?"

"None. We thought we might." They came to the side of the ambulance. "Mrs. Colton, may I present Mr. Scanlon, of this garrison?"

Ellen Colton gave the lieutenant her hand. She had taken off her veil. The lieutenant was all admiration.

"Our warm welcome, Mrs. Colton. Mrs. Stoker is waiting for you, at the captain's quarters. Captain Stoker is out on scout."

"Would you show us the way now, Mr. Scanlon?" she asked. "I am a fright, in this dust!"

The two officers rode ahead of the ambulance across the sand of the forlorn parade ground. They dismounted in front of one of a row of square, squat houses facing the barracks fifty yards away.

"Mrs. Stoker!" the lieutenant called. "O Mindy!"

The door opened, and a smiling woman came out offering her hands to the new post commander.

"Starke Colton! So long since the days at Union! How good to see you, to have you here! And the new Mrs. Colton! The bachelor overwhelmed at last. I'll bet she's a darling!"

"Mindy Stoker, how are you? We got here. To eat you out of quarters till the wagon brings our stuff." He laughed. "Don't worry, it should be here soon. Come meet Ellen!"

He led her to the ambulance. "With friends, Ellen! This is Mindy Stoker. She'll care for you."

When Colton and the lieutenant had helped Ellen from the wagon, she stood unsteadily on the blowing sand, the blessed military earth.

Colton dismissed the escort, and turned to the wagon driver.

"Bring in the traps, Williams. Then tend my mount and the mules. Tend yourself too, Williams. Thank you."

Mrs. Stoker put her arm around Ellen's well-shaped waist. "You come in this minute, darling, and rest. I'll bet you're dead. And this wind, isn't it horrible?"

Ellen did not think Mrs. Stoker really minded the wind. She seemed very sturdy in it.

"Your room is waiting and as soon as you have freshened, we'll have luncheon. How I wish Lefty were here! He'll be in any day now, from Stafford. Tonight we'll have more of a meal. I've invited all the officers for you both to meet the garrison." She turned to the lieutenant. "Thank you, Victor."

"Tell the adjutant to expect me after luncheon, Mr. Scanlon," Colton called.

Mrs. Stoker showed them to the bedroom that was to be theirs until the commanding officer's quarters should be established in the empty house across the parade ground.

It was a small, clean room with a double bed, a washstand, a chest of drawers, a small mirror, and two chairs, all obviously the best in the house. When the door was closed and the Coltons were alone, Ellen burst into tears.

"I will not appear out there for any luncheon! I will not! Oh I want only to bathe — to sleep — "

She sat on the bed to cry.

" — Ellen," Colton said. "It was a bad trip, granted." He sat down beside her. "But we're here now, you see. You'll get used to it. Don't cry like that."

She would not have his arm about her.

"Let me alone. Let me rest, rest, *rest*, Starke Colton! Can't you see? Can't you hear?"

"I can see. I can hear."

He left her, closing the door. The wind whined aloud around the corners of the house. He felt tired too. He found Mindy Stoker in the kitchen.

"She's going to rest," Colton said. "Going to bed, I think. Says she can't eat." He turned to the striker cook who was making dumplings. "I wonder if I could wash my face and hands here in the kitchen."

"Come to my room, Major, please," his hostess said. "There's soap and water and clean linen." She took his arm. "Please come."

When he had washed, and combed his mustache, and brushed his thick hair, he came into the living room. The table was set, and he was hungry.

"May I smoke?" he asked. He had a cigar.

"Of course you may. I'll join you." Colton watched her take a Mexican corn shuck cigarette from a box on the table. "I am going native, you see!" Colton held a match for her.

"Well," she said to be saying something in the silence when they were both seated. "You brought us a lovely girl." A gust of wind sished sand against the one small windowpane. "Aren't you a bear for bringing her!" She smiled, indicating the world with her hand. "What army wives put up with, Starke Colton, the army will never even investigate."

"Seems to agree with you, Mindy. Ellen will catch on. How's Lefty?"

"Lefty is wonderful." She almost added, "And still a captain," but she did not. "Tell me, where did you leave the cars? How near are the tracks?"

"Cantera City. We brought the ambulance from Langman. Far enough. We came fast, without waiting for that wagonload of stuff Ellen has collected. How's the post here, Mindy?"

She hesitated a moment. "It will be better, with Starke Colton commanding. As to the post itself, at least we're near some kind of town. Milk and eggs and people occasionally, to add a note of luxury. But I do worry about Lefty when he goes out, and he has been out so much. That Fuego is a hideous, busy Indian." She puffed her cigarette. "Tell me, how is Angel Island now? The green grass, green, green, and the bay, and the wet rain and the trees? Ah me. And the Occidental Hotel of sainted memory —"

"And the dress parades and the musicales." Colton said. "And the papers rustling across the desks? What a blessing to get to troops again!"

"Good Lord protect us from soldiers. Bringing brides from musicales to Fort Jefflin, Texas." She saw Colton's face. "But not really protect us, Lord. I remember when Lefty first brought me out. Second Lieutenant Bruce Stoker and Mindy, nee Clegg, by steamboat to Ehrenburg and big blue wagon to San Carlos — "

She served the new commanding officer chicken and dumplings, and fresh milk from town. They ate with relish. When the meal was finished, Colton stayed only for the least possible polite interval, then stood and took his hat.

"Thank you, Mindy. I'm going and see this post."

He saluted and walked out into the sandstorm, across the parade ground to the adjutant's.

Scanlon was there to introduce him. He met the adjutant, a serious lieutenant named Patino, and the clerk, and two sergeants. The commanding officer's desk was in a bare room beyond the adjutant's. Colton went in, looked around, and sat down for a try at it. Piled neatly in front of him were the five post books with the familiar labels, Order Book, Letters Received, Letters Sent, Morning Report, Guard Report, ready for his inspection. He looked at them with distaste. Punctiliously placed in the center of the desk top was the adjutant's correct, written request for relief from adjutant's duty. Colton glanced at it.

"Thank you, Mr. Patino, but this will be held in abeyance." He looked up at the lieutenant. "Good adjutants do not grow on mescal bushes out there in the wind.

"Have the trumpeter sound Officer's Call for me now, if you please. I want to see everyone. Mr. Patino, as of this date the supply people are getting the well-known 'timely notice' that we are going into the field after this Fuego brute until we kill him or he quits. I want to see the quartermaster and the commissary, with all their books, in the morning. And Annual Post Inspection and Report, Mr. Patino — this is the end of March. I'll discuss that with you in the morning too."

The adjutant was taking notes. The major obviously had been digging at the blue book lately.

"Dress parade, dismounted, tomorrow, to see the condition of troops," Colton went on. "I'll inspect stables briefly this afternoon. How about telegraph?"

"In town, sir. Not built to the post yet. A courier detail is on duty at all times, and a signal sergeant quartered in the office in town."

"I want to report my arrival to Roland this afternoon by telegraph."

"I'll see it's done immediately, sir."

"No," Colton said. "I'll go in myself. See how it's run. I'd like to have a look at that town down there too. I'll ride in before Retreat. How far is it?"

"A mile, sir."

Colton heard the duty trumpeter sounding Officer's Call, his trumpeter, calling his command, on his post.

CHAPTER IV

H<small>ALF DOZING</small>
under their hatbrims in the windy glare of early afternoon, it
seemed to the three riders on Joe Wakefield's buckboard that they
had been traveling the road by the river forever. Near now to the
end of their journey, they saw the rutted tracks in the blowing
dust twist and lose themselves southward where the gap of the pass
loomed ahead.

After a night of driving hard, dreading Apaches from every
bend of the road, and the tedious hours of jolting behind the trotting mules since daylight, the men on the wagon were shaky tired.
Bitter coffee and greasy mush for breakfast at Cottonwood Station had done nothing to improve the taste of travel in their dry
mouths, and they had no whiskey. Their eyes burned with the
sand that since dawn had whirled in gusts timed and aimed at

them with what seemed a personal, grit-edged malice whenever they looked out, or opened their mouths. With little to say to each other, and in no mood to shout it in the lashing wind, the three men rode tight-lipped, in the drifts of their separate minds.

Joe Wakefield's big fingers had sweated the lines damp as he drove. Employer of four mail riders and half a dozen rigs, he seldom carried the mail himself; this trip was special and it was a pain. He was so disgusted with the contract for United States Mail Route 39094 that he felt a wry satisfaction looking forward to the time when the railroad would run him out of business. He had been up to the north end of his route to claim three abandoned mail sacks, and to hunt for the rider, and a buckboard and a team, that last week had gone out of sight on the Stafford road. The rider had jumped the country. The buckboard and mules worth four hundred dollars had disappeared. The lost mail was a headache. Wakefield brooded over what he would do when he got his hands on the thieving brown bastard that skipped. He would fix his clock, permanently. He worked his jaw thinking about it and slapped at the mules.

Mr. Tedford Naylor, sitting stiffly upright on the seat by Wakefield, was having trouble with his bowels. All his thoughts now centered upon them. It was a humiliation to ask a man like Wakefield to stop the wagon so often, and Naylor considered himself very sensitive to humiliation of any sort. In his pockets he carried the names of twenty-odd new subscribers, and three more advertisements to run in the first issue of the Puerto *Eagle*. He had been hard put to find any but the papers upon which these were written, when he asked Wakefield to stop the wagon.

Naylor's editorial and canvassing trip up the river had been both profitable and pleasant until yesterday noon when the diarrhea had seized him. He had climbed on the buckboard at midnight in Charco shaken and uncertain. Thinking it over now, he was astonished. The expectation of attack by Indians, the tension of holding Wakefield's rifle and his own pistol ready for hours in cold threatening darkness, had been highly medicinal. Yet in the relaxation since daylight, his trouble had returned. He grimly awaited the comfort of a toilet in Puerto.

Chafing on the back seat with the dust-coated baggage and mail sacks, young Ludwig Sterner considered that a certain part of his anatomy was now almost leather; it must be as seamed as the back of Mr. Wakefield's neck. Across an ocean, a continent, Ludwig Sterner in four weeks had traveled from the banks of the Fulda to the Rio Grande. He could think back into what were surely cantos of this epic only dimly now, remembering pieces as in a dream, a dream of Ludwig Sterner on swaying, pitching seats that never stopped, never. The dear parents, Gimmeke, Minna not one of them at home in Kassel could imagine it, what he had seen since S.S. *Klopstock* carried him from the gray mouth of the Elbe out upon the sea.

Holding his wool hat on his head, squinting against the blowing dust, he was proud of his immense journey. Yet he must admit to himself, if to no one else, that Uncle Sterner now appeared to live nearly at the end of the world. The last of creation. He was anxious to see the store; he wondered if it was built of mud. Frankly it was a wild place to learn a business.

Around the bend where the grainy, thorn-studded hills fell away from the river channel, the white pole of Fort Jefflin appeared, and the flag.

Seeing it again, Wakefield felt better. He cleared his throat, ready for talk, and glanced at his passengers. That wool hat on the Jakey boy reminded him of the lid on a coffeepot.

"How you making out back there, son?" Wakefield called over his shoulder.

"Ya, thank you!" Ludwig answered promptly. English was very difficult in the noise of the wind.

"I'm turning in to deliver the Jefflin sack," Wakefield told Naylor, who frowned. He felt very uneasy.

For an instant Ludwig Sterner frowned too. He glanced at the flag whipping out straight in the wind seven thousand miles from Prussians and conscription, then he stared at the sentry. The American soldier was perhaps one of the former slaves!

With the mules pulled up and stopped in front of the adjutant's, Wakefield climbed down from his seat and limbered his legs. His right foot was asleep and he stomped it.

"Would you mind watching those scoundrels for me, Mr. Naylor?" Wakefield spit toward the mules.

"And would you mind finding out for me when they expect the new commander?" Naylor answered. He worked for the Puerto *Eagle* even when he had to speak through clenched jaws. "Will you?"

The clerk was alone in the office, writing at a long table when Wakefield walked in with the mail sack.

"What's the news from over Stafford way?" the clerk asked.

"Not much." The mention of Stafford irritated Wakefield.

"Where'd you leave old Fuego?"

"Didn't see him, thank Christ — "

Tedford Naylor walked in the door. "Is there a toilet here?"

The clerk looked at him. "Toilet?"

"I said toilet!"

"There is a latrine fifty paces to the rear, Mister." He jerked his thumb over his shoulder, and raised his eyebrows at Wakefield as Naylor hurried out.

"One of my fares. Got a slipknot in the puckering string. Been stopping the wagon."

"Who is he? Lord Chesterfield?"

"He is a highly educated hired hand of Judge George Heffridge's. Name's Naylor. The judge set him up, with a newspaper."

"Looks like he needed a newspaper. Say, did you hear the news? Colton's here."

"Is that a fact?"

"Got here at noon. You must of ate his dust on the road."

"If that was all his, he can raise it, son."

"He's raising it." The clerk indicated the deserted office and the stacks of papers on his table. "I'll need a gallon of government ink to wet it down."

"Is he a pretty good man?"

"He's got those gold leaves on his straps."

"People around here don't know a gold leaf from a screwbean. He bring any new troops?"

"Nothing. A squad of escort and a wagon that goes back to Langman. He did bring his wife. Man, a good-looker!"

Wakefield was folding a mail receipt when he heard a faint rattle and shout in the wind outside. He remembered his mules.

Ludwig Sterner had taken Naylor's place on the front seat. He was alone, holding the lines as if he had live snakes by the tails. He was alternately calling for help and addressing the mules, in German, and in anguish. Wakefield got through the door just in time to see the wool hat go in the wind. He saw it sail high, and come down with a kind of wobbling magic perversity, squarely in front of the kicking mules. They spooked, breaking sideward from the hat, tilting the wagon crazy on two wheels, stinging dirt into Wakefield's face as he lunged.

"Pull them, goddammit, pull!" Wakefield yelled with his mouth full of sand. "Hold them, Buster!" He managed to catch on the skidding wagon and swing himself up clutching, climbing over, yanking the lines from Ludwig's hands.

"Ho goddamn you. Ho!" Wakefield bellowed, and bore down on the brake. The pulling tendons stood out like thongs in his thick wrists. "Ho you wall-eyed wild bog-spavined black rattle-brain sons of bitches, ho there, ho boys, whoa!"

When he had stopped them, their sides heaving, he spit sand from his mouth and looked at Ludwig. Wakefield felt sorry for him. Such a goddamned gourd-green jake of a Jew kid. The adjutant's clerk was whooping out the door; the commotion had brought troopers.

Ludwig's knuckles were white from his grip on the seat. He felt the eyes on him and did not know what to say or how to say it. Wakefield slapped him on the leg.

"You done all right, Buster," Wakefield said. He looked out at his audience and raised his voice. "None of these drillyard skinners around here ever monkeyed with mules in Dutch, did they? It rattled their hocks, didn't it? And that hat, by God, it brought fever in the south! It was a sight, son. Say, where is that hat?"

Ludwig looked and pointed ruefully out on the parade ground. The hat was still rolling.

"Well get it, boy! Run! Fore it crosses the river and somebody sews braid on it!"

He could see the white teeth showing in the black faces of the troopers. Wakefield was enjoying himself. The sight of Naylor easing around the windy corner of the adjutant's, his scissortail coat flapping, was nearly as rich as Jakey jumping for his hat.

And Naylor felt better, weak but so much better. "I told him to watch them, Wakefield! What happened?"

"They non speaken the Dootch! I got me a new star route mail rider if I can just find him some squareheaded mules! Come on, Buster!" Wakefield waved his arm. Ludwig was trying to dust the hat. "Climb this driving seat! Let's carry the Dutch mail — git up you long-eared bastards! Hear that, son? Talk mule to them!"

"Is long ear bastard," Ludwig said. "*Verdammter Maulesel.*" He held his hat on tight.

Beyond the far corner of the military fence, Wakefield and Naylor squinted at the water backed up behind the ragged dam built across the river bed. From it issued the *acequias* that irrigated the fields down the river; no one in that dry land passed without a look at the water.

Wakefield nudged Ludwig and pointed. "Son, you are seeing the sights. Right over that water you now gaze on the great repooblica of Mexico. And that dam there's what grows the beans your Uncle Ike trades in his store. No water, no beans. No beans, and we're in a hell of a fix."

Ludwig looked at the few thin streams that ran spilling over the jagged lip and sloped rock face of the downstream wall of the dam. He could not see much of Mexico because of the dust; the water was surely nothing for one who had seen the Niagara Falls, or even the dam in the Diemel above Karlshafen; he did not understand very well about the beans, either. But he nodded his head and smiled at Mr. Wakefield.

The road turned. The mules' hooves thumped across the cottonwood logs over the *acequia madre*, the mother ditch that came from just above the dam. Under them they smelled the water thick with mud flowing on its way to moisten spring planting somewhere beyond the brown trees. The buckboard followed the ditch along its weedy bank, made a climbing turn in a gale that blew the mules' tails sideward, and topped out of the river bottom jolting around a rise suddenly, into town.

CHAPTER V

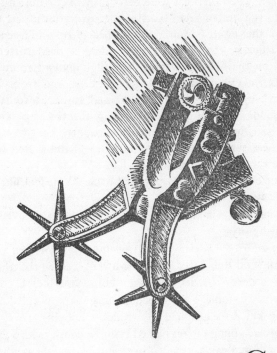

CAPTAIN John Rucker's black beard blew in the wind and the afternoon sun shone straight into his eyes. Forty-two days and seven hundred miles on the rough road west from Austin, he brought his wife and daughter and young son, his two wagons, his colored man, his livestock, and half a dozen of his picked men, into Puerto at last, to headquarters of Company E, Frontier Battalion, Texas Rangers.

The first sergeant of Company E, massive and steady Grif Miles who needed a big horse to carry him, had ridden down the river to meet Captain Rucker and his family, to welcome them, to show them the way into town.

Captain Rucker and Sergeant Miles rode talking, ahead of the spur-jingling rangers escorting the light spring wagon that moved along with the captain's wife and his daughter Louisa on the wagon seat. The horsemen were careful that their dust might not blow into the sunbonneted faces of the two womenfolk.

Behind the light wagon came a loaded freighter, and little Barney Rucker, the captain's son, riding a tired sorrel pony. Fastened on the bulging wagon sheet high above Barney's head, swayed a rickety coop of fighting chickens, and from this tall perch a red-eyed rooster suddenly crowed. It made a reedy sound in the wind. The colored man driving the towering freighter popped his whip over the mules and laughed.

"You hear that?" he called. "You hear old Rebel Red sing out to his new home? You reckon he like it?"

"How you like it?" Barney yelled back. "You feel like crowing?"

"I'm blowing! Ain't this dirt fierce? You can watch the world go by in the sky!"

Barney quirted his pony to a trot and rode forward into the horsemen. "Old Rebel Red, he just crowed! Telling the town — us rangers are here!" Barney shouted. "Hunt your holes, you rawhides, here we come!" He aimed an imaginary pistol down the street and killed six imaginary rawhides, whooping.

An angular young ranger named Print Ruebush, with a face like a good-humored eagle, reached over and playfully mashed down the crown of Barney's hat.

"Barney the button!" Print Ruebush grinned. "I'm about to turn you over to the tallow works. You and that sorrel lightning striker both!"

Print Ruebush was Barney's favorite ranger in the whole world, not only Texas. He wanted to be just like Print and he intended to be.

"Hey Print, is this here all there is to Puerto?" Barney felt he could ask Print serious things, man to man. "After coming all this way? I mean is this all there is to it, a few old mud shanties and that little bitty river?"

"What'd you have pictured off in your head? Ain't this pretty good compared to laying out in dry mesquite mottes with the tarantulars?"

"Aw, Print, I had it imagined better. I thought they was more to it. It's sure different from Travis County —"

"You'll be speaking spic and using a spade bit in no time, you ain't careful," Print said. "You'll turn cut-plug brown and eat chili peppers for breakfast and all your friends'll say, 'Why, that Barney Rucker don't even rig his drawers like a white man,' that's what they'll say. You get over there in that bad company across the river and I'll have to come after you with a rope."

"I want to see you ketch me."

"I'll bring a poker too. I'll straighten you out!"

Print laughed and ran his tongue along the grit caked on his front teeth. He wiped at them with his sleeve and looked up at the high branches of the cottonwoods. He could see the buds swelling, ready to push off last year's brown leaves.

> "Oh my trade was cinching saddles,"

he hummed, looking far away. The tops of the tall bare poplars by the *acequia* were bent in graceful curves by the wind. They were nearer leafing than the cottonwoods. Even in the dust, he could make out the first faint promise of green coming. He felt good.

> " — such a weary dreary life, .
> Riding through the heat and the cold."

Still humming, Print turned a little in his saddle and glanced guardedly toward the spring wagon seat. A look in the direction of the captain's daughter was a luxury he rationed out to himself only carefully and occasionally. Miss Louisa Rucker's face was hidden by the brim of her sunbonnet, but he knew just how it looked. He could see her pretty hands in her lap.

Captain Rucker rode in close beside his womenfolk and pointed ahead.

"Sergeant Miles tells me that's it — the place down there at the corner." He reached over and touched his wife's arm. "I'm proud of you, Kate!" he said. A smile showed in his black beard.

"I'm grateful to the Lord, John," his wife said. "Oh, I'm glad!"

"I thought we just never would get here," his daughter said.

They drew rein by the hitching rail in front of a low, plain-faced adobe. It walled the south side of the rough street for thirty sprawling yards. Barred shutters, their green paint almost gone, marked the four windows in the long wall. The only door was the *zaguán* at the middle, an archway pierced through the thick front side of the building, into an open patio, where a peach tree grew. It was in bloom, a flare of rich pink bright against the brown world and wind.

"John, look at the tree!" the captain's wife said. "It's like a welcome."

Booted rangers came from their quarters across the patio. They walked out the archway to shake hands with their captain, and stood around the wagons with their hats off, with the wind blowing their hair across their foreheads.

"Mrs. Rucker," Sergeant Miles said. Words to ladies came hard to him, but he felt the occasion, " — and Miss Louisa." Quiet and steady, he was down from his big horse. "These here are what there is of Company E. The whole front wing of this place is now your home, and we wish you a welcome. All of us are right proud that you are here."

"Thank you, Sergeant Miles. I am proud too." Kate Rucker blew her nose. Her husband helped her from the wagon.

Print Ruebush came forward hoping he could help Louisa, holding her hand, but he was disappointed. Her father swung her down and kissed her on the forehead.

"The west rim of Texas, Daughter." He looked around. "And not so lonely, either." Louisa was angry with herself for blushing.

"Wow, look at this old roost!" Barney yelled from behind the tree in the patio. He came out of the archway with his boots clomping. "Show me my diggings!"

"Barney. Settle down and be some help," his mother said. "Don't go running and calling. You help me here with the things from the wagon. Sister and I will be busy moving in and fixing supper. Land, won't it be nice to see a kitchen stove! And a bed!"

"And some place to get clean!" Louisa said. "This awful old dirt!"

"You and your warshing," Barney said. "I want to see the town!"

"Barney!" Captain Rucker called. "You see to your horse! See to mine too. The boys will show you around to the corral. Don't you go prowling this town yet, either."

Print Ruebush was meeting the Puerto rangers.

"They even got a piana on that wagon," he told them.

"A real piano. Can she play it?"

"God Almighty. Are you asking can she play it?"

"Well I'm all broke up on the first round."

"Look like fighting chickens in the coop. Does Rucker fight chickens?"

"No sir, he eats fighting chickens. He likes the flavor."

When Barney had unsaddled, and found empty racks in the saddle shed, and thrown rocks at the cowbirds by the hay pile, he went to see his room. He explored the rangers' quarters. He brought his box and his rock collection from the wagon, and he found his slingshot. When his mother called him from the kitchen, he sneaked to the horse corral.

The slingshot did not work very well in the wind. He climbed the corral gate and sat on top, looking out at the mud roofs through the branches of the trees. Westward he saw a street lined nearly solid with buildings; temptation took hold of him.

Regretting that he went afoot, without a spur at his horse's flank as he made his first appearance on the main street of Puerto, he climbed down the outside of the gate, put his hands in his pockets, and started.

Two glints from the lowering sun caught his eye. They were the insulators on a stubby telegraph pole. He saw the wires where they curved down swinging in the wind from the pole to the building on the corner, and he walked toward them.

At a narrow side window before he came to the corner, he stopped. Inside, he could see the telegrapher, and part of the brass machine, and some wires on a shelf. He put up his hand to shade the reflection on the dirty glass. He saw two more soldiers in there, with their hats on, and gloves. They had shoulder straps.

As he stood with his nose to the window, a cutting flare of wind showered him with dirt. He turned away spitting and squinting, seeing a big tumbleweed caught against the telegraph pole and the wall. He kicked the tumbleweed. It rolled toward the corner, angling into the street, gathering speed in a jerk of wind that whistled with the humming of the wires above Barney's head.

It was a lonesome sound, as if it came from a long way off and hadn't found anything.

CHAPTER VI

I N THE INSTANT
between the veer and the snort of his horse, Martin Brady saw it
coming, but it was too late. There was no time. The tumbleweed
struck the right foreleg and bounced under the belly with a swish
as Lágrimas jumped rearing. Martin Brady's hand in its reflex
pulled back, and the terrified horse came too high, pawing the air.
Brady saw it was too high. The wind-tangled black mane curved
up over him and he threw himself leftward seeing the mane
coming down. He fell with a white flash in his head and a cracking
stab in his pinned leg. He heard it pop as he hit. In his clenched
right hand the reins jerked as the horse came up again, towering
dark. Brady rolled with the pull, bringing himself to his feet for a

moment high and desperate. Then the ground rose up and hit him.

His eyes opened blurred and the reins were gone. He heard his
own voice telling him inside without moving his dry tongue, You
can't get up. They can take you. He wrenched himself hurting, so
that his hand was ready for the handle of his pistol.

"*Diego!*" His mouth said it aloud now. He knew Diego was
there, he saw his feet. "Bring Sterner!"

Diego's face leaned over him. "*Cabrón de los cabrones*, does it
pain? Lie still, be quiet, Martín!"

He heard other voices. He could not see well. A shout came to
him, "Patino! Gather those reins! Bring up that horse! The man
is down."

He saw the boots coming. He made out the yellow stripes up
the legs of the blue breeches. His hand was ready, close to the
pistol handle.

He snarled then at Diego. "You hear me? Get Sterner — "

"I go to bring him," Diego said.

Martin lifted his eyes. He made them focus. There was no
holster at the waist of the breeches with the yellow stripes. There
was gold on the shoulders. They came closer.

He heard the words. "Speak English?"

From flat on my back, Martin thought. The Union Blue. Asking
me if I speak it! He shoved himself up on his elbow, swallowing,
looking at the sunburned face above the brass buttons. He had to
decide if Martin Brady did speak English.

"Yes," he decided.

"Well don't move. You need help. Where do you live?"

"Not here." There were more faces peering down at him. "I
sent for help."

He fought the blur of rage with himself, caught, on the ground,
with the faces closing in like a cage. He saw his Chihuahueño hat
in the hands of a gringo boy looking down at him with big eyes.
He saw the yellow stripes standing by Lágrimas, oh that bastard
of a horse, and a burly man slouching out of the shade into the
street, armed. There were more men craning their necks, grinning,
strangers. The burly man came with his eyes fixed on Martin
Brady.

"*Qué pasó, hombre?*" the voice was hoarse, rich with liquor.

And he wants to know, he wants to know what happened, Martin thought, looking at him, watching his hand by the holster.

The Union Blue with the buttons spoke, crisply. "He talks English. Look at his foot."

Martin looked at it too. It looked like somebody else's, sideways.

"Whoof," the burly man said. He shifted the toothpick in his mouth, and looked up from the foot. He saw the gold leaves on the shoulder straps. "Say. My name is Tod Hogan. That's my place yonder, and you must be the new man at Jefflin." He put out his hand.

The Union Blue took it. "I am. Major Colton." His eyes were on Hogan. "This injured man ought to be off the street. Is there a doctor?"

"Doc Stovall. He's around here somewheres. Go get Doc, somebody. How'd this happen?"

"He got throwed on his Mexican ass." The man that said it laughed. Watery haze reddened in Martin Brady's eyes.

"Oh, he did?" Tod Hogan said. "You don't say." He looked at the horse Lágrimas, and he looked at Martin. "Some horse. Quite a horse. He throw you?"

"He fell on my leg."

"I saw it, Mister." It was the kid holding Martin's hat. "A tumbleweed, it — it come around that corner and boogered his horse."

"Where'd you come from, sonny?" Hogan asked. He saw a figure advancing from behind the boy. "Here's the doc, Major."

"I'm from Travis County," the boy said to Tod Hogan, who did not hear him.

The doctor had his hands in his pockets and a fresh cigar clamped in the middle of his mouth. He was short, like a horse jockey, but past his riding days. His nose had once been broken.

"Move back, will you?" he said.

His eyes were quick. He looked at Martin's face, then at the foot pointed the wrong way on the ground. Tilting his cigar with his teeth, he reached in his pocket, brought out a pocketknife, and opened a long blade. He squatted down.

Martin jerked, from the knife. "What you doing? Git away!"

"Oh, you talk English," the doctor said quietly. "I'm going to slit this boot and pants leg loose, my friend. So I can see what we've got. You hurt anyplace else?"

"No — my leg is —" He saw the doctor's hand and the knife moving down the leather going blurred. He held back the sounds trying to come out of his throat. The twist ground in, mashing. He heard Diego's voice by his ear.

"Martín, I brought the Señor Sterner. I brought him. Don't worry yourself." The words smelled of sotol.

"Take him to my place, Doctor."

Martin could not see the man who said it. He tried, but there was a red-hot wire. It pulled. There was more than one wire. The big one slacked limp, leaving him trembling cold. The doctor was looking in his face.

"Bad?" Martin asked.

"Not so bad," the doctor said.

Not so bad he says, *hijo de la madre*. He says.

"We're going to move you to set it," he heard the doctor say. "Don't try to do anything for yourself, or you'll hurt worse. Just let them carry you. They are going to lift you under the armpits. Now you hang on to their shoulders."

"*Ludwig! Diesen Arm!*"

That is Sterner again, Martin thought. He felt Diego under his other arm, and smelled the sotol, sour, just as the wires jerked burning tight and they lifted him.

"We have you," Diego said.

Martin was up level with the faces. They floated. There was the boy with the hat. He was leading Lágrimas. The Union Blue — the hoarse voice with the gun —

"Diego!" Martin called from far away. "My gun — "

"Shut up, man, I got it," he heard Diego say. "Hold me." They went up the street.

The raw fire dangled under him swinging as he went, the wind hitting icy on the sweat above his eyes. He heard his carriers grunt as they jerked him joggling, going under the bare tree in the dust to the head of the street, into the sudden darkness of the door where they twisted, O Jesus, slipping, with the sotol smell a part of the sick sweat when the wire flashed melting and went flat out.

He heard Diego's voice as if it had returned from a journey.

"This is the Señor Sterner, Martín."

"My gun," Martin said. "Give me — "

"You don't need it." Martin saw the dark face with the graying whiskers and the yellow teeth. "Casas has it. The doctor has gone to make splints. This is my nephew Ludwig. He helped to carry you."

Martin saw the young face and the blocky hands that belonged to it. They were the hands that put the wet rag on his face. The rag was cool.

"Thanks," Martin said.

"Do not mention it."

Diego spoke again. "Lágrimas is enclosed. There in the corral. All is arranged."

"A boy catch the hat," Ludwig Sterner said. He smiled, holding up the dust-caked Chihuahueño for Martin to see.

"Try some of this," said the elder Sterner. He held a tumbler. "Can you lift yourself?"

It was whiskey. Martin got up on his elbow.

"Drink it all. You will need it."

Martin Brady almost choked. He felt it go down sharp and ignite in his empty belly as he lay back on the counter top.

"These will do," he heard the doctor say, suddenly approaching. "Ike, have you got the bandages torn?"

The doctor was looking down at him again. "What's your name, my friend?"

"Brady."

"Well, Brady, you want another drink?"

"No. I want — to ask you. Can you fix it? Will it — get well? I can't not lay around. I — "

"Hell yes I can fix it. And like hell you can't lay around. That is, do you want it fixed? All right. First we cut these leather breeches clear off. Take his money here, *hombre*. Then this boot. Whooi! Now. Phew.

"Listen well, Brady, while I tell you. Here we go. Obvious crepitus — simple transverse fracture — upper third of tibia. Similar fracture — same level, fibula — no disarrangement ankle joint mortice — no avulsion fracture — no ligament damage — apparent. This is called palpation, Brady. It hurts like hell. And you're lucky. You're goddamned lucky. Breaking your leg near Herbert F. Stovall. Here we go now." He looked around at Diego. "*Hombre!* Hold your friend."

"Get by the arms," Isaac Sterner said to him in Spanish.

"Ike," the doctor continued, "you and the boy help me down here. Hold it exactly the way I tell you."

I wish I taken the other drink, Martin thought. The sweat is hot now. It is the lucky simple something of something. That is what he said. I wish I taken a barrel of whiskey. It was no damage to the something, no damage —

"Uh."

It came out of Martin Brady's mouth fighting with the big hot wire twisting. It scraped searing higher grinding into the gray almost gone, but it came back, with Diego gripping.

"Got it. Exactly like that. Now the pad. The splints up. Hold the end of the bandage. God Almighty, tell him in Yiddish or something, Ike! Hold it! — We got it, Brady. For Christ's sake don't move yet. Hold it — "

The counter top floated in a curve and came quick back, stinging the sweat. The big wire settled, quivering. Martin Brady was cold; his teeth chattered.

"You want that drink now?" he heard the doctor saying.

"Y-yes."

"I'll take one myself, Ike," the doctor said. "Fine as frog hair, Brady. Slug him good, Ike. We can move him to that pallet now, and put the robe over him. — Brady, you need a nap. Here's the medicine. I'll be back in a couple of hours and see if I got that binding too tight."

The four men lifted him and his stiff splinted leg onto the pallet in the corner of the warehouse.

"I got your blanket from the saddle, Martín." Diego put it under his head.

"Come on — *ándale hombre!* He'll sleep." Martin heard the doctor's voice going. They were taking the lamp away.

It was very quiet. The leg throbbed. It seemed far off with the whiskey and the matted hair of the buffalo robe. He saw blue twilight from the open crack of the sagging wide door to the corral. The black horse was out there in the blue twilight, in the wind. The wind. He listened. It was quiet.

CHAPTER VII

Martin watched
the first light of morning come through the crack above the corral
door. It was not blue like twilight. It was gray. It came slow in
the silence.

A thirst was in his throat, and his head ached. He could hear it
ache, pulsing on the sweated blanket. His leg throbbed, beating
time with the pounding in his skull. The rest of him, between the
ache in his head and the pain in his leg, felt melted, like candle
grease, with a rim where nausea threatened to cake and congeal.
When he pushed back the hairy robe, lifting himself on his elbows

and raising his head, the throb and pound and nausea all came tilting to spill his melted middle.

Out on a border beyond being sick, in a lonely place, he asked his mind to meet Martin Brady now. He had to meet him, on his back, crippled and cornered, with a left leg like a broken stick. He could not make his mind venture to a meeting place with such a sorry self; his mind stayed close by, lamed like his leg. He only sent his hand out, touching the pistol beside his pallet on the hard dirt floor.

The light brought him sounds of the day's beginning. He heard blackbirds, and hooves moving in the corral, and a voice in Spanish moving with the animals, a thump, and a bucket rattle. Beyond the closed door at the far end of the warehouse he heard footsteps. They went away a long time. Then he heard the door unbarred scraping, and the squeak of a hinge. Isaac Sterner walked up to him between kegs and a stack of hides. He had on a black hat.

"How do you feel, Brady? *Cómo te sientes?*"

"*Bien.*"

"I doubt that. My nephew is bringing coffee, and something to eat. He will help you." Sterner stood for a moment looking down at him. "I am going to the other side. To bring the cart through customs. Casas went last night to sleep on the ore with a gun — " Sterner hesitated. "The customs won't open those sacks at the bottom. They won't give us no trouble. No trouble at all." He turned away and opened the corral door. "Take some air," he said, leaving the door wide. "It will warm with the sun. Today no wind, Brady." Martin watched him walk into the corral.

Today no wind. He heard hooves going out the gate. Then the other Sterner came carrying a coffeepot and cup.

"How do you do, Brady?"

"I don't know."

"Ach, the carafe with no water! I get some."

Ludwig put down the pot and the cup, and went away with the *olla* he had placed by Martin's side the night before. When he came back, Martin lifted himself, and with his head hammering, he took a long drink, tasting the clay jar. He lay back feeling the weight of the water cold in his belly.

"You sleep the night?"

"I slept awhile. The whiskey — "

"You need to get up, Brady? Tell me and I help you."

Martin needed to. When he was flat again on the buffalo robe, he felt torn in pieces, dragged by a wild horse a hundred miles in the mountains.

"Coffee," Ludwig said. "Is hot." The smell brought the threat of nausea again to Martin's middle.

"You drink, Brady. I go to bring food."

Martin took a sip of the coffee. He had to set the cup down on the dirt.

The food Ludwig brought was a strip of fried beef, with biscuits and sorghum molasses.

"Put it down," Martin said. He fixed his eyes on the biscuits in the dark puddle. "I will try in a minute." He wanted to taste white bread and sweet sorghum again, on a china plate. Damn to his stomach.

"Is good. Eat more, Brady. Good — " Ludwig held the plate while Martin chewed and swallowed. "Is necessary the food — "

It tasted like Kingdom Prairie, all right. Martin put his head back on the blanket.

"I think I will try some coffee."

"The meat?"

"No meat. Just coffee, hot."

When Ludwig had put down the empty cup, he looked at Martin, shaking his head.

"I need some pants," Martin said. "Don't I, Chico?"

"Pants no difficulty." Ludwig grinned. "You get health more importance." He studied Martin's foot below the splints. Martin preferred not to look. The foot was puffed swollen, a strange dusky color that made the caked dirt look pale.

"The doctor," Ludwig said, looking at the foot. "You want me I bring him?"

"No."

A swallow flew in the open door and cut sharply around with a whirring sound, out again into the light.

"Chico. What is that name of yours, besides the Sterner?"

"Eh? Ah! Ludwig. Ludwig Sterner."

"How long you been here?"

"From Kassel in Prussia I came yesterday."

"Yesterday? You got here yesterday. Well, you didn't break your leg, did you, Ludwig?"

"*Nein.*" Ludwig smiled. He thought of the mules.

"Ludwig," Martin said. "The name Chico is better. Chico Sterner."

"Means small. I study Spanish."

"*Lo necesitas aquí, Chico.*"

"But English I know more. You have more name than Brady?"

"Martin Brady. *En español, Martín Bredi.*"

"Martin Brady. You United States citizen?"

"Sure, Chico."

"You live in Mexico expatriate."

"I live in Mexico."

"You work for rich Mexican, customer of Isaac Sterner."

"Very rich." He almost smiled. "Customer of Isaac Sterner, all right."

"What is your work, Martin Brady?"

"I ride."

Ludwig looked at the pistol in the holster and the belt of cartridges by Martin's arm. He looked at Martin's leg.

"Violent," Ludwig said. "Violent."

"What's your work, Chico?"

"The business of Isaac Sterner. He sent to Kassel, that I come."

"You like it?"

"Oy, is soon yet. I think I like it when I know more. Has great opportunity for riches, Brady."

"Your uncle married?"

"A Mexican lady. She gives him no childer. Isaac Sterner lives now far from Torah, from our custom. At this house door is no mezuzah of the holy writing — "

"What's that, Chico?"

"Morning, gentlemen."

It was Doctor Stovall, standing by the hides. There was a cold cigar in his mouth. He pushed his hat back, and came to Martin's side.

"Not so good, huh Brady?"

"I guess not."

"I thought I loosened it enough last night. Let's see here." He put his finger under the binding at the ankle. "Throb much?"

"Yes, sir."

"There may've been more vascular damage than I figured. You feel this?" He pressed.

"Yes!"

"I'm glad you can." He untied one of the bindings around the splints, and carefully rewrapped it, then got up and felt Martin's forehead, and took his pulse, looking him in the face. "Sick?"

"I think it was the whiskey."

Stovall laughed. "You do?"

"I am *crudo*. When I lift my head."

"Tell you what you do today, my friend. You lift your foot instead of your head. The reason I want you to do that is because blood's pumping into your foot faster than it's leaving. You help drain it downhill, see?"

Stovall had difficulty lighting his cigar. When it was drawing, he turned to Ludwig.

"Young man, let's get one of these little kegs over here."

They rolled it up on the edge of the buffalo robe, and the doctor lifted Martin's splinted leg so that his heel rested over the bulge of the keg. "Made to order," Stovall said. "Keep it there a good deal today."

"My head, it aches bad now," Martin said.

"Tell me, Brady. Did you strike your head when you fell yesterday? Is there a knot anywhere?"

"I don't think so."

"Well —" He felt Martin's head. "We have to decide which end of you we are worrying about. You do have fever. My advice is to stay on your back today, leg up. Drink plenty of water. And cheer up, Brady."

Stovall pulled his hat down, ready to leave. "See you later. I'm riding this morning. Saving lives. Drink a lot of water, Brady. Get some sleep."

Oh yes, thought Martin Brady. Have pretty dreams and cheer up, oh yes. I will do that.

A hen's squawk jerked him from a doze. He opened his eyes

seeing Diego striding toward him, with two good legs, against the noon glare of the open door.

"How does it go, Martín? How is my twin?"

"Bad."

Isaac Sterner and the peon Pablo followed Diego into the door. Pablo took off his hat, holding the brim with both hands in front of his belt as he came toward Martin.

"The infamy of the luck," Pablo said, looking down at the foot propped on the keg. "It gives me pain, to see it so!"

"The cart is here, Brady," Sterner said. He turned to Pablo. "Go ask Gregorio where to put the yokes and straps, man. Tell him to help you fork the feed."

When the peon was gone, Sterner looked at Martin and motioned Diego to come nearer. "The stage for Chihuahua leaves tomorrow. Casas, I want you to cross the river. You spend the night with Pancho Gil at the stage corral, and be on the stage in the morning. Without fail. At Chihuahua you report immediately to Cipriano Castro. You tell him about Brady. Tell him to write me new instructions for the return of the cart, with the merchandise. Bring those instructions to me with your own hand by the return stage. Find out whether he wants Brady back on the stage, or whether he wants him to get well here. You will be gone eight days, four going, and four to return. We wait. Meanwhile, we speak of this business to no one. You understand? No one — "

Sterner saw his nephew coming from the far end of the warehouse where the door opened into the store. A boy was with him. The boy had something in his mouth that made one of his cheeks bulge.

"What do you want?" Isaac Sterner asked.

"He buy candy," Ludwig said. "He ask if he can see Brady — "

"I better go," the boy said.

"Wait." Isaac Sterner looked at him. "What is your name?"

"Barney Rucker."

"Rucker. Of the family of John Rucker, the ranger. You are the boy yesterday that brought the horse to the corral."

"Yessir. I — jist came to see the horse, and to — " He pulled a lump of rock candy from his pants pocket and held it out to Martin. "Here, Mister — "

Martin took it. "I am much obliged to you," he said. He had to smile.

"I hope you git well."

"You come again sometime and see the horse."

"Yessir. He's some horse." Barney hurried between the kegs and hides.

"Little gringo rooster. He has style," Diego remarked, watching him go.

Martin was still smiling. He tried the candy with his tongue.

"Casas," said Isaac Sterner, "you and the peon of the oxen start those sacks of ore. Tell Gregorio from the corral to help. Put them along this wall. Ludwig, we will eat some dinner."

There were forty-seven of the heavy sacks tied shut with rawhide. Together they held more than two tons of picked ore. Keeping track of them as they were brought in, counting them as they were lined against the wall, watching the labor of moving them in from the cart, Martin tried to forget his leg.

"Any broken open?" he called to Diego.

"Not one." Diego was letting Pablo and Gregorio do the lifting and carrying. "A dozen on top were opened at the customs — those, with the rawhide loose."

"They opened a dozen," Martin said.

"To look inside and find rock. They took samples, showing the metal."

Martin did not answer.

"How was the candy, Martín?"

"I ate it. Listen, Diego, where is my money from my pants, my three *onzas?* What did they do with it?"

"I have it, all three. You want it, so I don't forget?"

"I was thinking of buying candy — "

"Yeee!"

Three gold *onzas,* forty-eight dollars, Martin thought. My fortune from Mexico. He put the money into the bottom of his holster and replaced the pistol.

"Candy gives me thirst," he said. "Can you get more water for this *olla?*"

Outside the corral door the shadows were long when Isaac Sterner came to see the ore sacks. He walked to where they were lined against the wall, prodded several with the toe of his shoe, and counted them.

"How far is the new shaft from the old Tigre Mine, Brady?"

"Two hundred varas, over a hill."

"I want an assayer should see this before I send it north. He can estimate — Here comes that doctor again, Brady."

An army officer walked with Stovall from the far door.

"Ike," Stovall called, "you know Lieutenant Heath. Just got in from a scout with Stoker. He wants to see Brady, and I brought him. How are you, Brady?"

Martin set a tight hold on himself, cornered, watching the Union Blue.

"How are you, Brady?" the doctor repeated. "Still *crudo?*"

"No."

"Looking better. Let's get it down now. Does it throb so much?"

"No." He was watching the Union Blue.

"What are the sacks, Ike?" Stovall asked, feeling Martin's foot.

"Ore from Chihuahua," Sterner said.

"Rich, huh?"

"They say. The Mexican smelter loses most of the silver getting the gold. The owner wants a trial up here. Eh Brady?" Isaac Sterner glanced at the sacks with a flicker of nervousness, as if the sacks might speak.

"Heath wants to talk to you, Brady," Stovall said. "This is Lieutenant Heath."

"Glad to know you, Mr. Brady."

He is glad to know me and I am Mister. Flat on my back.

"This afternoon we got an order by telegraph," the officer said. He pulled a paper from his pocket. "Would you like to read it? Or shall I?"

Martin's head pounded, waiting. "You read it."

"Addressed to Commanding Officers, Forts Jefflin, Langman and Camp Bourke, and operators on U.S. military telegraph lines at Silverton, Charco and Puerto. It reads: 'The Governor of the Territory of New Mexico under date 20 March invites the Commanding Officer of the Mexican troops recently in pursuit of hostile Indians across the border to co-operate with United States troops in further pursuit of these Indians. Commanding Officers of United States troops are notified invitation has sanction of Secretary of War. Any information of the whereabouts of the Mexican Commandant is hereby requested so that this invitation to cross border with troops can be officially extended. Signed, Halpert, Commanding Department, Fort Roland.' "

Martin felt the tension ease from his neck. He swallowed.

"Cordial of the Governor," Stovall said. "And the Secretary of War off the pot, that's progress."

"This thing," the officer said, tapping the paper, "doesn't name the Mexican commander. We don't know who he is. Major Colton sent me to see if you have any information, Mr. Brady. The major saw your accident yesterday. He understood you were from the interior of Mexico. Can you tell us anything about this Mexican commander?"

Martin looked for a sign from Isaac Sterner before he answered. He did not want to speak the name of Castro — owner of the ore sacks stacked against the wall — if there was risk. He read no risk from Isaac Sterner's eyes.

"I judge it means General Marcos Castro," Martin said.

"I see. Is he Commandant in the state of Chihuahua?"

"He fights the Indians with his own soldiers."

"How's that? A militia?"

"I don't know what is the right name you give them."

"Lieutenant," Sterner broke in, "of course I know about Castro. Cipriano and Marcos Castro are two brothers very prominent in Chihuahua. They have big holdings, land, mines, banks, business. Cipriano is the *administrador*. He is the older. The brother Marcos is the military. They are wide awake, the Castros. I hear they raise their own troops, to clear the Apaches from the state."

"I see. You suppose this General Castro would cross the line and take the field with us, to get Fuego?"

"A question," Sterner said.

Martin shrugged when the officer turned to him.

"Why couldn't you send the message to General Castro?" Sterner asked. "Tomorrow on the Chihuahua stage."

"You have the general's address, Mr. Sterner? Major Colton would appreciate it."

"No trouble, Lieutenant, to find a Castro in Chihuahua."

The officer folded the telegram and handed it to Sterner. "Fixes that. Intelligence in this matter has been — faulty shall we call it?" He grinned.

"See you and your leg tomorrow, Brady," the doctor said. Isaac Sterner was shutting the corral door for the night.

It was after supper when Diego came alone in the dark. He squatted down by Martin.

"To Chihuahua in a carriage," Diego said. Martin smelled the sotol on his breath. "Like the rich! I carry the word to Don Cipriano. And the official paper Sterner gave me for my General, that son of a whore." Diego touched Martin on the shoulder. "Wait for me eight days. Get well. And don't forget you speak Spanish, Gringo."

"Hear me, Diego. I might never ride with this leg. It makes me crazy thinking. It makes me crazy, lying here."

"Don't be crazy. That broken-nose doctor has the science, I see that. Take a rest, man. Dinners come here with regularity."

"Diego, before you go, bring me the Winchester and the scab-hard and the saddlebags from my saddle. And hit that black horse between the eyes with a rock — "

Alone again, Martin heard the far door open and then close latching. They keep coming, like on the Paseo, Martin thought. Isaac Sterner walked to where Martin lay in the dark.

"Casas gone?" Sterner asked.

"Not yet."

Diego brought in the things and put them down at Martin's side.

"You going now, Casas?" Sterner asked.

"Yes, señor."

Martin spoke to Diego. "Here," he said. "For a good trip." He put one of the three *onzas* in Diego's hand in the dark.

"*Tck*, Martín, thanks, and that you be with God!"

When he had gone, Sterner went over and barred the corral door from the inside. Then he lit a coal-oil lantern, turning the wick low.

"Brady, does Casas know about it?"

"I didn't tell him. That is all I know about what he knows."

Sterner's eyes had points of lantern light in them. "I didn't think he knew. We have to do this without delay. That is why I sent him tonight. Which sacks?"

"Look for the rawhide ties split for an inch at the ends."

When Sterner set the lantern down by the line of sacks, his shadow loomed angling on the beams high over Martin's head. Sterner opened his pocketknife and cut a rawhide tie. Then he pulled the sack so it fell on its side, spilling ore.

"Skins the hands," Sterner said, bringing ore from deep in the sack. "A damn heavy thing."

It came out an oblong of rawhide. It had been sewn up wet and shrunk tight drying, shaped like a crude brick and as hard, but much heavier. Sterner slit it open.

"That Leopold Koch does nice work at the mint," Sterner said, after a silence. "Five hundred. All new." He held one of the Chihuahua pesos, glinting the silver in the light. "Supposed to be 925 of fineness.

"Nobody complains, eh? Sacks of ore are legal, duty free. No trouble. And by arrangements, Cipriano Castro does not pay the Mexican export duty of ten per cent on coined or bullion silver. So he saves good money. The coins are in payment for merchandise I send him and I take his pesos at par of one dollar. Castro knows — but how can he complain? — that in San Antonio I make a little something extra over United States dollars on account of these nice 423 grains of silver at 925 of fineness — "

Martin looked at Sterner with the silver in his hand.

You like it, Martin thought. Old man with the beard and the money. It is all right with me if you like it. They told me to bring it and I brought it. It is all yours, Mr. Sterner, not mine. But I do not like it that much.

"I am going to get gloves," Sterner said. "Nine more sacks and the ore cuts. You brought a good load, Brady."

I brought a good load, Martin said to himself in the dark.

It seemed that his left leg was pinned under the load, under rawhide bricks of silver pesos in a pile growing so he could not move. He struggled against the weight, looking up at the empty sky, hearing the creak of the wheels on the big cart going away, leaving him. Marcos Castro with his cavalry made a dusty cloud along a far ridge but Martin could not make him hear in the wind, the terrible wind. He could not make him turn toward where Martin Brady lay alone, seeing the twisting line of the trees by the river, with his pistol gone, with his leg pinned.

"What is the matter, Brady?" He heard Sterner's voice by the rawhide bricks. "Brady! Take your hand from the gun!"

CHAPTER VIII

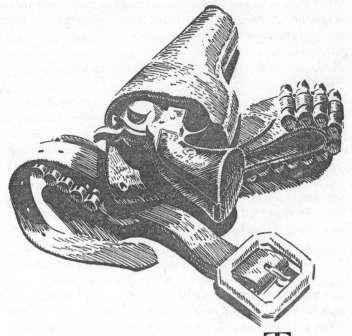

THE MILKY
overcast thinned the sunlight so that it came to earth weak and
shadowless. Inside Isaac Sterner's warehouse a silence brooded
over the hides and kegs and hardware, the high-piled crates and
boxes and dusty sacks. Martin sat on the buffalo robe with his
blanket drawn close in the cold, his splinted leg straight out before
him like a stick. He stared into the flatness of the pale glare outside the door, seeing the brown edge of the high corral wall harsh
against the colorless sky.

His mind had long since met the broken-legged Martin Brady.
He was no companion. He despised him. Now that he knew him,
he was not sure he did not despise all Martin Bradys, with one leg
or two, afoot or horseback, unarmed or with a gun. When he

looked for the one he wanted, the image would not form. The kind of Martin Brady he looked for was an empty place. There was nobody there.

You have plenty of time to sit and imagine him, Martin Brady. When the Castros get through with you — or maybe you decide you are through with them — how about it? Will you be there to get your throat slashed like a fat shoat? Or will they cut your pack off like an old donkey, drop a rock on your head, and leave you dead by the side of the road?

You have left some dead yourself. Do you think there would be a pile of stones by the wagon road out of Presidio to mark that place? I don't know, I never went back. What is that cross in the canyon of the Gertrudis, or that one in the round rocks behind Hormigas? The marble shaft in the graveyard at Nombre de Dios, you know that one, you have seen it. But they all go back to the first one, the gray evening, looking at your father by the wagon wheel, in the blood. When you grabbed his gun you got red on your hand. A solid sheet of red in your eyes with the tears. It brought you all the rest, that one did. You killed the others for other reasons. But you killed them. You like it? You, with the pegleg. It itches this morning, where you can't scratch it. You have itched for a long time where you couldn't scratch, where scratching did no good, you peon Brady.

You are having the time now, oh plenty of time, to sit and look at him.

What is that peon doing there? Where is he going, you Mister Brady? When he gets where he is going, what is he going to do then? Why, Mister Brady?

I will tell you why. He is trying to earn a living. Many people have not had to work so hard at it. He is trying to get along, earning a living.

So that is what it is. What do you want to earn a living for, Mister Brady?

To fill my belly.

But why?

So I won't die, Stupid.

Many people die, Mister Brady, every day. It is a common experience. Why do you fill your belly in order not to die?

That is easy, you sorry peon. I do not want to die, yet.

Is it so easy, finally, to die? And if it is not so easy — is it easier to live, the way you live? What do you plan, Mister Brady, filling your belly until you die anyway? Do you have any plans? Any engagements for yourself? Beyond the belly filling and a few fiestas? Beyond not wanting to do now what you absolutely must do later, which is die? Tell me.

I don't know, Peon, I don't know. I never asked myself honestly much beyond the belly yet, I never had time.

Whose time is it, anyway, before you die? Is it your time? Or do you fill your belly on somebody else's time, to work on somebody else's plans? Have you got any good plans of your own, Señor I mean Mister Brady?

That Señor and Mister, that is my trouble. I wish I was plain one thing. I wish in my mind I was not the stranger everywhere, like nothing was my own.

In Kingdom Prairie I know I was no stranger. Back there, I was like that little scoundrel with the candy who came to see the horse. He knows which side of the hill his house is built on. He can't think of things any other way. It is not so easy for the barelegged Casas kids at Valdepeñas. They haven't got much of a house. But they do know what is their own. They know where it is. I got it mixed. Not in my blood, in my brains.

Damn to your peon and your Mister Brady. Walking with eyes in the back of your head. And the people saying sideways "Do you speak English, Greaser?" — "*Quién es este gringo chingao?*"

"Morning, Brady."

Martin jerked around with a flaring anger at his own dullness. He saw Doctor Stovall. Where were those eyes in your head, you son of a whore what eyes, Brady?

"I hear somebody tried to steal your horse last night," the doctor said. "Ike was telling me." He sat down on a keg.

Martin spit.

"Says you scared them off."

"Yes, I got up on one leg. It scared them bad."

"Sorry you couldn't nail whoever it was. Mexican or American, you think?"

Martin looked in the doctor's face. "What about the niggers and

Chinamen? Maybe it was an Indian or a Jew. They didn't get the horse."

"On the prod, aren't you?"

"I'm going crazy."

"I called out good morning so you wouldn't jump." The doctor's eyes looked straight in Martin's. "Brady, there are just two things wrong with you."

"Besides the leg, what?"

"I don't count the leg. It's getting well."

Their eyes still locked. "What do you count?"

"You're dirty and you're talking to yourself."

"Is that so?"

"Wait a minute! You get cleaned up. You get yourself off that greasy ball of buffalo hair. You get that Saltillo blanket of yours washed, today. You get a bath and a shave and some clothes and crutches and it'll shake the world."

"Real smart," Martin said. He honed at the edges of the words, and looked around at the warehouse. "I could make it to the horse trough, sure." He spit again.

"In the back of his barbershop, Peeble has a bathtub. It's for hire. Real smart? You straddle the side with those splints out of the water, and give yourself a hell of a going over, with soap. You get yourself a new pair of drawers and pants and shirt. And a shoe — you won't need but one for a while. For about seven weeks. You have Peeble shave you and wash and cut that hair. First, you ask him for a little kerosene treatment, my friend. Christ almighty, you'll be a new man and smell like a rose. We'll find you some crutches. Then you can take your visiting card around. Meet the high society in Tod Hogan's saloon. You can come and have supper with me whenever you don't mind the company — "

"Doc," Martin said. "By God. But I ought to ask you now. I been wanting to ask you, about the money. How much you going to charge me for this leg?"

"I'm not worrying about it. You have any money?"

"Two *onzas*."

"I guess your employer wouldn't pay for setting that leg, would he?"

"He don't furnish anybody money for a mistake."

"What do you mean, mistake?"

"Not you. I mean breaking my leg in the first place."

"That was no mistake. You had an accident."

"It was a mistake. It was my own damn brainless mistake. I pulled back on that horse and you don't pull on a horse like that. An *arrendador* from Jalisco, where they know something about horses, taught that horse. You touch that horse to tell him. Like you were breathing on a feather. I jerked like I was on crow bait from Kansas."

"It's done. Why are you still worrying about it?"

"I guess I was nervous someway."

"And don't worry about my fee. None of my patients seem to, dammit, so I don't either. Those two *onzas* ought to carry you a way past a new rig and a cleanup at Peeble's. Beyond that, I'm thinking of your horse."

Martin looked worried.

"The horse broke your leg," Stovall said. "He ought to pay for getting it fixed. A lot of people would like that horse."

"I'm mad at the black bastard — but — not to sell him — "

"I don't mean sell him. Listen here. I have a pretty good mare, you know. She'll be horsing soon. A foal by that clean-legged Barb might be all right. Really all right. Would it be all right with you and the stud?"

"Doc, I'll speak for both! It would sure be all right."

"Done. I'll let you know when Madie's ready. What's that Spanish black's name again?"

"Lágrimas."

"Means Tears, doesn't it? Well Brady, let's quit crying. Take a bath."

It was midafternoon when Peeble finally untucked the cloth from around the neckband of Martin's new shirt. Peeble shook the cloth, folded it, and smiled. He handed Martin a mirror.

"Have a look," Peeble said.

Martin had a look.

Ludwig Sterner and the peon Pablo were grinning. Martin allowed himself an answering grin at the careful part in the slicked hair, at the smooth face that looked at him from the slanting disc of the looking glass.

"Never met him," Martin said.

He handed the mirror back, and shifted in the chair, to pull an *onza* from his pocket. The barber went to his black box on the table by the wall, and came back with a dozen silver pesos change. The rim of the pocket on the new jeans was stiff and the inside of the pocket felt starchy when Martin shoved in the heavy lump of coins.

"Come back, Mr. Brady," Peeble said, nodding and handing Martin his hat from the rack. "Don't catch cold."

Pablo picked up the wad of old clothes; then he and Ludwig took stations at either side of Martin, and helped him from the chair. Martin got his arms around their shoulders, standing with his good foot firm upon the floor. Peeble held the door open as they went out.

They stopped to stand resting for a moment twice on their awkward trip up the street, in the pale sunless light, under the high branching limbs of the cottonwood tree, to the doorway beneath the sign Isaac Sterner Genl Mdse.

"Tell me, who is this man?" Isaac Sterner said, holding the door open, showing his yellow teeth. "Sit him down in this chair, let him rest!"

Martin smiled as he sat down. He turned to his helpers. "*Mil gracias, hermanitos,*" he said.

"I wouldn't know this man," Sterner said. "Ludwig, you got a plenty good fit on the pants. How's the shoe, Brady?"

"Good," Martin said. "I don't need it much."

"Only thing looks strange," Sterner said, "is the Chihuahua hat. We have to fix you with something more *norteño*. How do you feel now? Do the pants bind, over the splints?"

"No, Mr. Sterner. I feel good."

Martin put his hat on the counter. He could smell the hair tonic, strong. He ran his hand over the smoothness of his face, and grinned.

"Don't look much like he's from Chihuahua," Sterner said. "Brady, the doctor was asking about the crutches. I have none in stock. I don't know where to get any here. We might find some, maybe. I think the quickest way is to get some made. We see about that. We have to measure you for the length." He made a motion from his armpit to the floor.

Pablo read Sterner's movement. "Pardon me, señores," the peon said. "I understand, that you are speaking of crutches. I can make them. Allow me to make them. It would give me pleasure to serve you, Martín."

"I did not know you were carpenter," Martin said.

"How not? Carving yokes for oxen?"

"Clearly Pablito, we forget! Yokes for oxen, and crutches for a sheep — "

"*Ándale* Martín! For a big goat, at the least!"

"Make them, *compadrito*. I would be grateful."

"We can find what you need for tools, Pablo. Make the crutches," Sterner said. "Ludwig and I have work now too. Here, Brady, try a cigar."

Martin felt well.

He sat smoking, looking past the bolts of calico on the counter, at Sterner's high desk piled with stacks of old papers. He drew lightly on the cigar, looking up at the horse collars on hooks, the shovels, frying pans, china pitchers, hatboxes, the pants suspenders, the spool of rope, the guitar hanging from a nail. Over the scoop of the weighing scales, he could see into the glass case with the cigars, snuff cans, cut plug, candy; and beyond that, to the groceries with the red labels on the tomato cans, the square sardines, the cracker boxes, the potatoes, the bean sacks and corn meal and pickle barrel, and the cheese and strands of chili.

Mixed with the cigar smoke and hair tonic, it all smelled clean, clean as Martin Brady. He still faintly smelled his soaping, and the goods-box smell of his shirt. His skin under the stiffness of the new clothes felt dry and newly tender. He ran his hand over his face, and back of his ears, to his neck. When he stroked upward against his clipped nape, the short hair on it felt stiff to his hand, like pliant bristles; downward it felt smooth, with no stiffness at all.

He brushed a flake of cigar ash from the pants leg that covered the splints, looking down at the new gray sock on his clean left foot, and the black box-toed shoe on his right. Holding the cigar in his teeth, he cleaned at his fingernails, using the thick nail of an index finger to dig under the nails on the other hand. He wished he had his knife from his saddlebags.

He looked up.

"This is Brady," Sterner was saying. "He brought the ore."

A short man with bushy eyebrows put out his hand, and Martin shook it.

"P. J. Ruelle."

"Pete is a friend of mine," Sterner said. "He assayed the ore."

"Sorry about your leg," Ruelle said. "I broke mine once. Fell in a shaft." When he smiled his eyebrows moved. "I say that ore you brought will run six to eight hundred a ton in gold. A couple of hundred in silver. Too bad we haven't got a little mine like that, ain't it, Ike? I guess you could use one too, eh Brady?"

"I never thought much about having one of my own," Martin said. "I could use one, I guess."

"Someday maybe you find one," Sterner said.

"Every white man in Mexico has a mine," Ruelle said. "Or knows exactly where one is. Surprised you haven't got a sack of samples, Brady. If you ever want to know what's in a rock, you bring it to me. I can tell you."

"You find a mine down there, and somebody else always gets it," Martin said.

"Rough going, toting a mine in your own skillet. I should know. But crooks don't live only on one side of a river. They're as thick as country rock. You have to work the mining game. And like you say, mostly it's a single-handed game of freeze-out. It can be done, though. Over at Silverton a — "

"Howdy, Buster!" It was a powerful voice for indoors. "When you going to drive my mules? You ready?"

"Howdy, Mr. Wakefield," Ludwig said. "Any day."

"Give me one of those plugs — that one."

"Glad to see you, Joe," Ruelle said. "Have you met Brady? He's from Chihuahua."

"Heard about that leg," Wakefield said to Martin. "And that black horse. Pleased to know you."

"What is the news, Wakefield?" Isaac Sterner asked.

"Git it from that fellow Naylor. He just tried to throw the hook in me again, for an advertisement. He spouts news. Says he's going to start printing it tomorrow. He must have hooked you, Ike."

"Newspaper means progress, Wakefield."

"A Heffridge Republican newspaper, huh?"

"Puerto is going to be something, with the railroad," said Isaac Sterner. "All changed."

"Running me out of business." Wakefield turned to Martin. "Son. When that leg gets well, if you want a job, you got an offer. I need me an honest-to-Christ mail rider. You look like one."

"Much obliged to you. You better wait and see can I ride anything but a chair."

"Say Joe," Ruelle said, "what do you hear from your long gone rider? What was his name, Flores?"

"I got a warrant out for that polecat every place including hell. If he's on this side, John Rucker says we'll catch him. Have you met Rucker yet?" Wakefield took a chew from the new plug, and offered it around. "But that Cruz Flores. He put it to me, I'll admit it. I never smelled a mice until the rascal took me in. He told me in pretty good English that he was an Albuquerque Mex, born up there. He wasn't. He wasn't named any Cruz Flores. He was some burnt-over brand from below the river. He was working some kind of a game."

"They call it robbing the mail, don't they, Joe?"

"Thank you. I'm glad to know. But that son of a bitch. He was up to something. He was robbing a particular mail. Maybe not for money, the way he treated the sacks. There's only one good thing about him. He's so ugly. With that hook nose and them narrow green eyes and that puckered scar on his jaw, he stands out plain as ratshit in a sugar bowl."

Wait a minute! Martin told himself, suddenly sharp. What did he say?

"If you boys see Mr. Cruz Flores, just let me know."

Abrán Rascón. So that is what he has been doing lately. Up here robbing the mail. Well, well. Maybe it was that *diablazo* last night, trying to steal Lágrimas. No. But he'd like it fine to try. Martin had to pull his mind back toward what Wakefield and Ruelle were saying when they went to leave.

"Buy you a drink, Brady, when you navigate to Hogan's," Ruelle said.

"You got that job, son." Wakefield winked.

"Thank you both," Martin said.

"You ready for some supper?" Isaac Sterner asked when it was time to close. "You come to the table with me tonight. You can sleep in the house too — now you are all clean, and better."

"I am going to sleep in the warehouse, near the corral door."

"Maybe a good idea, to keep an eye and a gun back there. We fix you a bed. Clean. O Ludwig! Get that Pablo and we help Brady to supper."

CHAPTER IX

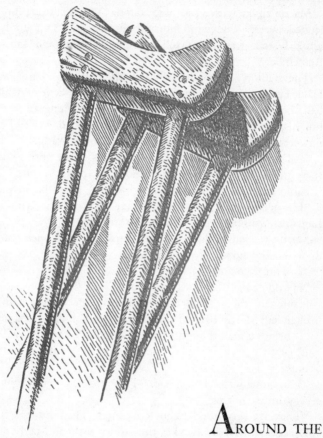

AROUND THE
crumbled adobe corner of the feed shed, the wind made a sighing
sound. It ruffled the mane of the black horse standing alert by the
sunlit wall.

Martin planted the crutches a step ahead and swung his good
foot forward in the blowing manure dust.

"Hu, Lágrimas."

The horse moved away another pace.

"Hu-u-u, Black," Pablo said.

Martin advanced again toward the horse, trying not to jerk as he swung himself forward on the crutches. A puff of the yellow dust blew from underfoot.

Martin spoke with a soothing sound. "You don't like this wood-legged man?" The wind blurred his words. "You don't know him? Listen, fool. You fell on him. You should know him. Remember?"

The stallion's ears pointed, with the lofty head turning. The black eyes rolled, showing for an instant a crescent of white eyeball, before the snort came from the wet lining of the flared nostrils, and the head moved on the arched neck. Lágrimas nickered, looking away, grumbling at Martin Brady.

"All right, Stud. Thou, whose fault it is. Wait until I am rid of these sticks. We will see who pronounces for Governor."

Pablo laughed. "The grain he gets now, he walks in the sky."

"He needs the mare of the Señor Doctor. She will fix you, Lágrimas, you big fraud of the two stones."

Martin turned in the wind and started for the open warehouse door where Ludwig stood watching.

"Is wild, Martin!"

"He don't like the crutches, Chico."

Inside, by the scuffed counter, where the doctor had set the broken leg, Martin backed around and got himself seated on a box.

"It brings a man thoughts for the cripples on the Plaza," Martin said, rubbing dust from his eyes, leaning his crutches against the counter.

"You move well," Pablo said. "They are better now, cut a little, a very little, shorter."

"They are very good, Señor Carpenter. The only lack is mine."

"Learning, Martín. It takes time to learn them. Maybe you will travel with them soon, to Chihuahua in the coach."

"I might."

"God granting."

Outside, a wild gust whirled down and hit as if its force dragged a weight thumping along the warehouse roof over their heads.

Pablo looked up. "Today I shoe oxen," he said. He pulled his hat down, turning toward the door. "*Vah!* This wind like the day we came." He walked out, grabbing at his hat.

"It is a native of this place, this *cabrón* of wind," Martin said. The wind flapped Pablo's clothes as he walked.

"You have seen this, Martin?" Ludwig pointed to the newspaper he had unfolded on the counter. "The first printing of Puerto. I study English on it. Maybe you like some news," he smiled. He pushed the paper toward Martin. "In Puerto I think is more *Käseblättchen* than *Zeitung!*"

"Look out, Chico, remember what you done to Wakefield's mules!"

Ludwig sat down at the other end of the counter where he had weighted a sheet of writing paper with a bottle of ink and a pen. "I write now, Martin, excuse me." He opened the ink, arranged his paper, and tapped the penpoint against the inside of the bottle.

Martin sat. The wind raced along the warehouse roof. It seemed to cry from great space. Martin stared out, at the top of the propped-open door wobbling steadily in the wind. Yellow sticks of broken straw whirled across the corral, over the wall. Between gusts he heard the small scratching of Ludwig's pen.

On the counter was the printed page with the bird and shield at the top and the block letters THE PUERTO EAGLE. Looking at it, Martin did not care much to try his ability with A Republican Newspaper Printed Weekly. In the near bottom corner A HORSE THIEF caught his eye.

Silverton.—A man left here on the night of the 18th named Handy Barton. He rode a cream colored horse, that did not belong to him. He is a tall slim man with rich black hair and a moustache. His trade is a butcher. He is low bred and uses much obscene language. Talks cards but is no player. Not gentleman enough for a gambler. Swindler from a drink up. Look out for him.

FOUND DROWNED

An unknown man was found drowned on Puerto St. today. Verdict: Drowned from the effects of falling into one of Hogan's 10¢ schooners at Hogan's Saloon, Puerto St. Adv.

Martin moved the paper, to try something longer.

. . . Captain Stoker, the best officer in this Department, the
man who saved the day at the Bear Canyon fight, returned to
Fort Jefflin with a troop of the 10th, unable to find a definite
trace of the wily Fuego.

At Fort Jefflin, the new commander, Major Starke Colton,
arrived last week from Headquarters, Division of Pacific. Colton
refused to divulge plans, but activity at the post indicates the
battalion may soon take the field.

Colton comes here without recent experience or reputation as
an Indian fighter. Citizens of this vicinity wish him success in
his new duties. Those duties are plain. After the Bear Canyon
conduct of his predecessor, a change is welcome.   -

It was slow work, to make out some of the words, and he turned
the page, opening the paper out flat, hunting for something better,
more like the swindler from the drink up.

The contract for carrying the mail from Puerto to Chihuahua
has been awarded again to the firm of Castro Brothers, Chihuahua. The line runs by Guadalupe, Carrizal and Carmen to Chihuahua, a distance of 350 miles. Time, four days. Fare, $25.

Diego Casas, Martin thought, is not paying that twenty-five
dollars. He is riding compliments of Castro Brothers, Chihuahua.
He is rocking along with the letter sewed next to his skin. He has
a little bottle of sotol, coming this way, past Carrizal by now. He
is having a time.

A rage of wind rumbling over the roof brought a sudden draft
that lifted the newspaper rattling. Ludwig looked up from his
letter.

"Made a blot," he said.

"Lift that pen when we sail away, Chico. Does it blow this good
in the old country?"

"*Pfu!* They would not imagine it."

Martin anchored the newspaper with his hat. He felt the grit
under his shirt collar when he turned his head. He felt the grit in
his nose, in his mouth.

"Tell them all about it."

"Ach, not all!" Ludwig looked down at his handwriting, hearing
the sound of the wind.

Waves on the sea as big as the Weser was wide, each wave. New York with the people like a milliard of ants, ten milliard, the prosperity, one retail store with a thousand employees. The timber left only to rot along the railroad to Chicago, purely wasting more than all the trees contained in Solling Forest. Oh the immense land unpeopled, the riches yet ungarnered. The prairies without a tree, days of flatness with the brown grass, the prairie dogs, the piles of white bones, the water stations standing lonely with tanks by the iron rails. Who could describe what one would call in Germany trackless mountain ranges? How would the dear parents consider the journey beyond the railway's end? Stopping three times daily twenty minutes to eat, and five minutes at intervals to change mules that went galloping, smooth road or terrible, over mountains, through desert wastes empty of all but savage Indians. To the end of the world, to houses of mud, in the wind. To the business of Isaac Sterner, now in the month of Nisan, at the time of the Pesach. Under the rooftree of Isaac Sterner who observes not the Seder of his people, who places not upon his table the unleavened Mitzvoth, the Cohen, the Levite, the Israelite, nor the bitter herbs, to celebrate the Deliverance with the bread of affliction. "Hear, O Israel, the Lord our God, the Lord is One." He is greater surely than the width of this world. "We were slaves unto Pharaoh in Egypt, and would still be so, had not the Lord our God brought us out thence with a strong hand and an outstretched arm."

Ludwig Sterner was not writing. Martin turned from the newspaper and looked at him.

"Homesick, Chico?"

"Eh? Excuse me, it means?"

"Homesick? It means you wish you were back home. Not away, in a new place."

"Now I understand."

"Are you?"

"No."

"I think you are."

"No. Think of it that someday I am homesick from this place, that I wish I am here! Ha. You can think of it?"

"I would have to work on it. Without the wind blowing."

"Martin Brady," Ludwig smiled, dipping the pen in ink again, "you are the one I think is homesick."

Martin laughed. "You got the word wrong! I haven't got no home."

Ludwig's pen began to scratch again.

Over the newspaper, the corner of Martin's eye caught movement in the doorway from the store, at the far end of the warehouse. It was the mining man, Ruelle.

"School took up?" Ruelle called as he walked toward the counter. The words merged in the noise of the wind.

Martin waved. "What'd you say?"

"Nothing. You look real studious, both of you."

"Chico here, he's writing the old folks. How the wind blows on the Bravo River."

"It damn sure blew my furnace chimney down! I'm out of business. I come over to see if Ike has got some heavy wire." Ruelle looked up at the beams overhead. "Rumbles like the racket wheels of howdy do. Say, Brady. You been to Hogan's yet?"

"These things — " Martin tapped the crutches. "Maybe I ought to try spurs."

"A mighty drying wind," Ruelle said. "Sounds like the cat walking the clothesline up there. How about a little something, to wet down the scratch?"

"I guess I'm not helping Chico any with his Dutch."

"Finished," Ludwig said, grinning.

"Come on, Brady," Ruelle said.

"Well. I'll try lifting the blindfolds on these stick horses." Martin put on his hat. "Here's your newspaper, Chico — before it blows away." He got up on the crutches and moved to his bunk in the corner. From beneath the clean, folded Saltillo, he pulled his belt and holster. Ruelle and Ludwig watched him buckle it on. He gave a pat to the pistol butt, in place on his right hip, his good leg, took a firm hold on the crutches, and started for the doorway to the store.

"How'd you like that Puerto *Eagle*, Brady? That newspaper."

"All right."

"Did you see the piece about two county attorneys for just one office?"

"I didn't pay no attention, Mr. Ruelle."

"So you haven't met Judge Heffridge, nor the Hights?" Ruelle watched Martin move ahead, into the store. "Ike — we're going to Hogan's!"

Isaac Sterner saw Martin armed, moving toward the street door on his crutches.

"Brady," Sterner said. "You be careful."

Ruelle held the door open; a puff of sand hit them as they stepped into the afternoon light. Martin stood for a moment, looking along the flat adobe faces of the buildings squatted down the uneven sides of the street southward, where he had ridden Lágrimas. Fading in the dust haze toward the river, it was like a street through a forsaken place, lifeless except for a few saddled ponies with their heads tied close to hitching racks, motionless except for the wind lifting ragged flurries of dust, tearing gray leaves from the cottonwood that cast a twisting shadow where Martin stood.

By the foot of the tree they crossed splintered planks over a narrow *acequia*. Martin handled his crutches slowly, watching the ground, bracing against the wind, until they came under the sagging portico, past the square-faced adobe columns with their dirtied whitewash flaking, to the door of Tod Hogan's saloon.

It opened before Ruelle reached the handle. A stumpy, red-faced man with white hair and bleared blue eyes stood in the doorway, rocking slightly.

"Howdy, Judge Bates," Ruelle said. He took him by the elbow and led him out the door, safely past Martin's crutches. "Can you make it all right, Justice?"

"Make it, young man, I can make it. 'Blow, winds, and crack your cheeks! Rage! Blow! Smite flat the thick rotundity of the world!' Young man, 'the tempest in my mind doth, doth from my fenses take all seeling' ump! Let it not be said — "

"Watch it, Justice. Go on in, Brady."

Martin put his good foot on the high sill, firmed his crutches on the hard-packed dirt floor inside, and swung himself in, out of the bright light and wind. Ruelle closed the door.

"Bates run over you?"

Martin remembered the hoarse voice, the burly man. He was standing at the end of the bar, looking at Martin.

"He had a load on," Ruelle said.

"The old fart. He hasn't been sober since Heffridge busted him off the bench."

A trim man with a goatee and piercing eyes turned from where he stood at the bar.

"Amend that reference, Tod. The Justice is not a fart. He is the wreck of a gentleman and a scholar. Wrecked on this damned sorry whiskey."

"Come on to a chair, Brady," Ruelle said. "I'll get you one by the layout. Tod, this is my friend from Chihuahua. Brady."

"I wouldn't hardly recognize you," Hogan said. His eyes had flicked toward Martin's right hip. "That day in the street, I thought you was *puro mexicano*. Right out from under a bear grass roof. Meet Mr. Travis Hight here. Travis, this is the feller has that black horse."

The piercing eyes looked in Martin's. "Pleased to make your acquaintance, suh. Brady is the name?"

Martin let go of the crutch to shake hands.

"Rest your shanks," Ruelle said. "I broke mine once." He brought a chair closer to the bar. Martin backed around and sat down.

"Excuse this crippled leg," he said.

"How about a drink?" Hogan asked. "Billy — " he called to the bartender.

"The usual," Ruelle said.

"No thanks," Martin said. "These sticks here. I don't want to tangle with them."

"Bring him a ginger beer, Billy."

"Another Stonewall," Hight ordered.

"Stonewall the nee pluss ultra." Ruelle winked at Martin. "It numbs you quiet as a nun."

Hogan's was like a long, dim square-walled cave. The sprinkled dirt floor lent an added dampness to the ripe bar smell. Beyond the far end of the bar, under an oil lamp chandelier, the lookout sat on his high chair over the faro layout. The dealer slid the cards out of the box, the checks clicked on the green, the case keeper moved the buttons, in a warm spread of light. Hogan's seemed well shored against the world outside.

"Three groans," Hight said, and drank.

"Brady brought a couple of tons of the prettiest quartz you ever saw," Ruelle said. "For the Tigre Mine people."

"Ah? The Castros?" Hight asked. "Are you certain you won't have a drink, Brady?"

"Much obliged," Martin shook his head. He sipped at the new taste of ginger beer.

"I met Don Cipriano Castro once, in Chihuahua City. I represent parties interested in building the Continental and Southern into Mexico. I must say in a negotiation Castro is rough as a bear fight. The man owns more than five million acres and great God knows what else. I would like to see the main hacienda, Valdepeñas. Have you ever seen it, Brady?"

"Yes, sir."

"Magnificent, they say. When iron rails carry Castro's cattle and wool and ore to the outside world, he will be golden Croesus himself." Hight took another Stonewall. "All this we see here — " he waved his arm — "is but the vestige of a crude and outworn time. The day the stakes of the C. & S. track survey are driven through this isolated, torpid — and corrupt — village of Puerto, that day the old order changeth and by God we — "

Glancing around as the door opened, Hight shut his mouth. The bartender's rag stopped moving. A quick, enveloping tautness in the air cut short the click of faro checks, the sound of voices. Ruelle and Hogan, caught between Hight and the three men who stood inside the door, backed stiffly, immediately, away from the bar. Martin sat in his chair. He watched the men advance, their eyes on Hight behind him. He could feel Hight, not seeing him, with his hand unmoving, ready. The three men walked behind Martin. He had an instant of not seeing, while he turned his head. Then they were past, past Hight who watched them walk to the far end of the bar.

"What do I owe you, Billy?" Hight said, turning. Voices began again, and a check clicked at the faro bank. Hogan went over and shut the door where the dust blew in.

"I leave you to your trade, Tod," Hight said. He walked out straight, with his back turned.

Martin glanced at the three newcomers, then over his shoulder, at Ruelle.

Ruelle came up to the chair and whistled softly through his front teeth. "Short! And standing close!" he said. Martin grinned.

"I was sitting."

"Yes you were!"

"What is this, Mr. Ruelle?"

"Politics! That's Gus Heffridge the U.S. Customs Collector, and Horse McFeeters the sheriff, and Naylor the newspaper man — all enemies of Travis Hight and henchmen of Judge George Heffridge. When the judge appointed a county attorney named Moore, the county commissioners turned around and appointed Travis Hight to the same office! Now the judge has Naylor printing rough language about the commissioners and they are all walking stiff-legged this morning like mungrels in a wagon-yard."

Tod Hogan had moved slowly, his hands at his sides, to where the three armed newcomers stood at the bar. They were having a drink.

Ruelle laughed quietly. "Hogan caught in the middle. Look at him. Heffridge's county attorney Moore has stuck Hogan with an indictment for gambling and running a public nuisance. Travis Hight says the indictment is illegal — he didn't draw it. He says Hogan's is a public convenience. But look at Hogan being nice to the Heffridge outfit — they got the court and the sheriff! The Hights got just a set of jackleg commissioners and the local bourbon Democracy. The Heffridges got the Federal appointments — and a right startling lot of paid greaser Republicans to vote at election time — "

Martin scratched his head. "Who was the old fellow, when we came in?"

"Hell. Old Bates was justice of peace. When he refused to recognize Moore as county attorney, Heffridge just pinched Bates off and put his own hundred-proof Republican justice of peace on the bench, fellow named Zinc. Hogan's trial comes up in Zinc's court — and if Travis Hight attends, somebody might — might blow some lights out — "

The ginger beer had gone warm in Martin's hand.

"A man wouldn't think there was much going on," Ruelle said, "just looking down the street. There ain't, I guess. This is a nice little wide place in the road now. But you wait till the railroads come. I've seen them come. There'll be hell busting tanbark — "

The door opened and Joe Wakefield stepped over the sill. He shut the door, spit, and rubbed his eyes.

"Howdy Pete! Hello there, Brady, I'll buy you one. Have you heard the news?"

"Which news?" Ruelle grinned.

"Rising in Chihuahua! Express just came to Del Norte. They're breaking the trace chains. Chili splattered all over the country. Some General Salcido had pronounced for Governor. They say he kidnapped old Governor Vega's son-in-law, that Jew Leopold Koch. Holding him in the mountains for a hundred thousand of those pesos Koch makes at his mint! Ain't it a riot? Gimme a drink, Billy! Brady, you're missing some excitement down there, ain't you?"

Wakefield and Ruelle were looking at him.

"I guess I am," Martin said.

I sure as hell am.

"You look kind of serious, Brady."

"My job's down there."

Wakefield laughed. "Why, I thought you were going to drive my mules! In white man's country."

"I might. I will take one of those whiskeys."

Ruelle's bushy eyebrows moved. He looked at Martin. "They're always fussing down there, pronouncing, aren't they, Brady? One right after the other. Is this a special one, you think?"

"Who's the army with, Mr. Wakefield?"

"Didn't say — or I don't remember it said."

"It depends on how the army goes, whether it's special. Has Sterner heard?"

"He has. He's worried about his wife, down there with her kinfolks. I guess it hits his business too."

Martin drank the whiskey.

Diego and the letter, Martin thought. I wonder if that stage is running.

"Howdy, Naylor," Wakefield said.

Naylor nodded, walking toward them. He stopped by Martin's chair.

"Your name Brady? I am Tedford Naylor, the Puerto *Eagle.*

I have been wanting to see you. To ask you about the Mexican situation. What about this revolt in Chihuahua? Is there anything to it?"

"I don't know."

"Who is General Salcido?"

Martin looked at Naylor. "He's a general."

"Indeed! Friend of yours?"

"No." Martin's eyes moved. They looked Naylor over and came back to Naylor's face. "I pick my friends."

"Do you? Thank you very much! Mr. Brady." Naylor walked back to his two companions at the bar.

"Well," Wakefield said. "Well, Brady. Have another drink?"

"I'm buying you and Ruelle one."

"No you ain't!"

"I am. Here, bartender — " Martin had his money out of his pocket. "Bartender, don't you take their money. This one is on me."

"Gitting along all right, feller?" Hogan asked, leaning over by Martin.

"Thank you kindly."

"Ever race that black horse of yours?"

Ruelle was relaying Martin's change over the bar when the door came open. They all looked around.

Ludwig Sterner had opened it. Only his head showed, gawking.

"Well, Christ come in or close it!" Hogan guffawed.

Ludwig came in, closing it.

"Hey, Chico! What are you doing? You want a drink?"

"Martin. *Oy!* Uncle Sterner. He want you should come. He send me I should tell you."

"He did?" Martin was smiling. "All right. If we can ride these sticks. Excuse me, folks." He rose, putting the crutches under his arms, holding the shafts tight, very tight. He had to blink his eyes, standing up, looking at the door. "We'll see what he wants, eh Chico?"

"Is trouble in Chihuahua, Martin — " Ludwig held the door. "Take care! The high place. Now — "

Martin swung out, into the wind. He was sweating, squinting

in an eddy of dust, moving in the cold windy shade out from under the portico.

"Hoorah for Brady!"

Looking up, Martin saw Doctor Stovall standing on the other side of the street, waving.

"Hello — Doc!"

"But watch those crutches, man!"

"Haven't got them — gaited good — yet."

"Keep'm in a walk, dammit!"

Isaac Sterner was alone in the store, shaking his head, when Martin moved through the doorway.

"My God, Brady. Drinking on crutches. My God, have you heard about in Chihuahua? — Listen, Ludwig. You go now to the post office — "

Martin reached the chair and sat down.

"That Salcido," Isaac Sterner said. "I didn't expect it. Did you?"

"No I didn't. Tell me about it."

"I don't know anything, only the express to Del Norte! Saying Salcido pronounced, saying Koch kidnapped! Some trick, eh? — Nephew! You going to the post office?" Sterner kept his eyes on Ludwig until he had gone out the door.

"What you think, Brady?"

"I don't think. I guess it depends on the garrison. Whether they stick with old Vega — "

"*Ach,* more depends! You know who sticks with old Vega. You know who keeps Serafín Vega sitting in that big chair signing the papers." The gray whiskers and yellow teeth were close to Martin's face. "You know it depends on Cipriano and Marcos Castro and you know they need that cart of merchandise *now!* While we wait around for a broken leg! My God!"

"Sterner, goddamn you."

"No offense, Brady, I am only nervous. You understand that. You understand the stage is not running from Chihuahua, maybe."

"Suppose it don't. Listen. Are you worried about the Castros? The Castros? You got your money, didn't you? They'll get their new guns. Won't they?"

CHAPTER X

Half dreaming, Martin heard the whistle. Stirring from sleep, he heard it repeated and he came awake fast, lifting up to look out into the darkness across the corral. The whistle came to him a third time, and he was sure. He answered with two notes twice repeated. A horse snuffed in the corral and hooves moved as Martin sat up, easing his splinted leg off the bed, throwing his blanket around his shoulders. He felt for his pistol, and reached for the crutches.

"*Oye!*" he heard the familiar pitch of Diego's voice. "*Qué tal, Martín, Pablo!* It is Diego! Open the gate!" He was knocking on it.

"*Qué tal, Diego!*" Martin called. "Pablo! You hear it?"

"I hear it!" Pablo called back. "Coming!"

Martin pulled the blanket closer in the cold, hearing the heavy bar slide on the corral gate, and the low voices and a laugh in the darkness, and the sound of hooves coming through the gate.

"Take the horse, Pablo — *Ai!* Pen him from the stallion," Diego said. "I go to salute Martín!" Silhouetted against the starlight, Diego came in the warehouse door.

"Ah Martín!"

"Dieguito! Over here! We thought you were not coming — "

"I was coming. Back again! In the dawn hours! How is the leg? I brought you a something, twin."

"Light the lantern. Here is a match."

It made a flare of yellow in the blackness, flickering as Diego lit the wick, steadying when he pushed the chimney down and turned smiling toward Martin.

"Sit down, man. Get warm."

Diego looked cold and dusty, grinning as he held his hands over the warmth of the lantern. He smelled of sotol.

"You getting well?"

"I'm better," Martin said. "It needs six more weeks. I go on sticks now."

"*Vah*, you have them! Look. From Chihuahua." Diego picked up the professionally made, varnished crutches he had carried in the darkness. "I did not expect you had them," Diego said, shaking his head.

"Diego, thank you. They are fine. Very light."

"I got them. I brought them on the coach, and by horse across the river. *Tck!* I did not know you would have some. But those — they are crude, like beggars on the Plaza. These are better!"

Pablo came in the door, squinting at the light. He saw the new crutches.

"They have elegance," Pablo said.

"They are much better. Where did those crude things come from?"

"I made them with my hands," Pablo said.

"Listen," Martin said, "both of you. Diego and Pablo. I thank you both for your help in all manners. I thank you both. Tell us,

Diego, about Chihuahua — eh, Pablo? Is it true? Is there combat? We thought the coach was not coming — "

Diego's teeth showed under his mustache. "The coach came. At the orders of Don Cipriano Castro." Diego tapped his hand over his heart. "Diego Casas, in a coach, with escort of twenty cavalry!"

"You brought the letter?"

"One to the Señor Sterner. One to the Señor Martín Don Bredi." Diego winked.

"Give me mine."

"Sewed in," Diego said. He patted under his jacket. "We unsew them in the presence of the Sterner, please, eh?"

"Well," Martin said. "So you have a guard for the cart now. Is it official cavalry or Castro cavalry?"

"Castro type cavalry, naturally — "

"Who commands the detachment of this Don Diego Casas and his cart?"

"My cavalry has much captain. El Verdugo, the Hangman! Now taking a little wine of Del Norte, in spite of the hour."

"El Verdugo," Pablo said. He crossed himself. "With the whiskers and the knife and the rawhide quirt."

"You don't like him?" Diego showed his teeth again. "He is a good man to have with us on the road, Pablo. In case of Indians. In case of Salcido. Very good!"

"There is combat?"

"The grand battle will be, they say, when Salcido comes from the mountains."

"What of the army, Diego?"

"All but the garrison regiment of Severo Cuevas for Salcido! You hear that, Martín? They say Salcido will start paying with the ransom of Koch! If he gets it — "

"They really took Koch?"

"Ha! Out of his carriage in the City, the night before Salcido pronounced. Hear me, my sons, there will be blood in the dung down there! They are raising the cry, 'Death to the rich!' "

"It results death to the poor," Pablo said.

"Old Pablo," Diego said, "angels in thy mouth, and the devil in Chihuahua."

"Severo Cuevas, and the Castros, for Vega," Martin said.

"Not many more, for the old *cabrón*. They say he makes water easier, now that Salcido is coming. *Hee!* Will you have cigarettes?" Diego pulled a wrinkled package from his jacket. He lifted the lantern chimney and held the lantern for them to light up.

"Was the coach molested, coming to the north?" Martin asked, tasting the smoke of the bitter black leaf. Pablo coughed.

"Delay leaving, but no trouble on the road. No trouble yet."

"This leg," Martin said. "This damned leg of wood."

"Shall we wake up the Sterner?" Diego asked.

"You should see the Sterner. Very nervous. — Dieguito! By God I am glad to see you, man!"

"I have the gladness, Martín!"

"The light comes," Pablo said. "With Holy Week gone, it begins to come early."

"Diego, I took an Easter dinner with the Señor Doctor."

"Myself, I heard no church bells," Diego said, blowing smoke.

"I did," Pablo said. "I crossed the river to Mass. Diego, do you know that the Jews do not keep Easters?"

"They killed the Christ, man! And they should keep Easters?"

"They do not keep them, but they have another thing. Martín told me. A holy day at the time of Holy Week! And the Señor Sterner does not keep that one either. Those Jews, they are supposed to have a holy supper drinking a little wine, and they eat a bread, something like tortilla, with horse-radish! Chico told Martín about it."

"Tortilla without chili, Pablito? No wonder that crowd killed the Christ! Who is Chico?"

"The nephew of Sterner, remember?"

"Ah! Who speaks *guc-shluc*. The language of pigs."

"He is a good boy," Martin said.

"Very droll," Pablo said. "With heart."

"Shall we wake up the Sterner?"

"Let me dress myself. Bring the lantern nearer. My shoe — "

"Yee, Martín! Look at the gringo, eh? The gringo clothes. All gringo."

"Where did you get the horse tonight?"

"The coach station. Pancho Gil did not want to lend it. I explained the importance. That Gil — listen, Martín! Before I left for the south — he told me something. Can you guess who has been here?"

Martin looked up from lacing his shoe. "For a peso, I will tell you."

"You know?"

"Green Eyes, eh?"

"Son of the goat! You have seen him?"

"No. But I will tell you something you don't know, Don Diego. Give me my peso. Abrán Rascón robbed the mail. On this side! How you like that?"

"*Tck!* How do you know that?"

"No one knows that I know it. Green Eyes himself was driving the mail coach. I heard the *patrón* of the mail contract describe him."

"*Yee!*"

"Why would he place himself on this side, as coachman for the mail? Why, one day, would he break open the sacks and leave them scattered by the road and disappear?"

"No mystery," Diego said. With his thumb and finger he made the round sign of money.

"He took very little. There is something peculiar about it."

"Rascón has fame as a thief of horses," Pablo said.

"That we know, at least. Speaking of thieves, Pablo, how will I watch Lágrimas at night when you go south?"

"Tie him close, at the door."

"Who ties him? I? With this leg?"

"I will tell Gregorio."

"Gregorio is better with milk calves."

"Well — " Martin pointed into the dark at the far end of the warehouse. "The Sterner bars that door at night. We have to go around to the kitchen. Blow out the lantern, Diego."

The leather band in Martin's hat was cold on his forehead when he got up from the side of the bed. Daylight showed the corral wall against the sky.

"You go well on crutches, Martín."

"We adjust those new ones later. You have to learn them, like a horse."

Gregorio was in the corral with his milk pails. He had Pablo shut the gate when Martin and Diego had gone through.

"Cold," Diego said, hunching his back.

Looking up at the gray light they smelled woodsmoke. In the quiet air it rose wispy from a black stovepipe against the paling sky.

"The cook beginning," Diego said. "A little cup of coffee — "

Their feet scuffed the ground in the silence as they came up to the heavy door. Martin knocked. They heard the bolt move and the door opened, with only an eye showing in the crack. When it opened wider, they saw the thick shape of the old woman against the lamplight inside.

"Good morning, Concha," Martin said.

She let them into the warmth beyond the door, and closed it.

"Wake the señor, please, Concha. Give him the notice he waits for. Go and tell him Casas is here, eh?"

They had taken only a few sips of coffee before Isaac Sterner came into the kitchen buttoning his shirt, smoothing his uncombed hair.

"Casas!" Sterner gave Diego's hand a shake. "The coach late two days, and the delay. You got here! The letter? The conditions of Chihuahua? Speak, man!"

"I carry the letter, señor, sewed in here. The conditions of Chihuahua, they — "

"The letter first! Then, all that you know. You come with me, to my desk."

Martin sat by the stove, with a cup in his hand.

"A little more coffee?" Concha asked.

"A little, please."

Fat beef sizzled in the frying pan on the stove. Through the window, Martin saw the light grow outside. Across the courtyard he could see the sun touching the top of the wall, bringing the day. Concha blew out the lamp.

"There is war in the south?" she asked, turning the beef with a black fork.

"They say so," Martin said.

"There are no wars here. There is lack of Christians, yes. It is true that I must cross the river to find a confessor. But on this side, nothing of war. It is better regulated. The soldiers, even those black ugly ones, do not go robbing respectables, nor carry away girls." Concha moved the beef off the fire.

Isaac Sterner, dressed now in his coat, with his hair combed, came through the door. He had a letter in his hand.

"Brady, for you — I opened it by mistake."

"Did you?" Martin looked at Sterner and took the letter. He pulled the sheet from the mussed envelope, seeing the ornate Spanish hand.

> *Martín Bredy*
> *Puerto, State of Tejas*
>
> Sir: —
>
> I have been informed of your misadventure and present inca-
> pacity. The delay you have caused, in transporting goods from
> Puerto, is a damage serious enough, in view of the present crisis.
> You will remain in the charge of Señor Sterner until you are fit
> for my service, when you will receive instructions for further
> employment. With your knowledge of both the Spanish and the
> English tongue, during your idleness at the border you will
> make yourself useful listening for such information as may be of
> interest to me. I remain, Your Attentive and Faithful Servant,
>
> C. Castro

Martin looked at the flourished signature and rubric. My attentive and faithful servant. Who kisses whose hand, who shits in
whose milk? Not any more.

"Castro writes me to keep you." Sterner stood looking at
Martin.

"Señor, the breakfast is ready," Concha said.

"Come on, Brady," Sterner said. "This is a busy day."

"I will eat here, in the kitchen with Diego."

"You both eat with me. — Good morning, Nephew! Casas got
here!"

It was afternoon when the big oxen stood with the yokes
strapped to their horns. The chains clinked as Pablo set them to
the yoke rings. Isaac Sterner stood with Martin by the loaded
cart, watching Diego saddle his bay horse.

"Fat!" Diego called. "And ready to throw me!"

Holding the reins up close, he swung on. The horse wheeled, the cantle rising from the blanket as the back humped, then settled, Diego seated straight, holding the head up. Grunting at the tightness of the cinch, the horse stood still. Diego swung down lightly, tossing the reins.

"I thought he was going to try," Diego said.

Pablo had brought the wheel oxen around to the cart tongue. Diego put the saddle on Pancho Gil's nag.

"You should make Zaragosa by daylight," Sterner said. "You should move fast." He saw Ludwig coming out the warehouse door.

"Uncle, a customer, she wants to see you."

"I am busy. You know it."

"Is a lady, with another lady, from the army, wants you. With a wagon from the army, and a black soldier, by the door."

"Huh? Well then, tell them I am coming — " Sterner glanced around at Martin, then at Diego. "O Pablo! Bring the cart around in front of the store. Gregorio, you bring my horse around. It is necessary to get started to the customs as soon as possible."

When Sterner had followed Ludwig through the warehouse, Diego walked over to Martin, by the end gate.

"The Sterner stuck close all day," Diego winked, "like a louse."

Martin pointed up at the loaded cart. "To the customs, eh?"

"Don't you know?"

Martin shook his head. "Where are you crossing the river?"

"At the customs, man! Don't you know? These boxes have dry goods! Cloth, buttons, maybe lace drawers. Don't you know?" Diego whispered. "We change boxes on the other side. We have cavalry to take us south because the other boxes carry arms for Marcos Castro. The Señor Smuggler Sterner arranged two hundred new Remingtons of the size of .44, with six thousand of ammunition! They have been waiting on the other side, at Pancho Gil's, since before we came with the ore! Gil told me."

"Oh," Martin said.

And I didn't know it. They were on the other side — that's why Sterner was having the fit! He was afraid somebody besides the Castros might get them.

"I learn," Martin smiled. "So Pancho Gil talked to you?"

"Without harm. We took a little cup together. — Look, you see how Lágrimas lifts the head? What a pity you cannot ride — " Diego stretched out his arm, opening his hand, to the south. "With cavalry!" He arched his eyebrows and touched his mustache. "I will carry Magdalena your regards. I will tell her to think of you in the north, when the music plays!"

"We are ready," Pablo said. He had his long pole. "You open the gate, Gregorio."

"I will see you, in front of the store," Martin said.

Diego mounted. "I will tell her to think of you when the band plays '*Adiós á Guaymas*' — tat tah ta *tah* — "

Martin waved him away. "You will tell the whores well enough — grandfather!" He moved on his crutches, toward the warehouse.

The ladies from Fort Jefflin were speaking to Isaac Sterner when Martin came through the doorway to the store. They turned their eyes toward him for a moment as he hobbled past the counter, and he saw their faces.

"The eggs, yes, Mrs. Stoker," Martin heard Sterner saying, "but the milk — "

Stoker, Martin thought, Stoker is the good Indian fighter.

"Surely you will arrange it for Mrs. Colton and the major. Won't you, Mr. Sterner?"

The one talking is the Indian fighter's wife, and the other one — that other one!

"I will do my best, madam," Sterner was saying.

The commander's wife. That one is Mrs. Colton. She is the wife of the one with the red face that asked me if I spoke English, that day.

Opening the street door, Martin could not hear what Mrs. Colton said. Outside, a Negro trooper held the door open, and shut it for him.

"Much obliged," Martin said.

She ought to be a general's wife, at least.

The cart was coming around the far corner of the adobe wall. The wheels on the cart were creaking, and the mules hitched to the trooper's army wagon had cocked their ears.

"Hope they don't git them Mexkin bulls too close to these mules," the trooper said.

"I'll tell them," Martin said. "Ho, Pablito! Don't scare these big-eared sons of generals!"

Grinning, Pablo halted the long line of oxen.

"Some rig they got there," the trooper said.

"These generals have strong wagons," Diego said, riding up smiling, reining by Martin, "and spavined sons. Look. And the recruits the color of mourning — "

The trooper had stepped over to help Ludwig with a big grocery box. They were loading it in the wagon when the ladies came out.

"Ellen! Look at that immense old thing over there!" Martin heard the Indian fighter's wife say. "Look at those grand oxen!"

Her name is Helen.

"Could you tell us, sir, what that is?"

And she is asking me something and I better take off my hat.

"Yes, mam," Martin said. "It's a freight cart. It's going back to Mexico."

"Ah, ladies!" Isaac Sterner said, coming out of the door, with his black hat.

"We are admiring that picturesque cart, Mr. Sterner!"

"Ah. It takes goods to Chihuahua — "

"What sort of goods would it take?"

"Dry goods, for the Mexican trade. Notions, and the like. Brady here, he — " Sterner kept talking — "he brought the cart from Mexico, full of ore. Then he broke his leg, eh Brady?"

"What a shame!" Ellen Colton looked at Martin. Both the ladies looked at him, but he saw only one.

When they were seated in the wagon, the trooper started the mules. The men standing in the street watched as the wagon turned into the afternoon sun, toward Fort Jefflin.

"We go!" Sterner called, mounting the horse Gregorio held for him.

"Good-by Pablito," Martin said, shaking the hard hand. "My thanks for all. Go with God, Pablo. And thou, Diego. Thanks, eh? Good-by — "

The wheels of the cart were creaking again. Diego looked down from his horse.

"I will not tell Magdalena — " Diego winked. He jerked his thumb westward where the army wagon had gone.

"Beat it, grandfather, with that Magdalena — "

"*Hola!* She waits a long time. I feel it. Maybe we all wait a long time for Martín. Who knows where his house is — " Diego spurred and wheeled away.

"Tat tah ta *tah*," Martin heard him singing, past the cotton-wood tree. "I think I will tell her — " Diego waved.

Martin watched them going south.

CHAPTER XI

JOGGING BETWEEN
the shafts of Wakefield's slat-bottom buggy, even the old horse
felt the excellence of the April sun. At the edge of town, Wakefield pulled up, and when the wheels had stopped, he turned to
Martin Brady on the buggy seat beside him.

"I just wanted to see it," Wakefield said.

They sat for a moment in the quiet, looking along the freshly
cut stakes driven at precise intervals on a compass line east and
west beyond the clustered adobes of Puerto. The brusque, mathe-
matical straightness of that line put a new, unnatural mark upon
the old winding build of the natural world.

"I can feel them rolling out the iron like it was on a big spool,"
Wakefield said. "I can hear the whistle blowing, coming down
the track. When she blows — it won't be long — it's time for the

old Charco Mail Stage, Joe Wakefield, Proprietor, to piss on the fire and call the dogs."

Wakefield spit over the front wheel. "Well. We better git for Del Norte — " As the buggy turned, he looked once more along the surveyor's stakes. "Brady, did you hear that six-shooter emptying last night? Travis Hight, when he came riding in from Ramblazo and seen those stakes, he let out a hoot, 'I salute the coming of civiliz-ation!' and starts down the street fogging the air. He sets up drinks for the whole survey party."

"I kind of like Mr. Hight," Martin said. "How did he come out of that trial business? I guess nobody got shot."

"The Hogan squabble? Hight took the cake. He walked into court unarmed, carrying a book. When they finally let him say something, he got up and started reading the law from the book. Nothing about Hogan. Hight was reading from the new Constitution of Texas, where it says no district judge like Heffridge can appoint a county attorney, nor no justice of the peace neither. Only county commissioners can appoint. None of the tomfool politicians had dug that up! Hight had Heffridge cold. The law threw Moore out of office, put Zinc off the bench, made Hogan's trial a joke. But let me tell you the funny part. That same law says a district judge can *remove* a county attorney or a justice of peace. That's his power. So Heffridge *removes* Hight, like he already done to poor old Bates! And we're right back where we started. No county attorney, no jaypee, no nothing worth a good goddamn. Except the rangers."

"Who do they work for?" Martin asked.

"The State of Texas! They ain't for sale. The United States Army ain't for sale neither, but it's mostly fools in it. Look at that fellow Colton out now chousing the country with his black-ass cavalry. Will he catch Fuego? He will not. He'll just wear out the seat of his pants, and need more mules. That's why I'm seeing my mule man over in Del Norte. I'm going to mule trading. The remount's crying for mules. And all that shooting in Mexico now, it ain't going to help Colton catch Fuego neither. What's that Indian fighter's name, down in Chihuahua? Doc Stovall told me you knew him."

"Marcos Castro. He won't help much."

"Speaking of Doc. He tells me he got the mare bred all right. I've wanted to ask you where'd you ever happen to buy that black stud of yours, Brady?"

Martin looked around. He was looking for something else, but the good humor was level and unmistakable in Wakefield's eyes.

"Much obliged." Martin almost smiled. "On twenty pesos a month, me buying it! But I'll tell you. So you'll know. Cipriano Castro, that general's brother, made me a present. One time, after I done something for him. He gave me the horse. Don't worry."

"I wasn't worrying a bit. It'll be a study now, seeing what kind of colt the doc gets. Putting Mexico on Kentucky. Say, Brady! It's kind of breeding weather, ain't it? It's a day!"

They came down the sunny tracks toward the river, smelling the water, seeing the green springtime shine of the tall poplars. A mockingbird sang from a budded cottonwood.

At the river's edge Wakefield led the horse and buggy onto the leaky plank scow that ferried over the river. "You haven't been on this thing?" Wakefield called to Martin.

"It was high and dry. The river was a seep spring."

"Look at her! Snow's melting, way up in the Sangre de Cristos."

The ferryman cranked at the cable winch, pulling them slowly along the rope stretched across the forty yards of water. The winch screeched with every turn of the handle. Sitting in the buggy, Martin looked out at the slow tan whirlpooled water over the side, feeling its power, its plash and suck against the planking.

"She's a bitch when she's high!" Wakefield bawled, above the complaint of the winch. "Someday there'll be a bridge."

When they ran up grounding on the other bank, the Mexican ferryman let down the slats at the forward end. Wakefield untied the horse, led it ashore, paid the ferryman a *real*, and climbed back in the buggy.

"The repooblica, Brady. Now, where do you find your man? The Chihuahua stage?"

"It's up the hill from the church."

"I know where it is."

Dogs came out to bark as the horse trotted the passage from the river to the town. Beyond a thicket of salt cedar, the passage became a street lined by the oblong faces of weathered adobe, with courtyards beyond open doorways, where green fronds of ferns and red splashes of flowers stood bright against sunlit walls.

At the head of the street Wakefield drove westward along the plaza with its broken walks and rusty benches, its faded bandstand, its chinaberry trees leafed out with pristine green. Above them the white bell tower of the church stood high against the sun.

The horse's hooves clattered on the cobbled way up the hill by the churchside, by the market, by the carved face of the city hall, the iron-barred jail, the bullet-marked garrison with its flag aloft, up the street to the tall wall and arched portico of the stage station to Chihuahua.

"I'll be back before long, Brady," Wakefield said. "While you talk to your man, I'll find mine. — Can you get down?"

"Fine," Martin said. "And thank you."

He swung his splinted leg out sideward, grasping with both hands at the side of the buggy, and let his good foot to earth. Wakefield handed out the crutches, and Martin waved.

The woman who answered his knock led him around to a narrow gate through the high wall. It opened into the wide corral where he found Pancho Gil by the granary, saddling a big flea-bitten mare.

"Great pleasure!" Gil said.

"Equally!" Martin answered.

Gil had a heavy body, and a heavy dark brown face that smiled. "They told me you were doing well."

"*Cojitranco!*" Martin smiled. "The doctor says four more weeks with these things."

"A good doctor, over there. He made a cure on my eyes. You had the good fortune, with that doctor."

"It was the good fortune." Martin moved to the stone water trough, in the sun, and sat down on the ledge.

"Come to the house, Bredi! Don't sit there, without comfort!"

"It serves well, thank you, Don Pancho. I see that you are about to leave and I will not detain you — "

"Without importance, Bredi. Come to the house. Take a cup of wine with me. It will give you strength."

"I came only to greet you, Don Pancho. To find how things are. Does the coach run?"

"One time, to Carmen and return. Beyond Carmen?" He shrugged his heavy shoulders.

"How is the news?"

"They took your cart to Carmen only. Cavalry of my General, Marcos Castro, met it there." Gil tapped a finger to Martin's arm. "There was much hurry — "

"What happens with the cart?"

"Still much hurry!" Gil wheezed when he whispered. "Especially bullets. A great lack — "

"While we speak, Don Pancho, and before we take that cup, for health, may I say a word?"

"I am at your orders."

"Abrán Rascón. He came here?"

"He made a visit. Very urbane."

"He said much?"

"It remained polite."

"You know what he did then, on the other side?"

"He drove the mail. Then he robbed it. Coyote!"

"Do you know what he did then?"

"Clearly no."

"I think he went to Salcido. Do you think he smelled the ox-cart?"

"Well." Gil's eyebrows raised, then lowered glowering. "Rascón can smell sharp. With that long hook of nose. I hope not sharp enough in the matter of carts."

"It could be bad, if the cart goes again."

"I do not like the cart. It is too slow, Bredi! Come — shall we have our cup?"

Sitting in the dim light of the thick-walled room where Gil received visitors, Martin watched his host take a bottle from the sideboard and pour two tumblers full.

They raised the heavy glasses, saying, "*Salud*." The wine of Del Norte was yellow, thick and sweet.

"How is the garrison here, Don Pancho?"

"Well paid. Loyal, unless the wind blows harder from the south."

"Where do they say Salcido moves now?"

"Toward the City. He received the ransom of Koch."

"He got the money! Did he return Koch?"

"Who knows? They say Salcido hesitates on the grand attack, because of artillery. Cuevas sits waiting to defend the City. Our General Castro does what he can, out on the flanks. The situation represents great danger, Bredi. More wine?"

"No thank you. I am going, Don Pancho. You were saddling a horse." Martin stood up with his crutches. "I am grateful."

"For nothing — " Gil arose from his chair. "You have means of traveling to Puerto?"

"A friend with a carriage."

"Have luck, Bredi. Heal the leg. I can stable your black horse here, if you wish it."

"Many thanks." They shook hands. "Until I see you."

"Until then."

Martin went out into the street, seeing Wakefield had not come. In an open space around the outside corner of the high corral, he sat down on a stone, to wait.

Sounds came to him in the sunny quiet, a dog's bark down the hill, a child's cry, the cawing of a crow high against the whiteness of a cloud in the blueness of the sky.

He looked out past the garrison flag, and the bell tower, over the loam of the planted fields with their green like a living springtime ribbon along the river's flow. With his eyes he followed the speckled sandy fold and slope of the hills to the level lines of the mesa tops, up the ridges to the mountainsides where the bare rock stood, faintly stained with red of iron, touched with subtle ochre, ribbed with the rich blue of shadow, paled with the high blue of distance. Beyond the notch of the pass, he saw the empty glare of the desert and felt the lonely space of the world.

The notes of a trumpet call from the garrison of Del Norte came floating silvery-mellow up the hill.

They even play a bugle different, Martin thought, like it spoke the tongue. Like it was music. Over at Fort Jefflin it sounds like work, like time was wasting, and it makes a different sound. It is all one valley but it has two sides. Two sides different as Wakefield is from Pancho Gil — and they both carry the mail. Different mail.

Martin Brady, you did well to cross the river. Breaking your leg, you broke that peon's back. Remember him? He was kissing whose hand? What do you care, which crook is the governor of Chihuahua? Look at old Mount Jefflin, over there on the other side. Look at Wakefield — there he comes. Him and his "breeding weather." And look at me, with nothing to do but take a glass of wine and a view of a valley and sit on a hill on a day like this.

"Tired waiting?" Wakefield asked.

"I liked it. Looking at the country."

"From here, two countries."

"That's right!"

"And auguring over mules, I wish it was one country."

When they had crossed the river and come up the sandy ruts by the customs house of Puerto, looking ahead they saw a crowd jamming the street in front of Hogan's saloon.

"What's all that?" Wakefield hurried his driving.

"It says 'The Great Professor Berg,'" Martin said.

"Hell. It's a show wagon!"

Turned toward the crowd, the side of the wagon was built in the form of a cramped proscenium, complete with a draggled curtain. Sun and dust had peeled and faded the once gaudy paint of the wood built up and over the little stage where, front and center, a plump girl was singing. She was dressed in red, and tarnished spangles. A ridiculous beaver hat with a bobbing ostrich plume sat high on her yellow curls. She was accompanied in her song by two blackface banjo players dressed in blue, and a tall, one-legged man in yellow tights, silk hat and Spanish cape, who played on a mandolin.

"Jesus Christ," Wakefield said. He pulled up the horse at the back of the crowd.

> "And when the will was read to me,
>   They told me plain and flat,
>   If I would have his money,
>   I must always wear this hat — "

"*Everybody!*" shouted the one-legged man, waving the mandolin. "Oh-h-h —

> Where did you get that hat?
> Where did you get that tile?
> Isn't it a nobby one — "

The plump girl took off the beaver. She waved it around her hips.

> " — And just the latest style?
> I should like to have one
> *JUST the same as that!*
> Wherever I go they shout 'Hello-o-o!'
> Where did you put that hat?"

The crowd whooped. Someone playfully shot a pistol into the air — Wakefield grabbed tight at the lines as the old horse jerked. A saddle pony broke loose from a rack and ran down the street in the noise.

"No place for nice girls nor horses!" Wakefield yelled in the howling. Martin had not noticed there were no women in the audience, none at all.

A big man, with a kind of massive agility, climbed the show wagon. He held up his hand. The music stopped. "Any more shooting and this show is over!" he announced. The crowd heard him. He climbed down.

Wakefield nudged Martin. "That's Sergeant Grif Miles, the ranger," Wakefield said. "He tells 'em, don't he?"

> " — To a chowder club
> To have a jolly spell — "

Martin watched the yellow curls. They were jiggling again. Diego ought to see this one. He ought to see it, him and his "*Adiós á Guaymas*," speaking of music *hija de la madre* a chowder club in Guaymas!

> " — Someone in the party
> Who's always sure to yell — "

"Oh-h-h-h — " the crowd bawled with the one-legged man —

> "*Where did you git that hat?*"

Someone reached up to touch Martin's sleeve.

"Hello Mr. Brady!" Martin looked down and saw Barney Rucker grinning in the racket. Barney pointed up at a rope stretched across the street from the ledge on Hogan's to the roof of Peeble's barbershop.

"The one-legged man — " Barney shouted. Martin leaned down to hear him. "He's gonna walk it, he says!"

The plump girl finished the song. When she had taken bows, showing her teeth, she held up her hand.

"Gentlemen!" she shrilled. "In a demonstration of skintillating skill — preliminary to the main exhibition by torchlight at eight o'clock this evening — Professor Berg, the one and only, the only one-legged rope-walker in the world, will thrill you now with his derring-do!" The banjos rattled out a fanfare.

Professor Berg had removed his cape and adjusted his peg leg. The crowd watched him come down from the wagon and climb a ladder leaning against the portico in front of Hogan's saloon.

"Any more bets?" Tod Hogan called, from the side of the wagon. Professor Berg picked up his balancing pole.

"Alley!" he shouted, stepping up on the rope, balancing. One of the banjo players changed to snare drum and beat a brisk ruffle. Professor Berg stepped out.

The crowd, with craning necks, scuffled pushing out from under the rope where the one-legged man came. Martin watched him come swaying, step by step against the sky, teetering, righting himself with little jerks and adjustments of his pole, moving along with his peg leg and his good one while the snare drum rolled.

He made it. Standing on the edge of Peeble's roof, the one-legged man bowed to the crowd. "That is all!" he shouted when the noise thinned. "Until this evening! At this time, uniformed musicians will receive any contributions you generous gentlemen may care to make for this performance. We thank you!" The banjo players came down with their hats ready, and moved into the crowd before it scattered.

"Where did you get them hats?" someone shouted, laughing.

"He really done it, didn't he, Mr. Brady?" Barney Rucker called.

Martin nodded, watching Professor Berg come down a ladder with his peg leg. "He sure did — "

The banjo player came up sweating toward the side of the buggy. He held out his blue hat to Martin. There were few coins in it. Martin reached down in his pocket and closed his hand over all he had — four silver pesos and three little *reales*. He brought them out hidden in his fist and tried to plant them unnoticeably in the hat.

"Many thanks to you!" the banjo player smiled.

"Hey Brady! What — " Wakefield said. His eye caught the splinted leg, the sock foot, the crutches. "Hell — "

"There's Print, Mr. Brady," Barney was saying. "And Sergeant Grif Miles, they — "

"Howdy Grif!" Wakefield said. "When'd you get in?"

"About noon. I wanted to see you," the sergeant said. "This is Ruebush. He was on scout with me."

"Glad to know you, Ruebush. This here's Brady, from Chihuahua. These fellers are Texas Rangers, Brady."

Martin shook hands with them.

My hands've got soft, Martin thought. So's my head.

"You're the man this scoundrel Barney tells me about," Print Ruebush's leathery young eagle face grinned at Martin. "And that black horse. Barney's figuring to steal it. You better watch him." One of the eagle eyes winked. "He's a bad one."

"I ain't no horse thief, like some I know!" Barney countered. He kicked at Print, who caught his foot and held it.

"I'm going to take the spurs off this shack bully yet," Print said.

Martin smiled. "Barney, you haven't been over to see me lately."

"They're making me go to school to Miss Tutt! I ain't learning a damn thing."

"You're just orgmathorial ignorant, Mister Turkey. I feel sorry for Teacher," Print said.

Wakefield touched Martin's arm. "Brady, listen — " Martin turned his head, toward the other side of the buggy.

"So Ruebush and me trailed him to where he crossed the river," Grif Miles said, "below Ramblazo. We picked up one of your mules. A Mexican had traded a saddle pony for it. This Mex spills something about the alleged Mr. Cruz Flores of Albuquerque. His name is Abrahán, I think that's it, Rascón. From Chihuahua. And he's long gone south."

"Well!" Wakefield said. "You ever happen to hear of him down there, Brady?"

"Yes. I have."

Here comes something and let it come but you be careful, you tell the truth to these people but you be careful.

"I put that scar on his face," Martin said. "The next one I put on him won't get well."

"I'll be goddamned — " Wakefield said.

Martin felt the ranger's eyes.

"Where'd you know him?"

"I had trouble with him."

"Where was that?"

"The El Tigre Mine. He worked there, for my boss Cipriano Castro. He was no good."

Print Ruebush and little Barney were listening now.

"Brady," Wakefield said. "I recall I described Cruz Flores. You didn't recognize him, behind the summer name?"

Are you going to stay honest now are you going to tell him?

"I recognized him."

"Then why didn't you say so?"

"I don't like talking unless talking does good."

"Goddamn it, it might have helped, knowing his name!"

"If you think it might have helped, I'm sorry. Rascón is no friend of mine. Don't you make a mistake about it."

"Small world," Grif Miles said.

"With a river running right down the middle of it," Wakefield said. "Tell me something else, Brady. Where did that chili-eating son of a bitch git all that English?"

"He clerked at Eagle Pass. He lived there for a while."

"If he'd just come back for a while," Grif Miles said, "we'd catch him." He looked at Martin carefully. "Glad I saw you."

If you're looking at me that way, Martin thought, what I done was a long time ago. It was a long way down the river from here, nobody remembers, including me, I don't remember.

"Guess Rucker will send some of us back here tonight," Grif Miles was saying, "to run a rope around a riot if the girl loses that hat."

"She ain't got much else to lose," Wakefield said.

"These braying jacks — reminds me, Joe, you claim your mule."

"I'm grateful to you boys!"

"Let's go, Grif," Print Ruebush called.

Barney Rucker stood by. He pointed at the rangers' backs moving toward the corner. "You know why old Print's so weedy?" The buggy started away. "He's stuck on my sister Louisa! Makes you puke — "

The street had emptied; the sunlight had gone. Wakefield drove by Sterner's door, and stopped.

"You can get down here," Wakefield said.

"I am obliged," Martin said. He wanted to say something right. He moved his legs around, very tired of them, the stiff one and the good one, and he held tight to the buggy to let himself down. When his foot was on the ground, he turned.

"I want to tell you, you treated me white from the beginning," Martin said. The words felt thin leaving his mouth. He wanted to say more. There was more to say and he wanted to say it. He reached up and got his crutches. "I tried to make a clean breast of what I knew — about Rascón."

"I been stung a lot of times, Brady, believing people. I guess it's why I'm not getting rich. I guess it's why I'd believe you. I'll be goddamned if I believe you'd sting me."

"I'll be goddamned if I would."

"I'll see you, son." Wakefield touched the lines to the old horse's rump, and drove away.

Martin stayed for a while in the gathering shadow, under the new leaves of the high-branched cottonwood. Standing there alone, he watched another buggy coming up the street. As it approached to turn westward, toward Fort Jefflin, he recognized Tedford Naylor in the driver's seat — Mrs. Colton, and Mrs. Stoker, drove with him. They were laughing, as if the newspaper man had said something funny.

The tavern bunch back in Kingdom Prairie, Martin thought, what was it, "Cut your peaches, gals, thunder ain't rain."

Martin spit, gazing down at the scuffed dirt at the points of his crutches, the ones from Chihuahua, the ones Diego Casas thought to bring him. He looked along the ground out the far end of the darkening street to the mountains of Mexico.

Isaac Sterner sat at his desk in lamplight when Martin walked in.

"Sit down, Brady. Anything new from Del Norte?"

"Nothing new."

Sterner turned from the open ledger on his desk. "Brady, I will tell you something on my mind. Last month I wrote an order to my friend who handles goods from Ilion, New York. The letter got lost." Sterner lowered his voice. "I think now for sure it was in that robbing business and that lost mail of Wakefield's stage!"

And I think now for sure, Martin said to himself, I am damn tired of Abrán Rascón —

"Naturally," Sterner said, leaning toward Martin, "I have not inquired too close. If the contents was known to some officials — they might be asking things, things not so good. It is on my mind. But I say nothing."

Me neither, Martin thought. I'm all through saying.

"I have written to my friend again, and he has received it. But the next shipment to the Castros is delayed. Your leg will be well, I think."

"I won't be climbing on any horse, not for a long time."

"A month maybe, Doctor says. He says you will be fine."

"I think I will be."

"For the Castros, we hurry all we can, eh?" Sterner eased back in his chair. "Well. Did you see the crowd in the street out there this afternoon?"

"I didn't know there was such a gang in this town."

"A hoorah town. Only beginning, Brady! Wait till the railroad — another world. I remember Puerto — " Sterner put his hand on the ledger, as if the book somehow contained it. "I brought a wagon from Santa Fé thirty years ago. Before you were born. When Puerto was maybe ten adobes and the *acequia madre* and the grist mill of Don Santiago McBee, with towers to look for Apaches. Oh the times change! Making opportunities. While a man — he gets old. A spring day, eh? We close up, and have supper."

A new Puerto *Eagle* lay unfolded on a box by the chair where Martin sat. The words BON TON headed a piece on the opened page. He wondered idly what BON TON meant.

Before their departure into the field, the officers of Fort Jefflin gave a social party Monday night. Only a few invitations were extended to those in the civilian walks of life. The Post Hospital was the place of amusement and was beautifully decorated with

American flags and military arms. A band furnished music for dancing, and delicious refreshments were served, the gentlemen waiting on the lovely ladies present. If there are any persons who entertain guests more pleasantly than the officers of Fort Jefflin, they have not been heard from!

Ludwig came through the doorway from the warehouse, carrying a lighted candle lantern.

"*Qué tal*, Chico!" Martin smiled.

"Howdy Martin!"

"Did you see the show, Chico?"

"Ha!"

"I bet you liked that girl — "

"Monkey business," Isaac Sterner said.

CHAPTER XII

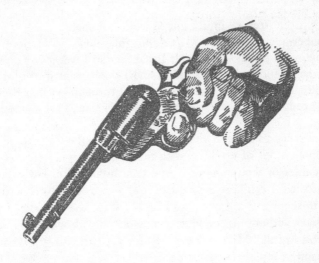

THE HEAT OF May baked the valley into a drowse. Afternoon sunlight struck the dusty streets and walls of Puerto with a dazzle that pierced into the eyes, a glare that made all shade cool and blue by contrast.

Martin sat in Peeble's barber chair, chin down, eyes fastened upon the faintly moving motes bright in the light beam cutting sharp against the shadow under Peeble's front window. The barber's scissors clicked and snicked at the back of Martin's head. Somewhere beyond the open door, the first cicada of summer tuned up a long raspy droning. The sound of it joined with the clicking of the scissors and deepened the drowse in the air.

Martin straightened his left knee, setting his boot heel out on the slanted footplate of the chair, feeling a twinge. Stiffly and uncertainly he bent his knee back again, flexing his left foot as he moved it, testing the weakness. He looked down at it, moving his toes in the unaccustomed tightness of the cheap new boot.

"You think it limbered any in that hot water?" Peeble asked.

"No."

"By golly, you know, the doc got a good set to it! Just as straight — "

"I lost the strength in it. I got to work it limber."

Limber in the head too, Martin thought, a long way from Chihuahua, with my mouth shut. If I told Sterner I was going on the drift, he would make me trouble, and I don't want it. No more trouble. Trouble was my study, and I'm through — when Peeble gets through, I will have two pesos to my name. That is another study.

I am sorry to leave, owing old Sterner. Not the Castros. They had enough out of my hide, with their book of lying ciphers on the counter of their *comisaría*. And their book full of law, handy on the shelf. I can hear the *capataz* read it to us yet. "It is permissible to shoot and kill one who tries to escape the custody of his employer without his employer's consent and without having paid all debts in full." My employer. His *ley fuga* and his happy land. His happy people. He can save a cartridge.

Peeble gave a finishing dab with the brush, took the cloth away, and stepped back to survey the work. "There you are," he said.

Martin got down from the chair. He put on his straight-brimmed Philadelphia hat, and put three pesos in the barber's hand.

"Hope we see you around town," Peeble said. "I hear things are mighty bad across the river. You going back right soon?"

"I'll be around until I can ride."

Favoring his left leg, Martin moved out the barbershop door, blinking his eyes against the light, feeling the sudden bite of the sun on his clean-shaven face. He felt faintly moist from the heat of his hot bath, itchy but pleasantly clean, and happy, standing on two legs.

Doctor Stovall stood under the sagging portico in front of Hogan's. "How's it working today, my friend?" Stovall called as Martin crossed the street, limping slightly, into the shade.

"Coming along, Doc. If I could bend this knee enough to get a foot up in a stirrup — "

"You can bend your elbow, can't you?"

"I better not," Martin said, thinking of the two pesos in his pants pocket. He smiled.

"Somebody might buy one to the noble science of osteology — Say! — The overdue mail from San Antone!"

The vacant sunlight of the street was abruptly peopled with a score or more of watchers as the dust-caked stage came wheeling, scraping the brake shoes, around the corner. The six mules slowed turning, trotting through the open wagonyard gate with the iron tires of the wheels clanking as they bumped over the stone threshold into the station, rocking the coach on its leathers, leaving puffs of dust.

When Martin and the doctor came through the gate and walked into the gathering crowd, a passenger was being helped down from the coach.

"That's Heffridge!" Stovall said, elbowing up. "Judge, you all right?"

The judge was a stout man. His red face glistened where rivulets of sweat ran down from under his high-crowned hat. He was in dirty shirt sleeves. Several turns of cloth stained rusty red with old bleeding were wrapped around his upper right arm. When his feet were on the ground, he took his Winchester, pushed away his helpers, and turned from the step between the wheels.

"Hello Stovall. I was going to send for you — " The deep voice wheezed.

A black-bearded man with a tall and calm authority came pushing through the crowd.

"Judge, those varmints winged you!"

"By God we wished for you, Rucker! And I nearly brought Mrs. Heffridge with me this trip! — Let's get to my house. Stovall, will you tend this? The flesh of the arm — "

"So I see. I'll have to go get my things."

"You come to my place, Doctor," Rucker said. "We won't let him go home hurt to an empty house. Where's your baggage, Judge?"

"That." He pointed the butt of the Winchester toward a valise the conductor had taken from the boot. "There's some papers in it for you, Rucker." Martin stepped over and picked it up.

"Let me help you," Martin said.

Rucker and Heffridge both looked at him, noticing him for the first time. He walked with them out the wagonyard gate.

"Somebody," Rucker raised his voice, "go find a buggy for the judge!"

Doctor Stovall had left the crowd; Martin stood by, with the carpetbag in his hand.

"Judge, I'm rolling out with my boys before sun in the morning," Martin heard Rucker say. "You had Fuego himself."

"Greer's men from Fort Horne, they pulled us out of the tight. The Indians had us. At Owl Spring station. I never saw the army look so handsome — making that column of dust up the road!"

"A telegraph came through from Colton this afternoon, from Silverton. He found nine dead and mutilated at Ivers' Ranch up there, everything burned. And he got there too late — " Rucker saw the spring wagon coming around the corner. " — There's my colored man — "

"Can I carry you, Jedge?" the wagon driver called. "Powerful pleased you ain't shot bad! I was going down the street for Mrs. Rucker's flour and a man said to — "

"Andy, help the judge! You take him to our place. Make him comfortable till the doctor comes."

" — I left my miserable coat," Heffridge said, "in the stage."

"I'll get it. Just a minute," Martin said. He handed the valise to the Negro, and turned to the gate. When he came back with the coat, the judge was up on the wagon seat.

"Young man, I thank you," the judge wheezed.

"I'll be along directly," Rucker called as the wagon started. He turned to where Martin stood alone by the wagonyard wall.

"My name is John Rucker." He offered his hand and Martin shook it, feeling the very pale, very quiet eyes leveled in his face.

"Sergeant Miles spoke of meeting you. I have Company E, Frontier Battalion, Texas Rangers."

On guard, Martin searched into the eyes.

"Your name is Brady?"

"Yes, sir."

He don't know, Martin decided.

"Brady, could I ask a favor? Are you busy? Could you come over to my office? I want some help from you."

It was impossible to read anything but quietness in the pale eyes, in the set of the mouth in the black beard.

"All right," Martin said.

They walked down the rutted street together, with their long shadows reaching out in front of them.

"The quarters are over there," Rucker said when they had come through the archway. Across the wide patio, half a dozen men sat talking, cleaning rifles and honing knives.

"Shoot me the oil — " Martin heard one say. "Howdy, Captain!" A flock of pigeons wheeled up into the sunlight above the shadowed far wall. Rucker opened a door.

"My office. Go right in," he said. When they were inside he closed the door.

"Sit down, Brady."

Martin looked up and saw it was too late.

"I knew your father," Rucker said. " — Watch it, Brady. I wouldn't try it." The westering sun, through the one small window, cut a yellow square of light on the closed door.

"Your father fought with Joe Shelby's Missourians. Slayback's regiment. I remember your father before the final muster when men were whining to quit and go home. I saw your father tie them two and two and send them under guard toward a Federal post, as men who had mistaken the command and enlisted in the wrong army. He yoked them like oxen. I recall James Brady well, with the captain's bars on the butternut shirt. He was going to Mexico with Shelby, unsurrendered, and offer service to Maximilian." Rucker smiled. "That was a bad dream. Those were bad times." He stood to the side of the yellow square of sunlight, with his back to the door, looking in Martin's face.

"I would keep my hands on that table, Brady. This is a friendly talk."

I walked into it. I walked into it. I walked into it.

"Years ago," Rucker said quietly, "there was a man named D. M. Follett. I had forgotten all about him. Sergeant Miles refreshed my memory. D. M. Follett was a freighting contractor on the San Antonio–Chihuahua Trail, right after the war. A Confederate veteran named James Brady was employed in Follett's wagon train."

I walked into it.

"Follett, witnesses testified, shot Brady in a quarrel on the Mexican side of the river, and crossed to Presidio. That night they found Follett by the side of the road with the back of his head blown off. No indictment was ever drawn for the murder of D. M. Follett. There was not sufficient evidence. Testimony stated that James Brady had no friends beyond a young son who traveled with him in the wagons. The boy disappeared." Rucker smiled again. "A long time ago —

"Now listen to me, Brady. I want to ask you a question. I have told you what I know so that you could answer my question in fairness to me and fairness to yourself. Would you like to enlist in the Texas Rangers?"

"What?"

"I am at times a very meddlesome man, Brady. But I do not meddle uselessly in old forgotten business. I see no good in it. I prefer the business of the day. I asked you about joining my company. I don't ask a scoundrel to scout with me."

Martin felt his heart pounding as he searched again into Rucker's unmoving pale eyes. In the silence a deep and sudden emotion of belief surged up to confront Martin Brady with the image of a man finding camp at last, lost no longer.

"A friendless boy," Rucker said with half a smile hidden in his black beard, "that could raise his spunk the way I think you raised yours, and make his way in a strange country with a strange tongue, has some makings —

"I'll tell you why I want you. I expect I will be crossing the river before long; the only way to get Fuego is to have my rangers free to operate on both sides. Judge Heffridge has been in Austin seeing the governor for my official permission — which I may say is not forthcoming yet from the Mexicans, from some felon called Salcido who appears to have burned and raped his way to the governorship of Chihuahua. We will get our permission. A few more Indian outrages will do it. When I cross the river I need a ranger — and I don't have him — with complete command of the

Spanish language and with intimate knowledge of those people down there.

"A private in the rangers gets forty dollars a month, and rations. The state furnishes ammunition, but you provide your own mount, rig, arms, clothes and blankets. If it doesn't appeal to you, say so."

"I — I never heard of nothing in the world I would like more."

"What about that leg, Brady? I understand you broke it."

"I did, but it got well. It is in good shape."

"You limp. Another thing — they tell me you brought a freight cart to Puerto. Who are you working for?"

"I did work for Don Cipriano Castro. I was going to quit. I made up my mind. I was going to stay on this side."

"I tell you what you do, Brady. You think this matter over. You get your leg all well. You square yourself with the Mexican you were working for. You watch yourself. When I get back from scout, I'll enlist you."

"I will do how you tell me — Captain."

Rucker smiled, opening the door.

" — Meet some of the boys out here. Well!" Rucker said, "I guess they've all gone to their mess." The big adobe square was empty.

Martin saw a lady with a white apron step out from a door on the other side of the patio. She waved her hand.

"Supper, John!" she called.

Rucker made a salute to her; Martin took off his hat.

"Brady," Rucker said, "come over here a minute. I want you to meet my wife. — Mrs. Rucker, this is Mr. Brady from down in Chihuahua. I may make a ranger of him."

She smiled at Martin. "Good evening, Mr. Brady. Would you have supper with us?"

"Why, I — yes, mam, I — "

"Then you just come right in. Judge Heffridge is with us, John. My, wasn't that awful, those Indians!"

"We'll be along in a minute, Kate. I will show you where to wash, Brady."

Clean and combed, Martin walked through the door into the Rucker parlor. He emulated the captain carefully, hanging his hat, then his gun belt, on the deerhorn rack by the door, and he turned toward the room with a kind of straight-faced, awkward excitement.

Martin Brady had not been in a room like it for more than half his life.

"Louisa, this is Mr. Brady," Martin heard the captain saying. "My daughter, Mr. Brady."

He heard her voice. "How do you do, Mr. Brady."

Martin felt his face burn. He nodded his head, not knowing what to do with his hands grown suddenly huge and hanging useless out of his sleeves.

"Gentlemen, good evening," Judge Heffridge wheezed, from a rocking chair. His right arm had not been brought through the sleeve of his black coat and he held out his left hand to Martin.

"How is the arm, Judge?" Captain Rucker asked.

"Stovall dressed it. I fear, Captain, that I am not seriously enough wounded to require many further ministrations from your good ladies. I deeply regret it!"

Mrs. Rucker came through the door. Her white apron was gone.

"Supper is on," she said. "Judge, are you real sure you can be comfortable at the table?"

"Certain of it, Mrs. Rucker — if you and Miss Louisa can overlook my awkwardness!"

"Why, we're so grateful you are all right!" Mrs. Rucker smiled. She turned to her husband. "John — Barney isn't home yet. His supper will be cold. I don't know what I am going to do about that boy."

"I do," Captain Rucker said. "Shall we go to table?"

In the lamplit dining room Martin was embarrassed that he had not helped Mrs. Rucker be seated. He had not known that he should until it was too late. The judge had done it, with one hand. The captain had helped Louisa. Martin sat straight and tense by Barney's empty place, acutely uncomfortable with desire to deport himself well.

Mixed with the desire was a confusing, acute happiness. The lamplight seemed golden. It seemed the very color of the sound of Miss Louisa's voice. His mind did not work with the meanings of the words of the conversation flowing around him. He heard them only as sounds. He covertly watched the captain's hands, to see how he buttered the cornbread, how he used the knife and fork on the gravied meat. The captain used a spoon with the beans; Martin imitated the example. He was sure the food was the best he had ever eaten, yet it seemed to have no actual taste. It demanded work in swallowing. He was startled feeling suddenly the eyes around the table turned to him, expecting him to speak.

"Have you enjoyed living down there, Mr. Brady?" It took him a moment to come to the meaning of the words. "Father says you have lived there so long."

"It is mighty nice, up here on this side, mam."

"What was your work in Mexico?"

"I worked cattle. I was a hand. On a big place called Valde-peñas. The last few years, I was riding the silver trains from the mountains, from El Tigre Mine, to the mint, at Chihuahua."

"What a rich country!" the judge said. "Governed by black-guards."

"I suppose you speak Spanish," Louisa said. "Oh, do you know any of their songs? Their songs are beautiful."

Martin swallowed. "They are," he said. "I can't sing very well. I wish I could."

"Miss Louisa is an accomplished musician," the judge said. "How you grace the pianoforte, my dear!"

"Judge!" Louisa said. "But I do wish I might learn some of the Spanish songs — "

"Daughter, might I have a little more coffee?" Rucker said. "Then I am going to be rude to you all. I am going to ask the judge if I may have a conversation with him about affairs in Austin. I am sure you are tired, Judge, yet this is my only oppor-tunity. I am pressed for time, with a number of things to tend to, leaving before daylight."

"We'll talk by all means, Rucker," said the judge.

When they rose from the table, the ladies carried the lamps to the parlor.

"Will you stay awhile, Mr. Brady?" Mrs. Rucker asked.

"I think I better leave," Martin said. He felt clumsy, going to the rack by the door while they watched him, buckling on his gun, taking his hat. Wishing he could stay.

"I thank you, very much," Martin said, standing with his hat in his hands. "Everything was the best that I ever had."

"Good land, Mr. Brady!" Mrs. Rucker said, laughing. "We just enjoyed having you!"

Louisa came from where she stood by the piano. "Good-by, Mr. Brady. I *am* sorry you can't give any Spanish songs."

"Mam, I could give the words sometime if you want me to. Maybe you could make out the tune."

"Good-by, Brady," Rucker said, standing at the door. He shook Martin's hand.

Martin Brady stepped out alone into the dark patio. Voices came across the darkness, from the rangers' quarters. He turned and went out the archway into the quiet street.

Some of the lamplight from the parlor showed golden through the shutter. It seemed a gold lustrous as the little rounded golden pin that clasped at Louisa Rucker's collar, a warm gold like the lights on her hair, the color of the golden flecks shining alive in her hazel eyes. He looked up into the sky, into the warm and quiet dark where the stars burned golden too, like many lamps. The branches of a cottonwood arched up above him in a kind of dance against the golden stars.

He walked away from where the walls lined the streets of Puerto, along a path by open spaces on a back way through the town. He wanted to walk not limping, on two good legs, feeling the plant of his steps and the print of his feet on the land where Martin Brady lived now, where Martin Brady belonged.

From somewhere in the dark streets westward, he heard the muffled pop of a pistol shot. Listening, conscious of the small sound of his steps along the sandy path, he heard two more shots from the same-sounding gun, a blurred shout, and quietness again.

He walked almost smiling in the starlight.

It is somebody celebrating, he thought. I am celebrating. Oh, I am celebrating. It does not come from any bottle nor a gun like that. It comes from people who were good to me. It comes from everything, everything better than I ever thought. Old Sterner will have a fit, the day I tell him, the day I have joined. They will have nothing to say to Private Martin Brady, the Texas Rangers. I am through with all the old times now.

When he came around the corner, nearly home, he saw a lighted lantern moving across the street ahead. It jerked in the dark, a small and yellow ball of light. It disappeared, behind black moving shapes, and bobbed abruptly, reappearing bright. The black shapes were men walking. The lantern went in Isaac Sterner's door.

Martin limped fast, toward the feeble line of light from the open door, toward the dark figures. He came up to them, ready with his right hand, ready to move. "What is it?" he asked. He could not see. "*Qué pasó?*"

"That you, Brady?"

"What is it, Ruelle?"

"Some son of a bitch pistol-whipped young Sterner."

Martin shoved into the door, into the light. Gregorio stood with the lantern in his hand. He pointed toward the doorway that led to Sterner's living quarters. It was open and there was light.

Ludwig Sterner lay on his back, on the bed. His uncle knelt with a towel, trying to wipe the blood. Martin saw the gash on the head where the red oozed through the wet hair. Blood welled from the cut in the swollen cheek, from the laid-open lip, puffed and pulling crooked on the battered face.

The cook Concha came with a pan of water. She knelt down trembling, and took the towel from Isaac Sterner. "Women know how," she said.

Isaac Sterner looked up, noticing Martin. Isaac Sterner was crying.

"Who did it?" Martin said.

"I don't know. The boy Ludwig, hurting nobody, walking in the street. Just walking."

"Vartin — " The name came queer from the bloody, crooked mouth. "Vardin Radhy — "

"*Dígame, Chico!*" Martin bent down. He put his hand on Ludwig's shoulder. It seemed very small. "Tell me who done it, Chico. Can you tell me?"

The puffed lip moved, but no sound came.

"We will see about him, Chico," Martin said.

He walked along the dark way through the store, hearing the sound of his own words, We will see about him, Chico.

He went by Gregorio's lantern, out the door, into the street. Ruelle was still there.

"I want to know who done it," Martin said.

"Some highline rider named Barton, somebody said, Happy Barton, Handy Barton, something. Tall. Just come to town. Riding a dun horse, if that's him — "

"They got him?"

"Hell no they didn't!"

"Why didn't they?"

"Nobody tried."

"Anybody know where he went?"

"Somebody said down there towards the tent saloon — "

"Where's the law at?"

"The law? The law named McFeeters is at Hogan's drunk as a skunk. I told you there would be hell popping tanbark when sons of bitches started filling this town! I'm about to pack a derringer myself. They shot at the little Jew's feet making him dance and calling him a shitass sheeny — Look here, Brady, you be careful — "

Martin moved away into the dark.

He moved fast. The street was very dark. He heard the footsteps following him, and he jerked around. *"Hijos de putas! Cobardes! Stay back there!"*

Around the corner of the last wall, through the salt cedars, he saw the glow of the lights shining through the tent top. He smelled the river in the darkness beyond.

In the dim light by the tent door, he heard the music inside. He saw the horses at the rack, a dun horse. He untied it and cut hard at the face with a rein. The horse plunged loose, out into the dark; Martin stood still a moment by the door flap, adjusting his eyes to the light.

He stepped in casually, calling out above the music, "Whose dun horse out there?"

A dark whiskered man turned from the bar.

"What about the dun horse?"

"Broke loose, kicking!" Martin said. "Thought I'd tell whoever it belonged to."

"Why, goddamn the goddamn goddamned hell, go catch him!"

The crowd had turned to look.

"Don't like to touch another man's horse," Martin said.

The man moved toward Martin, standing in the door.

"If the goddamned horse was loose — " He saw Martin was armed. "Couldn't you bring him up?"

"I got a bad leg here, but I will help you head him — "

Beyond the canvas flap outside, the man looked at the rack. He moved out into the dark. "Ho — whoa! You boogered goddamn bastard, I'll blow your goddamn — Christ!" he said, turning. "You catch him. Buy you a goddamn drink."

Martin moved carefully. Not shoot him, not kill him. Catch him. Hurt him, not shoot. Take him to Rucker.

"Say!" Martin whispered. "I saw you work over that kid, up the street!"

"What about it? Wasn't that a goddamn caution? I made the goddamn yellowbelly Jew boy — "

Martin swung with his doubled left fist, hitting with all his weight. The punch struck solid in the face — too high — too high. He saw the shape in the dark topple back half twisting, hitting the ground with a grunt, with a hand scrabbling, and Martin knew it was not enough. He sprang to kick the face and grab. The face jerked away as he sprang and he saw the split-second glint in the hand coming up. Martin fired, feeling the recoil jump solid in his hand, with the cracking flash down into the shape on the ground and the burning smell, and the shape moved. Martin fired again. He fired again, and the shape did not move, and he ran around the corner of the tent as they came out the door.

Bent low into the darkness of the thicket, he moved carefully, furious with the tornillo thorns that snagged scratching across him as he worked down the slope, through the musty brush to the open place of the river.

He came to the soft bank unbuckling his gun belt, seeing starlight shining in the black water at his feet, hearing a shout from somewhere in the thicket at his back.

Jamming his hat tight, gripping with his left hand the gun belt high and dry, he eased down unsplashing into the quiet current, feeling the breath jerk in his throat with the shock of the water's cold. He moved out into it paddling underwater with his feet and his right hand, slowly, with the drift downstream, working, with the breath coming hard, out across the space of the murmuring rippled darkness toward the line of the black bank on the other side.

He thrashed up to it in a shallow matted with a tangle of high cattail, and climbed out through the stinking ooze, splashing, grasping at the sharp-edged, rustling reeds, holding his gun, holding his gun high and dry in his stiffening left hand, reaching dry ground with water slopping from his jeans and his boots squishing as he hobbled with his leg hurting up the claybank away from the water. He turned for a moment and looked back. In the sticking sharp wetness of the clothes that bound him, he trembled with the cold, feeling scalding tears come burning on his face.

PART TWO

CHAPTER XIII

M<small>ARTIN</small>
climbed from the gully, hearing the sound of his breath in the
silence. He came up at the back of the tall wall and moved around
it to the corner, to the street. It was empty. His damp boot soles
made a faint scratch as he stepped along the dim arches of the
portico in the starlight. When he raised his knuckles to the shadowed face of the Chihuahua stage station door, his hand stopped.

I got to have Lágrimas, he told himself.

Looking over his shoulder, Martin rapped on the door. Pancho Gil, you got to bring me my horse.

Martin rapped and waited. He rapped louder, hating the sound, and waited. No answer came to him and he shifted his feet, pulling his gun. He tapped on the wood with the pistol butt.

"Don Pancho! *Oye! Don Pancho!*"

Martin put his ear to the door. He stood listening for a long time. The stillness, the blackness, seemed suddenly bad and he struck at it with the gun butt, banging on the door.

"*Don Pancho! Tu amigo! Bredi!*"

From the silence a town dog howled baying; the vacant face of the lightless door stood unmoving, soundless. Pancho Gil made no light in the stage station, made no answer.

Slipping the gun into the holster, Martin limped away from the door. His shirt clung damp to the small of his back, and he shivered clenching his jaws, moving slowly along the tall wall. At the high and heavy double gate of the corral he stopped and raised his eyes at its dark solidity. He kicked at it with the side of his boot, and turned to lean against the wood.

He ached with weariness. His leg hurt. He felt the swollen left wrist, flexing it.

If I'd just hit him hard enough, he said to himself alone in the dark.

He rubbed at the skinned knuckles.

But I didn't.

"And I shot the son of a bitch." He said the words in English, aloud. "I had to."

"*Who is it?*" a voice whispered from the other side of the gate timbers. Hackles stood on Martin's neck as he jerked around.

"Don Pancho?"

"*Shhh!* Who speaks?"

"Bredi. From Valdepeñas — open it!"

He heard the bolt slide and saw the gate open a crack. The dark tube of a musket barrel came pointing out.

"All right. You are Bredi. Pass in."

He stepped through the gate. When it closed again, and the iron bolt was thrown, the figure with the musket turned. The voice whispered, "I heard the words of English. Otherwise — "

"I want Don Pancho."

"I know you from the day you came with the cart. With the black horse."

"Wake Don Pancho."

"You think he would not wake with your noise? He's gone! When they came to take him, he was gone."

"When who came to take him?"

"Are you making jokes?"

"Answer me — when who came to take him?"

"*Salcidistas!* Who else? As soon as they had the garrison and the city hall, they came to take him!"

"Mother of Jesus, they got this town! When?"

"Now. This evening. The captain of the garrison gave them the key! They drank all the wine in the customs, then rutted. Didn't you hear bells?"

"I came around the town, from the other side. I didn't know it." Martin brought one of the two silver pesos from his wet pocket and put the coin in the dark hand. "Take me to Don Pancho."

"How? He is gone — "

"Listen to me! Listen well. I am man of confidence of Cipriano Castro, the *patrón*. You take me to Pancho Gil."

"He's far, señor."

"You take me. You understand you are taking me?"

"There is no horse, no mule — the Salcidistas took — "

"Shit of that. We go afoot. We go any way."

"Señor. I speak truth. I am afraid. I am also guard of this property, for Don Pancho. I cannot go. You are not of the Salcidistas, so I can tell you something." He made a cross of thumb and forefinger. He kissed it. "The truth," he whispered. "On the main road to Zaragosa, a league more or less, is the farm of the Asunsolos. You will find it by asking. Don Pancho hides at the Asunsolos', by the river. In secret. He awaits developments."

"And if you have not told me? If he is not at the — the Asunsolos'?"

"I have told you. By this Cross."

"Open the gate."

"That you go with God."

He went quietly in the quietness, skirting the huddled lines of houses on the sleeping streets, stopping still, waiting in the dark when dogs barked. He labored along the dim broken spaces of fields and thickets of brush near the river, hoping he walked the Zaragosa road, moving in a kind of fever southward toward the dark line where the valley met the sky. He limped as he moved tensing the soreness of his leg, dragging the heel scuffing as he swung the weak foot ahead. Sweat ran from under the band of his hat. The bunchy dampness of his clothes dried hot. He smelled the breath from the staleness of his mouth, and he swallowed often, turning his eyes, expecting the morning star over the trees beyond the river. His mind moved circling, cutting arcs, hovering the effort of his flesh.

Night silence suddenly coiled with the whirl of his thought, spinning, crying out with the black earth tilted away, withdrawn from his step. It came back reeling from space, banging dizzy on the sole of his boot. Martin Brady sat down. He felt the great black curl of the tree and the sky twist over, and with the palm of his hand on the grainy ground he closed his eyes.

A padded flutter and shuffle soft in the sand sent sound from dream to shaken wakefulness. In the gray light, gray burro legs moved too near his face. Packsaddles cinched with knotted *mecate* joggled squeaking; a rock hit and bounced from the ragged rump of the last donkey in the file.

"*Arre!*" said a voice.

Martin sat up by the side of the road and saw the wood hauler trailing the beasts.

"*Qué hubo*," Martin said. He coughed, dry in the throat.

The wood hauler stopped in his tracks. "Ah," he said, after a while. "Juice. That's it. Juice of the vine. Juice of the mescal."

"Neither," Martin said, standing up.

The wood hauler's lips were open in an expressionless grin, as if wires pulled at the corners of his mouth. He saw the holster at Martin's hip. "Excuse me. Sleeping out. I believed it was the juice."

"Is this the road to Zaragosa?"

"It is the road."

"Do you know the farm of the Asunsolos?"

The wood hauler looked at Martin, surveyed the tree, the *acequia*, the field beyond. "Asunsolos," he said. "Asunsolos."

"Where is the farm of the Asunsolos?"

"You ask where? Excuse me, señor?"

"Do you know where is the farm of the Asunsolos?"

"An oddity. Asking for Asunsolos."

"What oddity?"

The wood hauler moved his hand upward as if he used its edge to slice the air carefully, over the *acequia*. He sighted along his arm at the field beyond. "The farm of the Asunsolos."

"Huh!"

The wood hauler looked sideward at the gringo with the gun. "With your permission — "

As Martin walked along the edge of the vineyard, sunlight touched the top leaves of the vines. A congregation of jangly blackbirds flew from a dead cottonwood. By the corral, a dog came snarling. Martin picked up a broken wagon spoke from the clutter by a tumbled adobe wall, and stood waiting, while the dog barked.

A man came from around the corner of the house under the trees. He was armed and wore spurs. He walked forward with his eyes fastened on Martin, kicked at the sidling dog, and spoke.

"Who do you look for?"

"Señor Asunsolo."

"At your orders."

"Martín Bredi, at yours."

"What do you want?"

"I am from Valdepeñas, Hacienda de Valdepeñas."

"You appear to be from Texas. Without horse."

"I have been there. I crossed the river last night, late. I went to the station of the Chihuahua stage. I went looking for a friend of mine."

"Well? Who told you to come here?"

"The peon of the station corral. He knows me."

"I don't."

"I understand that, señor. In that case — could I drink from your well and rest myself — before I go?"

"In that case suit yourself."

When Martin had both hands on the well rope, the man with the gun and spurs moved briskly around the house, and disappeared.

I did it wrong, I'm tired, Martin thought, tipping the dented bucket to his lips. Señor Pancho Gil. But if he's here, they'll tell him. And if they tell him, he'll see me. If he's not here —

He set the bucket down, and moved around the tumbled wall. Seated in the long shade, with his back to the adobe, he took off his hat, and rubbed his eyes. He felt his belly gnaw for food. A line of ants marched by his boots, out over the wagon ruts in the sunlight. A beetle went by.

Hearing footsteps, Martin turned his head, alert. Pancho Gil stepped from around the corner of the wall.

"*Andale Bredi!* A loyal man. We need you! The goddamned Salcidistas —" The eyes in the heavy brown jowled face surveyed Martin as he rose to his feet. "Swimming rivers? No horse?"

"I came to ask your help. I left my horse on the other side."

"What?"

"I had trouble. We have to get the horse. It's at Sterner's."

"What trouble?"

Martin tapped the gun. "I left."

Gil clicked his tongue. "Shooting? With gringos, eh? Ha!"

"A gringo. He abused the nephew of Sterner. Maybe I killed him. I came over here —"

"Good! Now you can kill some Mexicans." Gil's heavy shoulders drew up as he laughed. "Don't worry yourself."

Martin checked at the surge of anger. "Just get me the horse. If they haven't taken it away."

"Who?"

"Texas police."

"Milk of Texas police! I need you with that black horse. I was sending for you."

"Were you? One thing is necessary. Right away, get the horse. Sterner knows you. You tell him about me and you bring me the horse."

"All right, Bredi. Enough horse. What do you say of breakfast?"

"I could eat."

He sat outside the door of the smoky kitchen, breaking off limp pieces of tortilla, with them scooping the beans and chili, the shreds of strong meat, from the clay bowl to his hungry mouth.

When he had finished the coffee, pale with bluish boiled milk and not hot, he thanked the barefooted cook handing her the cup and bowl, and walked to the shed where Pancho Gil and the man Asunsolo saddled horses.

" — Raising the dead in Del Norte this morning, with their forced loans. Their writs, their Salcido *préstamos*, their documents — " Gil spit in the manure dust, and tightened the saddle girt. He put his rifle in the scabbard under the stirrup. "They will not find Señor Gil. Señor Gil is gone. He is among gringos. He keeps one foot on the bank of the river. Ready to jump. *Que viva Méjico!* Eh, Bredi?" Gil swung up on his horse.

"My Winchester is with my saddle, over there, and my saddlebags — could you get them filled with .44–40s? Sterner knows the size."

"Are you ready, Don Rubén?" Gil called to Asunsolo.

Martin opened the gate, looking up at Gil. "If you could find out how things are, over there. So I would know — "

"A quantity of things to find out today, Bredi. Maybe the armed mother whore of Salcido, on the way to the river crossing. Or on the way back. You stay here. Quiet."

The two horsemen rode fast across the field, toward the river.

A hot wind stirred along the valley as Martin sat waiting by the tumbled wall. He waited in silence with the slow climb of the sun, with the sound of the wind, with the sway of the shadows. The wind brought a veil of thin dust across the sky. The dust faded the color, leaving only the glare of the high lonely emptiness enclosing the empty world.

Southward the sandhills danced blurred in the heat, waiting, in an old desolation. In the hazy noon sunlight north beyond the trees by the river, the waiting shape of Mount Jefflin stood pale and unsubstantial as a ghost.

The sun inched with an agonizing slowness down the sky, and set with a fading yellow shine. Killdees made a faint crying over the river while the light and the wind died. The gloaming sound of the work stock enfolded for the night, the footfalls, the dim voices, moving from fields to wisps of smoke from kitchen fires, the murmur of twilight, enlarged the loneliness by the tumbled wall.

Martin's thought traveled out the invisible space beyond the black line of the hills westward to the Sierra Madre, the mother mountains of Mexico. He rode the black horse over the top to where the sun still lit the western slope, to Sonora. He left Chihuahua dark at his back forever. He rode away from it, from the reach of the Castros and the old times, and came to another place.

The evening star went down and crickets chirred. Martin sat in the dark facing the river, listening for the sound of hooves. Dogs barked from across the sleeping fields, and were answered, muffled with night and distance.

Martin half sensed the sound beyond the vineyard suddenly, and stood up. He moved to the gate by the saddle shed; Asunsolo's dog ran gruff-throated past the corral. The soft shuffle came, the click of a hoof, a snort, and a squeak of wet leathers, before he could see. There were three horses.

"Thou, Bredi?" a hoarse voice said.

"Here! And you got him!"

"Goddamned outlaw with his two stones and scared of water!" Gil came down from his mount. "Don Rubén had to ride him across. Don Rubén is all a horseman."

Rubén Asunsolo swung off and handed Martin the *ramal*. "Much horse. If I had him, he would be a mount." Asunsolo was soaking wet.

Martin smiled and said, "Lágrimas," seeing the lather white on the black jaws in the dark. He whistled two notes quietly, repeating them, while his arm went over the black neck. "Lágrimas." He patted the neck. "Old one, it's Martín."

"We unsaddle," Gil said, loosening his cinch.

"We go to the kitchen. To get dry," Asunsolo said.

Martin untied the wet Saltillo, and took the heavy bags from the saddle on Lágrimas.

"You got them," Martin said, hefting.

"Two hundred rounds, .44–40," Gil said. "Compliments of the Señor Sterner — at least, he extends you credit. Here, your rifle, dry. I carried it myself."

Asunsolo turned his horse loose, and went out the gate toward the house.

"That black threw Asunsolo in the river," Gil said.

"I hope the cartridges are dry," Martin said, unsaddling.

"Examine them by the light inside."

"First I rub this horse."

"He is drying well."

"I am glad to see him."

"Listen, Bredi. That business of the Señor Sterner with the Castros is finished. Until better times, until arrangements. Now, nothing travels south, the mail coach, nothing! With that horse you are rubbing you travel very well. And fast enough, against Salcidistas on the road, against Apaches of Fuego. You ride now with a letter to the hacienda at Carmen, for the Castros. Fifty leagues. If the hacienda is fallen, ride on, to Valdepeñas. I tell you I cut the testicles of the party of Salcido here in Del Norte — with a little help! If I get a little of that metal which is refined from the El Tigre Mine of Don Cipriano Castro. If I distribute a little of that metal. It is urgent. You leave in the morning? The Señor Sterner says you have not yet ridden the horse. You are able?"

"I also swim, eh? Swim rivers. What else did the Señor Sterner say? About last night — what did he say?"

"He says for you to stay on this side. The law is very strict, he says. Don't go back."

"How is the nephew?"

"Bad. He is wounded sadly."

"And the one I shot?"

"Well shot. Buried. One less *gringo chingao*."

CHAPTER XIV

THE MEASURE
of difference, the height of spirit, between a foot on earth and a
foot in stirrup, was manifest in the centaur line of his back, in the
easy, faintly swinging frame of his shoulders.

He rode alone, his eyes sharp, among dry scourings strewn like
gigantic bones of stone and ancient crumbling grit from the bare,
ruined carcass of the world. A noon glare bent down upon it,
melting its edge in a blur and shimmer of waving heat. The enor-
mous dazzle knifed at him, under his hat; his mind pulled back into
the last small shade of his skull. At a landmark called the Crossing
of San Isidro, he touched rein and turned along the flinty slant into
the pale wash of the Río del Carmen.

South beyond the rim of the plain, the unreal shape of the Sierra Mojina loomed blue above the fluid tremor of the heat. The worn walls of the hacienda at Carmen waited for him somewhere at the foot of the blue, and he frowned, squinting into the south.

It is the wrong sierra, Martin Brady told himself, the wrong blue, coming closer. He heard the words far back in the silent shade of his skull. ¶ did stop, at the edge of the dunes, that second morning. I looked so far west it ached in my eyes and I thought about it, on the horse, with the fifty pesos from Pancho Gil in my belt, with the dried meat and the cornmeal, the two hundred rounds tied on the saddle, everything for Sonora.

I remain your attentive and faithful servant. That is how they write it, with the rubric. It ought to be your honest and brainless fool. No rubric. Not so honest either, but foolish enough. I came south with the damn letter of Pancho Gil because I said I would and I wish I taken the road to Sonora.

"Lágrimas," he said aloud, for company, watching the ears, "foolish horse. How are you?"

You did this to me. When Pancho Gil got you across that river, Pancho Gil got me. Now the Castros get us both.

He slowed along the gravelly rise of the wash upstream, crossing the trace of the stage road, watching for sign, for moccasin tracks. Through stunted thickets of gray granjeno and wilted clumps of sacahuiste he came to the glittering bed of the waterless stream, and crossed over, turning south, away from the ruts of the road, to high ground where he could see over the breaks into the empty furnace of the plain with the dry gash of the watercourse sloping up to the Sierra Mojina. He turned in the saddle for a moment and looked at what lay behind him.

San Isidro, the crossing of the saint of farmers, he thought. San Isidro, he would find it a little dry. The old man at Potrero said water was upstream and we will wet our nose, Horse, when we find it. I hope it is better water than the scum at Alamo de Peña, or that water at dawn when I saddled you in the dark and rode down to Potrero with the old man telling us the road by the ditch and the people sneaking behind the walls afraid. Two days past, the old man said, the Apaches of Fuego rode into the *plazita* laughing and got off with rifles cocked. They were insolent, as if the people of Potrero were beneath reason. That is what the old man said. The Apaches walked into the houses. They jerked blankets from the people's shoulders, from the beds of the sick. They took all the blankets. They took three girls and held them crying on the horses. They said they would come back to Potrero and they rode away carrying the girls and the blankets. The people did nothing. They awaited the return of Fuego. They awaited a new cruelty. These were bad times with war in the south and Apaches in the north, the old man said. He said the citizens were sheep. Not all the citizens, Martin rode thinking. There were some wolves around. Enough coyotes. Maybe a few sheep dogs that starved or got belted to death for their trouble, while the sheep bleated. And that is enough about animals, he thought, but this is a sad and sorry country. Something holds it. It has got too much patience. It don't expect enough. In my country — say! — there is too much expecting and not enough patience. Your country. You had your chance. You had supper once with Miss Louisa Rucker. You walked out of her house and shot a man. And ran. She thinks a lot of you. She remembers you well. She is waiting to hear all those songs. Her father and her mother would be so glad to have you teach her the words.

> *Ai chinita que vente conmigo*
> *Adonde vivo yo.*

It means in Spanish, Miss Louisa, that it's a love song, about a dove. It says, that you come with me, to where I live. Come with me to where I scratch fleas at El Carmen and sleep by the horse corral.

The clack of a hoof on a glancing stone was the only break in the beat of the soft sound treading the silence, the long space, the long hours. The muscled black shoulders moved in their smooth alternate thrusts with the sway and push from the lift and swing of the steady black driving haunches.

The sun moved. Shade grew edging into the flat glare, adding a depth slowly, building a form and a solidity into the outreaching fall of distance. Shadow reached across the hoofprints of a horse. Shine cut under the brim of a hat.

The Sierra Mojina became more than a prophetic silhouette of mountain. It stood with its detail revealed, on the visible feet of its upthrust slope from the plain, frowning from its blue-shaded crags, its jagged turrets and smashed cupolas of high stone. Below, the wash of Río del Carmen made a pale twisting scar. It was laced with a rim of green as it turned from the plain into the roughening hills and went from sight beyond a shouldering bluff.

Lágrimas, smell water. Remember the place? When we came with the cart? It took us a day from the hacienda, with the oxen. We will make it in two hours, we —

He pulled up stopping sharp, with a tall mesquite for cover at his back. Squinting into the sun with his hand projecting his hat-brim, he watched the black dots circling slow in the sky, beyond the far side of the green bend in the Carmen. He strained his eyes until they watered, looking for movement, for telltale dot or hint of dust in the brush or on the slopes along the wash or under the wheeling buzzards, and beyond, to the shoulder of the sierra. Under him his horse's breath came timed with a faint repeating squeak of sweated leather in the unmoving silence. When the horse moved again, answering the spur, the first step of the hoof seemed cracking loud in the quiet.

Two days past, the old man said this morning. Maybe it was Fuego, leaving that souvenir for the birds, Martin thought as he watched, maybe it wasn't. Maybe Fuego has moved on to another water, maybe he hasn't — but I'll south the long way around with room to run. If they jump me.

He turned abruptly into the sun, riding low ground, through the long breaks to the edge of the gravel, to the big tabacón leaves in the slanting light, with the musty smell, and the bright green jarilla, and the dusty tall willow, watching. At the far side of the open wash, in untracked silt, in the shade of a flood-marked stone, stood water. The horse blew, smelling, as the hooves rattled the gravel.

I'll let you, Horse. You need it. You might need it more. Don't waste time. This is not a good place.

He sat with his eyes first running along the way he would jump the bank into the brush, if he had to. Then he turned, watching around the sides of the draw, hearing the pulling suck at the horse's lips, the fluid gugging up the rings of the gullet, the sudden break of liquid plash as the horse's head came up with the munch of teeth on dripping bit.

And I might as well take my chances too, you damn horse, it sounds good. It sounds wet.

He slid off. Scooping with his hatbrim cupped, he lifted it and drank, tasting mud with the stale felty smell of the wetted brim, swallowing the tepid wetness running it over his tongue and the back of his teeth and down his throat. He dipped to drink twice again, fast, and jammed his hat on while he rinsed his mouth and squirted water. Wiping his chin, he stepped into the stirrup and swung around, up the bank into the brush.

He came out across the ruts of the mail road into the dry open, seeing no sign, moving away from the road, working out from the circling buzzards in a wide loop westward on the flat before he turned south again. He rode in a fast rack, turning his eyes, sensitive to the pitch of the points on his horse's black ears.

That is too many birds, he thought as he looked back. And not enough sign. We have missed their sign, Horse, whoever they were. We are not going back to see.

Over his right shoulder the plain swept west to its hazed horizon under thunderheads fire-edged with the lowering sun. At his left the broken scarp of the Sierra Mojina pitched up cobalt-shadowed and immense over the tangled line of brush along the Carmen's wash. He watched the menacing tangle darken, out beyond the far-legged joggle of his horse's stretching shadow, as the light moved down, reddening, in the west.

The sign — more sign than he looked for — came suddenly, and he bent over, reining, to read a churned swathe of horse tracks. The hooves that made them were all shod. They marked the ground in a regular order of files. The files moved long-strided, toward where the buzzards flew.

He swung down from Lágrimas, and squatted to study the soil grains edging the tracks. When he had examined them, he remounted and rode on, puzzling along the backtrack of the many prints southward.

They weren't Fuego's. They were a troop or more of cavalry from the direction of El Carmen, early yesterday, or the day before that. They hurried, and somebody left something for the birds.

The sun dropped over the horizon, lifting its red stretching fire from across the ground, from across the horse tracks, leaving blue shade. The blue turned purple following the last reddened light up the Sierra Mojina. Dusk came flattening all shape under the deepening sky.

Another dry camp, Horse, no El Carmen tonight. No El Carmen for us until we know which cavalry —

The buzz and the jump came in the same instant. Lágrimas broke wind as the hooves struck and lifted high again, with Martin rebalanced. He looked back at the ugly shape coiled dim on the ground, still buzzing.

"Good horse," Martin said.

There is trouble around El Carmen this evening. There is not even a man moving goats to a pen for the night. There is nothing but horse tracks and a rattlesnake and it's getting dark.

The great star of the Lyre stood over the Sierra Mojina as Martin turned toward water. He rode down through the brush, picking his way quietly to the cottonwoods. As he moved under the branches, a breeze rustled in the heart-shaped leaves dark above him. He came to the edge of the water and smelled the damp grass.

The horse drank long, without hurry, while Martin stood in the softness of the grass, hearing a frog sing with the rustle of the cottonwoods. In the cool, he felt his face still burn from the long glare of the day. He got on his belly and drank.

From the saddlebags he pulled a tin cup and a canvas bag of *pinole*, parched corn ground and mixed with sugar. When he had scooped up water in the cup, he poured some of the pale meal into it, and stirred it with his finger. Sitting in the grass against a tree he ate his sweetened gruel from the cup, while his horse fed strongly, pulling grass and munching, moving faintly, in the dark.

The bright star stood high above the sierra when he put the reins over the black neck and swung into the saddle. He cut across the shallow water, up the slope at an easy walk in the starlight, through scrub oak and cardenche, into the hills. As he came over the rounded crest of a rise, he saw what he looked for in the south — campfires at El Carmen, points of orange light flickering in the dark. He sat the saddle for a while watching, wondering for whom they burned.

When he stepped down from the stirrup, he uncoiled from the pommel the slender line of the *cabrestante* and with it tied Lágrimas to the trunk of an oak; then he unsaddled and unbridled, and hung a nose bag, with cracked corn in its bottom, on Lágrimas' black nose.

He put his saddle and rifle and the unfolded Saltillo on a clear place, and stretched out on the ground, resting his neck against the saddle seat, with his hat off, looking up at the stars, hearing the muffled sound of the horse's teeth grinding on the grain. When the sound had ceased, he got up. The campfires at El Carmen were almost gone. He took the empty *morral* off the horse's nose, and looked around, listening in the quietness, then went to his blanket, unstrapped his gun, and slept hungry.

CHAPTER XV

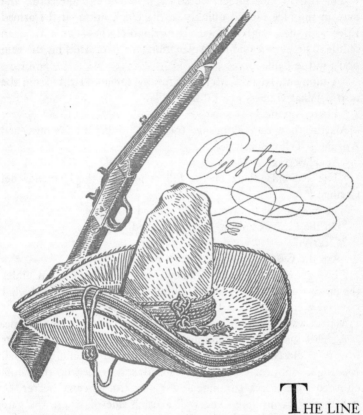

THE LINE
of mud huts and the stage station by the road were barely touched
with light when Martin came to the edge of the settlement at El
Carmen. In the gray quiet, El Carmen bore no visible scar of
violence. Smoke from dim chimneys rose thin and straight up the
windless air. A calf bawled from behind walls.

Martin rode into a thicket by the lane that led to the straggled
village. He sat waiting, while the light grew from behind the
looming Sierra Mojina.

He waited a long time, sitting the saddle, before the straw-hatted rider on the thin pony came trotting up the lane.

"Good morning," Martin called as casually as he could, coming from the mesquite.

The brown face under the straw brim showed concern. The eyes in the face looked quickly at the black horse, at the armed rider with the gringo hat, with the gringo clothes — on a Mexican saddle. The eyes found no explanation; the bare heels hit the thin pony in the flanks.

"A moment, friend." Martin carefully smiled. "I ride from the north. What is news in El Carmen?"

"There is none."

Martin rode out, alongside the thin pony. "El Carmen had Apaches? Tell me, man!"

"Apaches, no."

"The hacienda, there on the hill, who holds the Hacienda del Carmen?"

The eyes under the straw brim looked sideward.

"Do the Castros hold it?" Martin asked.

"Clearly."

"Are the Castros on the hacienda now?"

"The general." The eyes glanced sideward again, from under the straw brim. "The general, riding a black horse. Of which I now see a copy."

Martin watched the back of the hurrying hat joggle up the lane.

A high wall of thick adobe, with musket ports and corner towers, enclosed the Hacienda del Carmen on the hill. The wall was edged with early sunlight when Martin headed up the hoof-churned road to ask entrance at the gate. As he came nearer, he saw there was no gate. The wall at each side of where the gate had been was darkened with the stain of smoke. A guard with a gun stood alert in the opening. The guard wore the standard wide-brimmed felt sombrero with the scarlet *barboquejo*, the red chin string, of Marcos Castro's cavalry.

"Who lives?" the guard challenged.

"Mexico." Martin took the chance. "And the Castros."

"What do you want?"

"I have an express for the general."

"Improbable. With the Texas hat."

"Who is your captain? El Verdugo?"

"Do you know him?"

"You tell him Bredi is here. Bredi. Riding from Del Norte."

"That is a Castro horse you ride."

"Without doubt."

"Dismount, and I will have you taken. — *Hei,* Pito!" he called.

A bandy-legged little cavalryman stepped toward the guard.

"Take him to the captain." The guard turned to Martin. "He will carry your firearms. You lead the black — "

Martin walked leading Lágrimas, following the bandy legs cased in their worn leather. A long sheath knife wagged out over the seat of the breeches. The knife's horn handle was snugged above the belt, in the small of the trooper's back. He walked examining the Colt and Winchester he had taken from Martin.

"Good arms," the trooper said, hefting one in each hand. "Very good. We have the Remington of one shot. Without pistol — but with knives."

Martin felt the strangeness of being in a crowd, encircled by a wall. Cook fires were burning on the tracked dust. The tang of mesquite smoke and the flaming drip of fat from beef spitted over the fires, richened the air. Martin felt his nostrils move and his belly reach for the sizzling hot meat. A few old women moved among the scores of big-hatted men. The women carried clay bowls of beans, chili, tortillas in stacks.

Over the crowd stood the massive shape of the hacienda's big house. Fire had licked from its windows; beneath their smoked lintels the windows were black holes behind blackened iron bars.

"What happened, Maestro?" Martin asked his trooper.

"The Salcidistas happened."

"When?"

"Six days past."

"When did you come?" Martin indicated the men at the fires. They were cutting broiled beef with their long knives.

"Day before yesterday."

"I saw the buzzards north of here, and the horse tracks."

"And the tracks of Salcidistas?" The trooper spit. "They made them going out. Only going out."

The ruined blacksmith shed stood at the battered end of out-buildings between the big house and the maze of adobe corrals. A smith worked at the anvil in the ruin, by a dented iron tub of red coals and a peon pumping at a patched, wheezing bellows. Past the corner post of the shed, horses were tied along a line awaiting the smith's attention. As Martin came toward them, he saw El Verdugo's thick back and spindly legs in their sheaths of dusty leather. He stood with a quirt in his hand, watching a farrier measure shoes for a high-headed bay.

"My captain," Martin's trooper said.

El Verdugo turned, in the sound of the clanking anvil and the spark-blowing wheeze of the bellows. His hat sat on the back of his head, spilling a thick jet forelock in the beads of sweat on his brow. The eyes under the bony jut of the brow were as black, as impassable, as the burned, iron-barred windows of the big house. They fixed on Martin, then moved over him in a flat stare. A hint of stained teeth showed from under the twists of a sweeping mustache.

"Very oddly dressed," the captain remarked. "Still mounted on that black."

"I brought a letter. From Señor Gil in Del Norte."

"And how is Del Norte?"

"At the orders of Salcido."

"This hacienda was likewise at the orders of Salcido." El Verdugo's eyes moved slowly, staring, surveying the evidence. "The day before yesterday in the morning, the orders were changed. You came late for the fiestas. — Hand me the damned letter. I'm busy."

Martin pulled the paper from the money belt inside his shirt and handed it to the captain, who took it and turned his back, without a word, to watch the farrier nail a shoe.

Martin stood waiting, eyeing the thick insolence of the un-moving back.

"My horse has come fifty leagues," Martin finally said, between his teeth. "Is it possible to issue orders for forage?"

The back turned and the eyes leveled, not at Martin but at the trooper who stood holding Martin's guns. "Give *Mister* Bredi his tools and take him to the devil or the forage sergeant." El Verdugo turned his back again. "Bredi — you understand you are at the general's orders — move on!"

Martin swallowed, keeping his mouth shut. He felt the sweat in his hand as he slipped the pistol into the holster. The trooper put the carbine in the scabbard under the stirrup, and they led Lágrimas away, along the pitted walls, to the opened gate of a corral.

The trooper pointed beyond a haycart. "There is the sergeant," he said.

It was Diego Casas.

"*God of my life!*" Diego came with the red chin string of Marcos Castro's cavalry biting his cheeks. "Son of the mother!" He embraced Martin. "On two good legs!" They slapped dust from each other's backs.

"You are acquainted," the trooper observed.

"Not with a sergeant!" Martin said.

"Of the valiant!" grinned Diego. "In charge of corn and hay."

"I will leave you, with your permission," the trooper said.

"Thanks, Pito," Diego said, "for bringing him. He is my twin."

"It was a pleasure." The trooper walked away.

"Can we pen Lágrimas well, and feed him?"

"You came to the place, Martín! I want you to wait here a minute. I go to arrange something." Diego disappeared around a corner.

Martin stood with the worn *ramal* of the reins in his hand. "Horse," he said in English, patting the black neck, "do you like this?"

When Diego reappeared through a gate, the peon Pablo came with him.

"Martín!"

Pablo pulled off his hat, smiling with the wrinkles creased deep in his face. His eyes glistened. He put out his brown hard hand.

"The times are better," Pablo said, "with our friend Martín! Like old times."

"With our friend Pablo," Martin said. "Much better!"

"Tend the stallion," Diego said.

"Old times, Martín," Pablo said. "And the leg all well! *Hu* Lágrimas! The same. The same."

"I will find my corporal," Diego said. "I will give him charge. We will divert ourselves with novelties from the north! Hast thou eaten, Martín?"

"Not in twenty years."

"We have the remedy!"

He sat in the shade with Diego, chewing, tearing the savory meat from the bones with his teeth, licking the yellow fat from his fingers, drinking the fiery juice from the frijole bowl, dipping beans with eatable scoops he made of rolled tortillas, and chewing more meat.

"Diego, it heals me. Fifty leagues with a bag of *pinole* and a little *carne seca*."

"Ah, the belly grows, there in the north, with the rich food of Texas! With all that food and drink. With all those women of the aristocracy. How did it go, in the north?"

Martin looked carefully at Diego.

"My twin, I thought we lost you. And you come back."

"I'm back. Here I am. Tell me about Sergeant Casas. How did he happen?"

"He happened on the journey from Del Norte with the cart and the guard of cavalry and the Remingtons of the Sterner brand."

"I finally saw those Remingtons this morning."

"They are very good. And how did you leave the Señor Smuggler Sterner?"

"The same."

"How is Pancho Gil?"

"I brought a letter from him to the Castros. Del Norte is lost and Pancho Gil is hiding, with a wet foot, waiting for better times."

"The times are disordered."

"How much longer will the fighting go?"

"Who knows? But I will tell you something true. This cavalry of General Castro has force. One, we are better armed. Two, we are better mounted. Three, we are better fed. Four, we are better led."

"*Ándale*, what a sergeant!"

"The general is making a battalion of infantry with Indian recruits from the south. They are a different crowd from our people. I have seen them, pure Indians, brutes. The general gives them a musket and a hundred rounds, and a knife the size of a wagon tongue. They get a little corn — and all the loot they can take, and they are like a plague. They are tougher than dun horses. Don Cipriano sits in the big house at Valdepeñas and Salcido is afraid to go fight him. You see what happens, when Salcido bothers Castro land?"

"What happens?"

"The people of this hacienda and the village of El Carmen ran to the sierra when they saw the Salcidistas coming, and that gang, that *chusma de canalla*, burned down the gate and made a carnival of barbecues, and fireworks inside the big house. You saw.

"We were with El Verdugo at Hormigas, bringing arms from Presidio, when a rider brought word of El Carmen. Three days later, we came. We caught that gang, by a bend of the Río Carmen. *Tomate, tomate!* Blood! We saved out six captives. El Verdugo sent for the General Marcos Castro to come see the hacienda, to come see the captives. He came yesterday.

"A bad thing yesterday, Martín. You remember what El Verdugo did that time to the cow thieves at Valdepeñas, on that flat place out there at the section of La Novia? And how the foreman made us ride out, all the vaqueros, to watch it?

"We watched it yesterday. The six prisoners. Our general saw the condition of the big house, he saw the dead stock and the barbarities, and he ordered the six holes dug. We knew it from the kind of holes they were digging, in a line."

Diego spit on the ground, and looked at Martin.

"I was not ordered to ride," Diego said. "The First Platoon rode. The rest of the troop, and all the people, were ordered to watch. So we watched. As you and I did at Novia. A hoof hit one of the heads as it screamed. '*Death to the* —' it started. And ended, like dropping a rock on a melon. The Señor *Teniente* of the platoon got permission to march to the Río Carmen afterwards. The troopers rode their horses through the water several times.

"So I have no sotol to offer you. Yesterday I drank all I had. General Castro is not liberal with beef of the Castro brand, you know that. But today you see us with plenty of good meat. The general rewards us. Why?" Diego shrugged. "I tell you, that running over the heads is excessive.

"Martín — I will tell you about being sergeant. It concerns an old acquaintance. With green eyes. With the remembered name of Abrán Rascón."

"He wasn't one of the heads yesterday?"

"No," Diego grinned.

"Continue, my sergeant."

"It was at Carrizal, coming with the cart. You recall how you mentioned Rascón when I was in Texas? I went with eyes open. As we moved south, El Verdugo put me to the employ of riding ahead, to the settlements, to arrange for corn for the horses. It is a sometimes profitable work, making arrangements with farmers." Diego winked. "I am learning. I am now forage sergeant of the troop.

"I knew a good man at Carrizal, and I saw him when I went there to search for grain. We were chatting and he mentioned Abrán Rascón, who bought grain in Carrizal. He *bought* it! I knew it was odd.

"I will not make a bother of detail — but I saw an opportunity. Through my friend in Carrizal, I was able to find Rascón. He made an approach to me, and I told him, like an assassin, the cart was coming. He asked me what it held — fix yourself to this, Martín — I told him I thought it bore arms."

"He already knew that."

"Clearly. Well then, he asked about the guard of the cart. I told him it went unguarded, as usual, like a load of petticoats and buttons, to avoid attention from authorities along the way. I told him more of the same mark, after he promised to warn me of the attack — and to spare me — it was for me a great risk!

"You see? So I rode north to El Verdugo and I told him. We fixed a trap. The guard, and the horses without riders, stayed behind, out of sight of the cart. When Green Eyes and his criminals came riding around a bad point — he gave me no signal, the son of a whore — I raked my nag and went like a bird. Eight criminals were killed by the heavy fire from the troopers hidden in our cart. — It was our bad fortune to see Abrán Rascón escape — he had a very good horse. But that was not my fault! El Verdugo hit me across the back with his quirt and made me sergeant.

"The story has grace, Martín?"

"The grace is evident, Sergeant Casas."

"And this cavalry life is better than riding hungry in the hills of Valdepeñas!"

"With the great Captain Verdugo."

"It is the same, that part. El Verdugo or the foreman of vaqueros or who else. It is the type, and for us it does not change."

"How do you like the bullets of the cavalry life?"

"I have a rule. Those you hear whistling, do not touch you — eh Pablo?"

The peon Pablo had come in from the sunlight, and squatted to take the empty frijole bowl from the ground by Martin.

"It is a just rule if bullets come from distance," Pablo said. "From close they do not whistle, they come *zas!* When the horse thief Rascón fired at the cart near Carrizal I fell on the ground like a dead man."

"What has happened to that cart, Pablo?" Martin asked.

"It is here, in the corrals. I thought it would be ruined by Salcidistas. But no. It remains." Pablo shook his head. "In Lent we left Valdepeñas. Now in a little time it will be Day of San Juan — "

"He misses the favors of his old lady," Diego said.

A bugle blew, with a ruffle of drums, from beyond the big house.

"Troop muster." Diego got to his feet and straightened his hat. "Rest yourself, Martín. I will be back."

"Pablito," Martin said when they were alone, "how does it go?"

"They say men live only because God is great. And I am alive, eh? How is it with you, Martín? How is the north? The corral of the Señor Sterner. Gregorio and his family. The warehouse of goods. The cook Concha. That wine of Del Norte. And how is the nephew Chico? It was an amiable time, in Texas." Pablo smiled. "You came back to serve the Castros. You are a man of good faith."

"Pablo. You be sure it was not good faith that brought me south. Tell me, is Lágrimas well tended?"

"Stabled with grain. It was a pleasure to watch him roll, *qué macho*, clear over his back, three times!"

"Is the saddle safe, with the gun and cartridges?"

"Very safe. I have been at El Carmen a long time."

"I could sleep, Pablo, with this full belly. Do you know a pile of corn shucks in the shade where I could throw my blanket?"

"Let me show you."

Pablo led him to a brush *ramada* near the bottle-shaped stone granary on the far side of the adobe corrals.

The shade was cool and quiet. Martin lay on his back, on straw that crackled as he moved. His clasped hands on his chest raised and lowered a little as he breathed. The weariness humming his ears seemed to move away from inside his head. His body came slowly loose from the taut springs of its sinew and floated, weightless upon the upholding softness of the straw. As his eyes drowsed half closing, he looked out into the space of sky framed beyond the shady poles and dry boughs that made his shelter from the sun. A hawk sailed across the space on unmoving wings.

He is looking down on Mexico, Martin thought, losing the thought.

He threw the crutches away and gathered the rawhide bricks one by one, loading them higher and higher in his arms. Then he walked down into the water. The bottom shelved off. He clenched his teeth as he pushed out swimming with the load in his arms, and it glided queerly, like the breast of a swan, across the water. The people all saw him and he was ashamed, lifting the load from the river with the rags dripping muddy on the nakedness of his legs. He felt her hand touch him as he came under the tree in the rustle of the heart-shaped leaves. He put the load on the ground at her feet. In the dark arch of the leaves she watched him. He slid the long knife from his belt and bent down to slit the rawhide husks and bare the treasure he brought her, when the wind rattled the leaves all suddenly dead and he dropped the knife as he hit at the sharp dry shapes with Louisa Rucker crying.

His eyes batted open. He jerked up slapping, to knock from his face the prickle-footed crawl. It landed squirming with a many-legged small rustle on the straw. He stumbled to his feet and mashed it with his boot heel, stomping it to pulp in the dirt.

"Bastard," he said in his dry mouth. He rubbed at the itch still sticky hot across his cheek, and looked outside, sweating, focusing his eyes, seeing afternoon shadows stretched out long from the walls. "I slept all day." He saw Pablo peering around the corner of the *ramada*.

"A damn centipede, Pablo — "

"You were bitten?"

"I bit him first." Martin picked his hat up from the straw. " — And I slept all day! Why didn't you wake me, man?"

"There was no reason. You rested well?"

"I dreamed. Is there water to drink, Pablo?"

"It is a lack. I have a little *olla* — come with me. When the Salcidistas were here, they broke down the hacienda dam. They threw a dead burro in the well of the big house. A part of my employment now is the hauling of the water from the Río Carmen. — Here, Martín, drink."

"My thanks," Martin said when he had drunk long. "You think there is enough to pour a little on my head?"

"Here it comes!"

"Ahhh," Martin said, shaking the rolling drops, blinking water from his eyes, and blowing. It was cool and good.

"It refreshes," Pablo said, hanging the *olla* back on the peg. They sat down in the long shade.

"Pablito, what did you do when the Salcidistas came?"

"I was with the oxen, down the Río Carmen, when I heard shooting. Then I met people coming to the hills. We stayed camping for four days, in poor conditions until El Verdugo came and we saw the battle from the sierra and we came back to El Carmen."

"You knew the Apaches of Fuego were in the country?"

"We knew it and we were afraid. But they went away! I think they smelled the cavalry of El Verdugo coming."

"The hero Verdugo."

"The devil and his horns — "

An armed trooper appeared from behind the granary. "Bredi?" The trooper's voice was hoarse. "I hunt for a Bredi."

"My name is Bredi."

"Man, I looked in all parts of this pizzled hacienda. The General Castro is waiting! Jump!"

Martin stood up. He tucked in his shirt, tugged at his belt with his thumbs, and adjusted his hat.

"And leave the pistol," the trooper said.

Martin looked at him. "As you wish — " He handed the pistol to Pablo. "Watch it, Pablo."

The trooper led past the sentries, through the archway, into the patio of the big house. The open square formed by the smoked walls had been cleared of debris and swept clean. The flagstones had been sprinkled for coolness. By a column in the shade stood a camp table and two chairs. At the table sat General Marcos Castro and Captain Verdugo, with a bottle of cognac between them. They smoked cigars rolled from the pungent black leaf of Querétaro.

Quick eyes, rimmed with spiky lashes like spider legs, peered from Marcos Castro's rigid face; a clipped mustache made a gray line above his gaunt brown mouth. He dressed in tight breeches and short jacket of gray buckskin embroidered with gold. There were gold spurs at his heels, and ivory-handled pistols in gold-fretted holsters at his bony hips. He wore a gray, gold-embroidered sombrero, with the red chin string thrown up over the brim. It bobbled faintly when he talked.

"Bredi," he said, when Martin stood before him. He tapped Pancho Gil's unfolded letter by the cognac cup. "Answer some questions. What were the evidences of Salcido's force south of Del Norte?"

"I saw none."

"Did you see anything of the Apaches of Fuego?"

"Nothing, except mules butchered and rotting. At the sand dunes of Samalayuca."

"Nothing more?"

"There was a raid at Potrero two days before I passed. The Apaches took blankets and stole three girls."

"Did you find sign south of Potrero?"

"No, señor."

"When you were in Texas I received an invitation to cross my cavalry and join forces with the army of the United States, to fight Fuego. I was busy. I never answered." The general took a sip of cognac. "Did you hear them speak of it?"

"I heard of it."

"What kind of *Yanqui* swindle was it?"

"I believe it was an invitation to fight Fuego."

"You believe that. The marvelous *Yanquis*, calling for help. Tell me, what army force did you see at Puerto? Describe it."

"A battalion of cavalry, well equipped. The troopers are Negroes."

"I have heard they use blacks. But I never believed it. Who commands? Is he black too?"

"He is not. His name is Colton."

"Did you ever see him?"

"Once."

"Is he enough man?"

"I could not judge."

"My brother Cipriano, your *patrón*, asked you to observe conditions in Texas. For example, who is the power at Puerto? That army commander?"

"He is the military power. It is distinct from other power."

"You are saying a commander of a district carries no civil power. Who polices their damn civil government?"

"It is done by voting. My people make their own civil government. They vote for it and they have it. My people more or less police themselves — Señor General."

"Your people, eh? Very interesting. Voting themselves to order. More or less. With no police. A marvelous people!"

"They have police. I meant to say it is distinct from the army."

"Go on, please."

"The Texas Rangers, they act as police, sometimes."

"There are Texas Rangers in Puerto? How many?"

"A company."

"And who buys them? That is what I mean by the power."

"They are not bought."

"You don't know that everything is bought? *Shit!*"

"The Texas Rangers are not bought."

The general puffed at his cigar. "You have a rare opinion of that pack of assassins."

"It is my opinion they are not a pack of assassins."

The general sipped carefully at his cognac. "A hired *pistolero* is in no position to have opinions about assassins. You watch yourself. I will watch you myself. I notice your style of dress. You passed a pleasant time in Texas?"

"Very pleasant."

"It is pleasant to see you back." The general's eyes shone unpleasantly. "I presume you yet ride the stallion my brother gave you, after you killed Arriaga at Nombre de Dios. Where do you go now? To my generous brother?"

"I await the orders."

The general glanced at Captain Verdugo, who sat silently with his quirt in one hand and his cognac in the other.

"Bredi," the general said. "That oxcart you took to Texas — our captain has a project for that thing, a project in the terrain of the enemy, His Excellency the magnificent Governor Salcido. You will fill that cart with something counterfeit, and take it south. You will go with only the ox driver, as an innocent carter on the Chihuahua road. More innocent than you now appear, in those clothes. I suggest you dress more appropriately to Mexico. You ride guard with that cart and avoid suspicion. In the load will be three sealed canisters, concealed with care. You will deliver the canisters to a man near the City of Chihuahua, detour the city, and proceed south with the cart to Valdepeñas where you will report to your *patrón* —

"Captain Verdugo, what is the name of that friend, that expert, who waits for the canisters?"

"Juan Pardo. Waiting at the village of Minillas. Juan Pardo, Minillas."

"You understand that, Bredi?" The general smiled. "Frankly, I cannot regard this project with seriousness. It is unlikely to succeed. I do it to humor my brave captain who made the arrangements. Nevertheless — " the general's smile faded. "You have my orders, Bredi. You deliver those canisters. That is all."

"My general," El Verdugo said. "Juan Pardo will explode His Excellency, venereals and all, right through the palace roof."

CHAPTER XVI

MARTIN RODE
up, past the hulking crawl of the cart, and came alongside the peon Pablo carrying his pole by the slogging oxen. Pablo turned and grinned.

"They look at the Texan Bredi," he said. "And then, they believe it."

"It gets harder. Too many lies, Pablo."

"I believe them! When I hear you explain it. I can see our little mine in the sierra. I can see us taking this ore from our mine to the smelter of Chihuahua. In our cart. I look at my new *patrón*, the miner Bredi from Texas. I see the black horse he won playing monte with a rancher from Galeana. I hear him talking and I believe each word the miner Bredi tells." Pablo's eyes glistened, looking up at Martin on his horse. "I wish it was true."

Martin took off his hat, wiped sweat from his face with his sleeve, and turned in the saddle, to look back. The governor's road patrol was out of sight, beyond the twist of the canyon.

"It gets harder," Martin said.

The cart wheels screeched a dry duet as they unrolled their broad tracks along the furrows of the road. The yoke straps squeaked chafing on the oxhorns. The big splayed hooves moved slowly along the dust.

Martin looked up at the blaze of the June sun, white-hot overhead.

"Pan Pintao is laming maybe, Pablo. I think he might be laming. What do you think — shall we noon?"

"Pan Pintao is a wise ox. He lames near that pretty grove, eh? *Ándale*, Pan Pintao!"

Pablo turned the oxen out of the ruts and the dust, and the cart scraped complaining down the easy slope to the walnut trees and the trickle of water in the bed of the Arroyo Varas.

They unyoked and watered the stock. Martin unbridled Lágrimas, tethered him at high grass under a tree, and helped Pablo hobble the oxen.

While Pablo moved around the propped cart tongue, rummaging at the iron cook pot, Martin built a little fire in the shade. Squatted on their heels, Pablo's bare, Martin's in battered Kansas sole leather, they broiled slabs of dried mutton on pointed sticks, and ate it with tortillas and fried beans Pablo brought from the cook pot. When they had finished, they dipped water from the stream and drank.

"*Contento*," Pablo said, wiping mutton fat from his hands, leaning back, with the thick mat of his black hair against the trunk of a flowering mimbre tree.

"The good life," Martin said, drawing designs with his finger on the shady sand.

"A man needs very little," Pablo said. "And the little is hard to get."

"And to be *contento* is the hardest."

"It is simple. *Contento* comes from the belly. It lasts a little while. And reaches to the heart."

"Does it ever reach to the head?"

"The head is more distant."

Martin lay back, looking up at the rocky canyonside across the far bank of the stream bed. As he squinted at the hot glitter of the stones beyond the green leaves, a cloud, boiling high and white-topped above the rim of the bluff, reached across the face of the sun. It plunged the canyon into a flat and sudden shade.

"Pablo. We ought to go to our mine."

"I believe it."

"When we have delivered those three powder cans at Minillas, then we keep going, the other side of Valdepeñas, right over the Sierra Madre."

"And fill our cart with gold."

"I am glad we are going."

"With the exception, there would be no gold. My woman would starve alone at Valdepeñas. The Castros would catch me and shoot me."

"That way, our mine does not sound so well."

Pablo shook his head. "You tell it much better. I wish our mine was true. What day is it now, Martín?"

"I lost the count."

"I think it is near the fiestas at Valdepeñas. Near the Day of San Juan."

" — Not very near to Minillas," Martin said. "Shall we start that cart moving?"

"The cloud is fat," Pablo said as he got to his feet. "Growing fatter."

The air was sultry when they came out upon the road and moved south in the shade of the gathering cloud. A league beyond their nooning, they passed the dozen wretched huts of a settlement with its patchwork dam and its pocket of rocky cornfields along the Arroyo Varas. Beyond them, the road began a long climb from the narrowness of the canyon.

New clouds bulged with unspilled rain above the rimrock as the cart inched up the winding slant of the hill. The oxen set their heads out stiff-necked shoving at the yokes; silence lengthened between each slowed creak of the turning wheels. Martin rode the slope glancing at the sky, watching the double file of muscle-legged beasts lean straining with the cart against the long incline. Above them, the clouds moved fast. Their solid rounded edges melted fading in misty gray fingers and coils of lowering scud.

Grasshoppers flew from under Lágrimas' hooves with a yellow skitter and rasp of wings strangely bright against the darkening ground, strangely loud in the silence. A dove called its woe from a hillside thicket, and called again. The first far boom of thunder rolled. Martin rode in toward the cart.

"We ought to make ready — it's coming!"

"Not yet, Martín! A bad point to stop oxen — and worse with mud!"

"It's coming, man!"

"I see it. We have time."

"I'm going up to look — " He touched spur and Lágrimas bounded, clattering stones along the slope.

"*Arre, bueyes!*" Pablo whacked with his pole. "Get moving, oxen! Tortas! You, Pan Pintao! Get to the top — before the water! *Arre!*"

Fifty yards up the rise, Martin wheeled at the crest, and looked back. He eyed the sky, and Pablo working his pole, and he made a hurrying motion with his arm. The sound of Pablo's voice, the creak of the wheels, even the scuffle of the ox hooves came to him clearly as he sat the saddle waiting. Not a leaf, not a stem of grass, stirred in the sweating hush.

The flame jumped high and fiery before his eyes. The blast knocked him in a slamming wave of engulfing great sound as he fell, seeing shapes spurtle from the flash. A torn piece whistled, and he ducked down, hearing it thud, hearing another, and another. The black horse Lágrimas screamed and stood riveted, trembling in the sigh of the wave of sound as it settled to silence leaving the smoke and the shapes and the hole in the road.

Martin got up staring, shaking as he stared. A sudden wind puff jerked at the smoke where the cart had been. A fat drop of rain splashed burning cold on his face.

"Pablo!" he yelled. He started to run on his shaky legs. "Pablo!"

Shapes, pieces of shapes, lay unmoving, smoking, smelling of gunpowder and burnt hair. A spotted ox with its side torn open lay working its legs patiently, scraping in a pool of blood. A dun ox lunged suddenly to its feet, and bawled. One of its hind legs dangled broken.

"Pablo!" Martin called, searching. The ox bawled.

A quick gust swept the slope and the rain came slanting, thick, thumping the ground with a padded roar.

He found Pablo down the hill near a tazcal bush and a splintered piece of a wheel. He came to it stumbling, seeing the rain spatter glistening on the brown naked back, seeing the black tangled mat of hair in the mud. Blast had torn the clothes away, ripped the right arm from the naked trunk, leaving oozing pulp and white shattered bone.

Martin bent down in the lash of the rain. He turned the broken flesh gently, with awkward compassion, and looked at Pablo's face. The rain hit washing at the blood from the mouth. The rain thinned the thick red, in little splashes. It struck into the staring eyes. With shaking wet fingers Martin tried to close the lids. They opened. He propped them closed, with two flat rainwashed pebbles.

"Wait here," Martin said aloud. "Pablo." The rain ran between the opened lips. "I will bring you my Saltillo."

He turned away and walked up the slope, where Lágrimas stood trembling in the drive of the rain.

"You all right?" Martin's voice croaked. He cleared his throat, shaking his head, shaking blur from his eyes.

"Black horse. You all right?"

He smoothed at the wet hair on the black neck, feeling the animal heat in the palm of his hand as he patted.

"You're scared."

He went around the horse, looking for sign of hurt on the dark shine of the hide.

"You're scared, good horse. Huuu — " He swung up in the saddle.

The cold wet of the seat touched sharp on his buttocks. He rode talking, soothing, down the hill to a stumpy juniper where he tied the black frightened nose close to the shaggy trunk.

The dun ox bawled, calling the pain. Martin walked fast to

where it stood with its crooked leg dangling, and he shot between the eyes. The ox dropped, silent in the splashing rain, and he walked on, to the spotted ox. It was dead.

Lightning flashed, with thunder pounding in the canyon. A hurtling fork of blue fire cracked close on the rimrock and shattered in the seethe of rain. Lágrimas jerked at the tether and quivered as Martin untied the wet strings from the Saltillo behind the cantle.

He carried the folded blanket to the place by the tazcal bush, by the piece of the splintered wheel. He spread the blanket. He covered all the broken nakedness, he covered the face, the pebbles fallen from the eyes, tucking all of it in. He anchored each corner of the blanket with a wet stone, and stood over it without thought, without words to form thought. He heard the rain hit plumping at the tight-woven blanket. It made a faint hollow sound; he stared at it, watching the drops run from the sides of the shrouded mound. He felt words form slow, building from daze toward thought.

It turns the rain. It has turned the rain many a time. It keeps the rain off. It is all I got, that you can use. Pablo.

You won't ever get back to your woman at Valdepeñas and all I can do about it is blame myself and wrap you in my blanket and dig a grave and put you in and go tell your woman how it happened and help her if I can. I wish I could help you. I wish I could show you that Bredi was your friend. I don't know what happened. But it's my fault. I should have made you get away from the cart. Before God, I didn't know those cans could explode unless the lightning hit them. But they did. Someway it's my fault. I rode to the top of the hill to watch the storm and I'm alive and you're not. It was no lightning. I know it wasn't. I was looking. It just blew up. And it killed you. It didn't kill the governor of Chihuahua. Nor the general who said he didn't take it seriously, nor that brave captain who thought it up, nor this bastard Brady in the dirty business. No. It killed Pablo. It killed the good and decent man. I don't know why.

He stood shivering by the horse and the dripping juniper tree, with the scattered lumps and shapes dark on the hillside in the thinning rain. When the drizzle stopped, he kicked dry trash from

a rat nest by a runt tazcal, and lit a fire. His teeth chattered and
his nose dripped wet with the cold as he fanned at the smoky
reluctant flame.

He had his shirt off, trying to dry it, when the two farmers
on the burros came riding the road, from the settlement down the
canyon. Martin stood up, and waved the wet shirt. The burros
set their feet daintily along the mud and the two riders were silent
as they came up to the popping of the flame. Martin looked at
them, sandal-footed, in their ragged *petate* hats, their soggy shirts
and drawers of dirty *manta*. They looked at Martin with his bare
white chest and the gun strapped on his hip.

"Good afternoon, sons," Martin said.

"Good afternoon." The farmers looked around. "What happened?"

"You can see. The ox driver — the oxen — the ore cart. Leaving
only the black horse. And myself."

"The grace of God," the older farmer said. He crossed himself.

Martin pointed to Pablo's body under the blanket. "Is there a
priest in your village?"

"It is too poor."

"Is there a graveyard? Holy ground?"

"No, señor."

"Are there shovels?"

The farmer who talked showed his teeth.

"I have no shovel," Martin said. "I have nothing."

"I heard a great roar. *Zum!* Before the rain. It was not as thunder. It was very distinct. I came to see."

"You see now, my friend. Can you help me with shovels?"

"The shovels are far. It is late —"

Martin eased two pesos from the money belt around his belly.
He showed the silver, holding it in his hand.

"These wait for you. It is also a matter of mercy."

The farmer looked up the slope. "And the matter of oxen?" he
asked.

"Oxen?"

"The meat."

Martin looked at the two faces.

"For shovels, yes." He hung his shirt on a bush and threw a
rotten branch of damp tazcal into the blaze.

CHAPTER XVII

I T SAT
like a crown upon a crest. It faced out commanding the immense
plain of grass; at its back the folds of the hills lifted, rise on distant rise to the pale line of the Mother Sierra.

Martin Brady looked along the course of the stream that issued
from the hills and flowed through the gardens, out upon the fields,
into the plain. He looked up the long sweep of the easy slope, to
the white wall of the great house and the pink stone of the carved
church tower, in the trees.

I am glad I am seeing it again. Not thinking about anything else, only how it looks, I am glad I am seeing it, Hacienda de Valdepeñas. It was where I lived.

He rode Lágrimas up the slope into the shade of the straight avenue lined with the ancient trees. Their leafy benevolence arched over him, green, whispering in the breeze from the hills, as he went riding toward the turret-flanked gate. The guard with the gun strapped on his hip waved and stood grinning.

"*Tocayo!*" he called. "My namesake!"

Martin reined and reached down to shake the hand of the guard named Martín. "*Qué tal, Tocayo?*"

"You got here for fiestas. You were gone a long time, but you got here."

"Don't tell me I got here on Day of San Juan — "

"Don't tell me you didn't! Double fiestas. Very double. Five barrels of tequila for tonight, man, a real drunk. Barbecue and fireworks this year. In honor of the Saint — and the new governor. Mostly the new governor, eh? You got back at the right time. All the girls with a bath and their hair washed, smelling good — "

"How is that about new governors?"

"Are you joking?"

"*Tocayo*, I have been in the hills. I lost count of days and I heard of no governors — "

"Then, friend, there is news. Don Cipriano Castro is governor of the state!"

"Since when is that?"

"Since four days. When he, when all the family of Castro, when the infantry of the General Marcos, when the whole crowd, went to the capital!"

"What happened to Salcido?"

The guard shrugged. "Who knows?" He grinned. "Something, without doubt. Our *patrón* is governor."

"What happened with the old Governor Vega?"

"You have been in the sierras, man! He's dead."

"And his loyal General Severo Cuevas of the garrison?"

"Killed, man!"

"Leaving the Castros — "

"Leaving the free tequila tonight! How was it in the north? You are dressed very *Yanqui*."

"It is a long way north. Who stays in charge of the hacienda? Is the mayordomo here?"

"The same. Don Fulano. Report to him, *Tocayo.*"

"Until I see you — " Martin touched rein.

"At the tequila barrel — "

Martin looked along the upper fork of the roadway. It led through an inner wall topped with broken glass in a thick and jagged glitter, toward the church and the great house beyond. The gate in the forbidding wall stood open, for the holiday of San Juan.

I ought to take a look, Martin said to himself, my last look.

He rode the smoothed gravel into the cool of the gardens, by the long borders of maguey. Three women in poor black came down the steps of the church, and Martin tipped his hat.

"Good afternoon, señoras," he said.

He thought of Pablo, looking up at the mellow crust of stone saints and scrolls, the pink carved tower of bells, the blue tile dome, the cross of bronze.

He thought of Pablo wrapped in the blanket, with the shovels scraping by firelight, with the cross of cart planks set in the pile of stones at the side of the road, with hungry people butchering dead ox meat at midnight, quarreling in the dark, with Pablo quiet in the ground, and Lágrimas on the dim trace, through the hills to Mala Noche, to Sainapuchic. To the church of Valdepeñas on day of fiesta.

Beyond the lacy line of pepper trees, sunlight touched upon the western wall of the great house standing quiet, alone in the flowers. Under the engraved stone of the entrance archway, the iron grilles and bossed mahogany doors were locked shut.

Martin rode by them.

You need all of it, Governor of Chihuahua. You need a nice church of your own and plenty of house. *Patrón* of Valdepeñas, Carmen, El Tigre. *Patrón* now of the state. With your brother and your business maybe you can be *patrón* forever. And have more churches, and more houses. I leave you to it, *patrón.*

He came back through the gate, on his way to find the woman of Pablo.

Be sure you have plenty of wall, *patrón.*

The lower fork of the roadway into Valdepeñas was neither smoothed nor graveled; its ruts were printed thick with the marks of heavy wheels and hooves and bare feet. Martin went the back way, not looking for those who knew him, among the storehouses, stables, shops and barns, along the sprawled tangles of adobe corrals. He moved clear of the dusty plaza, the heavy walled quarters of the mayordomo, the work office, the commissary, and made his way toward the crowded scores of huts and shacks where the people lived who performed the toil within the hacienda's walls, in its gardens, orchards, vineyards, fields, its pens and pastures and camps, on the million stretching hectares of Castro grass and timber to the mountaintops.

The people did not toil on San Juan's day. They bathed the required bath of the year, early in the morning, and washed their hair and picked the lice and put on clean clothes if they had them and went to Mass with the bells ringing. Women cooked in their dirt-floored kitchens, spicing the air faintly with a smell of plenty. Men sat in clean clothes after church, and talked in the shade, impatient. Girls hummed, and put flowers in their hair. Musicians tuned fiddles and guitars, blew at brassy cornets, made a few trial tunes, ready for a night of music. Ropers and riders brought their stock to the carnival field across the stream, to wait for the crowd, for the starting guns in the cool of the long afternoon. Don Teófilo of the commissary set up his stand of candy and cane and aguardiente of Valdepeñas. Don Lázaro, foreman of vaqueros, bossed the men sweating with the sides of meat and the fires at the barbecue pits. Don Fulano, the mayordomo, set his police ready, patrolling the carnival field with guns at their belts, roping off spaces for dancing and for rooster fights and games of *chusas*, draping the pavilion, guarding the fireworks and the tequila barrels, for the evening. The kids of Valdepeñas ran everywhere with their clean shirts long since dirty.

In the sound and smell of holiday, Martin rode looking for the shack of the ox driver Pablo.

"*Oye, Bredi!*" The voice was peremptory.

He turned. The mayordomo came at him on a groomed chestnut stallion, sitting a saddle trimmed with silver.

"Where do you come from?" The mayordomo's eyes were yellow like a cat's.

"The north, Don Fulano." The two stallions snorted at each other and stood restive.

"When?"

"This moment."

"What are you doing?"

"I am here on orders General Marcos Castro gave me at El Carmen, some time ago."

"And the orders were?"

"Confidential. And to report to Don Cipriano here at Valdepeñas. I have been in the hills. I did not hear of the new governor until I arrived at the gate."

"The governor and his brother are both in the City of Chihuahua. When will you leave?"

"I would like to see my horse rested a little, and get some grain, before I go on."

"Still with that black, eh? — Tell me, what happened to the big ore cart and those first-class oxen you took north? Do you know?"

"The cart and oxen were destroyed carrying out orders. The ox driver was killed. I came to report it."

"You were responsible for the cart and oxen?"

"And the ox driver."

"Well, the ox drivers are not so expensive. But your report, it does not concern me. It is no hacienda matter. You understand you are employed now by His Excellency the Governor. A situation of promise for you, Bredi. For us all, eh? Report to the governor as soon as possible." The mayordomo spurred and the chestnut plunged away, toward the carnival field.

Riding the dirty lane, Martin called to an old man sitting in the shade.

"Do you know the house of the ox driver Pablo?"

"Over there," the old man pointed, with his chin.

"Where?"

"The next to the last — on the other side."

Martin rode to the wattled shack with the leaning wall and the mud scaling from the chinks. It was hot in the sun as he dismounted and stood on the bare ground. There was no door to knock on; he knocked on the scuffed post that framed one side of the opening.

A woman finally stuck her head, her hair uncombed, around the edge of the ragged cloth that hung in the doorway.

"Pardon me, señora," Martin said. "Are you the woman of Pablo who went north with the oxen?"

A vague flicker of some feeling between suspicion and fear touched at the stolid black Indian eyes.

"Yes."

Martin took off his hat.

"I am Martín Bredi, of this hacienda. Pablo was with me in the north. He mentioned you many times. He thought of you. I came to tell you — "

The woman waited, unmoving. She did not ask Martin in from the sun; he stood with his hat and the *ramal* of the reins in his hands.

"There was an accident, in a place called the Arroyo Varas, in the north. Pablo lost his life. I came to tell you."

The woman's eyes looked at him, without expression. She let loose the door cloth for a moment and crossed herself, then held the cloth tight again.

"I was with him, when it happened," Martin said. "I put him in a grave. There is a cross over it. I was his friend. Do you have any people to help you? For necessities of life?"

A tear rolled out of one of the Indian eyes, down the brown cheek.

"I came to say if I could help a little, señora, with a few pesos if — "

"*Aee*, woman!" a man's voice called from somewhere behind the cloth door. "Woman. What goes on — thou — come here!" The tongue was thick. "Hear me, woman?"

"An uncle," the woman said.

Martin swallowed. Pity rose to smother at his anger. He turned away and climbed into the saddle. "I came to tell you that Pablo is dead." He put on his hat and did not look back, riding away. Old Pablo, he worried about his woman.

Martin spit on the ground, and rode around a corner, up another lane, toward the familiar hut of the Casas. Seeing it ahead, he stopped Lágrimas suddenly, wheeled and went back. He rode fast, over the bridge of the stream, to the stand by the bunting-draped pavilion on the edge of the carnival field.

"I have not seen you for a long time," the storekeeper said. "Bredi." He remembered every name in every account book on the hacienda.

"I have been riding. Give me the worth of a *tostón* in candy, please, and a small bottle of aguardiente. Can you put the candy in paper, to ride with it?"

The storekeeper slid the brown slices of quince candy into the rolled cone of the yellowed newsprint, and folded the top over. He pushed the package and the brandy bottle across the counter, and opened his book.

"This is for cash," Martin said, pulling the peso and the *tostón* from his belt.

"We prefer to put it in the book."

"This is cash. It does not go in that book." He threw the coins on the counter and looked the man in the eye.

"As you like. Bredi."

He put the bottle and the candy in his shirt, mounted Lágrimas, and rode again across the bridge and up the lane to the hut of Mateo Casas.

Three of the Casas children, playing in the sun, saw him as he came.

Their voices shrilled. "Martín, Martín, here comes Martín!"

"*Chamacos!*" Martin waved at them.

The little girl ran in the door to tell the news. When Martin got down, the two boys hugged him around the waist, scuffling, and asked to hold the *ramal*.

"We'll tie Lágrimas," Martin said, ruffling the boys' hair. "Then you watch him for me. How is everyone? How is your daddy Bartolo? And your mama, and the grandfather, and the grand-mother and the aunts? Are you having fiestas?"

Old Mateo Casas stood in the door, stocky, with his great gnarled hands and craggy brown face. He was dressed in a white blouse and leather breeches. Coffee had spilled down the front of his blouse. He held out his arms.

Martin saw that Mateo Casas was blind.

"Don Mateo," Martin said. He embraced him.

"I felt it. I felt you arrive." The voice was still deep, still rough — without the power it once had. The two great hands gripped Martin's shoulders and the blind eyes looked in Martin's face.

"You see how I am, Martín? But I can see you, behind these eyes. I am glad to see you, my son."

"I am glad to see you, my father."

Diego's wife and baby and the brother Bartolo and his wife and the two Casas daughters and a husband crowded into the little room by the old man's rawhide chair. Martin embraced each one. He looked around. "Doña María, my mother?"

He knew, the instant he had asked it.

The Casas daughter Lola began to cry in the silence. "Four Sundays past," she said. "That she be in the Glory — "

"God gives. He takes away." Mateo Casas spoke roughly. "Who has more right than God? *Andale!* This is day of fiesta and Martín is with us! How are you Martín?"

"I am well. Does Diego know of his mother?"

"No. Diego was here with the cavalry, two weeks before the death. We do not know where he went."

"I saw him at El Carmen. He is probably in the City of Chihuahua, with the troop. With the new governor."

"Are you riding that way?"

"I don't — know."

"I wish you were."

The little girl Belita hugged at Martin's leg. She whispered something.

"What is that, Belitita? What?"

"Martín. Did you bring us something?"

Everyone laughed.

"Mmmm," Martin said. He stuck his hand in his shirt and rattled the paper. "You think so?"

"I think so."

"Here. Your mama will let you have some. And some for the boys."

Belita smiled and hugged his leg.

"And here is something for the grandfather. A little something for day of fiesta." He put the bottle of aguardiente in old Mateo's hand.

"*Guay!* We wet our throats. We drink with the news. Open it, bring cups! — Listen, Martín, where is your horse?"

"Outside."

"The black? The stallion Lágrimas?"

"The same."

"Bartolo! Tend the horse! Take him to the stable."

"I will," Martin said. "It is trouble for you, Bartolo."

"It is not trouble. It is pleasure."

"I want you to stay with me and tell the news," said Mateo Casas. "Bartolo will tend the horse."

"Then let me unsaddle — keep my saddle and the carbine in this house." He got up and went outside with Bartolo and his boys.

"The blindness, man!" Martin kept his voice low. "When did it come?"

"The night of the death. He could not see. He has not seen since."

"How does he do? In his heart — "

"He is much man. *Mucho hombre.*"

"He is the most man I know. — Something for the house, Bartolo." He put the silver pesos in Bartolo's hand. "Don't tell the old one. Are you getting along? Do you have enough?"

"We eat. Many thanks, Martín."

"I wish it was more. It came from the boss of the mail coach in Del Norte, a man named Pancho Gil. He lent it. I have not been paid by the Castros since I went north."

When Bartolo and the boys had led Lágrimas toward the stable, Martin brought in his gear and sat by old Mateo. The aguardiente was opened, and there were cups in their hands.

"*Salud* — " the old man said. "*Y fuerzas* — " They drank.

"Tell me first, my son, how is the leg? Diego told me how you broke it. I cannot see how you use it."

"All well."

"Not crooked? No pain?"

"In no way. It was stiff when the doctor took off the sticks. It hurt for a while. Now I forget it was broken."

"Luck." The old man drained his cup.

"It was a good doctor. I was worried enough, sitting crippled, waiting." Martin smiled. "Don Mateo, the doctor bred his mare of Kentucky to Lágrimas. It was all the — "

A volley of guns popped in the distance; there were shouts from the field. The bells of the church tower began jangling.

"The *jaripeo!*" The little girl Belita took Mateo Casas' hand. "Grandfather! Martín! Can't we go? Can't we?"

A band of musicians came down the lane; the guitars were playing in the sunlight, moving toward carnival. The little girl started crying.

"Shh! No, Belita. Not this year. Child — " her mother said.

"We wear black," Lola Casas said, watching the musicians go.

"God knows there is enough mourning," Mateo Casas said. "The world is full of it. Martín! Help me and my chair outside, if you please. Where we can talk. Bring the bottle!"

They sat in the shade, around the corner. Martin poured aguardiente. The sound of the crowd on the rodeo field came drifting up the empty lane.

"Day of San Juan." Mateo Casas lifted his clay cup and drank. "I have seen my first one and my last one, Martín. At the earliest one I remember, there was a miracle on my tongue and I never forgot it. I tasted for the first time the sweetness of a crumb of brown sugar. And at the last one when I still had my eyes, I watched you win the 500-vara racing your black Andalusian horse. I can remember the greatest fiesta of San Juan. There was never any like it, the one when the General Santa Anna came, with all the wine. The old Castro was *dueño* and Cipriano and Marcos were round-faced boys in velvet and silver, on dapple ponies. I won the forefooting and bull-tailing both, it was forty years ago. Days of San Juan. I remember your first one, Martín. I have always remembered it. I found you sitting alone in the corrals, big-eyed, hungry, saying words of English aloud. And when I asked you why, you told me you were practicing your tongue, for the time when you would return." Mateo Casas showed his jagged teeth. "Did you remember your tongue, when you crossed that river?"

"It came to me."

"You liked it. There in the north."

"I liked it."

"They didn't remember about Presidio. About the boy I found holding the pistol that night by the river."

"They remembered it. They remembered."

"And they did nothing?"

"They pardoned me, Don Mateo."

"And why didn't you stay, son?"

"I wanted to. The last night I was there — I shot a man and I had to leave."

Mateo Casas sat silent.

"Martín, it was not all good when they chose you from the vaqueros, and armed you. I do not speak as one without guilt. I have spilled blood for personal reasons and I have been in war. Blood is sometimes necessary. It is sometimes desirable. But the life with firearms, it grows — to a habit of blood. Much blood is much sorrow. I have seen it. You are seeing it. It is the sorrow of my Mexico. Will you live your life in it?"

"I don't know. I wish I knew."

"We gave you what we had. Yet — it was not your own. I see that, blind."

"I am grateful for what you gave me. It is much. It is all I have."

"No. You have more. Do you know the word *castizo?* Do you know what it means in this tongue you have from Mexico?"

"*Castizo?* Good breed? Good style?"

"When it is *castizo* it stays good breed, it stays good style. I told you that, sitting in the dark. My son, pour me one cup, and then I want to hear music, and taste barbecue. We live, all of us, only a little space from death."

The music was playing when he led Mateo Casas into the crowd at the edge of the field.

"I can hear it and I can smell it." The old man's great gnarled hand gripped Martin's arm. "Dust. What are they doing?"

"They are tailing bulls."

"Big bulls?"

"Big enough."

"Not as big — as they used to be. Who's riding?"

"Fausto Marocho — and he tailed it! The bull flopped and

landed skidding. Fausto is riding back. He lost his hat." In the cheering Martin had raised his voice.

Mateo Casas grinned. "The Day of San Juan is the best day of the year. Who's next?"

"It looks like Ángel Contreras."

"He is not horseman! A little crazy. He is better in a sheep pen — "

Bartolo Casas appeared suddenly, and put his hand on his father's shoulder. "How do you like it?" he asked. "I have been looking for you." He carried little Belita in his arms, so she could see. She was eating quince candy. Her brothers were edging toward the front of the crowd by the fence.

The crowd whooped and Mateo Casas boomed, "Tell me!" in the whistling.

"That bull tailed Ángel! Before he could get the tail under the stirrup, it jerked him off — "

The musicians had changed tunes, banging happily at their strings, tooting the brass, singing "The Best Vaquero."

> The foreman was very worthy,
> He stopped and said to me,
> "How are you at handling cattle,
> Riding the rough terrain?"
> *Eee — Ha! What did you tell him?*
>
> I said, "I am the best vaquero
> That ever roped a cow!" *Eee — Ha — Ha!*
> So he showed me an ox and a muddy field
> And told me, "Start to plow!"
> *Eee — Ha! That's what he said! Eeeee!*

"The best day of the year," old Mateo said.

Bartolo put his mouth close to Martin's ear. "Martín — " he waited until there was less noise. "Don Fulano is looking for you. He sent word, at the stable."

"The foreman was very worthy, eh? What does he want?"

"I don't know."

Martin looked toward the box in the pavilion. The mayordomo was there, watching the gate, for the next bull.

"They told me to tell you," Bartolo said.

"Thank you."

The ropers built their singing rawhide loops in the last sunlight. They forefooted wild mares in clouds of dust like luminous haze. The distant line of the Mother Sierra stood sharp against the glare in the west, then dimmed, fading. The *charros* ran their fastest horses in the early dusk. When the winner of the 500-vara rode to the pavilion in the shouts, and the first bonfire was lit, the people moved to the fiesta of the night of San Juan, to the barbecues, the barrels, the dancing, the games, the cockfights, the music.

An armed police touched Martin on the shoulder.

"The mayordomo wants you."

"I have been told."

Martin walked to where Don Fulano stood alone by the chestnut stallion.

"Bredi, when do you leave?"

"Any time."

"Could you take an express? A matter of urgent information from the mine of El Tigre. I received it after I saw you this afternoon. The governor awaits it. Where would I find you when I have the message written and sealed?"

"Here. Eating meat."

The mayordomo mounted his horse. "Thank you, Bredi. This needs a trusted man." He paused. His cat's eyes moved toward the crowd at the barbecue pits and the barrels. "You know these people, night of fiesta. Even my police — "

"Don Fulano, could I ask a favor?"

"Speak."

"The woman of the ox driver Pablo who was killed in the north, she lives in a shack near the end of the second lane. Very humble. With nothing. Could the hacienda give her a way to earn bread? The ox driver Pablo served the Castros well."

"I will remember it."

"I will carry your express."

He found Mateo and Bartolo Casas, and the husband of Lola, in the firelit crowd.

"Martín! Get some!" Bartolo held up browned goat ribs.

Mateo Casas turned his craggy face. He was chewing. "Where are you?"

"Here, Don Mateo. And hungry!"

"Eat! The *chamacos* have taken meat to our women at the house. Sit down. What did the mayordomo want?"

"He wanted me to carry an express to the *patrón*."

"When?"

"Tonight."

"And you go. To an excellency. To a palace of a governor. And if it happens that you find my son Diego — " Mateo Casas stopped. He turned his blind eyes toward the sound of the music. "They sing 'Memory of Valdepeñas.'" The old man's voice roughened. "And I hear it. With meat in my mouth — smelling smoke of the fires — "

> I carry in my heart the land I knew
> When I was young and sorrows were not mine.
> I wish I could ride singing across the plain,
> And come to the fair place there by the wooded hills,
> And have my youth again.
>
> I belonged to that land, it was my mother earth.
> I was content with the things it gave me.
> There I felt the enchantment of the world,
> The sun was gold on the walls of my house,
> And I had my love.
>
> > All my youth,
> > All my love,
> > Are far away,
> > Far as the house
> > That sheltered me
> > At Valdepeñas,
> > The land I knew.

The fiddles cried and the voices sang in the flickering light. The sound drifted into the open darkness beyond the people.

CHAPTER XVIII

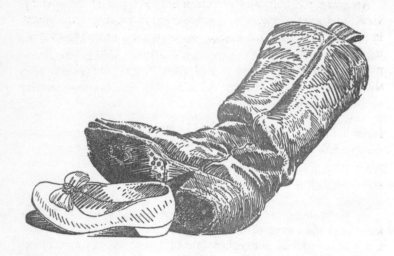

MARTIN BRADY had breakfast by a farmhouse door at dawn, three leagues from Chihuahua. The taste of the greasy *gordas* the woman gave him, and the stale coffee, stuck sour in his throat. His bones ached unrested, he felt dizzy from the long motion of his ride, and his eyes stung. When he had given the woman a *real*, he went to the well in the farmyard and from a leaky bucket dashed water on his face. Then he mounted Lágrimas and rode tired, on a tired horse, toward the city.

Other travelers moved along the road in the early light. He passed drivers with loaded burros and files of trotting pack mules, sagging wagons and thin-shanked country nags, haycarts, ox drivers, riders, walkers. Some of them called morning greetings and their dogs barked.

The sun climbed up with a summer blaze; Lágrimas paced the dust along shortening shadows, into the heat of the day. New sweat caked in the hair of the black hide. Insects hummed in the sun-flooded brush by the side of the road. Sweat ran stinging from under Martin's hat.

Around a climbing turn of barren hill, he watched the opening view. The scars of mines on the slopes above the city were bright in the glare ahead; a thin smoke rose high from one of the workings. As he rode on, the aqueduct appeared, strung out on its masonry arches. The tops of the twin towers of the cathedral showed suddenly. Then, over the last of the rise, set in a crescent of tan mountains, he saw the walls and roofs and towers and domes. A leaf-bordered stream wound around them; their sharp-faced build of tawny stone and pale mud brick stood graced with the green of trees and pleasant gardens. He rode along a fringe of willows by the chapel of Guadalupe, hearing the sound of water, and entered the shade of the Alameda lined with cottonwoods to the city's heart.

He did not ride to the Plaza. A block from the cathedral wall and the portico of the palace beyond it, he turned Lágrimas into a side street flanked with shops. Porters had sprinkled the cobbles; he smelled the morning fragrance of the damp stones and he rode them with his horse's hooves clacking. He reined before he came to the familiar, tall, polished, bronze-knobbed door. A soldier stood armed at each side of it, under the neat sign with the gold letters C. CASTRO Y HNO.

The soldiers watched him as he dismounted, and he stood on the cobbles, feeling short, stiff in the legs, dry, dirty. Leaving the *ramal* around the pommel so that the horse stood with a stylish arched neck, he tied Lágrimas and moved by the guards, feeling their eyes, into the dimness beyond the tall door. His spurs clinked as he walked the worn flags to the grilled window of the banker's cage at the end of the long, high-ceilinged room.

"Good morning, Señor Roa," Martin said.

The man in the cage shoved his spectacles up on his forehead. He peered. "Where did you come from? Hm."

"Valdepeñas."

"Only Valdepeñas?"

"I was farther. I came to ask you, señor, where it is best to encounter the governor. I carry an express to him."

"The governor still has residence in the family house. Inquire there."

"One other thing, Señor Roa. I have not been paid since January. I have been in the north. Can you pay me?"

"Certainly not." The spectacles dropped into place. "It requires a written order. In your case, from His Excellency Señor Don Cipriano Castro de Ibarra y Zámora, Governor of the State, hmm."

"Thank you. Does the cavalry of General Marcos Castro happen to be in the city?"

"Billeted in the former mansion of Salcido, hm. The General Marcos prepares — at great expense — a campaign against the savage Apaches of Fuego who persecute the north."

"I am grateful for the information, Señor Roa. I will come back when I have seen the governor."

"When you have a written order."

He felt the soldiers' eyes again as he walked to Lágrimas and mounted.

There were other guards — they wore big gray hats with red chin strings — standing their posts in front of the house of the Castros. Martin rode past a line of saddled horses, through a crowd of loungers and beggars, by a waiting carriage, and swung down at an iron gate that gave entrance to the garden before the house.

He walked to the sentry in the gateway. "I carry an express to the governor. From Valdepeñas."

The sentry eyed him. "Who speaks?" he asked, solemn-faced.

"Come on, man. I remember you at El Carmen." Martin pointed his thumb over his shoulder, at Lágrimas. "And you remember that horse."

"It is a Castro horse. Tie him. I will tell the authority."

The authority was a lieutenant in a tight uniform with gold braid. A dress sword dangled at his side as he walked across the garden toward Martin, halted in the gateway, and clicked his heels. "Lieutenant Zuñiga," he said. "Aide-de-camp to His Excellency. May I serve you?" He tinged the word "serve" with his own quality.

"I have an express to the governor. From Fulano Zarco, mayordomo of Valdepeñas. My name is Brady. Tell the governor my name: Brady, with an express."

"I will take your express."

"I am sorry, my orders are to deliver it myself."

"So you have orders. You must know it is very difficult to arrange an audience with His Excellency. What does your message concern?"

Martin looked at the lieutenant. "The message concerns the governor of the state. Do I speak clearly?"

"Guard!" The lieutenant raised his voice. "Seize him!"

Martin moved back a step and laid his hand on the butt of his gun.

"Seize the man!"

Martin stood planted; the sentry made no move at him.

"Insolence! Gringo! Seize him, *you* — " The lieutenant's voice brought the sergeant of the guard.

"*Qué hay*, my sergeant," Martin said quietly. "Tell the lieutenant. Tell him I ride for the Castros."

"He does," the sergeant said. "I know him."

"*Are you going to seize him?*"

"*Señor Teniente*," the sergeant said. "Why should I seize him?"

"Mutinous militia! Rogue! You will see why — when I have you also in irons — " The lieutenant made a very military about face and strode toward the house with his hand on the sword. He had attracted a gallery; there were grins at his back.

The sergeant stepped over to Martin and asked, "What happened?"

"Nothing. I have an express to the *patrón*. I have orders to deliver it by my own hand. It offended him that I did not offer a slight fee, a little *propina*."

"That the bad lice eat him! The *patrón* is governor and you see what we encounter? We encounter the military of the parlor. The jokers of girls, the drinkers of cognac, the players of guitars."

"Where did he come from?"

"The garrison. He is official. We are all very official. We have toy swords to screw with." The sergeant shoved his big hat to the back of his head. He put his mouth close to Martin's ear. "How did it go with that cart? With those cans we loaded?"

"Bad," Martin said.

"Bad? Did you — " he stopped.

The lieutenant strode toward them.

"His Excellency — will see you," the lieutenant said, tight-mouthed. His face was pale. "Leave the side arm — "

"Here," the sergeant said, "let me hold it." Martin handed him the pistol.

"Follow me," the lieutenant said.

Martin followed him, through the portals, into the courtyard. The exigencies of office had made its privacy public: seekers of favors, imparters of news, takers and givers of bribes, carriers of grievances, of compliments, messengers of good, of ill, sat waiting on benches by potted palms and jardinieres of ferns. Guards walked armed among them. A guard opened one of the double doors at the far end of the courtyard as the lieutenant approached. Martin took off his hat and followed the lieutenant inside, to the private sitting room of the governor of the state.

Cipriano Castro sat in a carved chair with his back to a tall shuttered window. At his side stood a table holding a breakfast tray from which he had just taken morning chocolate and sweetened breads. He was alone.

"Lieutenant Zuñiga — " Cipriano Castro said. The voice was resonant, cultivated. It gave the z more than a trace of Castilian lisp. "Look well at this man. His name is Bredi. He saved me from the assassin Arriaga at Nombre de Dios: I am indebted to him for my life. For your further information, he rides a black stallion, full brother to the Andalusian mount of the General Marcos Castro. When this man Bredi asks to see me, arrange it. Understand? That is all. When you leave, close the door."

Martin stood looking again at the *patrón*, at the hard elegance of the bony olive face with the black lustrous eyes and the graying, sharply trimmed Vandyke. He was dressed in a suit of immaculate white linen. His pointed boots were as black and polished as his eyes.

"You have an express for me?"

"Yes, señor." Martin handed him the message.

Castro broke the seal and unfolded the paper. Before he started to read, he looked up at Martin. "Sit down, Bredi."

It was the first time a Castro had ever asked him to be seated. He sat stiffly, holding his stained hat, conscious of his dirtiness. The sole had broken loose from the toe of one of the cheap Kansas boots; in the silence he looked up, away from himself, at a big picture on the wall. It was old and dark, of a Spaniard in armor. His gloved hand rested upon the hilt of a sword and his bony face peered at Martin with lustrous eyes. The beard was gray, sharply cut — Martin glanced at Cipriano Castro, guardedly, from the corner of his eye. He looked up again and made out painted letters dim on the black background: EL EXC. SR. DN. BALTASAR CASTRO AÑO DE 159 — he could not make out any more.

"You bring good news," Cipriano Castro said, folding the paper and pocketing it. "Bullion from El Tigre is on its way. I may say that a principal ingredient of government appears to be silver — and cries for silver — Bredi, we shall talk a few moments."

The lustrous eyes fastened on Martin's face. "Your return from the north is proof of an attribute I mentioned both to my brother Marcos and to Fulano Zarco: your personal loyalty. I put you in a position of trust in sending you north. You did not abuse my trust. Meanwhile, our situation has altered very considerably, and fortunately. There are many opportunities for those who serve me now. I shall without doubt need a man of your — background, to aid in certain relations that exist between my interests and the Americans with whom I shall increasingly deal. I trust that I may continue to depend upon you. You will be properly rewarded.

"To speak in less general terms, your orders at this time are to remain in readiness until I call you. Inform Filiberto the house man, that you are stabling your horse, that you are to be fed and bedded in quarters here until further notice. Is that clear? — You are attracted by the portrait, Bredi? The first Castro in New Spain — " Cipriano Castro's eyes moved beyond the painting. "For reasons unknown to me, though I suspect they were commercial, Aurelio Salcido did not loot this house during his — tenure of office."

"May I ask a question, señor?"

"Speak."

"What happened to Salcido?"

The luster in Cipriano Castro's eyes sharpened. "The garrison commanders of Chihuahua became persuaded that Salcido was unfit for office. He was somehow informed of his troops' new persuasion, and feared for his life. He fled."

"He got away?"

"We will find him, Bredi."

"One other thing, señor, I — "

"Bredi, there is another point that will probably interest you. The Rascón whose face you disfigured when he stole your black horse at El Tigre — you saved him for the summit of a career. That same wretch carried the arrangements between parties of good government and garrison commanders. I suspect he also informed Salcido at the last moments and caused his escape. Treachery compounded!"

"Where is Rascón?"

"We will find him."

"Señor, I would like to mention that since January — "

"Ah Bredi! One other thing. The General Marcos told me about a mission, with an oxcart. He was angry that you were late — at Minillas, I believe. Would you explain it?"

"I never got to Minillas. On the road the powder exploded."

"Amazing."

"It killed the ox driver. It killed the oxen and ruined the cart."

"Shocking."

Martin looked straight into the lustrous eyes. "It was hot and still, just before rain. I happened to be looking, and it was no lightning. It exploded itself. The force struck me off my horse."

"Fantastic."

"There was no warning. It blew the clothes off the driver. It blew his arm off. I never found it."

"And you escaped as in a miracle."

"It was on a hill. I was waiting at the top, telling the driver to hurry, the storm was coming, and it happened. I buried the driver by the road, his name was Pablo. He served you all his life. His woman is at the hacienda, with nothing. I spoke to Don Fulano about it. Pablo was a faithful man. I felt his death. And I do not know what caused the explosion."

"It is necessary to believe this story, Bredi?"

Martin clenched his teeth. "I have said what happened. Believe what you wish."

Cipriano Castro was amused. "Actually — I wish to believe you." He leaned forward in his chair. "Let us say merely that it exploded. You lost my cart and oxen. You killed my driver." Cipriano Castro leaned back again. "Yet one might consider it fortunate. The palace was damaged enough. Plots of gunpowder are puerile; they kill the wrong persons or no one at all. I told the General Marcos it was a barbarity when it was mentioned. — Enough of it." Cipriano Castro rose from his chair.

Martin stood up. He made a last dogged effort: "I have not been paid since I went north and it requires a note to Señor Roa from your hand. I need the money. You see my — "

"I see them indeed. Very Texan! Bredi, there is neither pen nor paper convenient, forgive me, I shall arrange it at a less busy time — " He pulled the bell cord and a guard opened the door. "Guard! Send for Filiberto. The Señor Bredi here wishes to see him."

Martin walked out. He put on his hat.

Like hell I wish to see Filiberto.

Lieutenant Zuñiga brushed by, with his sword, leading another caller into the presence of the governor.

The guard touched Martin's arm. "Wait here. Filiberto has been sent for."

Martin stood waiting, angry with his mind's confusion, his body's weariness. Fool, he called himself, fool, fool, damn fool. They get me with no money and a tired hungry horse. Fool, it is what I deserve. Coming like a fool to see what a governor is like. I saw.

Filiberto came from around a potted palm.

"Don Cipriano asks me to tell you I am stabling my horse here. I am eating and sleeping here. Until further notice."

"Mother of God, the way we are crowded? Where is the horse, eh?"

"In front."

"There is no remedy! Bring the horse around and I will tell them to let you in. The Chinaman will feed you. You find your own bunk. As usual eh?"

Like hell as usual eh, Martin thought, crossing the courtyard. He walked out the portal, into the sun, through the garden, to where the sergeant of the guard and two of his men stood at the gate.

"You saw the *patrón?*" The sergeant handed Martin the Colt .44.

"I saw him. Thank you."

"A friend waits for you, outside — "

Leaning against the wall in the shade, by Lágrimas, Diego Casas waited for him.

"*Hah!*" Diego grinned wide, with the red chin string creasing his cheeks. "I was passing by. And I saw this horse, and I knew — "

"Diego — " Martin pulled his mind away from himself. "I was coming to find you. I have been to Valdepeñas."

"When?"

"I left there night before last."

"How did you find — but that was night of San Juan! You rode *crudo* all the way to the City! *Ehaah!*"

"Not *crudo.*"

Diego's face sobered. He looked at Martin. "What is it?"

"Your wife sends affection. She and the baby are well. She waits for you, she told me to tell you."

"Good. I am glad to hear it." Diego winked.

"I tell you that first," Martin said. "The rest is not — come over here, Diego." He took him by the arm and led him around the corner, away from the people at the gate.

"Two weeks after you were at the hacienda. You lost your mother. They say she died without pain, and your sisters are happy that the priest was there. There is something else. The night of the death, your father could not see. He is still blind. Bartolo and the girls take care of things, they take care of him, the best way they can. Your father told me to find you. To tell you. It is the real reason I think why I rode to Chihuahua. To tell you and I am sorry to tell you."

Diego Casas sagged, against the wall. He sat quite suddenly, on the cobbles, and bent over, under his big gray felt hat. Martin looked down, watching the hatbrim shake while Diego Casas cried without a noise. Martin stood still, until the hatbrim quit shaking.

Then he squatted, so he could see under the hat, and he put his hand on Diego's arm.

"Dieguito. It strikes us all. You know it. Some with more luck than others. You had the good luck. For instance, better than mine. I do not remember my mother. You had yours, until now. You still have your father — "

Diego came to his feet. He took off his hat, and wiped his face, his eyes, with his sleeve. "I know it, Martín. Excuse me. Now — " he shook his head. "*Así es la vida.*"

"You help Bartolo. He is a steady boy. He has the mouths to feed. And when you can get leave from your Captain Verdugo, go to Valdepeñas. It will do them good, all of them. They are proud of you."

"I will go. *Ai!* What are your orders now?"

"I don't know. I am asked to stay here. By the governor."

"What do you think of the governor? A surprise?"

Martin shrugged.

"He had enough to *buy* the garrison, all of it! You know who carried the arrangements, singing the coyote tune?"

"I know. And he got away."

"And I do not like to have him loose. Green Eyes has no love for me since that trick at Carrizal — tell me, how did it go with that cart, from Carmen? I wanted to ask."

"All bad. Our friend Pablo is buried in the Arroyo Varas."

"Really?" Diego spit, and shook his head. "*Tck!*" He put on his hat and looked at Martin. "Let's go and take a cup together. For old times. I need a cup."

"Diego, thank you. But I had a ride. The horse needs care. I need to make a plan."

"I can find you here?"

"Ask for me at the back gate."

"Good." He put his hand on Martin's shoulder. "Thou art a brother."

Diego went to the rack, and mounted his horse. He rode down the street without looking back.

Around the opposite side of the block from the entrance to the house of the Castros, a guard let Martin ride through the carriage gate. Inside the high wall, Martin led Lágrimas to stable. He unsaddled, and saw the black horse watered and rubbed down and fed, safe in a stall with clean straw. A crippled stableman carrying a brass ring of keys unlocked a harness room, and Martin racked his saddle and saddle blanket, his carbine and saddlebags and bridle. At a table in the shade by the kitchen, a Chinese in a white apron fed him frijoles and meat stew with green chili, coffee, and hard-crusted white bread dusted with sugar and cinnamon. When his belly was full, he went to the cubicle the crippled stableman had shown him. He took off his shirt and hat, unstrapped his gun, pulled off his boots, and lay down, with no blanket to put under him, on the rawhide straps woven as springs on the battered frame of the bunk. He wadded his shirt for a pillow at the back of his head, put the gun within reach of his hand, and lying straight on his back, invited the sleep his body cried for. It came to him, with the mournful sounds of pigeons murmuring in their cote by the stable wall.

It was a heavy and dreamless sleep.

He awoke from it knowing he had slept for hours, and he got to his feet feeling a kind of gratitude to his body, stretching the stiffness from his limbs and his back. Then he sat on the edge of the bunk, and rubbed his eyes, and tried to plan. He looked at the dirty wrinkled wad of his shirt, and he shook it out trying to smooth it, and hung it on a peg by the door. He tugged on his boots. He tried to knock some of the dust from his jeans, from his draggled Philadelphia hat, and he ran his hand over the rough stubble on his chin.

Two *reales* to do anything about it, he thought, feeling in his pocket. I could have borrowed maybe from Diego but it was no time to ask that. The governor can buy garrisons but the *hijo de puta* has no pen nor paper convenient —

He went to the horse trough and ran water from the pump over his head for a long time, rubbing at his face and neck, wishing for soap, for a towel when he was done. Smoothing his wet hair as best he could without comb or mirror, he went back to the cubicle and put on his hat. Then he put on his shirt, tucking the tail in tight, pulling his belt up an extra notch, squaring his shoulders.

It damn sure needs no sitting in a stableyard worrying about a man with whiskers. Maybe I can get credit. At the Amigo de Los

Pobres. Or someplace. At least for a shirt. At least I can try. At least I can get a shave and a shine for two *reales*.

He buckled on his gun and started for the carriage gate. "I am going to the Plaza," he said to the guard. "Make sure you tell your relief about me. If I come in late."

"The girls, eh?" The guard winked. "The town is full of them!" He opened the gate. "*Con chichis!*"

Martin walked the cobbles, through hot strips of sunlight slanting from the west, along lengthening cool shade beside the walls, under the boughs, of the quiet afternoon streets to the city's heart.

In increasing traffic, he came past the tawny wall along the side of the cathedral and crossed the street to the shade of the Plaza's high trees. A shine boy with his box slung over his shoulder ran up pointing at Martin's boots.

"Give me a good one," Martin said.

He sat down on an iron park bench in the shade, by a bed of bright flowers. The boy put his box on the walk, and lifting Martin's foot to the scuffed cleat, began work. The clock hands on the cathedral pointed to five, and a bell rang from one of the towers. It blended with the pleasant murmur of the fountain at his back, with the easy sound of voices, of hooves, clicking along the street. Martin sat at ease, unthinking, idly watching the horsemen, the carriages, the pedestrians as they passed. The shine boy worked with his black paste, rubbing it into the marks of the long rough road from the north.

Martin did not notice the hack until it had passed, until the driver had pulled up at the curb. He saw the man step from the hack door. He noticed the Panama hat, the tailored trimness, the slight unsteadiness as the figure turned. Then he saw the face. Martin's foot jerked down from the cleat on the shine box, and he rose up ready. The lawyer Travis Hight from Puerto walked toward him. Martin heard the drawled Southern timbre of words in another tongue.

"Brady! By God — from the corner of my eye, suh — and I told the hackman to stop!"

Hight came proffering his hand. His piercing eyes were hazed faintly, his lips smiled above the trimmed goatee. Martin shook the hand, and smelled the liquor.

"How are you suh?"

"I am all right, Mr. Hight."

"You have been riding. Out in the brush. I see that."

"Yes sir."

"Just get in?"

"Yes sir."

"Where from?"

Martin looked at Hight carefully. "Hacienda de Valdepeñas."

"By God I finally saw that place! Beautiful. We were down there ten days ago, during the *coup*. I inquired for you from the Castros. I wanted to see you. Do you have plans for this evening suh?"

"No sir. Just to get cleaned up, some."

"Why don't you come over to the *mesón?* I'd like mighty well to have you meet some friends of mine, gentlemen from Saint Louis, the Continental and Southern Railway."

"I don't look good, Mr. Hight."

"Devil take that! I want to talk to you. A business proposition." Martin looked in Hight's face.

It is a chance. I want to know. I got to take my chance.

"You will have to excuse my looks, Mr. Hight. I couldn't draw my pay when I got in. I been out where I couldn't get paid. I haven't got no other clothes but these."

"Rats! Get in the hack." Hight tossed a *real* to the shine boy, who still knelt on the walk, looking up at them. "There, *muchacho.* Come on, Brady, we will ride over to the *mesón.* We will have a thin touch of this brandy we seem to encounter in Mexico. Clean up over at my place."

"You do not want the shine completed?" the boy asked, worried.

"He wants to finish the shine, Mr. Hight."

"Goddammit, *muchacho*, get on the hack! Let's go! I need a *muchacho* today anyway. *Vamos!*"

"*Vámonos*," Martin said to the boy. "Finish it at the inn. Get on the carriage, with the driver." The boy grinned.

"Brady," Hight said when they were seated in the hack. "High cotton, by God, the high cotton and we're in it!" He jabbed Martin's knee with a forefinger.

More liquor than cotton and I am in a jam and I want to know —

"Continental and Southern has the agreement, signed and sealed! A right of way from the City of Mexico to Puerto on the Rio Grand'! A new age!"

Martin sat waiting, smelling Hight's breath.

"The last link in the line was Chihuahua. To negotiate it we had to have a governor we could count on and we backed your Cipriano Castro. Not only because of his political strength, but because the man owns an almighty parcel of land through which the roadbed must be built. I told my clients. Irrefrag-irr-ir-*re*fragable logic! Well, suh. We got to the ear of the President of Mexico. The Chihuahua garrison commanders got notice to drop their bandit Salcido. Castro got from Continental and Southern a thumping fine sum of money in good faith and in consideration for the future right of way. And it all came to pass! Practical politics in Mexico? Godamighty godamighty!"

Hight jabbed Martin's knee again. "Before long, the survey party will be running the line. We want a man like yourself with that survey. You know the country, the people, the Indians. You know the way the rascals operate down here. I have mentioned you to my colleagues from Saint Louis. That is the business we want to discuss with you. There is also the matter of a little contract for furnishing railroad ties later. I believe that a team like you and myself could handle that very profitably, Brady. This country is opening up suh. For a man who knows Mexico — "

The shine boy had opened the hack door.

"Home from the hills," Hight said. "Feeling very dry." He got out. "*Espérame!*" he called up to the hackman. "Come on, *muchacho!*" Hight led the way across the wide wagonyard of the inn, to the door of his rooms. He got the key in the lock, and opened the door.

"Brady, if you want it, tell the boy to go get the *mozos* and to bring water for your bath, hot or we will cut some throats. Do you want to use my razor, or do you want a barber?"

"I'm not much good with a razor, Mr. Hight."

"*Oye, muchacho*," Hight said. "*Traiga barbero también. Pronto!*" He turned to Martin. "Come in suh. At this point a little bottled French wake-robin might be in rousing good order." He stepped to the table and poured two big ponies of cognac from the bottle sitting on the tray with the glasses.

Martin picked up a folded square of paper from the floor. "Something put under your door," he said. He handed it to Hight.

Hight read it, tilting his head, turning the paper carefully.

"From my colleagues," he announced. "Another *parranda!* By God, the Castros entertain us! 'Nothing formal' as they say." Hight winked. "Don Cipriano apologizes in most courtly style for the lack of state dinners and formal entertainments in his yet unorganized administration but I find no apology necessary. On the contrary. Lord God these parrandahs! Your poison, Brady. Three groans — " Hight tossed off a pony.

Martin took a bare sip, and Hight looked at him. Hight's eyes went to the gun on Martin's hip, and Hight smiled as if he had remembered something suddenly.

"Why didn't you claim that reward, Brady?"

"What was that, Mr. Hight?"

"The reward. I think it was a hundred dollars. For killing that scoundrel in Puerto."

"You mean — " the words would not come.

Martin felt his whole mind tighten, his whole body go tense, looking straight into the hazed eyes. "Mr. Hight," Martin said. His heart pounded and he stood ready. "If you are making sport out of me I am going to kill you."

Hight's eyes came leveling, remarkably clear of the film that had hazed them. "I am armed myself, Mr. Brady. You are welcome to try."

"I want to know, *I got to know* aren't they waiting for me up there with the law?"

"I see you didn't know. *You know now.* I told you. You happened to nail the tinhorn that murdered the clerk and stole the payroll at the Silverton Mine. The company had a reward up for the scoundrel dead or alive."

Hight's eyes pierced at him now, wise with a thousand courtrooms. "I see you didn't know. If you had been indicted — which you were not — no jury in Texas would have convicted. You had a witness. Mr. P. J. Ruelle followed you that night. He saw you hit the man with your fist to avenge young Sterner. He saw the man draw on you and he saw you fire in self-defense. I will say this, Brady, had there been a trial it would have been a pleasure to defend you. — You want a drink?"

"I have one."

"Drink it. — Here's how."

The fire went down Martin's throat as the *mozos* came in the door with the smoking kettles and the tin tub.

"You still want that bath?" Hight asked.

"I need one."

"You need another drink."

"Shall I throw my gun out the window, Mr. Hight?"

"Forget it. Here's how. *Salud*, as they say."

"*Salud*. Did the young Sterner, did he get well?"

"I never heard the contrary."

And the old Sterner, Martin thought, with the fire of the cognac and bitterness burning, I see it. He didn't want me around because I knew something on him. And Pancho Gil, he wanted me to ride — and the two of them, the two bastards, they got up that lie and told me I couldn't go back. *But I can.*

" — What a peroration in final argument suh. Gentlemen of the jury, there sits a man, a *man* unafraid to defend a friend, a helpless, battered, an innocent friend victimized by a vicious, verminous bully. There sits a man who risked life, who risked all, to right a heinous wrong. For a friend. A friend. Gentlemen, greater love hath no man — good God, Brady, the world and the Bar of Texas are losers! Have a thin one. Let us prepare for a parrandah!"

Martin sat doubled in the hot water, working with the soap, with the fire burning in him.

"And how are the Ruckers — I mean, how is Captain Rucker?" Martin called.

"Fine, fine," Hight answered from the next room. "Ruckers are fine people. Charming daughter. John Rucker is friendly with that blackguard Heffridge, but John Rucker is no less a damn fine fearless Christian gentleman. Fought with Hood's Texans. Did I tell you, Brady, we whipped the damned black Republicans from office in Puerto? Justice prevails. Our little city is booming. Soon to be bound with ribbons of iron to the commerce of two nations.

" — Would you like a touch of this for your glass while you dry? Want you to meet my friends from Saint Louis. A profitable enterprise suh. Tell me, are you interested?"

"I will have to see about it, Mr. Hight."

"See here, Brady, you can't wear those drawers. Or that shirt. Just a minute — " Hight came into the room. "Try these. A little short-legged and short-armed — otherwise — perfectly proper for a parrandah I believe."

"I couldn't go with you, thank you, Mr. Hight. I — "

"The hell you couldn't suh. A parrandah is just what you need after a ride in the brush. I can't say I right vitally need a parrandah myself, after three nights running, but I am still interested. When Travis Hight stands uninterested in the materials of a parrandah, Travis Hight stands ready to die."

It was difficult to keep the chair from floating out the door while the razor scraped. It was very difficult. Martin tried opening his eyes. The room tilted. He tried closing his eyes. He tilted, himself. He breathed deeply, filling his lungs, emptying them, carefully, and he held on, with his eyes open, then closed, then open, while the barber — also breathing deeply — bent over him and the razor scraped.

" — Day after tomorrow in the morning, Brady. The first stage to Puerto since the troubles. Do you think you might ride with us?"

"I have my horse, Mr. Hight."

"Splendid animal. Do you race him?"

"Hardly ever."

"That rascal Tod Hogan would be delighted to arrange something. When we get to Puerto."

The shine boy helped Martin on with his boots. They were blacked, and almost shining. Martin stood up. He felt his smooth chin. He focused his eyes. He looked down on himself, in Hight's snowy shirt. There were pleats on the bosom.

The shine boy had brushed the jeans, the Philadelphia hat, and he was grinning. Martin gave him a *real*.

"Keep your money in your pocket suh. It's all taken care of. But you need a tie. Here — And *muchacho*, you can take those spurs off his boots — *quita las espuelas*, son!"

Hight tied the bow in the black string tie, and backed off admiring his handiwork. " – One thing more, Brady. Unarmed. Leave your gun here with mine."

"Hate to move without it, Mr. Hight."

"I do recall you were going to throw it out the window."

Martin smiled. "I sure was – " He unbuckled it.

Hight put the gun belt with his own shoulder holster. He stuffed them both into his traveling bag, and shoved it behind the bed. "Under official auspices of the governor of the state I trust we need no firearms suh. Exceedingly official auspices. Parrandah, *March!* We are off, the captain shouted – Come on, *muchacho*, you're still hired! Blow out that lamp."

The keeper of the *mesón* stood by the door, grinning as they went out into the dusk. "Is everything well?" he asked Hight.

"Christmas a long way from Chloe's house suh!"

The lantern on the hack was lit.

"*La parranda!*" Hight called. "*Tú sabes!*" The hackman grinned and saluted, and they got in.

"Cigar, Brady? Havana. None of that bilious black leaf – "

They lit up, and sat puffing, driving through the darkening streets. A high moon stood in the clear sky. It appeared to be two moons when Martin looked up at it. The carriage appeared to move with a marvelously strange roll through the evening air.

And I can go back, Martin told himself. The warmth was hot in his middle, it reached to his heart. Going back, going back, the hooves clacked on the street. Going back, going back to my people to my country going back.

They were out of town when the hackman stopped at the *huerta* and they got out hearing the music of strings, and walked under the trees with the moon on the leaves, on the big felt hats of the two guards with guns and leather breeches, by the door.

"*Buenas noches, señores!*" the guards said.

"*Muy buenas noches!*" Hight said, pulling the bell rope.

"Ah the Señor Lo!" Martin heard the voice say. The tall woman was handsome. She had a spangled gown and raddled cheeks.

"I wish," Hight said in his best Spanish, "to present my intimate friend the American Señor Green."

"I have much pleasure, Señor Gree!"

"The pleasure is mine, señora," Martin heard himself say.

"Ah and such Spanish! Come in gentlemen please!"

The patio was lit with Japanese lanterns and moonlight, and crystal lamps on a long table draped in white napery and spread with a plentiful buffet. By a trellis of honeysuckle, the music played. The girls were dressed in bright gowns, with glitter at their throats, and white slippers, and they smiled.

It seemed that there were girls named Tina, and Chepa, and Mariquita and Cotita and Lencha and another and Ana who was pretty stout and Dolores and María Luisa and two others and Trini who was something. It seemed she had a little mole on her neck like Magdalena used to why remember that? It seemed that the gentlemen from Saint Louis were very glad to meet him delighted these parrandahs fine old Latin custom talk some business tomorrow these little brown queans suh on swivels it seemed like on swivels. It seemed that the waiter by the other table kept bringing the cold wine in the long-stemmed glasses bubbling tickle your nose that Trini really believed he came from Nueva York only did they speak such good Spanish none of the others talked true Spanish Señor Gree it is because I am a true man and I speak true Spanish to a truly beautiful girl. It seemed that oysters were a nothing more like calfslobbers and the goose liver Mr. Hight said that is what it was was better but the ham and turkey was the best damn good with the little white bread and butter and the fish eggs not bad salty with that cold wine Trini —

Martin straightened. He brought his eyes to bear.

"This is Lieutenant Zun-unigah —" he heard Hight saying. "Aide to His Excellency. Lieutenant may I present an intimate friend of mine very well known in Texas my friend Mr. Brady."

"I have had the pleasure. Good evening Mr. Brady."

"Good evening."

"I trust you find the entertainment pleasant."

"Very agreeable, *Señor Teniente*."

"I am enchanted."

"I am enchanted equally."

He watched the lieutenant's back moving across the patio. He saw other uniforms, other gold braid, by the long white table.

"Had no idea you knew him," Hight was saying. "Quite a lad

with arrangements. Especially these arrangements — you have them, Mariquita, your arrangements are superb — "

No good and I shouldn't, Martin tried to think, but the lanterns doubled, then tripled and what is the difference anyway I am leaving the country it seemed more cold wine better Trini you are a trick with everything all built in of course Nueva York is bigger than Guanajuato Trini everybody there has houses big as cathedrals true the carriages are gold plated big steam trains with a thousand cars run on tracks up over your head they whistle like mockingbirds but they do not have *jarabes* Señor Gree Greegree *ai* that naughty Mariquita and Cotita see what champagne causes without clothes what a pretty barbarity do you like that my *chulito* they have no *jarabes* like that in your Nueva York but they do have them here Trini not here my *chulito* here and all the hot suns the long times the rough roads the loneliness forever the empty world rose up in fire and died quenched dead clinging in the dark.

"*Señor!*"

Both the title and the voice awoke him. He opened an eye and squinted, painfully, against the glare of sunlight from the open door. He saw the girl in the wrapper standing by the bed. She shook him by the shoulder.

"Señor! They call for you! Now!"

Both of Martin's eyes came open.

"Who?"

"Soldiers! Of the governor."

Martin sat up, and wished he hadn't. Stone hammers pounded inside his head and his mouth felt full of rusted iron. Its fumes choked and he coughed with the hammers cracking at the bones of his skull, the sick meat of his brain. He groaned and put his bare feet on the cool tile floor.

"I will help you dress yourself," the girl said, and she helped him. The boots were the worst.

"The *dueña* is holding the soldiers, señor. She wishes you to hurry. — Here, the shirt." The girl buttoned him and he stood swaying.

"Ready?" the girl asked. No powder covered the tan skin of her young face. Darks like faint bruises spread under both her eyes, from the inner corners of the lower lids outward to the bones of her cheeks. She put her hand on his chest. "*Ai*, last night!" She brought her head closer. "Will you come back? Please?"

Martin looked down at her, ready to be sick. He held himself.

"Something to tell me, so I will know," he said, with the fuming iron in his head. "Art thou clean?"

"I am clean."

"The truth?"

"Believe me, señor."

"Huh," Martin said, "I am sick, forgive me." He stumbled out the door and was sick by the honeysuckle. He straightened up with the hammers and the anger in him raging, with the iron in his throat. "Show me to the backhouse."

"Now," he said, when he had crossed the patio again.

The tall woman gave him his hat at the door. Two armed soldiers in garrison uniforms were waiting. There were three horses tied at the fence beyond the orchard.

"What do you want?" Martin asked.

"The aide sent us. To bring you."

"I would like to go by the *mesón*. To wash, to — change the shirt."

"I feel deeply. That is impossible. The governor waits. The Señor Governor."

The sun was hot, the horse was rough. Martin was sick again, in the street. At every pound of the horse's hooves on the cobbles, Martin felt his backbone ram into his skull.

"I have to wash myself," he said when he got off at the iron gate, in front of the house of the Castros. The guards in the big hats were grinning.

"Tell the lieutenant."

Lieutenant Zuñiga's face was ravaged with his night before, but his gold braid was neat. He stood straight.

It straightened Martin.

"His Excellency asked for you early," the lieutenant said. "When you were not in your quarters, it gave him no pleasure, I assure you."

Inside the double door at the end of the courtyard, Cipriano Castro received them. He frowned.

"Bredi. I am surprised. I am not pleased. Are you drunk?"

The hammers pounded. "I ask your pardon for the way I look." He tried to clear the roughness from his throat. "I was not permitted to clean myself before I came. But I am not drunk."

The lustrous eyes appraised him. "Very well. You are sober. I have something sober to discuss with you. Sit down." Cipriano Castro motioned the lieutenant from the room. When the door was closed, the governor of Chihuahua seated himself and looked in Martin's face.

"You give me to understand you are in condition for sober discussion. Am I correct?"

The hammers pounded. "Yes, señor."

Here it comes.

"Aurelio Salcido escaped by way of Coahuila. He crossed the river at Eagle Pass. My informants brought this news late last night. They state Salcido is on his way to San Antonio in Texas where the remains of a revolutionary junta await him, with funds. As long as he is alive, Aurelio Salcido is a threat and a danger. To me, to my government!"

Do it right. Do it right, the hammers pounded, you better do it right. The worst morning of all your life to think do it right and you better do it right or you are gone.

" — And my attendant confidence in your ability, in your loyalty — or I would not have you here. You understand I am prepared to reward you."

Cipriano Castro turned. He brought a buckskin purse from a table drawer and held it out, offering it casually to Martin.

Do it right.

Martin took the purse. It was heavy.

"Thirty gold *onzas*, Bredi. I assume this amply pays you for your recent time in the north. I assume it amply provides expenses for your journey to San Antonio. I assume you know this is a mere token — upon your return, with proof, there will be many *onzas* awaiting you, or title to a respectable ranch property or such other concession as you may sensibly desire from a governor of a state. That is my promise. I assume you know I do not break a promise."

The hammers pounded. Martin licked his dry lips, tasting the iron, holding the gold in his hand.

It seemed the picture of the Spaniard looked at him from the wall it seemed Cipriano Castro sat wearing the armor suddenly and might have a sword — Martin focused his eyes, tearing at the blur in his head, fighting it.

"You understand, Bredi?"

"I understand."

Do it right.

"Thank you, señor." Martin stuffed the purse in his pocket.

"There is another thing you must understand clearly. I assume you know your — odd position. I assume you know that you have enjoyed my personal protection in the face of the law, both of Mexico and of the United States." The lustrous eyes surveyed him. "I am fully informed of the circumstances that brought you to Mexico. I am informed of many matters, such as the disappearance of a valuable cart and oxen and a driver, to mention a recent example, that might demand explanation in the face of the law. I mention this only to assure you that I am confident your conduct will warrant my personal protection in the future. You understand?"

I have to do it right. "Yes, señor."

"It is a matter for immediate and decisive action. The sooner, the better. There is a stage to Presidio this afternoon."

"Señor. I will ride the horse. It is necessary. A fast horse."

"I leave the method to you." The lustrous eyes bore in upon him. "I shall receive reports of your progress in the direction of San Antonio, of course."

"You will have them, señor."

"I say no more. — Bredi, Lieutenant Zuñiga surprises me with information that you were with the Americans McQuigg, Hight, Peters and the other, last night. Why?"

"Señor Hight was an acquaintance in Puerto. He is a cordial man."

"Is that so? What passed between you yesterday?"

"Nothing. Nothing but drink, mother of God! Somehow I left my pistol at his room in the *mesón*. I will see him again before I leave this afternoon — "

Cipriano Castro almost smiled. "If you had champagne, I advise no water this morning. You will regret it."

"Señor, I already regret it."

Cipriano Castro did smile. He stood up and offered his hand. Martin shook it. The smile faded. "Good luck, Bredi."

"Thank you, señor."

You did it right, so far, you did it right. Do it all right.

He walked to the stableyard, and washed his face at the horse trough. The Chinese cook gave him a cup of hot black coffee, and his stomach held it, in doubt. With his head pounding, with his pocket bulged and heavy with the buckskin purse, he walked the street to the tall, polished, bronze-knobbed door. He put the purse on Señor Roa's counter.

"Señor, I have some *onzas* here."

"You have indeed, hmm."

Martin stacked them. "These eight are my pay for the months in the north. Four of them I take for my spending. Please change them to silver pesos. These other four I wish to send to Mateo Casas of Valdepeñas. Can you send them to him with the next messenger to the hacienda?"

"It can be arranged. The charge is one *tostón*, hm."

"I will pay it. Change this peso."

"Very well. The four *onzas* go to?"

"Mateo Casas, vaquero, Hacienda de Valdepeñas."

"Any message?"

"Say only: From Martín. *Salud*."

Señor Roa wrote it carefully. "Very well," he said.

"Now," Martin said.

Do it right.

"These twenty-two *onzas* making 352 pesos I wish to deposit here with you. I am riding. I wish you to keep them until I return. Until I return to Chihuahua."

"Very prudent, Bredi, hm." When Roa had finished writing he peered at Martin through the spectacles. "Prudent. And rare, for a man who rides. Thrift is the base of good fortune, hm. Here is your receipt."

"Thank you, Señor Roa."

Martin walked sweating to the store beyond the Plaza and stepped in under the sign LA TORRE DE BABEL. He bought a pair of drawers and sox and a handkerchief, a heavy gray shirt, a pair of leather breeches, and a blanket — not a good Saltillo, he could not afford it — and he paid twenty-three pesos and walked out with his big package.

Beyond the trees on the street by the palace he caught sight of the hangman El Verdugo, the captain of cavalry with the quirt on his wrist, riding the high-headed bay. Martin watched the thick back ride away down the street.

Mateo Casas called it something, Martin stood thinking. "It is the sorrow of my Mexico." There goes the sorrow of my Mexico. In one package. No. It can't be wrapped in one package. There would be no Verdugo without a Marcos Castro. There would be no Marcos Castro without a smart brother. The sorrow of Mexico, it goes wrapped in many packages. But the pain of Mexico — this morning it goes wrapped in one package for sure, it goes wrapped in this damn fool head —

But I am doing it right.

A hack from the Plaza took him to the *mesón* and charged him two *reales*.

The shine boy answered the knock on the door. He looked tired.

"Brady! Glad to see you!" Hight was in shirt sleeves and needed a shave. "Just in time for a morning soother — some fine *menudo*, God bless it, and a little hair of the dog. How did you fare at your parrandahing suh? Here is Mr. Peters, Mr. Gibb, Mr. McQuigg. Sit down, Brady. Have some of this. You leaving with us tomorrow, to Puerto?"

"I wish I could, Mr. Hight. I found out I have some things to tend to."

"But we will see you up there? Won't we?"

"You will when I can get there."

"We are counting you in suh!"

"I am sorry I can't go with you. I came by to thank you. To bring your shirt and drawers. Mr. Hight, I lost your necktie. I want to pay you for it, and pay to get your things washed up, and for my shave and everything, yesterday."

"Good God, man, I am paid by the pleasure of your company! I will hear nothing further about it."

"I like to pay my own way."

"Nothing more about that, Brady! This gruel is mighty strengthening, isn't it? I recommend a public monument, gentlemen. To the Inventor of *Menudo* Restorer of Mankind on Grim Mornings — damned sensible recommendation. Brady, I trust at least you will be with us for the final grand and glorious parrandah this evening. General Marcos Castro will be our host. The general himself led our escort when we came up from Zacatecas to Valdepeñas. The general is a *bon vivant*. Quite a host."

"I have to ride," Martin said.

Hight and the gentlemen from Saint Louis were interested in Martin's rig when he came from the next room wearing his new shirt and leather breeches. He had on his Philadelphia hat and his spurs and his gun again, and he carried his new blanket over his shoulder.

"Mr. Hight, please give that old wad of my clothes to the shine boy. He can use them. I left your shirt and drawers in there separate — and I am obliged to you. I want to say that was some *parranda!*"

"Have a thin one with us, Brady, before you go."

He had the thin one. He said good-by.

The thin one helped his head, and he had a beer, cool, alone in a saloon by the Plaza.

It was midafternoon when Lágrimas stood saddled in the stableyard and Martin loaded on the saddlebags with the ammunition, the dried meat, the full bag of *pinole*, the *morral* with cracked corn. He tied on his new tin canteen, filled with water, and his new blanket, behind the cantle. He mounted, and rode out the carriage gate.

At the edge of town, he did not take the Presidio road, nor the road to Coahuila. He put Lágrimas in a long-paced rack, and took the road west. His head pounded again as he went, facing the sun, facing the mother mountains of Mexico.

Tell Chihuahua good-by, black horse. Say good-by to all *señores de horca y cuchillo,* all the lords of gallows and knife — *adiós!* The shortest way out of the state of Chihuahua is over the sierra and we take the shortest way, Lágrimas black horse. The lonesomest way. Tell all the roads good-by, we will see big country. Over the big slopes to the top, to Sonora. We will see clear out to where the sun goes down — and move north, black horse, I will teach you English on the way.

A league on the road west from the city, a bullet sang over his head. He heard the gun report and the faint shout at his back.

Swerving into the brush he touched spur, and felt the drive of the black legs under him. He looked back. He had a glimpse of the big hats, the gray hats he was sure. They shot again.

"Git us!" he shouted. "Try and git us. If you think you can. That's English, Lágrimas. That's the way they talk up there. Remember?"

PART THREE

CHAPTER XIX

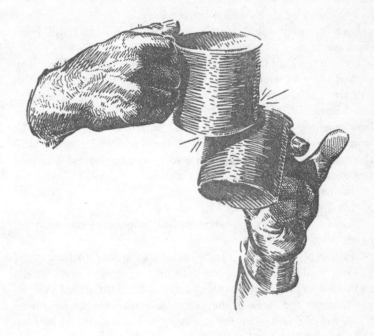

HE SENSED
rather than saw the movement on the slope above the trail in the
twist of oak trunks and tangle of leaves. Then he saw it, the white
patch on the rump, the antlers moving, and he slipped down from
the saddle, easing the carbine from the scabbard, watching. He
saw it again. It stopped to look back, head up, its big ears twisting
forward. He aimed. The sound crashed in the silence and he saw
the gray shape struck. It tumbled in the echoing sound. There
was no movement at the place in the leaves as he stood watching.
Lágrimas snorted.

Martin turned and motioned to the man on the little mule, with the four loaded pack burros, standing still in the trail a hundred varas down the hill. Then he stepped into the stirrup, swinging up with the gun still in his hand, and rode the slope to the place he had marked with his eye.

The buck lay dead with a broken back.

I am shooting high, Martin thought. Uphill, and still I am shooting high —

He got off, cleared the empty, uncocked the hammer, and slipped the gun back into its scabbard. With the knife from his belt, he cut the buck's throat and pulled the head around to bleed downhill. He cut the glands from the legs, and made the long opening, with care not to slit a gut, from vent to chest. The warm entrails were out, smoking in the shady grass, by the time the man came up from the trail leading the big burro. The man was grinning under his stringy mustache. He pushed his straw hat on the back of his head.

"How good!" he said to Martin. "Big! And fat!"

"Your meat, Justo." Martin smiled, wiping blood from his hands on a clump of grass.

"Plenty of meat now," Justo said, "all the way to Bacanora."

They loaded the butchered deer on the squeaky pack saddle and tied it in place with cords of *mecate*. Sunlight angled yellowing through the trees as they entered again into the shadowed trace, and rode on, with the empty mescal barrels retied high on three of the packs and the venison joggling on the other. Half a league over the slope they came down into pines by the side of running water and made camp under the high rocks on a shelf above the stream.

When the animals were unsaddled, and Lágrimas and the little mule were tethered and the burros hobbled for the night, Justo built a fire in the chill of the sierra's October dusk. Martin sliced tenderloins from the buck. He and Justo ate them broiled on sticks in the firelight, with tortillas, and frijoles from a pot. The stars came out and they saw them between the black boughs. They heard the wind in the pine tops and the water moving on the dark rocks.

"The trouble of the world," Justo said, "comes from the hand of man. The sierra is not troubled. I have thought about it. The sierra is too big for the hand of man. I carry mescal from Bacanora over the summits to the towns thirsty in the east five and six times in the year, and I see the sierra always in peace. It has the wild beasts, yes. And the wizards and some things of magic. But the affairs of men are small in it."

"Every night you mention wizards, Justo. You have seen wizards?"

"*Guamas, chiseras, naguales.* There are many. I carry this against their powers." He showed a metal cross on a string around his neck, and sat silent, looking into the fire.

"What powers do they have?"

"Many." A knot popped in the fire, scattering sparks. "Only a fool doubts their force."

"I have never seen any wizards, of those names."

"I have told you," Justo said, "in this sierra there are also bandits. One time they robbed me of my cargo and entered upon a great drunk. But bandits are few. And Indians? Only Tarahumares and God in His wisdom made them timid! In the matter of fierce Indians, here it is too far east for Yaquis, and too far south for Apaches. Thanks to our Lord Savior."

"You believe Apaches never come to these sierras?"

"Who knows? They might. But I have not seen them. I do not want to see Apaches."

"I have told you how they catch an unarmed man and crack his head open with rocks."

"But that is in Chihuahua. I do not go far in Chihuahua, I have never been beyond the mine of Yepachic. These sierras are better. The Apaches stay north of here. Señor, tell me, you still have strong desires to go north?"

"Very strong."

"Tomorrow the best trail forks. And if it forks, this is our last fire together."

"I am sorry. It has all been good."

Justo looked into the fire. "It is understandable, that a man wishes to go back to his own country. But going north — those Apaches — *fiuu* —"

Martin smiled. "But you, Justo, here in your sierra with wizards. *Guamas, chiseras.* What were the others?"

"*Naguales.*"

"What are they like?"

"They make an odd sound in the air. They are great thieves, señor, robbing up to life itself. I prefer not to discuss them."

Before the fire died, Martin went into the dark and took the *morral* from Lágrimas' nose.

"Good horse," Martin said, in the huge darkness.

Up the slope, the bright stars of Orion lifted above the rim of pines.

That is an old hunter, Lágrimas, I used to see him at Kingdom Prairie when I was a boy and he came climbing over the hill the first fall evening. A hound dog goes with him, with a big bright eye. But that hunter coming over the sierra now — he's from back there in Chihuahua. He don't see us. He better not: we will plug him right between the eyes. Must be his gray sombrero up there — see the red stars? Chin string. It's no sword he carried now, it's a knife for sure. And there's his Remington — I guess that dim star is a fly speck from Sterner's. The dog hasn't come over the sierra yet — but it won't be a dog. It will be a horse. One of the geldings from the horse pasture at Valdepeñas and he will run his legs off and wink his big eye and never catch us.

Lágrimas rubbed bumping his cheek against Martin's chest; Martin ran his hand on the black hide of the neck, down to the foreleg. He patted the foreleg.

That hunter nearly got us. You know that? You hidden in that sheepshed at Pacoromachic with your hoof full of pus. Over there on the bad side of the sierra. You a cripple and me a damn *pelado* pushing a plow for our keep and trying to stay hid out. Don't you never throw another shoe! Look where you go throwing those hind feet, you worthless old stud horse. They nearly did get us. But they can't now. We are in Sonora. Sleep good.

The coals glowed red, thinning, in the silence beyond the sound of the wind and the water. Martin lay down to the comfort of the earth, wrapped in his blanket, with his guns by his hand. An owl awoke him in the dark, and the wind blew harder before he and Justo rose in the blackness and rebuilt their fire, with the morning star above the rim. They cooked venison in the growing light, hearing wolves howl from beyond the dim ravines.

They had been on the trail an hour, their blankets wrapped under their chins, their animals' legs wet with dew, when the sun came showing at their backs, over the trees from Chihuahua. Martin looked through the pine boughs, down at the sloping tumble of the mountains opening out westward under the pale pink of the sky. As the sun warmed him, he folded his blanket to his saddle and rode the trace in the silvery light with Justo at his side on the little mule, driving the burros with the barrels and venison, among the trees.

In the midmorning they came down a steep slope to a long plateau rimmed with mountaintops. They rode out upon the level, in grass faintly gold from first frost. The stalks were stirrup high and they rustled with the tread of the hooves in the sunny quiet.

Justo turned in his saddle, and reined. "Here it is," he said. There was regret in his voice. "This is the Mesa del Tabaco. On the one hand —" he pointed — "the trail goes for Sahuaripa, for Bacanora. On the other —" he used his whole arm to cut the air like a slow knife — "a trail points through that notch called Paso del Águila, to Bavinuchi, and beyond —" he shrugged — "to all the north. You will not decide to continue with me, señor? In Bacanora my house is yours."

"Thank you, Justo. My direction is north."

"Come to my town someday. Make a proof of hospitality. Make a proof of the finest mescal in all the world, which I will furnish you — *mescal de pechuga* distilled through the breast meat of wild turkey. It is exquisite."

"I would like to taste it with you. Tell me, Justo, do you know what I will find first on the trail that goes north? Is there any settlement before Bavinuchi?"

"You stand on land pertaining to the Santos family. Over the edge, toward the notch —" he pointed — "following the water — so — you will find a rancho of the Santos. There are workers living at the rancho. They will tell you the way to Bavinuchi. The Santos have fame as good people. You will find them."

Martin put out his hand. "I am grateful, Justo. For everything."

"The gratitude is mine," Justo said with the handshake. "That God our Señor take you by good road."

When she had gone fifty varas, Justo's mule turned her head toward Lágrimas, and brayed. The men waved, grinning.

Martin watched Justo and his animals grow small across the widening plain of grass. They shrank to five little dots. They disappeared. Martin felt his own smallness, alone in the immense mountains under the immense sky.

He felt the southing autumn slant of the sun at noon as he came over the edge of the mesa and rode under trees again. By a high oak on the stream bank he unsaddled, and dozed for an hour while his horse grazed in the shade. Squirrels and bluejays chattered at him. Cloud shadows moved, patches of rich blue, along the slopes. He washed in the cold water of the stream, and drank, before he saddled again and rode on. Cow tracks were thick along the trace he rode, but he saw no stock.

As the tangle of tracks climbed from the rocky stream, up the shoulder of a hill, a familiar sound came to him and he stopped to listen. Herded cattle bawled in the distance. Over the hill he came into a wide glade shelving to groves by the water. The glade was a grassy cup set in timbered slopes and at its far side a hint of dust hung pale in the trees. From it came a rise and fall of bawl and bellow blended by distance into a rustic music.

Martin rode toward the dust and the sound. He saw a corner of a big adobe cabin, and a fence. He saw an edge of cedar-post corral gray in the shade, and then the cattle, many cattle, of many colors. He heard a faint shout, and smelled cedar smoke. He smelled a thin whiff of burnt hair, and an armed vaquero rode toward him, under the trees.

Martin reined and waited, carefully. The vaquero, in leather and a ragged hat, came toward him.

"Good afternoon," Martin called.

"*Qué hubo!*" The vaquero was young. His face was scratched from wild rides in thick brush. "Where from?"

Martin made a motion eastward and upward. "The sierras!"

"Where do you go?"

"The United States!"

"*Eeee!* Far. What do you do?"

"Vaquero, miner. A little of many things."

"You are Mexican?"

"No. I lived in Chihuahua, but not any more. You see me headed for my country — riding the sierras on my way."

"Hunting mines, eh? How did you come?"

"From Jicachic. Using trails to Sahuaripa. I came with a *mescalero* from Bacanora."

"You came on a good horse. Andalusian."

"A very good horse."

"What is your name?"

"Martin Brady, at your orders."

"Agustín Santos. I am at yours."

"You are the family of Santos of Bavinuchi?"

"That is my family."

"Would you tell me the trail to Bavinuchi, Señor Santos? Does it follow this water to Paso del Águila? And beyond?"

"You are riding for Bavinuchi?"

"I am on my way."

"Why? You see us here finishing our *corrida* — with a good camp. My father is with us. He will talk to you — travelers from Chihuahua are rare!"

"Well," Martin said, "I smell the branding. I can help, if you need another hand. Your father is the *patrón*?"

"Yes."

They started toward the dust.

Agustín Santos' father stood by the branding fire. Martin knew he was *patrón* the instant he saw him: authority stood written in the set of his head on his shoulders. It was a working authority, inherent in the stamp of the man, without pretension or solemnity. The leather clothes that cased him bore the rips of rough rides and stains of many camps. Iron buckles clinked on the outer rawhide *metazas* sheathing his bowlegs to the thighs and he wore spurs with long rowels and steel jingles. Strapped on his hip was a black-handled .44. "*Is that all?*" he bellowed at the bellowing herd.

A mounted roper came dragging a roan bull calf at the end of his rawhide.

"The last!" shouted the roper.

Martin watched a vaquero go down the taut reata and spill the jumping calf. The vaquero's hat bounced off. He swore in a high tenor, laughing, with a twisting grip on the doubled foreleg, and two men ran to help him hold. One of them slipped the reata from the bawling calf's neck when the roper gave him slack. The *patrón* himself took an iron from the fire.

In a fetid puff of white smoke, he burned his mark on the stretched flank. He cut his *señal*, an underslope from both ears. Moving with a practiced skill he turned and took hold of his calf's big scrotum, sliced off its end, squeezed out its testicles, cut its cords, rasped "Go, ox!" and strode to the fire. He threw the testicles in the pile that broiled on the coals at the edge of the flame, wiped his hands on his leather breeches, and bellowed again, "*Is that all?*"

"That's all!" came the answer.

"*Epah!* Turn them out, Calixto! Set a guard to hold the steer herd, and those heifers!"

"Exactly!" Calixto shouted, riding.

"*Oye*, Father!" called Agustín Santos, in the noise. "Look!"

"Eh!"

Martin saw the eyes. They were the color of wild honey. They turned at Martin quick and sharp — with good humor in their amber lights. There was no suspicion in them. Martin was not prepared.

"Santiago Santos," this *patrón* said, offering his ungloved hard hand. "At your orders."

"Martin Brady, to serve you."

"He hunts for mines," Agustín Santos said. "And rides that black nag — " he pointed at Lágrimas tied to a corral post, his neck arched.

Santiago Santos looked at the horse, and then at Martin. "Well," Santos said, dry, "enough pony for a ride to a mine — " The voice was loud. It carried some sound of the winds, the herds, the rocky canyons. Martin liked it.

"To tell you the truth," Martin said, "I am not much miner."

"I did not hear your name precisely, señor."

"In English, Martin Brady. They say in Spanish Martín Bredi."

"Martín. Clear enough. You are English?"

"No señor! American."

"You speak good Spanish, man. You are Texan?"

"I have passed some times in Texas."

"Angels of Christ, they say even the people that pass some times in Texas are like bisnaga thorns. Well, we manage. With thorns of all types. Have a little egg — " He stooped and stabbed on the end of his knife a nicely browned spheroid split open by the fire. He offered it courteously.

"Thank you, Don Santiago."

The *patrón* stabbed up another, for himself. His son Agustín and half a dozen vaqueros were helping themselves from the coals.

As they stood by the fire, Santiago Santos looked up at the sky, at the gathering clouds in the late light over the trees. The tilt of his head exposed a sharp Adam's apple covered with a grizzled stubble. It bobbled as he blew on the hot testicle before taking a bite. "Rain tonight, the sky says," he announced, taking the bite. "Camp with us, Señor Martín, and stay dry. Pen that stallion where he will not chew ears from my *remuda*, and camp with us. We can offer you what we have, a little something to eat, to drink."

"Many thanks, señor. Are you holding a herd tonight?"

"Why do you ask?"

"If I could help, with the night guard — "

"*Vaya!* What are my vaqueros for?"

"I am vaquero and I have been riding lazy. Tonight I could relieve a tired man who has thrashed the brush all day — to help, señor — "

Santiago Santos grinned under his big mustache. "*Qué raro!*" He looked in Martin's face. "You are my guest, not my vaquero."

The rain came thick, straight down in the twilight. It soaked Martin as he unsaddled and penned his horse. The man with the high voice, who flanked the calf, came to help. He brought Lágrimas cured mountain hay from a tumbled rick, and a little corn, while Martin stowed saddle and bags and blanket and rifle under the roof of the shed by the rancho's cabin. He watched his horse feed alone under the lean-to in the corral, and he checked the gate again, before he moved cold and wet toward candlelight.

He came into the cabin too late for the counting of the ears. Each man had brought his string from his saddle, each hairy pair of pendants on that string proof of an unbranded outlaw he had caught alone in the sierra and taught for the first time the jerk of rawhide and burn of iron. In the bragging and joking on this last night of *corrida*, the *patrón* — alert for chicanery — had counted the strips of ears on each string; the champion of the *corrida*, according to custom, had been proclaimed. His whiskers were curly, his name was Domatilio; he carried a knife strapped in a sheath on his left forearm. He would get a golden *onza* in Bavinuchi, and he grinned, and bragged the most.

They ate in the light of tallow dips, a dozen men in soggy leather, laughing and chewing, with the rain sounding on the roof, and cold drops leaking through.

There were succulent yams, new and good to Martin's taste, and fiery meat floating in chili on the tin plates. There were tender dainties to pick from a bull's head that had roasted caked in clay and buried in hot coals since dawn. There was coffee with milk and sugar, in tin cups. There was a scarred little cask of mescal for the cups when the coffee was gone.

Santiago Santos belched and clicked his cup to his guest's. "We say in Bavinuchi:

> *Para todo mal, mescal.*
> *Para todo bien, también!*"

Martin laughed and drank. "I listened to much mescal from my friend in the sierra. He came from Bacanora."

"Then he can speak! In Bavinuchi I can give you something from Bacanora: *mescal de pechuga!* It is the best."

"I have been told. Don Santiago, do you leave for Bavinuchi tomorrow?"

"Before the sun. You ride with us?"

"With your permission."

"With pleasure."

"Do you take that herd down for other pasture?"

"The pastures up here are the best I have! You see the beginning of our *equipatas*, our season of winter rains. They keep this grass strong all winter. No, tomorrow that herd starts a little trip. This year I send heifers to a rancher near Ures, and beef steers to market at Hermosillo."

"That is called a little trip, Don Santiago?"

"*Oye*, each year in the fall, since the times of my grandfather's father, the Santos make a drive. Some years as far as Guaymas and the sea. It is a custom. It is a good business. We miss only in times of war, or Indian trouble. This year my two sons, Agustín and Andrés, go in charge of the herd west from Bavinuchi — Andrés is in Bavinuchi now, you have not met him. Here in the sierra last week he roped a wild one. Taking up slack with a *vuelta*, his rope jerked — you guessed! — it sliced off a finger on the saddlehorn. He now carries the *señal*." Santiago Santos laughed and held up his own nine fingers. He looked over at Agustín. "That Santos lacks the mark!"

Agustín grinned. "I prefer the mark of a good roper, my father. A good roper! Five on each hand, eh Martín?"

"Many lose them," Martin smiled. "You know, in Texas they keep the end of the rope tied on the saddlehorn, and save their fingers."

"And break their thick heads jerked to the ground," Santiago Santos said. "Holy God, how intelligent! The ten-fingered Texans. Do you rope?"

"Not in the class with Santos."

"*Vaya!* Where did you learn?"

"At the hacienda where I worked in Chihuahua."

"What hacienda?"

"Valdepeñas."

"I have heard of that." Santiago Santos scratched his ear. "Wait — that is property of the new governor of Chihuahua. Castro. You worked for him?"

"Many years."

"And you only a vaquero?"

"I was one of a hundred vaqueros on the hacienda. But I have not worked cattle for a long time. Castro armed me. He made me guard on his silver trains from El Tigre Mine. That horse I ride is a gift from Castro. I carried a pistol for him."

"It appears more fitting to your type, carrying a pistol. More fitting to that horse you ride." Santiago Santos pushed his hat back and Martin saw the shiny baldness of the brown head. "What type is this Governor Castro?"

"I left his employ this summer after he got to be governor.

I owe him nothing. He owes me nothing. I want to carry my own pistol. In my own country. Where I belong."

Santiago Santos' tawny eyes regarded him.

"A man should live where he belongs."

Santiago Santos carefully made a corn-shuck cigarette. From his jacket pocket he pulled the buckskin from which he unwrapped his tindercord, his flint and his steel *eslabón*. He struck fire in the tinder, blew on it, lit his cigarette, pinched out the fire in the tinder, rewrapped his equipment in buckskin, inhaled on the tobacco, and looked at Martin.

"We Santos," he said, "we live where we belong, I think. We have lived in Bavinuchi since the times of the king Carlos III. He granted us the land. A Santos was *Marqués* of Sonora. We do not produce any damned *marqueses* in these times, nor any damned politicians either. My grandfather said it was better to own land than to govern it. We Santos produce *rancheros*. I wish there were more of us. By the time there is fuzz on our cheeks we have learned the music of the bull pens, we know horses and firearms and these sierras. We like them. I would not be content elsewhere. Nor would my sons! — When were you in Texas?"

"When I was a boy — on my way to Mexico with my father. But in the spring of this year I took an ore cart north for the Castros and I spent more than two months on the Río Bravo at the town of Puerto. There are good people at Puerto. I have a job offered me there. That's where I'm going."

"And you go by all these sierras — "

Martin searched the honey-colored eyes.

"I have good reasons to go by way of Sonora. I have good reasons to leave Chihuahua. I am not ashamed of my reasons."

"A man is entitled to his own reasons," Santiago Santos said. "Decent men have decent reasons."

"Where is your father?" Agustín asked.

"Murdered at Presidio. Fourteen years ago."

"Fourteen years, and you have gone alone?"

"No. A vaquero and his family at Valdepeñas treated me as a son. I was lucky."

"*Vah*, you appear more Mexican than Texan!" Santiago Santos looked at him. "Fill your cup."

Three guards, relieved from their watch with the herd, came in for their supper. Water dripped from their hatbrims, from the blankets they hung on pegs by the door. The big spurs on their sandals clinked as the men moved piling their plates with meat. Squatted on the floor by cups of mescal in the dim light, vaqueros were singing. The high tenor led off with —

> "Here comes the spotted bull,
> Son of the blue roan cow — "

and the verse unwound with harmonic howls from all the throats, all the coyotes in starlight celebrating a sierra that reached to the sky.

> " — Shouting at the vaqueros:
> *'Leave that wild bull to me —* ' "

"Don Santiago — " Martin called, smiling in the racket, "I would like to stand a guard — "

"Angels of Christ, forget that! — *Oye* Calixto!" he said to the dripping foreman who had begun to eat, "is the rain thinning out there?"

"It's thinning," Calixto said. "And the cattle quiet."

It was quiet when Martin lay down with his blanket, by his saddle, under the shed. Ragged edges of clearing cloud moved fast above the trees, and stars showed. The air was sharp and clean, pungent with the washed boughs of pine and cedar. A faint breeze came stirring the bough over the shed; the last dripplings of the rain fell in a flurry on the roof, pattering with small sound. Santiago Santos and his men, and his herd, were quiet in the cold dark of the sierra. Martin closed his eyes and slept.

He dreamed, as he had not dreamed in years, of Kingdom Prairie, of his grandmother's house, and the barn. It was very plain. There was Minny with a new litter of pups rooting at her dugs — seven pups, and the runt not getting a thing. He saw them through the planks of the corn crib, and he knew he was in the cow house. Gray light showed between the warped shakes of the low roof, and he could hear the wind sigh. There was something warm and comfortable about the rich smell of the cow in the stall; and there was Lady, the buggy mare, half asleep by the door, with her tail tucked tight. He smelled the harness as he squeezed close, through the frosty door crack, and walked out into the snow. In the silence under the lowering sky, he saw Kingdom Prairie, and Brady Grove, and the line of Sugar Creek. It was strange how he heard snowflakes hit with the faintest small hiss as he walked past the hot ash hopper in the white quiet, around the corner of the familiar house. He knew he was a little boy. He climbed the snowy porch steps and opened the parlor door, and saw his father. He saw him with his black beard, with his uniform.

His father said, Christmas Cheer, Mart! Hug your old dad—

Martin reached up in his dream. Is the war over? he asked his father. Is it? Are you home with us now?

No, the war isn't over, Mart.

When will it be over?

I don't know. The uniform was frayed, muddy. The straps, with the two bars, were tarnished on the gray shoulders. We will have our Christmas and then I go back. You smell that goose your granny is cooking?

Dad. Are we winning?

We are trying to win.

Don't track the floor, his grandmother said. She was basting the goose. The kettle of greens from the cold cellar cooked steaming. He could see the pan of high-rising yellow corn bread.

I brought you a gourd of popcorn and a jew's-harp, Mart, his father said.

But Santiago Santos, with his blanket to his chin, came to the door in the dream.

I have brought the horse, my friend, he said. Martin heard the words in Spanish.

Oh Jim, his grandmother said to Martin's father, Mart can't go with you. You can't take that boy. She was crying.

Martin's father said, The Kansas redlegs are going to burn this house, Mother, and you are going to die and I have to take this boy wherever I go.

I want to go with you, Martin said.

It is necessary to go now, Santiago Santos said. That horse will take you. It is a good horse for war.

Martin saw it was Lágrimas, very black in the whiteness of the snow.

That is my horse, Martin said.

You will never ride it, his father said in the dream. Until I am dead. The words were in Spanish and Martin cried.

CHAPTER XX

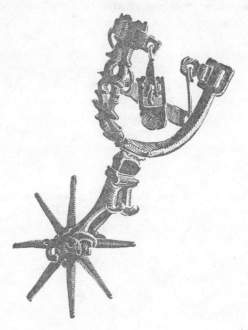

A RIDER
coming toward us," Martin said.

Santiago Santos had reined. He sat straight in his saddle, squinting into the mountain light, the mottle of shade through the oak brush, the broken outcrop of granite down the tilt of the slope.

"Just one," Santiago Santos said. He touched spur, and they moved on, watching the dark speck bobble climbing toward them between the trees, along the far foot of the granite.

They rode with the lead steer's steps rattling on the rocks behind and above them. The herd came following, a slow flow of spotted hides down through the timber. The hundreds of hooves moving brought a dull rumble and scrape into the air; their noise made a steady undertone to accents of sound down the pitch of the slope, a pop of a branch breaking, a shout, a vaquero's whistle peeping like a chick, a slap of rope on rawhide, a clatter of rock gone tumbling, a heifer bawling. It was a continuing stream of sound, alive, in the mountain silence.

The bobbling dot on the trail grew bigger.

"A sorrel," Martin said. "With light mane."

"Andrés rides a sorrel. *Hu!* I think that is the sorrel! That is Andrés — " He pulled off his hat and waved it wide, with the sun gleaming on the bald top of his head.

The horseback figure waved back, and they moved faster toward him, down the slope. Martin could see the white on the left hand as it waved.

"My boy Andrés. My eldest. With the nine fingers. — *Epaaah!*" he bellowed down the trail. "I thought you were home — " he took breath " — with sucking calves!"

Andrés Santos came riding to where they could hear his voice plainly.

"More damned noise up here," he grinned, "than a saloon on Carnival Tuesday — "

The point of the herd moved past them as they met in a clump of mountain mahogany beside the trail.

"How is the hand, son?"

"Good. Nearly well."

"I am glad. This is Señor Martín. From over the sierra — My son Andrés Santos, Señor Martín."

They shook hands leaning out from their saddles.

"Listen, Father," Andrés said. "Some news last night. I thought I — "

"Wait a minute — " his father jerked around to shout at the foreman Calixto — "*Capataz!* Ride the point! Keep them moving! Andrés is here! Wants to talk!"

Calixto waved acknowledgment and spurred, knocking stones as his horse jumped, down the slope.

"Now. What news?" Santiago Santos asked.

"Hey, Brother!" Agustín Santos sang out. His horse came bounding toward them from the flank of the herd.

Andrés waved with his bandaged hand, and turned to his father. "They say we have Apaches."

"Who says?" Santiago Santos frowned. "Apaches where?"

"Last night a rider came in, to Bavinuchi. He says the Apaches have come over the sierra. They had them in Techapic four — five — days past. Seventeen of the people killed. This man was from Techapic. I don't doubt him. His teeth were still rattling."

"Thunder of Jesus, Techapic is too close! Which way were they headed?"

"The man said north — they left going north — "

"*Vah*, coming over the sierras here and going north — they don't do it! They don't come in here!"

"They did this time! There is word why. Some damned Chihuahueño general whipped them and ran them over the sierra."

"I doubt that."

"It is what they say. You haven't seen any sign, up there?"

"No sign of a sign — " Santiago Santos turned to Martin. "Did you see anything, farther up? Heh?"

"Nothing. The man of Bacanora kept saying the Apaches did not come in here."

"Not for twenty years! Nearly twenty years. The last time they came we gave them something to remember. It was at a narrow place called La Trampa below the Mesa del Tabaco. We had Yaquis help us and we made an ambush and we killed sixty, sixty brutes of damned Apaches and they never came back. God, I am sorry to see them back! The last times they came you boys were still at your mother's skirts — "

The drags and the camp pack mules had gone by. The noise of the herd came from the canyon narrowing below.

"We get those cattle down — We set lookouts around Bavinuchi — "

"I have already set them," Andrés said.

"Good. One of the vaqueros must ride back to the rancho and warn our people up there — "

"I will," Martin said.

"That is for me," Agustín said.

"The devil," Andrés said, "I am — "

"Shut up!" his father said. "None of you! You are staying with the herd." He spurred and they followed him down the hill.

When they caught up with the drags, Santiago Santos shouted.
"Domatilio!"

Domatilio wheeled his pony and tipped his hat.

"Listen, Champion," said the *patrón*. "How is that knife on
your arm?"

"In good health, Don Santiago."

"Listen to me, Champion. I have something for you to do. You
ride back to the rancho. Tell my people up there that I have
received report of Apaches on our side of the sierra — at Techapic! Tell them I do not think there is much danger now. Tell
them the Apaches must have already moved north, toward their
own range. But you tell my people up there to watch! To live
prepared. To keep the horses up. To send word if there is anything we should know! You come back to Bavinuchi tonight and
report to me. Your *onza* will be waiting. *Ándale!*"

Domatilio tipped his hat again, and started fast, up the swath
of muddy tracks. "I will tell them — "

"See that you do!"

They rode in the drags, with the herd moving down the canyon ahead.

"How is your shooting eye, Martín?" Agustín grinned. "For
Apaches."

"Bad without doubt."

Santiago Santos turned in his saddle. "Who is that *cabrón* of
a general in Chihuahua? Who could drive Apaches into our lap?
Martín — do you know if there is any such type?"

"I think so, Don Santiago. Named Marcos Castro. He has
fought Apaches before. He has his own picked troops. He is
brother of the governor over there."

"Castro. And you know him. I would not believe they could
produce any such thing in Chihuahua. If they have — God damn
them! Putting Apaches on us! Castro. May rats piss the milk of
Castro."

"Well, señor — " Martín half smiled, "I have those sentiments."

"Hah! I knew that."

As they rode following the herd into the deepening notch of
the canyon, an eagle came sailing above the bluff.

"Paso del Águila," Santiago Santos remarked. "Well named."

The eagle turned gliding down on its great quiet wings, over the treetops, to tilt in a slow airy climb again against the blue, and hover, and glide again circling.

"In Chihuahua — " Santiago Santos' eyes cut around from the eagle to Martin — "they shoot well?" He asked it fast, challenging.

"Shooting is noisy."

"The devil himself has already heard us!"

The three grinning Santos jerked their pistols, with their heads thrown back watching the sky. The eagle came curving again.

Before the Santos had aimed, Martin drew and fired. He knew when he touched the trigger: it was that fast snap shot a marksman makes a few times in his life when the ball seems guided beyond fallible act of eye or hand, with the target in the mind and the hit known queerly, foreseen before the flash. In the cracking bang feathers popped loose high in the air, and the Santos horses jumped. Lágrimas stood steady, trained — the Santos noticed it. The eagle hit the ground twenty paces up the trail.

"Angels of Christ — "

A vaquero came thrashing from the drags. He was craning his neck, inquiring.

"Nothing!" the *patrón* shouted at him, waving him back to the herd. "Foolishness!"

Awkward with his bandaged hand, Andrés cut a wing from the eagle and tied it on his saddle. Agustín pulled big tail feathers and stuck them in his hatband.

"For the kids at the house," Andrés explained. The stretched curve of the eagle's wing was a feathered perfection.

"This Pass of the Eagle — " Agustín said. "*Paf!*"

Martin felt good. "This pass of the pure accident — " He had to laugh. "No more eagles, señores! Never!"

Santiago Santos guffawed. "That was the eagle of the history — " he looked in Martin's face — "with documents. Passport from Chihuahua, eh? *Vaya*, it was the passport from that damned Texas — and enough petards, sons!" He spurred again. "Welcome to Sonora, Martín! There are Santos cattle going to Bavinuchi — "

In the smell of pine and cedar, in the light of late afternoon, in the haze of late October, Martin looked down and saw summer, suddenly. He was not prepared for the depth of the Barranca de

Bavinuchi, for the steep fall of shade on the bluffs that walled it, for the sparkling river that watered it, for the loamy banks that nourished it, for the fields, gardens, orchards, groves, and houses that adorned it. Martin looked across the ravine, at the darkly timbered continuing wilderness of sierra, blue beyond blue, ridge beyond ridge, paling to the lost edge of the world; and he looked down again into the depth before him, upon the miniature, ordered cluster of white walls and bright greens and rich browns, upon Bavinuchi nestled along its clear water, certain of its haven in the shelter of the riven stone.

Martin felt Santiago Santos' eyes, and he turned toward them.

"What a country!" Martin said.

"You like it?"

The heads of the grama grass were little golden sickles in the sun as the horsemen rode toward shadow, where the herd raised dust now on a dry slope, down where the trees thinned to runt tascal, and farther down, where the earth stood bare by prickly brush and sacatón. Tall branching pipes of patahaya and tangled plates of thorny nopal grew from the broken canyon rock along the slanting zigzagged trail.

Downstream from the walls of Bavinuchi, the trail led them at last into the rank foliage on the canyon floor. It brought them down a narrow lane between cornfields, to the road along the river. The herd broke, bawling, through the willows to the water's edge, and drank, wading, roiling the clearness of the stream.

When Santiago Santos had issued orders for holding the stock during the night — with guards in a rock-fenced hayfield under the bluffs across the water — he motioned to his sons and to Martin, and they left the herd. As they paced up the river road, a muffled fall of tumbling water made a soft sound in the warm sundown quietness. The sound grew louder; Santiago Santos turned in his saddle and called to Martin.

"How do you like our mill?" He pointed. He had to raise his voice in the noise of the pouring splash as they rode by. "My brother Domingo built it!" The pale foam spilled from the high turning wheel.

The mill stream ran through a grove of dark-leaved trees.

"Oranges?" Martin asked.

Agustín reined. He reached over and pulled at a branch. "Here," he said to Martin. "Try one."

Martin held an orange in his hand. He smelled it. He smiled. "I never have seen an orange growing. I never have eaten an orange since I was a boy."

The spicy redolence of the little globe in his hand was as strange as the summer dusk in the canyon. He thought he had never tasted anything so good as the sweet running juice in this orange of Bavinuchi.

"We had oranges at Christmas," Martin said.

The Santos all laughed at Martin with his orange.

The timbered world of the autumn sierra above the darkening bluffs seemed to Martin a thousand leagues away.

The house of Santiago Santos was a rambling thick fortress in the trees; its whitewashed walls were pale in the last daylight. Beyond the house, in a corral of high stone, the horsemen unsaddled. The curved fronds of a date palm stood dim above the wall. When the saddles were racked and the horses stabled, Martin walked with the Santos toward the glow of candle lanterns, in the sound of shouted greetings and barking dogs. The tang of green chili pods roasting, and cedar smoke, hung rich in the dark balmy air.

The family of Santos were gathered to greet the leather-clad head of the clan, to eat and drink with him, upon his return from the sierra, from the reported terrain of raiding Apaches. Agustín Santos politely led Martin into a great confusion of introduction, with nods and short handshakes, to sisters, uncles, aunts, cousins, to married relations, to nieces and nephews and infants and children playing with eagle feathers and ancients in chairs. When the gauntlet of names had thoroughly confused him, Martin stood aside, smiling in the warmth, the cordiality, the noise. He looked around the long candlelit room.

It was floored with hewn timbers smoothly joined, spread with bright Indian blankets and tanned skins of bear and mountain lion. Yellow and black upon one of the thick whitewashed walls was a great jaguar hide. Fastened to the opposite wall was a weatherstained silk banner embroidered with the eagle and serpent of Mexico and the words COMPAÑÍA MILITAR DE BAVINUCHI —

EQUIDAD EN LA JUSTICIA, and beyond it, hung on pegs, a country arsenal of muskets, rifles, pistols, swords, knives, and their accoutrements. In a niche at the far end of the room, beneath a carved ceiling beam, two candles were lit before a gilded wooden image of the Virgin of Guadalupe.

"Enough Santos, eh Martín?" Agustín smiled. He had his arm around his young wife. She was pregnant and laughing. Andrés held a black-haired baby, chucking its chin with his bandaged hand. Santiago Santos, his voice louder than ever, disclaimed to his heavy-set brother Domingo, and the frowning thin rider from Techapic, any sign of Indians in the sierra.

Martin saw musicians coming in the door. One carried a homemade harp, and there was a guitar, and a fiddle. There was a drum made from a bladder skin stretched on a big wooden bowl.

Santiago Santos' daughter Elena — and Martin remembered her name clearly — came passing a tray of little mescal cups to the men of the family. Martin took a cup, and she smiled at him. Her teeth were very white, her eyes were very black, her waist was very slender.

"Will you dance to the music tonight, Señor Martín?" she asked him.

"I wish I could," Martin said.

"Why can't you?"

"Martín!" Santiago Santos bellowed in his big voice. "Come here! I was saying something to my señora."

Martin saw the robust woman in neat black standing at Santiago Santos' side. She had a high comb in her hair. She had just come into the room.

"This is our guest from the sierras," Santiago Santos said to his wife. "He kills eagles blindfolded at three thousand varas. I think we need him with us while our boys and vaqueros are at Hermosillo. In case of Apaches. Martín, this my señora, Doña Adela."

"I am at your feet, señora," Martin said, bowing his head to the matriarch of the Santos.

"Welcome to your house," she said smiling.

"Listen, Martín," Santiago Santos said, with the candlelight shining on his brown bald head. "That is *mescal de pechuga* you are drinking. Tell me, do you like Bavinuchi?"

CHAPTER XXI

DON MARTÍN
de Bavinuchi, Martin thought, lying in the soft bed, with the
first light touching his room.

Don Martín was a gringo, they say, but he never went back.
He liked Bavinuchi better. Old Don Martín, he is one of us. He
is of the Santos family. They have fame as good people. Old
Don Martín, with his children, his grandchildren. He married one
of the Santos. Doña Elena, she was a beauty in those days. She
was the prettiest of all the Santos girls, and Don Martín, he made
the best *ranchero* of all the Santos sons. He worked harder. Don
Martín was the one that found the mine, the Lost Mine of the
Holy Name, that made the Santos so rich. The old Don Santiago

Santos possessed a chart made by the Society of Jesus a hundred years before his time — you know the story — when the Jesuits were driven from Sonora. The chart was in the Santos family papers. Santiago Santos showed it to Don Martín when he was a young man, when he first came to Bavinuchi, he trusted him that much, and Don Martín, he finally found the mine in the sierra. That was when he built the big house for his Doña Elena.

Martin looked up at the dim beams of the ceiling, in the daybreak silence.

That was when, he thought, when Don Martín better get up and go soak his head in cold water. Now.

The black *chanate* birds were gathered, fluting their jangled morning songs under the pomegranates and figs as Martin walked from the house. A sunrise breeze rustled in the date palm by the high corral wall; first rays touched coppery on the top of the western bluff high above the shadow along the quiet river. Bavinuchi awoke in the growing light. The first cook smoke rose fragrant from its chimneys.

Martin lifted the rawhide thong that held the gate where Lágrimas was penned. The black horse's head went high, and he blew, showing the white of his eye, as Martin came toward him.

"Don Martín and his fat horse," Martin said. "You like your new shoes?" He looked down at the four black hooves he had shod the day before. Whistling softly between his front teeth, he patted the slick hide. He lifted the left forefoot and looked again at the healed marks by the frog on the sole rimmed with square-edged new iron.

Remember how that looked at Pacoromachic? And now look! The two tubbies of Bavinuchi, letting your cinch out, letting out notches on my belt. Where shall we go on the new shoes, tubby? You think we might hunt again for *tigre* and bring home another big spotted hide for you to snort at? Shall we kill another bear? Or will we go again to Techapic looking for Apaches that aren't there, or to Sahuaripa with Don Santiago to buy more sheep? Or will we just lay around Bavinuchi forever and court the girls with serenades and eat our heads off and call each other Don —

He heard a sound at his back, and turned.

The old harelipped herder Torquato, who tended the milk

cows, grinned at him over the gate bars. He held up something in his hand. "Get one! Come on!"

"Get what?"

"Get a spoon."

"What for?"

"Listen, man. Don't stand asking, with the mouth wide, like church doors on Day of Corpus! Follow me! For something exquisite." Torquato kissed his spoon.

Carrying a spoon he got from the cook in the kitchen, Martin went with the old man, to humor him.

"The breakfast of the saints," Torquato said. "In heaven." He ran his tongue along the edge of the harelip.

Potbellied Domingo Santos stood waiting by the cowshed. He had on his iron-rimmed spectacles and he was smiling.

"Ha, Martín! Torquato cooked it for me in the night. It makes us think of when we were young!"

On the lid of a feed bin Martin saw two halves of a ripe pumpkin. It had been split open and roasted. A sugary brown crusted at its golden edges. It still smoked faintly.

Torquato put down his spoon, and picked up a half of the pumpkin, holding it underneath with one hand, a pad of sacking in his palm to glove it from the heat. He went to a cow in a stall, and he milked. He filled the golden cavity of the roast pumpkin with foamy white spurts rich from the udder.

"*Calabaza á la Bavinuchi —*" Domingo Santos chuckled at it when it stood propped on the feed bin lid. He dipped in his spoon. "Ah!"

"Ah!" said Torquato, wielding his own spoon.

"I learn something every day," Martin grinned. "All good!" He spooned at the sweet pumpkin meat in the hot creamy float.

A rooster crowed morning in the corral.

As they stood eating, they heard the jingle of spurs; Santiago Santos came striding around the corner of the shed. He stopped, shoved his hat to the back of his head, and burst out laughing. "I get invited to this crime?"

"We were going to send you half, Chief!"

"Criminals! You were not going to send me a damn thing! Lend me a spoon. Hah! Martín, you know pumpkins in Bavinuchi are not so bad as pumpkins in proverbs? But they taste better in a corral! Torquato — fill the other — "

A vaquero jerked through the corral gate. He left it open. "*Patrón!* PATRÓN!" His eyes were round. He ran. He did not tip his hat.

"Ho!" Santiago Santos gruffed, frowning.

"Indians! The Apaches — "

"What?"

"The rancho — Rancho del Tabaco — up there — "

"Calm yourself. Then speak."

"*Patrón* — " the vaquero swallowed, breathing hard. "At the first light, when I was at the lookout, the one in the rocks toward Paso del Águila, I heard it. Then I saw. It was, I thought it was Indians, it was the boy of García from the rancho. His horse foundered, that black-nosed gray. He could not speak, the boy. He fell in a fit. When he saw me. Then he told me. The rancho. Burning. Killing the people screaming! His family, his mother, God guard us! He — "

Santiago Santos turned to his brother. "Ring the bell, Domingo. Man, woman, child, to the big house! You are in command there. Get them together! I will order the armed party — " He turned to Torquato who was pale in his leathery face. "Saddle my horse. Then come to me."

Martin started away, to saddle Lágrimas.

"Come back here," the *patrón* snapped. "You stay with me until I tell you!" He turned to the vaquero. "Where is the boy from the rancho?"

"I left him, with the other man in the lookout. The man Pancho Silva. The boy is in a convulsion of fear. If the Apaches are sighted from the lookout, Pancho Silva will fire the gun of alarm. I rode down only to tell you."

The bell at the big house began to clang.

"You did well," Santiago Santos said to the vaquero. "You are mounted. Go find the horse herders. Give the word that every horse and mule comes to this corral! Now! With the devil riding your buttocks. Then report to me."

The clapper of the bell pounded fast, racking the air with a steady clamor.

The amber lights in Santiago Santos' tawny eyes were very sharp when they turned at Martin. "If that scared boy tells truth, Jesús María, that poor crowd at the rancho! But we can't go. Wasting our force up there. Not until the threat to Bavinuchi itself — is past.

"Listen, Martín. There are two ways the Indians can get into this Barranca from the Tabaco side. They can come by the trail from Paso del Águila. Or they can sneak down the rough wash two miles downstream. We could ambush them at either place, and angels of the sweet Christ, I wish my boys Andrés and Agustín and that Calixto and his gang were back from Hermosillo! Without them we haven't got enough to cover the approaches and still have good men to defend the big house if the Indians break through. But maybe we have enough. If we are organized —

"Go saddle your horse. Ride to the El Águila lookout. You and Pancho Silva hide yourselves high and watch the trail. As soon as I can, I will send you a few armed men. You know how vaqueros are when they are armed: watch them. You are in command. You keep them up there, and you stay! Until you are relieved. Keep your party hidden high in the rocks, over the trail. If the Apaches come, make your people hold their fire until the Apaches are under you — and then lift the lid of their brains! If they do not break under your fusillade, fight them any way you can, sell yourselves dear — keep the brutes from this valley, Martín! A lookout on top the house will be watching, in case you fail. Domingo will be ready with what he can muster behind these walls. I will command a party over the dry wash downstream, and I will try to keep contact with you and with the house, for what develops. Send that boy from the rancho to me as soon as he can come. I want to find out what he really knows and what he imagines. You understand everything? Good! I know you understand my trust. Hurry! — I am going to quiet the women and arm the men — " He started through the gate. "Take every cartridge you have!" he bellowed, over his shoulder, with the bell clanging. "See that you kill Apaches — like you kill eagles — "

There were no Apaches to kill.

There was nothing but the quietness with the horses tied in the scrub oak behind the ledge, with the seven men hidden in the rocks, with the guns and the loads ready. Martin stationed his vaqueros with care, in two groups for crossfire on the trail close below, and the men took their places, and waited for his signal, and watched. They watched at first with an excitement, an impatience.

In the long hours the impatience changed to boredom, and then to doubt. The sun moved up, stood high, and moved down changing the shapes of the shadows on the broken slope. The watchers tired their eyes, running them a thousand times, and then again, along the climbing sweep of the hillside and the drop into the canyon of Bavinuchi. Nothing moved. They listened, alert for firing in the distance, for nearer click or clatter, for voice or sign or clue. No sound came beyond the faint stir of wind along the rocks, the far call of a bird crying in the rise and fall of the stillness. There were no Apaches. The sun quickened over the bluffs westward. It plunged down reddening the sky, dimming the slope, the rocks, the ragged brush, the familiar twist of the trail, into twilight.

Now they will come, Martin thought. They come at crack of day or sundown when the light is bad and the shooting is hard and they come jumping. Now is the time for Apaches.

A chittering flock of parakeets whirred suddenly up the hillside, shaking the half-lit silence. In the still-lighted sky above, a flight of *guacamaya* parrots made a wavering long file, two and two, mate and mate, then a single, then more mates, two and two, dark specks moving across the emptiness. There were no Apaches.

In the early starlight vaqueros spoke low-voiced.

"Those *guacamayas* from down by the ocean, flying up to the sierra, going that far to eat pine nuts! Mother of God, it appears reasonable to me. Me with nothing to eat since the supper my old lady made me last night, in former times!"

"The Apaches heard my bowel. It frightened them. That's why they didn't come. They heard my bowel crying for a *gorda*."

"Listen, *gorda*. If you had Apaches today, you would not have hunger."

"Having neither Apaches nor chilis, I remain with hunger, with hunger, man!"

"You think we will shoot these guns?"

"With all the bellywind blowing, it is not necessary — "

"*Ssss*, listen!"

From down the slope, hooves rattled in the stones. Martin stood up, trying to see. Close by, in the silence, a vaquero cocked a gun. Martin jerked around. "Uncock that! Use your head, son, the sound comes from downtrail — use your head!"

The sound climbed toward them.

"*Hei!*" It echoed in the rocks.

"Who is it?"

"Santos! And don't thou shoot!" There was a pause. "*Hei*, Martín!"

Martin moved down the rocks. He saw the shapes of the two horsemen in the trail.

Santiago Santos put his gun away and leaned down from the saddle to shake Martin's hand. "How does it go?"

"Quiet. Too quiet."

"The same with us. Here is Domatilio. Carrying food. The women fixed it. You hungry?"

"We could eat."

The two men dismounted. In the quiet Martin heard their horses breathing from the climb. Domatilio carried a rawhide *alforja* bulging from the pommel, and a water jug slung in straps.

"*Qué tal*, Champion," Martin whispered. "Take it to the men up there. They're gnawing sandals."

"And you?"

"After I talk to the *patrón*."

Domatilio climbed the rocks with the food and water. Santiago Santos spit, and squatted on his hunkers, by the horses. Martin squatted beside him.

"What you think, Martín?"

"I think I ought to ride to the rancho. And find out. Tonight."

"I have thought the same. But not you: Domatilio and I are prepared to go."

"And I with you."

"What about this post of men?"

"Pancho Silva can handle it. Your own post, down there — you are leaving it, señor?"

"Teresa's husband Antonio has it. He is capable."

"So is Pancho Silva."

"Um. That boy from El Tabaco — " Santiago Santos' voice did not lower easily into a whisper — "when he came riding in from pasture up there he says he saw something burning, he heard shots, he says he heard screaming, and he says he saw an Indian horseback. That is all we know. It is not enough. I am going up there to find out what we face. It may be nothing. It may be the Apache nation."

"Let me go, señor. If you prefer, let Domatilio go with me, but — I hope you will stay down here to command the defense."

"Listen, *niño*. My people know what to do! And I don't send riders at night and stay home myself."

"In that case, *patrón*, take two riders with you."

"Go eat something. Send Pancho Silva to me. I will talk to him."

Sitting in the rocks, Martin filled his belly with cold meat and tortillas. He ate three oranges and drank water and walked down into the scrub oak with his carbine and the cartridge bag. He loaded them on the saddle and untied Lágrimas and led him to the trail.

"When we return you will know it," Santiago Santos said to Pancho Silva. "At the top of that ridge up there we will fire three shots, pafpafpaf. Listen for it. Don't be shooting at us when we come down that hill! You understand everything?"

"Very well, *patrón*."

"I leave it in your hand." Santiago Santos mounted his horse. "Domatilio, you lead with your cat eyes in the dark. Martín, follow me. We stay bunched, close."

They moved out into the dark.

As the three men rode, a taut peering watchfulness and acute care for sound seemed slowly to merge their minds, so that they lost separate thought and were like one, not three, climbing together with single intent through the shape of darkness, the sound of silence, into the sierra.

They worked up the slopes into the trees, into the night chill of the mountain, easing their way along rough sidehill breaks away from the narrows of the trail. They stopped often to breathe their horses, and choose a way. Then they moved, breaking the quiet with the click and scuff of hooves, the squeak of leathers, the tink of bit rings and spur rowels, the huff of the breaths under the cinch straps. Martin rode seeing the dim shape of Santiago Santos' straight back; farther ahead the pale stocking on the right hind leg of Domatilio's horse moved like a small ghost along the ground.

The minutes stretched laboring to wordless hours. The horsemen scaled the black rising twists and folds of stone and foliage through the notch of Paso del Águila, feeling a way for the hooves through the threat of shapes unseen.

In the hour beyond midnight when the Dog Star stood highest, when the horsemen rode with jaws clamped to keep the chatter from their teeth, when their eyes ached stinging in the dark and their bodies rocked stiff from the cold in the saddle, a November moon rose wasted and sickly between black clouds. The yellow moonfire brought an edge to the night shapes, cutting wan patches along blurred deeps of shadow, paling a wisp of mist low in a ravine. Wind came sighing in the timber, rousing at the stillness, giving it voice, blowing cloud across the moon. Cloud thickened above the trees. A harsh invisible rain came striking in the wind as the riders worked their way, with the last ridge at their backs, down a slope into the black cup that held whatever they might find at Rancho del Tabaco.

They could not see what they would find. Sitting their wet seats, they peered down the slant where Santiago Santos pointed, with the drops splashing on his hand. He touched rein then and turned, and pointed to a clump of pines. They rode into it, and got down from the horses under the boughs in the dark wet, and stood stiff and numb-footed on the slippery needles, and cold, with the reins in their hands, and their hatbrims almost touching.

"This rain is good cover," Santiago Santos whispered. "You think they are down there?"

"If they are gone, so are their tracks," Domatilio said. "Two hours of night yet."

"From here, how far to the house and corral?" Martin asked.

"A thousand varas, more or less."

"If you wish to go nearer and will stand ready with the horses, I will move in afoot and look around and come back and tell you."

"A risk. And you don't know the ground."

"I know enough. I will strike that horse-trap fence from this side and work in from there. For a look."

They rode to the bottom of the hill. As they came into the black shadow of trees thick along the stream bed, a moan wailed long-drawn through the rattle of the rain. The horsemen stopped. From close by, a hoarse chorus joined with the moan in a wavering throaty yammer. It died abruptly. The horses stood trembling.

Santiago Santos leaned toward Domatilio.

"Authentic?"

"To my ear, yes!"

They rode across the shallow stream a step at a time with the rain seething on the water. They got down from their horses under the dim tangled spread of a great oak.

"How far to that fence now?" Martin whispered.

"Two hundred varas. That direction." Santiago Santos pointed his dripping arm. "That direction exactly."

Martin hitched his belt around so that the pistol rode up on his right buttock, so he could crawl. "All right. It may need an hour. Watch for me. You will hear me whistle when I come close. Don't shoot. And if I don't come back — don't let Apaches get my horse."

"If those were wolves we heard, you will find no Apaches. Nor Christians alive."

Martin walked alone up the stream bank to the open edge of the meadow in the rain.

Clear of the trees he stopped and turned to study the shape of the great oak. Then he memorized the dim line of the humped ridge beyond the black cup, and when he was sure, he bent and started into the high, drop-laden dark grass. He counted his paces, straight on the bearing, crouching down, stopping, moving again with his eyes reaching, aching for the form of the formlessness around him. When he had counted off the paces, the fence was not there. He moved on straight, in doubt. The grass shortened, and thinned, and gave out. He flattened to the mud with the rain tapping on his hat. Lying still, he made himself close his eyes. He counted thirty, and opened his eyes, seeing better, and he moved in the mud. The fence was there.

More than three hundred, not two hundred damn him, Martin

thought, but here it is fine fence along the weeds good weeds fine weeds. Plenty of time. Lower. Stay lower. Goddamn to these burrs. There. There it is. The Apaches came they really came they left the gate open. There is nothing in that corral. Nothing. If you can get in the cover of the trees there at the edge. Flat down this time. Flatter yet God it is a cold slime. It is better than a bullet. Not much better. You couldn't hit a barn shaking this way. Don't shake. Quit it. Those people are dead. Or gone. Dead or gone. Dead and gone. You have to quit shaking. Now. Up to that tree that fine tree if you can mash your nose against — they did burn that shed you slept in. They burned it. They burned that house LOOK *low by that wall*. Listen to them. Gobbling. Gobbling what. Do something. Do what. Nor Christians alive he said. Poor Christians. Do something. All right. Go tell Santos his people are dead and the Apaches are gone and the wolves are here. Go tell him.

At the corral he stood up and walked. He walked along the fence to where he thought he should turn, and he walked out through the grass with the rain tapping harder on his hat. He shook and he heard mixing with the rain the sound of the gobble snuffling snapping, the imagined sound, he told himself. Imagined. He knew the great oak. Walking through the icy grass he looked into the blackness under the tree. He whistled. He whistled twice.

"No Apaches," Santiago Santos rasped at him. It was a statement, not a question.

Martin's teeth chattered. "They came."

"You got to the house?"

"Close enough. The house is burned, and that shed. The corral is empty."

"No people."

"The wolves are in front of the house."

Santiago Santos and the vaquero Domatilio brought their hands from their blankets and crossed themselves.

"I did nothing about it."

"What could you do? We wait until day."

Martin walked to Lágrimas. He was glad to see Lágrimas. The blanket at the cantle was soggy wet, but he untied it and wrapped it around himself, wiping mud from his numb hands. He leaned against the tree and waited for warmth.

"The boy didn't make up anything. The orphan."

"There is some remedy for this hour," Santiago Santos said. He went to his saddlebags and came back with a bottle. He uncorked it and handed it to Martin. "*Mescal de pechuga.* Then we will make cigarettes, and wait."

Martin felt the fire spread through him. It made his eyes water.

"I am grateful," he said.

"Have another."

Martin had another. He and Domatilio spread their blankets over Santiago Santos as he squatted making three smokes, lighting them with his flint and steel, and the three men huddled near the horses by the great tree, cupping little fires in their hands, drawing the smoke in their lungs, feeling the warmth of their liquor, waiting in the rain for the night to end.

The first gray came above the humped ridge. Through low murk the gray came late and it came slow. But it came. It touched at the black cup, building wraiths of coming form half tangled yet with unformed dark. Then the black cup filled with gray. It fashioned edges upon the wraiths and they stood in leaden pallor freed of night.

Born into day, the three men looked at the gray rain, and they looked at each other, at the gray faces under the sagging hatbrims, at the gray light on the dripping blankets they held to their chins. They looked at the three horses standing humped with the wet cold, half asleep in the dim brush under the black branches of the oak.

Santiago Santos' voice came hoarse. "We can see plenty."

"And they can see plenty." The vaquero Domatilio's eyes were black slits in his wet face. "*Cabrones*, I put no trust in the *cabrones*, but I am ready."

"You, Martín? Ready?"

"When you say."

"We ride with guns in our hands. If we get a welcome, we break for the trail straight to Paso del Águila, and we stay together — understand? Angels of Christ, I am cold. And stiff. And old."

Fumbling with numb fingers, they tied their blankets to the saddles, and they mounted, jerking with cold. Martin drew his pistol and with the soggy wad of handkerchief he pulled from his pocket, he wiped around the hammer, and checked the action. The three men rode up the stream bank, with the rain tapping, with the hooves sounding in the soaking high grass.

They came to the corral. They looked at its gray emptiness, its open gate. Past the tumbled hayrick and the feed pen with its sagging lean-to, they rode around the trees, watching, feeling the rain in their hands on the gun handles. They saw the black hump of rubble where the shed had been. They came past a scorched tree. Beyond it stood the roofless walls in the rain, the window holes with the gray showing through, the gaping ruin of the door.

The horses snorted in sudden veering panic. Reining, spurring in an arc wide of the ruin, the riders moved with their guns gripped, their eyes darting at the threat of the gray walls, the gray cover of the trees. But their eyes saw most the gray ground with the stained lumps, the draggled rags, the noisome black-blooded scatter torn from cream-pale bones in the mud. Then around the corner of the charnel house they saw the two naked bodies gray on the rusted meat hooks by the gray wall, the whole bodies, hung head down on the tearing hooks, above the reach of wolves' teeth, in the rain. The bodies of two children.

Santiago Santos wrenched his horse around. He stopped dead still, staring into the grayness. "Infamy!" he shouted at it. "Brutes! Come out! Fight me! *Fight me!*" The bawling anguish rolled out into the unechoing quiet. The rain tapped on the riders' hats.

Martin saw it was not rain on Santiago Santos' face. The water came from the red-rimmed, honey-colored eyes. They looked straight at Martin. They moved on, and leveled at the vaquero Domatilio.

"The *cabrones* have gone," Domatilio said, not knowing what else to say.

Martin ran his tongue over his dry front teeth, and turned Lágrimas with the hooves splashing in the mud. "You noticed?" he said. "When we rode by?"

"Notice what? Jesus Christ, those poor people!"

Martin got down stiff from the saddle. He handed the *ramal* to Domatilio, and walked toward the gray walls, clamping his jaws, hating to breathe. He picked up a muddy rifle from the ground. With the barrel he prodded at a wet, torn lump, feeling his gorge rise. When he had prodded enough, he reached down and took hold of the peak-toe on the moccasin, and pulled. A part of the knee-length rawhide legging came with it. He found another rifle, and picked it up. The horses shied when he came close with the things in his hand. He dropped them in the mud, and walked on, to another scatter near a tree. He came back to the horses with another rifle. He threw it on the ground by the others, and looked up at Domatilio.

"The scalps are over there yet. If that knife on your arm itches — "

The vaquero's teeth showed like gray fangs in the curly black whiskers.

Martin turned to Santiago Santos. "What guns did your people have?"

"They had a French musket. A thing from the time of Maximilian."

Martin got on his horse. "It was a lot of musket."

Santiago Santos shook his head, frowning, grinding his teeth. "We see what else they had."

The three horsemen rode wide around the ruin, cutting for sign, finding no sign readable in the rain-whipped mud. Then under the trees fifty yards from the walls they found a dead Apache pinned under a dead horse. They found two more dead Apaches, and a dead pony with rawhide shoes. The bodies were all on the south side of the walls.

"The Apaches left their dead," Martin said. "They left their dead on the field — Apaches don't do that. They left going south, and they left running — "

"Who chased them, *Jesús María*, your Chihuahueño again? My people didn't chase them. My people are up there at the walls."

"As for the Chihuahueño, he is not mine. Neither have we seen his Remington .44s in this mud. But: Apaches don't leave their dead."

"Neither do Christians," Santiago Santos growled. He looked toward the walls in the rain.

They tied their horses under an oak near the corral. Prodding in wet black rubble where the shed had been, they found two spades. The handles were charred away.

"Make handles," Santiago Santos said. "Some kind of damned handles, Martín. Domatilio and I will prepare what we can — over there — while you cut handles."

There was no wood. Martin went to Lágrimas and mounted, to ride searching. He rode up the slope and he thought of the peon Pablo and the hungry people digging the grave in the dark Arroyo Varas; he rode fast, wanting the wood for the handles, wanting the dead buried away from the jaws of the wolves, wanting the Rancho del Tabaco behind him, wanting the trail, wanting beyond the trail the canyon of Bavinuchi. He rode suddenly foreboding with the cold hand of the rain on his back, and he glanced around, down the hill.

He could see Santiago Santos by the ruined house. He could see Domatilio moving by the lean-to at the feed pen, prowling for shrouds. He could see south, over the rise where he had come for the first time — it seemed long ago — to Rancho del Tabaco.

Down from the saddle, he pulled the short *machete* from its sheath in the coil of the *cabrestante*, and he walked to a pine sapling to trim from it a spade handle. Drops like ice showered thick on him as he grasped it, bending over, and he hacked at the trunk. A shadow of mind, a sense beyond sense, stopped him. He looked south. Less than a hundred varas away, on the rim of the rise, he saw the horseman with the gun.

Gray in the rain, the quick image sliced at his mind. It came sharp. It was very clear in the grayness: he understood it. But he did not believe it. He swallowed the jump of his heart in his throat, he gripped the knife tight in his hand, and he stared. It was necessary to believe it, to believe the shape of the hat, the saddle, the packroll, the build of the wracked nag, the color of the shape of horseman who sat still in the saddle, watching him, holding the unslung carbine. The Union blue, the black Union blue.

Martin set his knife down. He brought both his empty hands up, above his head, and gripped them together, and shook them for the horseman to see. With both his empty hands clearly above his head, he stood waiting. The horseman came holding the gun on

him, slow. The hooves scraped approaching in the murmur of the
rain. Martin saw the black face under the black hat, he saw the
two black letters on the canteen at the black pommel, US.

The horseman reined, pointing the Springfield. "Soldados — "
he jerked his chin toward the rim of the rise — "fight Apache!"
The teeth showed snarling white, and the tongue showed red, in
the wet, black face. "Kill Apache! Savve? No speak espanyol,
humbre!"

"I speak English."

"Lord God Jesus!"

"Will you lower that .45–70?"

"You ain't Mex!"

"No."

"You wouldn't try to lay no trouble for soldiers, would you?"

"Can't you see my hands? I'm friend — will you lower that
gun?"

The Springfield lowered. Martin stooped and picked up the
machete. He walked to Lágrimas, slid the knife in its sheath, and
climbed into the saddle. The trooper's eyes were fastened on him.

"What you doing, this goddam country, white man?"

"I work here."

"*Hei!*" The shout came sharp, from the trees by the ruin.
"Martín! Who is it?"

The trooper jerked his gun around. "Who that? What he say?"

"My boss down there — trying to bury his dead — keep your
gun off!" Martin cupped his hands and called, "Friends! All well,
Don Santiago! All well!"

"Who is it?" Santiago Santos shouted again.

"Soldiers!"

No answer came.

Martin saw the shambling file appear at the rim of the rise. He
saw the slumped horsemen, the makeshift litter hitched between
the two mules, the men on foot, the pack animals, slow in the rain.
He heard a blurred command, and he saw the carbines unslung.

"Tell your officer, soldier," Martin said. "Three of us alive at
the rancho, all friendly!"

Facing the dark file along the rise, the trooper held up his arm.
The file was halted. The trooper turned to Martin. "Tell them

greasers down yonder to show theirselves. Show peaceable if they don't want no Springfield balls."

"Get this in your head: you are with friends."

"We ain't seen no friends in this goddam country, white man."

"Goddam you see them now! — *Don Santiago! Come out! Friends!*"

Nothing moved in the open spaces around the ruined house.

"I will go and tell them," Martin said.

"Git them in plain sight, white man! This gun barl is looking at you."

Martin touched rein and moved down the slope. He stopped in the open near the ruin, where the trooper could see him, and he motioned to Santiago Santos and Domatilio who stood watching with their guns under the scorched tree. He motioned again, until the two men walked out to him.

"They want to see us here in the open," Martin said. He got down from the saddle.

"What soldiers are they?"

"American soldiers."

"What? Here? What are they doing here?"

"Fighting Apaches."

"*What* are damned gringo soldiers doing in Sonora? My father in his time killed the son of a whore the filibuster gringo Crabb who came with gringo soldiers making trouble in Sonora! And by God I — "

"These make no trouble."

"No trouble! Raiding into Sonora!"

"This is no raiding — they come with permission of your government to fight Apaches! These men fight Apaches, they come only to fight the common enemy, they kill the enemy and now after a killing they come here with their wounded and you — and they — "

Santiago Santos slapped the butt of his pistol, and spit in the mud.

"*Chingaos*," Domatilio said, "I put no trust in the *chingaos*."

"All right," Martin said with anger surging suddenly hot and white in his head, "fight them! You have guns! Go ahead! Fight them!"

"*Vaya, Martín!*" Santiago Santos' voice grated deep in his throat. "*Vaya!* We won't fight them! We won't trust them but we won't fight them." He had reached back with the flat of his hand to touch and to check the knife sheathed on Domatilio's ready arm.

Martin looked straight into the red-rimmed, honey-colored eyes. "You trust me?"

The eyes did not waver. "You know I trust you. Since the day you came."

They stood together in the silence with the rain tapping on their hats when the horseman came riding through the trees.

"Eh Martín! Black like that?"

"Black gringo! Eeho!"

"We have black ones," Martin said.

The horseman was powerfully built. Twenty paces away he reined and dismounted. He walked to them leading his jaded, rain-plastered horse.

"Picket up there say you talk American. Which one?"

"I'm American," Martin said.

"Well! Major wants to see you. He is up there, in them thick trees. This all of you? Just three?"

"Just three." Martin pointed toward the gray walls.

"We done seen it," the trooper said.

"Did they give you a fight?"

"We jumped the goddam *siquisns* while they had this place afire."

"This man is the owner," Martin said. "He would like to know about it."

"We come too late to help the people. They was dead."

"We counted six dead Apaches — "

"You can go about five miles south and count twenty-three more of the dead sons of bitches!"

Martin jerked his head around toward Santiago Santos. "*Todo muy bien, Don Santiago!*" He turned again to the trooper. "Which Apaches were they? You know?"

"Magues' band. Magues is subchief of old Fuego. I know that devil Magues, from duty at Warm Springs! This time he was leading all fighting bucks, no squaws nor camp doings."

"Did you git Magues?"

"No, goddammit. We killed all but him and two or three others that made the break when we flanked them. He got away. But he ain't looking for trouble about now. He had his trouble."

"Don Santiago," Martin said, "the threat to Bavinuchi is past! It was the band of Magues. All but three or four are dead."

"You believe it?"

"Yes I believe it! *Why?*"

"Good! I thank God for it."

Martin turned to the trooper. "How did you catch them?"

"They caught us! When the sun raised yestiddy morning our goddam Teewer Indian scouts was acting queer and boged off, skeered. The Apaches shot down into us sudden — the first volley give us hell in a black basket! Then we rallied. Both sides firing from cover. My Lieutenant Scanlon, he finely led eight of us crawling clean up high around the hill. Took till almost noon. Crawling. We smoked them out! Them we didn't hit, had to move, and they moved jumping for their horses, and the main body cut them when they jumped. We put the blue fire in them dirty docks! Finely. That major like a crazy man leading us forty-four thousand miles. We finely done it, my L Troop done it, and where are we? My Lieutenant Scanlon, dead. Contract surgeon, dead. Packer Boggs and his two men, dead. Nine of my good niggers, dead! All buried mighty shallah. In this goddam country. The four Teewer scouts, all dead, what knew the trails or said they did — I think my own niggers killed them for boging. Nobody now to tell you where you is and is you going the right way. Nobody now to speak the Spic so's you can trust it. Short of mounts, and what we still got, unfit for the duty! My three wounded niggers. And the major in a litter, shot in the side, still like a crazy man. I druther be in hell with my back broke than gitting my L Troop outn this, back to God's natural country! How far are we from the You Ess?"

"A long way. You the sergeant?"

"Tobe Sutton, first sergeant, L Troop, Second Battalion, Tenth Cavalry, Fort Jefflin, Texas."

"And Major Colton is in that litter."

"How you know that?"

"I was in Puerto. Maybe the major will remember me."

"My Christ, let's go see! What is your name, suh?"

"Brady. Before we go, let me tell Señor Santos here."

"Tell him. Bring him and the cowboy along."

"Don Santiago. This is the sergeant. There was a bad battle, about five miles south, yesterday in the morning. The Apaches are destroyed, but the troop is hurt. It moves now for the United States — with only one officer alive. He happens to be a Chief of Battalion and commander of the fort at Puerto, Texas, and I know him! He is wounded and they carry him in a litter. He wants to see us."

Santiago Santos abruptly held out his hand to the black sergeant. The sergeant looked surprised. He shook the hand.

"Santiago Santos, a sus órdenes."

The sergeant grinned. "No speak espanyol. Tell him, Mr. Brady, I thank him."

Santiago Santos turned to Domatilio. "Bring our horses! We ride to the commander. — Martín, ask the sergeant where the cavalry first encountered these Indians."

"He wants to know where you first jumped the Indians."

"This time, at the foot of the Hatchet Mountains, right near the Mexico line. When we come south at Púlpito Pass the Indian sign forked. The major split our force. He brought Scanlon with L Troop and the packers and the four scouts after this Magues bunch. Cap'm Stoker took H and K and a company of Cheericow scouts east of Púlpito after Fuego's main band. G Troop made supply camp at Púlpito. They are guarding the wagons there. Goddam I would like to see them!"

"Don Santiago, he says they trailed these Apaches from near the boundary."

"Forty leagues! They had permission from the State of Sonora?"

"Mr. Brady," the sergeant said. "I know that word! They all ask it. Tell him we got *permiso*. I wish to Christ we didn't, but we do. It says: 'pursuit on a trail, and not more than one hundred miles below the line.'"

"They have the permission. Completely official."

"What did he say of Púlpito?"

"The army wagons are camped there, waiting for the troop."

"The Púlpito is thirty leagues from here."

"Sergeant. Don Santiago says you are about ninety miles south of Púlpito. The line is thirty or forty miles north of there."

"Jesus loves me," the sergeant said.

They got on their horses and rode into the trees. Beyond a guard detail standing with carbines unslung, rain-darkened horses and pack mules stood with sagging heads along a picket line stretched between two pines. Gray smoke boiled thick from camp-fires of wet wood. Troopers in their sodden brown canvas fatigues and drooped black hats hunched over the first thin warmth of the fires, preparing to boil coffee, slicing pale salted sowbelly into a few blackened pans. Beyond them, a tarpaulin was thrown over the low branch of an oak and fastened slanting to pegs in the mud. Under its sloped shelter a few men stooped and sat around a litter made of pine poles and a blanket, propped up from the mud by piles of stones.

"Here are the people, sir," the sergeant said, leading Martin and Santiago Santos toward the shelter, away from Domatilio who stood holding the horses, shivering, alone under a tree.

The rain patted on the oily canvas and rolled along it in little winding streams. A trooper with bandaged head and a trooper with an arm in a stained sling moved aside. Martin looked down at the face of the man lying on the litter. The face was thinner. It was not red now: it was pale. The whiskers were not dusty: they were wet. In the dimmed light under the canvas, the eyes in the pale face seemed unnaturally bright.

"I recognize you. The black horse broke your leg. You were lying in the street."

"I was — and you told them to get me a doctor — "

"I have forgotten your name."

"Brady."

"I am Major Colton."

"Major, this here is the man I work for, Don Santiago Santos. He owns the fine hacienda of Bavinuchi. This rancho is his, and most of the country around here. And you won't find a better man."

"Is that so?" Colton's eyes looked up apprizing the figure in dripping rough leather.

"Don Santiago," Martin said. "*Quiero presentar, como amigo, el Señor Comandante Colton.*"

Santiago Santos reached down offering his hand.

"Buenas dias mucha gusta," Colton said.

"*El gusto es mío, Señor Comandante —*"

"Tell him I don't speak it, Brady." Colton spoke with his jaws clamped shut.

"He has no Spanish, Don Santiago."

"Nor I English. Angels of Christ, I thought he would be black, Martín! I want to thank him for his vengeance on the brutes who killed my people. Tell him I am grateful! Ask him of his wound. He is in pain!"

"Don Santiago is grateful to you for killing Apaches. He wants to know, are you hurt bad?"

"Certainly not! The wound started bleeding again, jerking in this litter. I have ordered a halt until this blood stops —" He pulled back the blanket and stared at the red splotch on the binding around his waist. It smelled of carbolic acid. "Just under the ribs on the left side — the ball traveled through and came out clean in back. I can't think the bowel is punctured. But — I lost my surgeon — in the first volley —"

"He can't travel with that," Santiago Santos said. "He is my guest. Offer him my house. Tell him I will also care for his men and his stock until he is well enough. Tell him! Let them carry him to Bavinuchi!"

"Don Santiago says you are his guest. He offers you his house in Bavinuchi. He wants to quarter your men too, and put your stock in shape while you get well."

"I have heard of the Latin punctilio," Colton said, after a silence. "It doesn't mean what it says."

"Let me tell you something. Get it straight. This man means just what he says. He is trying to help. He is a damn fine man and he can help plenty!"

Colton looked up. His eyes moved to Santiago Santos' face and back to Martin's. "Thank him. I am leading troops to base. Without malingering or delay. As soon as this bleeding stops, we will push on."

"He thanks you. He says he is leading troops to base without — delay. He will move as soon as his bleeding stops."

"If he wishes to die in the sierra — that is his affair. Does the troop have a surgeon?"

"He was killed in the battle."

"Tell the commander I regret he will not accept my very poor hospitality. Tell him at least Domatilio can help the wound. He can find cobwebs. He can find nopal."

"Don Santiago is sorry you won't stay and get well. He says before you go he would like to have his cowboy gather some spider web to put on the wound. That will stop the bleeding, Major. We use it down here. Don Santiago would also like to fix you a poultice of a cooked cactus leaf to put under that binding. It draws out the matter. It would help you."

"I don't think we need any primitive remedies, thank you. We have the surgeon's chest. Carbolic acid seems to deaden the pain somewhat. Mainly, I believe my use of a litter is all wrong: it is not only slow, it is uncomfortable. I would do better to bind myself tightly and ride horseback. I intend to do that — " Colton sat up abruptly, gripping the pine poles of the litter. " — Get moving. These troopers of mine are hurt too. — Does the señor have any corn here for stock feed? And does he have any hard liquor to use for medicine?"

"Don Santiago, he does not want the cobweb or the nopal. But he wants to know if you have any corn for his stock. And if you have any strong drink, as medicine."

"Tell him to send men to the feed pen and to take all the corn they find. As for drink — a pity there is so little in the saddlebag!" He moved out of the shelter, toward where Domatilio waited with the horses.

"He says for your men to take all the corn they can find, down there at the feed pen."

"I expect to pay for it," Colton said.

Martin said nothing.

Colton looked at him. "Do you know the country north of here, to the Púlpito Pass?"

"Only as far as Techapic."

"How far is that?"

"Maybe thirty miles."

"You don't know it farther on."

"I am new to this side of the sierra, but — "

"I may as well mention my situation. My four Tewa trailers are dead — and Boggs, the packer, who spoke Spanish and knew something of this general area. I had hoped to get from you some dependable information as to the most direct march back to the Púlpito."

Santiago Santos came under the tarpaulin. He carried a bottle. He put it in Colton's hand.

"Gracias," the major said. "Cuanto?"

"Eh?" Santiago Santos asked Martin. "What? Tell him I am sorry there is not more. All he wants awaits him at Bavinuchi."

"That is all the liquor he has here, Major. He is sorry there is not more. At Bavinuchi he could give you plenty."

"What is this stuff?"

"Mescal."

"Villainous!" Colton looked up. "Cuanto?" he repeated. "How much? And for the corn?"

Martin hesitated. "He is wanting to pay you, Don Santiago — and for the corn."

"Tell him," Santiago Santos said. His voice was very dry. "It is a gift. Gift. Martín, thou comest from very strange people."

"What?" Colton asked.

"He don't want pay for anything. No pay. But you could lend him shovels, if you carry any. So he could bury his dead people — "

"Sergeant Sutton! Order out two details. One to gather the corn you find at that pen by the house. The other with spades to dig graves. Get them moving!"

"Yes suh!" The sergeant glanced at Martin, and started away.

"Don Santiago," Martin said, "the sergeant is taking men to get the corn. And men to dig graves — "

The tawny eyes turned at the major. "Good. Very good."

"He better tell the sergeant what he wants done," Colton said. "Perhaps you will go with him. When you return would you both share my mess? Not much — but at least the stump-water coffee will be hot. I will see it's hot!"

"Thank you, Major." Martin turned to Santiago Santos. "We ought to go with the sergeant."

They walked out of the shelter, to the tree where Domatilio stood alone with the horses.

"Don Santiago," Martin said. "One thing is clear to me. These people ought not to be in Mexico."

"Nothing could be clearer." Santiago Santos started to mount his horse.

"Don Santiago. Wait — If that major will not stay to receive your help, I ought to go with him to give him mine."

"That major!"

"I don't know much about majors. But I saw that sergeant — he is about to have more than he can manage. I feel it, it is strange, I feel it. I ought to go — "

"Man! You mean you would leave us? Leave Bavinuchi?"

"Señor, believe me. These times at Bavinuchi — I want you to understand me — but these people — from my own country, in trouble — you see it!"

"Listen to me, Martín. Something I would not say. But I say it now. I think of you like a part of — of Bavinuchi. I will tell you: like a son, like Andrés, like Agustín!"

Martin looked down, at the muddy hooves of Lágrimas in the wet pine needles. "There is something I have said all my life in Mexico: I say it to you for the first time from here, from my heart: I am at your orders. Do you want me to stay?"

The honey-colored eyes had bright amber lights in them as they looked in Martin's face. "No. We once said, 'A man should live where he belongs.' A man has to decide."

They got on their horses and rode toward the gray walls.

CHAPTER XXII

By DISCIPLINED effort of will, Colton gripped at the big pommel of Martin's Mexican saddle, grasping it with both his desperate hands. He held on, rocking in the twist of the pain, the fevered weakness, feeling the spring of the driving sinew under him, surrendering the urgency of his pain, his weakness, to the pace of the horse Lágrimas carrying him north, north where at last the familiar line of the mountain was the shape of his hope.

Sitting an issue saddle on a tough dun cavalry jade, Martin rode using his spurs, jolting at Colton's side. He rode watching Colton's gripping hands. Behind them a squad of troopers and a pack mule hammered a punishing trot unequal to the pace of the black stallion's swinging rack or the half lope of the heavy-footed dun.

He might, Martin thought, carefully keeping his eyes from Colton's gray rigid face, he might. I never believed it. But he believed it. Maybe he can. He might after all. He asked for this — he would not stay in that wagon at the Púlpito; he pulled his rank, he said he could make it. He said he had to make it. And now he might. By God he might. I hope he will.

Watching the hands grip, Martin felt his mind pull tight, like a rope, a rope frayed against the unrelenting edge of Colton's agony.

I wonder if I will, Martin thought. I wonder if we meet the big gray hats along this road, the red chin strings and the Remingtons — and him riding my horse — before we cross the river.

"Looks familiar — up there — " Colton forced the words from his dry mouth, and turned his head.

"The spring of Samalayuca is at the edge of these dunes."

"Brady. Keep pushing."

"We will make it, Major. This is the stage road now."

The westering winter sun cut steely lights on the stone of the mountains in the north, on the hazed shapes at the far side of the emptiness, at the pass where Puerto stood. Long shadow slanted from the dry December skeletons of mesquite, from the moving legs of the horses. The hooves touched quiet in the emptiness.

"Brady — " Colton said. Martin saw. He knew it suddenly and it tore his heart.

"*Hu* Lágrimas," Martin said. He swung off the dun horse fast, and came around, to the rein by Lágrimas' jaw. He reached up with his other hand trying to hold Colton on the saddle.

"Tobe!" Martin called. Lágrimas jerked and Martin almost lost his hold. Sergeant Sutton sprang from his horse to Martin's side.

"Ease him," Martin said. His voice came hoarse. "Foot — out of stirrup — there — "

The powerful Negro took Colton from the saddle as if he were a child. Jumping down from their blowing horses, the other troopers came. Martin handed Lágrimas' reins to one of them. Their eyes rolled, yellow in their black faces, in the sunset light. Martin kneeled by Tobe Sutton, over the figure on the sand.

"Get him water," Martin said. He untied the dirty handkerchief from Colton's neck. When the trooper came with the canteen, Martin wet the handkerchief and bathed the stiff, dusty face.

Colton's eyes opened. They looked up, at the black men, at the black horse, against the yellow sky.

"Hopeless," Colton said. The word came through the clenched jaw. "I can't hold on. Here —" he fumbled at his finger, at the gold ring with the scratched stone, the worn spread eagles and the numerals '61. "Sergeant. The ring goes to my wife — Mrs. Colton — take it." The effort of lifting his hand seemed very great. Tobe Sutton took the ring from the finger. "It is — important," Colton said.

With the resolute effort of will that had sustained him horseback six days and two hundred miles bleeding inside with a bullet hole at the edge of his spleen, bleeding slowly to his death, he tried to finish what he had to say in his loneliness. He tried to finish his life.

"Tell Mrs. Colton this was the training, to wear it. *Ellen!* In Long Gray Line we follow, close order, where —" Colton labored at his fading thought, trying to lick his lips. Martin wiped them with the wet handkerchief, and waited. "Thank you," Colton said, very clearly. "Seven bad months in the field but — when I found the enemy, I engaged him —" The jaws came suddenly open.

It was intolerably quiet.

Tobe Sutton looked at the gold ring in the dirty palm of his hand, and he stood up, and looked at his troopers. "You niggers, you went to Mexico with a soldier. I be goddam if you didn't."

"We ain't going to leave him," a trooper said, half asking. His rusty hat was in his hands.

"We are going to take him home," Martin Brady said.

It was biting cold, in the faint light of first stars and a new sickle moon in the west, when Colton's body was wrapped tight in canvas from the mule's pack, and lashed over the back of the tough dun, ready.

"I liked the major, finely —" said Tobe Sutton. "I will lead him."

Martin went to Lágrimas and reset the stirrups, letting out the leathers to fit himself again. When he climbed into his saddle, he felt the good familiar seat, the good familiar response from the *ramal*. He patted the slick hide on the warmth beneath the tangled mane; he had to whisper to Lágrimas, privately, in his own tongue, "Thou art horse —"

"Fix that halter rope," Tobe Sutton said to a trooper. When it was fixed, the sergeant leaned from his saddle and took the end of the rope in his hand.

"Forr'd — " he called. He led off, with Martin and the troopers and the limping pack mule in a silent file behind the dun horse and the burden. They rode the pale mark of the stage road around the mounded dunes to the seep of Samalayuca in the dark.

The moon was down when the stock stood drinking at the stagnant pool. The troopers eased themselves, standing with the reins, stamping their numb feet, blowing their numb hands. They used words, in a kind of shorthand of comradeship.

"By morning, this tank gonna be stone froze — "

"My Jesus I'm stone froze now."

"This nigger is starving to death."

"Naw he ain't. He done et. Lass year over at Sonory."

"He alive, ain't he? More than some — "

"Shut your mouth, that live and dead talk! Don't want it."

"Howbout barrack talk? This time tomorrow: *Tattoo* — "

"Joobus but I likes to hear the nigger talk that. Talk it!"

"Talk's cheap, takes money to buy the whiskey — "

Martin drew the sergeant away from the voices. "Tobe. This is no place to be. We can cut northeast off the road and hit the river in twenty miles. We can be in the States by midnight."

"Mr. Brady, if these 'public animals' breaks down now, we'll walk, and if we can't walk, we'll crawl."

"One thing — " Martin said, "we don't want *no* Mexican patrols on us! If we move straight across from here, we will come out below Ramblazo on the river. On the other side, the men can build a fire. And eat. And get to Fort Jefflin in the morning."

"God's natural country, Mr. Brady."

It was more than twenty miles, and it was later than midnight when they came around the foot of the hills and felt the slope that tilted eastward into the open, into the valley. The sand was deep and the gullies were rough. The gaunted animals toiled, weak in the legs, stumbling often; the riders sat their saddles, aching in the frosty cold.

Slowly, under the winking high stars, they came to where they saw beyond the paleness of the sand the darkness of the brush that lined the river, and they rode toward it. They worked across a dry flat of alkali white in the starlight, with the hooves scuffling the crust in the windless silence. They filed along blurred thickets with thorny arms of tornillo snagging, scraping at the canvas on the dun horse's back. They moved through the brush to the bank of the river, to the edge of Mexico.

Martin rode to the wet lip of the stream dark in the sandy bed.

"I'm trying it first," he rasped to Tobe Sutton, "to see — It don't look bad — "

Lágrimas stepped in, snuffling, grudging the faint tap of the spur. The bitter cold flow splashed with each deepening step. It came eddying to the stirrups and Martin lifted his boots. Then it shallowed fast. The wet hooves stepped out climbing dry sand to where salt cedars grew. Martin's heart pounded when he reined on solid ground. It seemed no different. It looked the same, it smelled the same, it was just as cold, just as dark. But his heart pounded.

He turned to watch the troopers. They crossed churning, quick. He saw the dark shape on the dun horse joggle in the splashing. It came moving up the bank behind Tobe Sutton, who looked back, beyond the horse he led, beyond the black water.

"I wish," he said, to nobody, from deep in his throat, "we never have to go over that river no more."

"I looked over Jordan," a trooper said, "and I seen the You Ess Aigh."

"We will ride up in the bosky," Tobe Sutton said.

They made a rough camp by a fire they built of rotten cottonwood dragged into a pile. Colton's bent body was stiff, and the canvas was wet, when Martin and the sergeant unlashed it, and lifted it from the worn dun's back, and laid it on the ground at the edge of the firelight. The shaking tired troopers set a picket line, and unsaddled, and took the pack from the lame mule, and hung the nose bags on. Martin tethered his stallion away from the horses; he poured all the corn he had into the frayed *morral* before he fastened it on the black nose.

Warming themselves, too tired and too cold to care about the telltale brightness of the curling gold flame, they drank scalding coffee and ate hardtack and sowbelly the mule had packed from the G Troop wagon a long way back, a long, long way back, at Púlpito.

Tobe Sutton looked at the Dog Star high in the west. "You niggers: rest on your arms. I'll stand a guard for you — me and Mr. Brady, we stands your guard — while you catches a nod till day."

Sitting close by the red coals, Martin shaded his face from the bite of the heat, feeling the scorch on his shins, on the front of his shirt. His outstretched fingers pulsed tingling. His nose ran and his eyes watered with the warmth. It merged with his weariness to make him dizzy.

"Tobe. If I fall to sleep, pull me out of the fire."

"I feel a little bit noddy myself but — I'm too spunked now to shut my eyes. I could of kissed this old ground. Old Texas ground!"

"Tell me something, Tobe. You heard what the major said: 'Long Gray Line.' What did he mean? I thought he was a Union man."

"Course he was! He fought to free us niggers. You got it wrong — I hear plenty shoulder strap talk in my time! Major meant about the West Point. Where the rank goes to learn. They wear gray going to school."

"Oh," Martin said.

"Lots of pride in that school, for white gentlemen."

"You finally liked the major, you said."

"Mr. Brady, this afternoon look to me like I found out why Colton take us chousing all over the creation looking for Indians to fight. You see, the battalion commander before him at Jefflin didn't take to no battling. And it finely come to Bear Canyon. The bullets flew so thick he like the boy that caught the yellow jacket and let it go again glad to git out of it. He stay off on a nice hill giving orders where it take a Gatling gun to touch him. He think his hair is too good to be lost. Old Fuego run off our horses and would of cut us all to pieces if Cap'm Stoker lucky hadn't come shooting about that time with K Troop. It was bad. Battalion commander got relieved after that one. He was a diss-grace to the Tenth, and then here come Colton. Everybody think Cap'm Stoker was in line for the command. But here come Colton. From the Division Headquarters, one of them gilt-edged detail boys. This evening when he try to talk before he die, I got the idy. He just been trying to prove he was all right. He want the West Point to know he was all right — and he sure want his wife to know."

"I don't see how he lived — or rode a mile, Tobe. Last night when I helped him his belly was swelled hard as stone. Stone! Then today, when we got so near — I thought he was going to make it. He kept saying he was going to make it."

"He try to see his wife, before he die. Lord — " Tobe Sutton checked himself. "Mr. Brady, you ever see the major's wife?"

"Yes. I have. I am glad I don't have to see her tomorrow. With that ring."

"Will you go with me when I takes that ring? I druther butt my brain on a stooping post oak — Mr. Brady, you got to help me!"

"We better get there first."

Light came with coyotes crying, and the cold sky hard and clean. When the troopers had been roused, and the horses with their breaths smoking were saddled, and the bent canvas bundle was tied stiff on the dun again, and the hitch was trim on the mule's back, the horsemen mounted, springing their achy knees, cursing. As they moved to the river, to water, Lágrimas shied at the sudden racket of mallards rising noisy from the marsh at the edge of the tamarisk. Martin looked north. Beyond dark bobbling dots of duck and honker V's in the lighting sky, pink sunrays touched the top of Mount Jefflin.

The hoarfrost was melting on the low ground beneath the salt cedars, on the tan cattails along the ragged slews, when the horsemen crossed a dry *acequia* and came to the first cornfield of Ramblazo. Skirting the lines of broken yellow stubble, they rode with the climbing sun straight in their faces, to the sandhills rimming the valley's eastern edge. A haze dimmed the tall trees over the nestled settlement; the tang of mesquite smoke and burning leaves hung faintly acrid in the pale sunlit air. It warmed as the file of riders moved jogging around the bare fields, past vineyards with each cut vine mounded in its brown cone of loam for the winter, by lanes of leafless tall poplars, to where they entered again the ruts of the road north, to Puerto. Tobe Sutton put his draggled, weary detail to a trot.

Martin saw the buggy coming. Dust boiled from under the wheels and drifted thinning up into the branches, the brown leaves, the clumps of green mistletoe, on the arching cottonwoods over the road. There was something about the angle of the buggy driver's hat — Martin touched spur. Lágrimas sprang forward, away from the trotting file.

The driver was waving, long before Martin reined and jumped from his saddle, at the side of the road.

"*Doc!* How are you?"

Doctor Stovall had the cigar from his mouth, grinning. He was holding out his hand. The sun cast a crooked shadow beside his broken nose, on his long upper lip. "I knew that black before you started to run! How in hell are you? That leg! That stud horse! By God!"

"Doc, I am glad to see you! You well?"

"Out saving lives. This is my day at Ramblazo — what're the troops?"

"Tobe!" Martin called. The sergeant pulled his file off the road, and halted. He dismounted and came to Martin's side.

"Doc, this is Sergeant Tobe Sutton. I been camping with him and his army since the big mountains of Sonora. Tobe — this is the best damn doctor there is."

"Pleased to know you, suh! We been needing a doctor — "

"What you been up to? Scouting Cocomonga wine from officers' mess, and working Brady over?"

"We pretty near made him a trooper, at that — "

Stovall put his cigar in his mouth, and pointed at the dun horse. "I didn't see that! What do you have there?"

Tobe Sutton looked at Martin, to let him answer.

"Doc. That is the body of Major Starke Colton."

"*No!*"

"Yes it is. He had a damn tough fight with Apaches. He come close to wiping out Magues' whole band. Down in the Sierra Madre. Colton got a ball in his side. He tried to get home and he near made it, riding horseback — two hundred miles! He died just below Samalayuca yesterday evening."

Stovall was obviously moved. He looked down the road, saying nothing.

"Well Doc — I didn't know you were such a friend of Colton's."

"I hardly knew the man."

"It's pretty bad, I know, carrying him doubled over like this, into the post. And when he almost made it. Bringing him to his wife, without warning — "

"You are not bringing him to his wife."

"What?"

"His wife is dead. They found Mrs. Colton last week, drowned. At the dam in the river, there below Jefflin."

"Drowned? How?"

"She apparently committed suicide. I was called for the inquest. There was no surgeon at the post."

Tobe Sutton looked at Martin, then at the doctor.

"My Jesus. That pretty woman — And this ring now, I was taking her this ring, Doctor."

Stovall looked away. He pulled a match from his pocket and tried to light his cigar. "The way things go," he said.

"Doctor, is there any troops at the post?"

"The adjutant, and a guard detail. The battalion is still in the field. I guess Stoker will get the command now."

"Colton was all right, Doctor suh."

"Who said anything about that? Of course he was all right."

Martin looked toward the dun horse. "We better go on. This sun, it's — "

"You're correct, Brady," Stovall said. "When you get through, why don't you come by, and stay with me in town? I would like to hear the story, my friend."

"I'm much obliged, Doc, inviting me. Say — how is that Kentucky mare? I see you are not driving her."

"Madie's fine — her colt's due along in March. She's getting shod this morning, and I borrowed a horse."

"Isn't this Wakefield's old bay?"

"You remember a horse, don't you?"

"Maybe better than a man, sometimes. But how is old Wakefield?"

"Same old Joe — he's started up a livery stable. Brady, you won't recognize Puerto. Oil your gun well before you arrive. The C. & S. grading crews are this side of Charco now! Puerto is a goddam lot of honkytonk, hardly room to walk in the streets. If you don't want to sleep on the ground, bunk at my place."

"I have slept on lots of ground, Doc. But I would sure like to take you up. I expect you'd like to see me with some of the ground washed off, before I walk in."

The corners of Stovall's mouth lifted, creasing wrinkles at the corners of his sharp eyes. "Hell. Glad to see you back on this side."

PART FOUR

CHAPTER XXIII

Big WET FLAKES
tumbled thick from the night sky. The snowy streets of Puerto
were queerly neat and quiet in their luminous shroud.

"Reminds me of Missouri," Martin said. His toes were numb
and his boots crunched as he stepped.

"Reminds me of chilblains," Joe Wakefield said. His breath
smoked into the fall of the silent flakes. "Damned if it don't make
Puerto nearly pretty."

They turned a corner and walked another block in the muffled strangeness of the whirling snow. A crack of light glowed along the sides of the drawn curtain in Doctor Stovall's front window; Wakefield rapped his big chapped knuckles on the doctor's door, and it opened. Yellow lamplight made a golden swarm of the snowflakes.

"Come in!" P. J. Ruelle, the mining man, greeted them. "You froze?"

"Cold as a welldigger's butt," Wakefield said, knocking snow from his hat. "Where's the doc?"

"Somebody come for him. He said he would be right back. You git up to the fire while I fix you both a little hot priming toddy. Doctor's orders!"

Martin stood by Wakefield warming at the hearth. The pleasant room smelled of mesquite smoke, and the drugs of the doctor's pharmacy cabinet, and the whiskey Ruelle was pouring from a jug into the toddy glasses. He added steaming water from a pitcher on the table, and stirred the sugar with a spoon.

"Shine the light!" Wakefield said as they lifted their glasses together. "I guess we would have missed this party if Mart hadn't whipped the empty wagons down the road while I augured with the gotdummed purchase agent. We took four hundred bushels of corn and three wagonloads of hay to that gang up there — they must have a couple hundred head of mules dragging scrapers on those fills."

"Where are the tracks now?"

"Coming! The other side of my old Cottonwood Station."

"Brady," Ruelle said, "did you git your reward money from Sheriff Mathews yet? He told me this afternoon that he got it for you, in the mail from Silverton."

"I got it. That's why we're late. I am sure obliged to you and to Wakefield, and the sheriff."

The front door squeaked opening, and they saw the doctor. Snow was caked on his hat, on his long buffalo coat, on the top of the scarred satchel in his gloved hand.

"Toddy for you!" Ruelle called.

Stovall hung the hat and coat on the rack by the door, by his guests' pistol belts. "Why didn't you help yourselves to cigars?" He walked to the mantel and took one from the box.

"Doc. We appreciate your having us for a feed. I am damn tired of my own fried grits."

"I thought us sorry singles ought to eat us a roast goose for good luck and watch the New Year in. And try to stay out of trouble with saloonkeepers, pimps and newcomers — " He took the toddy from Ruelle. "Thank you, Pete. Here's how — "

"Any trouble over there on the street? Is that where you been?"

"No trouble. Just delirium tremens and pneumonia in the barrel shed of the Acme Saloon. His mother would scarcely have known him." Stovall drained his glass. "Well. He wouldn't have known his mother either. I suppose Puerto is suffering from what our departed friend Travis Hight used to call 'the coming of civiliz-ation.' Let's fix another drink all around."

"I hear Judge Heffridge came back."

"Got back before Christmas, while you and Brady were up in Charco. He brought two additions to the town. 'Capitalists' the Judge calls them, from up north somewhere, Illinois or Indiana. Good strong Republicans like the Judge. They are going to get a charter for a National Bank and buy up town lots and start a lumberyard and take over what the Judge calls 'the development of a great frontier.' "

"When Heffridge got whipped at the polls, he just moved out of office into taller grass!"

"After the big shooting. I figured the judge might not come back to Puerto."

"Why not? The bitterness against Heffridge died with Travis Hight. It's a different bunch now."

"A roody bunch. What's the matter, Mart? Old age got you?"

"Mr. Hight must of let whiskey get the upper hand of him."

"He done the town a big last favor when he killed Gus Heffridge and that sorry Horse McFeeters! And if he'd been a fraction faster whipping around at Horse — "

"Travis Hight would be dead anyway. The judge would see to that."

"I saw Gus Heffridge once," Martin said. "Recall that time, Mr. Ruelle? It reminds me of the newspaper man. I forget his name. What happened to him?"

The doctor's eyes glanced quickly in Martin's face. Martin noticed it.

"After the elections," the doctor said, "that Republican newspaper was a lost cause. Then the shooting match of Heffridge and McFeeters against Hight finished off what was left of the Puerto *Eagle*. Naylor left town."

"Tell you one thing, Brady," Ruelle said, winking, "that Naylor took lots of buggy rides with the army woman they found behind the dam."

"Pete," grinned Wakefield, "you sound like Miss Tutt talking."

The doctor's gray-headed Mexican cook opened the door from the dining room.

"*Lista*," she said.

"I guess our goose is cooked. Drink up, and we'll eat."

"Where'd you shoot the bird, Doc?"

"The slew behind the McBee place. While I was down there I got some bottles of Don Santiago's red wine. It might be a little sweet for Burgundy, but it's still pretty good with a goose for New Year."

"How is old Santiago McBee?"

"Not so strong for civiliz-ation. He used to own all the land this town is built on. Now all he has is the old house in the grapevines. He's still telling the stories about how he ground corn in his mill for Alexander Doniphan, and how he gave a banquet in his house for Benito Juárez — who wouldn't cross the river to the party. Let's eat."

"Some spread, Doc."

The doctor's table did not seem to belong in Puerto. It was set with a white tablecloth and china, silver and wineglasses, with smoking plates of plenty by the brown roast goose.

"Sons — " Wakefield said when the doctor finished carving, "bless the meat and damn the skin, throw back your ears and all pitch in."

"We got a parson in Puerto now. Be careful."

"Just sing me 'Pull for the Shore' while I git outside this goose!"

The four men ate. Contrary to their desire and their expectation, vague as shadow in the corners of the room, a constraint compounded in their separate thoughts came touching around the table. The old cook brought hot biscuits and gravy; the doctor poured wine; for dessert there were holiday *buñuelos* dusted with sugar and cinnamon; yet the feast never mellowed to festivity.

"Brady," said the doctor, "I saw Ernest Mathews. How does it feel to have a hundred dollars gold in your pants pocket?"

"Feels peculiar."

Martin knew he should be glad to have the money. And it bothered him. Suddenly he understood: it was the wry, heavier weight of the buckskin purse on his leg the day he walked to Señor Roa's. Remembering it, Martin took a drink of the wine. Lamplight caught in the wineglass making a shining spot red as blood.

"You going to buy a town lot and get rich?"

"Well," Martin said, "I owe a fellow in Del Norte fifty pesos. And I'm going to buy my nigger sergeant Tobe a bottle of gin for New Year's. He's coming by the stable tomorrow. And I think I'll get me a new saddle blanket and some boots with thick soles and a new hat and stand treats for you all."

"Mart, you won't never be rich. You'll be like me."

"You know — " Martin spoke trying to put vague shadow into words, turning the stem of the wineglass, peering at it, "this evening is peculiar. The way things go. For instance, if Mr. Ruelle hadn't seen me that night by the tent saloon. If Mr. Hight hadn't told me, down there in Chihuahua, how it was. And if — well, I would be on the other side somewhere tonight. Eating tortillas if I was lucky. Instead of goose. I guess I ought to feel rich, right now — "

"Brady — " the doctor left it unfinished. Instead, he looked at his watch. "Right now, the old year has ten minutes to go and the old Puerto goes with it. The Puerto I came to. Right now, I get a fairly clear whiff of the odor of mortality."

"I can't smell it from here, Doc," Wakefield finally said, "but I can hear it."

The sound came to them, across the distance of the snow-muffled air from Puerto Street.

"Hell. If we're not going to hoot, or holler, or shoot — or sing — " the doctor grinned, "shall we drink? Here's to tomorrow: don't look back."

"Happy New Year."

"I believe the Honorable Joseph Wakefield, proprietor, Star Livery Stable, will now rap out a ditty."

"Clear the gate, boys —

> Little black bull come down the mountain,
> Hoorah Johnny and a hoorah Johnny —

Join in, gents —

> A long time ago,
> A long time ago.
> He run his horn in a white oak sapling,
> Hoorah Johnny and a hoorah Johnny,
> A long time — "

They heard the loud knock, and followed the doctor into the parlor as he went to the door.

"Come in," the doctor called.

A gaunt-faced stranger stood holding his hat. "Doctor?" he asked. Stovall nodded. "The Diamond G has burnt. A couple of the whores has been crippled in the stompede. Can you come?"

"Yes," Stovall said. "I can come."

"They was a shooting also," the stranger said. "In front of the Boss Billiards. A Chinaman. Look like he has lost his liver and lights in the snow."

"I expect he has," Stovall said. He turned to his three guests. "Anyway, we had our goose. You boys sit by the fire and work on that jug. I'll be back."

"Doc. Mart and me have been on the road since daylight. I'm gitting old. If you don't mind, I'm going to roost. On a full stomach and thanking you — "

"I thank you too, Doc," Martin said, "very much. I will move along with the boss."

"We'll all go," Ruelle said. "We'll walk over with you, Doc. It was a fine evening."

"There is a cowboy riding," said the stranger, "on Puerto Street in a pair of woman's lace drawers."

"Nothing I can do for him," the doctor said, "until they shoot him."

Only a few vagrant flakes fell upon them when they walked out the door into the cold, into the white street.

"Are you going to take a look before you turn in?" Ruelle asked. "I want to see what happened to the Diamond G."

"Fire's out," the stranger said. "It just burned the ceiling off. The stovepipe got hot."

Wakefield stopped at the corner. "I don't think I will go looking for any loaded buzzards on the shoot," he said. "That's my New Year resolution."

"Make that mine," Martin said. He turned with Wakefield up the side street, toward the livery stable, and they walked alone in the unmarked whiteness.

Dark in the whiteness ahead, two unsteady figures came wavering, talking, down the middle of the street.

"My boy — "

"It's awright, Justice, jest a little ways now. Less go home."

"Lord, it's old Bates!" Wakefield whispered. "And he hasn't been drunk since he got his court back, since election — " Wakefield raised his voice as the two figures came closer. "Evening!"

"Evening gennulmen," the colored man said, holding Justice Bates up.

"Need any help?" Wakefield asked.

"We is almost home — "

"Uh-h-hk," Justice Bates said, sick. The vomit made a smoking black place on the snow.

"My boy," the justice said as he straightened.

"Less go home now, Justice."

"My boy." Justice Bates' voice was steadier than his gait. He lurched with the colored man's arm around his waist. "My boy. Tender yet in years. Remember this counsel ere folly o'ertake thee to thine own self be true and thou canst not be false to any man."

"Less go home now."

The dim figures wavered away.

"That's the nigger boy from the Senate Saloon," Wakefield said. He unlocked the livery stable gate and Martin followed him inside.

When they pulled it open, the door to the buggy shed marked

a dragging arc on the drift of snow. Wakefield lit a lantern; Lágrimas, quiet in the stall with the straw, turned to look into the light. In the shadowy dimness for an instant the black horse's eyes glowed blood red.

"I guess everything's all right for the night — what's left of the night," Wakefield said. "See you in the morning." He started away with the lantern. At the door of the office where he slept, he stopped and looked back. "Ain't much home, Mart. But it's yours. Happy New Year."

"It's plenty home. Happy New Year to you, Wakefield."

Martin sat down on his bunk in the dark. He pulled off his boots, and his breeches and shirt. He put his gun under the tick pillow, and took off his hat, and got into the blankets, shivering. Warmth came to him sooner than sleep. In the last hour of the night he stirred troubled with a dream blur-figured beyond memory.

Mount Jefflin seemed a higher mountain, dazzling white in the sunlight, when Martin finished breakfast by Wakefield's cook stove, and crossed the corral to his stable chores. He had to drop the bucket hard to knock a hole in the ice when he drew water from the well; he broke crusts from the watering troughs. A glaring silver sun warmed the air as he worked. Snow softened watery, dripping, trickling in muddy streams from adobe walls. Roof boards leaked. Mud caked on Martin's boots. The tops and corners and sunlit open places of all of Puerto's rawness melted dirty through its white masquerade.

Martin was carrying hay on a fork when he saw the black sergeant closing the gate. He was in dress blues. His chevrons were big and bright.

"Mr. Brady! Look like you working on legal holiday!"

"I'm about through. How are you?"

"Off the duty, and got me a day pass from the post! Happy New Year!"

"The same for you! Like I told you yesterday, I hoped you would come see me."

The sergeant pulled a lump from inside his blue blouse. The lump was wrapped in wrinkled brown paper. He handed it to Martin. "I brought you a little something."

It was a minutely patterned hatband plaited of black and white horsehair.

"Tobe, is that for me?"

"I made it for you, Mr. Brady."

"Made it? Where'd you learn this pretty work?"

"Cow camp work! I was cowboy fore I enlisted. You know that. Live Oak County, Texas."

"Tobe — thank you. It makes my present to you look sorry. I was going to buy you a bottle of gin for New Year's."

"Mr. Brady, ain't nothing noway sorry about a bottle of gin! Only thing — I can't take it, suh, thout I offer you a drink from it so's to kind of think back how glad we was to see the wagons at Púlpito, and how it was when we come to the river."

"I am going and get that bottle and we will have that drink. You come on in the shed and sit on my bunk, till I get back from Hogan's Saloon. It won't take long."

"I'll wait with the black horse, Mr. Brady."

When Martin came back with a bottle from Hogan's the blue blouse with the chevrons was carefully hung on a peg by the stall. Tobe Sutton was currying Lágrimas.

"Happy New Year, Tobe." Martin handed him the bottle.

"Real happy," Tobe Sutton said. "This old stud is show horse. Just like a peacock. We ought to braid his mane!"

"Legal holiday, you said! Put down that comb and pull the cork. I am going to the kitchen to get cups. Just one drink with you. You save the rest for yourself."

Tobe Sutton put on his blouse and buttoned it before he poured the drinks in the tin cups.

"What do they say down there in Mexico, Mr. Brady?"

"*Salud!*"

"That's what we drink it to, Salute!" The cups clinked. The gin was raw.

"Tobe. How's things going?"

"Shall I tell you? My old L Troop has got a letter of commendation, from the commander of the United States Army, General Cump Sherman! For what we done against Magues down there in the mountains. It make me proud."

"The way they say you crawled around that hill with Lieutenant Scanlon, and then led your men on without him, you ought to be proud."

"That ain't it!" Tobe Sutton hesitated. "Somebody colored, got to teach colored people! That's why I'm proud. My L Troop show colored people how to do. It show white people we do it."

"You keep on, showing them."

The black face grinned. "They ain't going to see me work over this gin! Have just a short one, Mr. Brady."

When the drink was poured, a crease came on Tobe Sutton's black brow. "Something I want to tell you. I ain't no rotten talk peddler. But I am going to tell you what they say at the post. About Major Colton. While he was out fighting, a man put tracks in his yard."

Martin thought of Stovall's glance. He thought of Ruelle's remark.

"What are you talking about?"

"The major's wife was running around with the man that wrote the newspaper. Two days after the man left town, the major's wife drownded herself. Let me tell you something. I talked to a corporal named Parvis, one of the guard detail at Jefflin while we was gone. Parvis was the one pulled the body from the water and he said they was no doubt. The major's wife was in the family way."

"This Parvis ought to have his black mouth sewed shut."

"I threatened to club him to death if he said any more! And he ain't. But he had done talked. That ain't all. The striker at Cap'm Stoker's quarters, he talked. He heard a plenty one evening. The major's wife come crying to the cap'm's wife. Talking loud how she hate the major, sobbing she's going crazy, can't stand the noise of the wind, can't stand the noise of the water running over the dam, can't stand dirty black niggers looking at her, can't stand nothing about the army. Wanting to go to San Francisco, wild. And then when Cap'm Stoker got home, the striker hear Miz Stoker break down crying, telling the cap'm the troubles. The striker hear Miz Stoker say the words, 'she was, Lefty, she went to the civilian doctor in town and he told her —' "

"That pukes me. Shut it off."

"Only reason I say this much, you and me was kind of tied in with the major at the last."

The major and the peon Pablo, Martin thought. They both worried about their women.

The door rattled open from Wakefield's office.

"Well," Tobe Sutton raised his voice, "old Fuego is down south stealing Mexkin horses in nice weather. The battalion is refitting. Clerk say Stoker going to be wearing gold leafs any day — "

"Hey Mart!"

"Here I am."

"Look who come to see you — "

Martin turned. He saw the stubby build of the figure coming through the door. He saw the smile. It was Ludwig Sterner.

"Martin Brady — "

"Those whiskers — I didn't hardly know you — "

"The face looks better with beard."

Martin saw the waled scars.

"How are you Brady?"

"I'm fine."

"Howdy, Sergeant."

"Howdy, Mr. Sterner."

"You know each other?" Martin asked.

"Why, I seen Mr. Sterner at the post gate the day he come from the old country! They say he was driving Mr. Wakefield's mules for a while — " Tobe Sutton winked. "And Mr. Sterner seen me plenty since: he kinely give me credit!"

"Your credit is good, Sergeant!" grinned Ludwig Sterner.

Tobe Sutton had wrapped his bottle in the wrinkled brown paper. "Gentlemen," he said, "I am going to amble."

"Don't go, Tobe. Where you going?"

"Legal holiday!"

"Don't get in any fix — "

"Don't you worry, Mr. Brady. Jim Crow won't give me no trouble neither — I got a little make-out of a place here in town." Tobe Sutton smiled. "My thanks, and Happy New Year."

"Come see me, Tobe. Thank you for my present."

Tobe Sutton, carrying his wrapped bottle, crossed the mud and went out the gate.

"Martin Brady," Ludwig Sterner said when they were alone in the buggy shed, "I am glad to see you." His eyes were in Martin's face. "I came to Puerto three times to see you. But you was gone on the road with Mr. Wakefield. You never came to see me in the new store in Del Norte. You never came to see my uncle over here in Puerto. I — want you should know you got Ludwig Sterner — Chico — for good friend. No matter what, I owe you always."

"You don't owe me a damn thing."

"Yes. Always."

"Let it go."

"*Ya hablo mucho español, Martín.*"

"*Qué bueno. Ya puedes platicar con los Castro!*"

"The Castros are business. The store in Del Norte is because of my uncle and the Castros. I understand that. Ah Martin Brady. I understand also what you mean, I understand. I have learned. Since you went to Mexico."

"I went to Mexico because your uncle and Pancho Gil lied. That's all right. Forget it. It's just business. I learned too. Since I went to Mexico."

"I am sorry you do not think me as friend."

"I got nothing against you, yourself. Forget it."

"Martin Brady, the Castros got something against you. I do not forget it. I came to find you, to tell you. I came to warn you. Don't never come across to Del Norte," Ludwig Sterner whispered. "They try to get me to invite you to my place! They tell me you are wanted by police in Chihuahua for stealing the ore cart and oxen and killing the man Pablo. That you have murdered many in Chihuahua and go unpunished. Martin Brady, *I do not believe it.* I know — I know it here — " he touched at his heart with his stubby fingers. "I come to tell you. They will send somebody to kill you. In Del Norte surely, in Puerto if they get the chance. You believe me?"

"Yes, I believe you."

"Then if you believe me I have done something. I am grateful to do something."

Melted snow dripped steadily from the shed roof in the silence.

Out the rickety open door, the top of Mount Jefflin stood above the walls, high and white in the sun.

"How are you getting along?" Martin said, to be saying something.

"You ask. The Del Norte branch does well. American goods, retail in Del Norte, wholesale to Castro Brothers in Chihuahua. With the railroad — then it will be immense! I have my own place next to the store, with a cook. Martin, I have a dog now, it came to my place and is fine friend. I wish you see it! White with black spots, and long tail and brown dots over the eyes, like double eyes! I name my dog Figge," Ludwig smiled with the scar twisting his upper lip, "after my cousin in Kassel." Ludwig paused, and his eyes went to Martin's. "This summer, when my face — was better, I went for visit to Santa Fé. On Sabbath there I read Torah with my people. It was nice. I stayed with the Lindfeld family. In Santa Fé Mr. Abe Lindfeld is wholesale merchant. There is a daughter Irma, Irma Lindfeld. *Ja.*" Ludwig's head was nodding up and down. "*Gemütlich!*"

Martin felt himself smiling. "Good for you. Chico."

"Listen, Martin. I want to tell you something I came to tell you." Ludwig frowned. "Don't stay in Puerto."

"Will you do me a favor?"

"You tell me and I do it."

"I borrowed fifty pesos from Pancho Gil. I have the money now to pay him back. Will you take it to Del Norte?"

"Don't you pay Gil nothing! He is agent of people to do you harm! You owe him nothing! You save the money."

"I am not owing a plugged *tlaco* to any son of a bitch in the State of Chihuahua. Will you take it to him?"

"I do it," Ludwig said, "but is foolish."

Martin counted the coins from the money belt under his shirt, and handed them to Ludwig. "Tell Gil you did invite me to Del Norte. Tell him I ain't coming. Tell him I send his money, and thank him."

"Don't stay in Puerto, Martin. Why do you stay in Puerto?"

"Maybe I like the place. Not exactly the way I thought I would, either."

"As a friend I ask, what plan do you have?"

"I'll tell you. I'm waiting around. When Captain Rucker gets back from Austin, I want to see if he will enlist me. In the Texas Rangers."

"Rangers." Ludwig shook his head. "And violent. You want to be violent yet."

"I guess I carry a gun for a living if that is what you mean."

"You never try anything else, Martin Brady?"

"I never had the chance, to speak of."

"You have it! Leave for another place. Go now without the gun. Go away from old troubles. You know the care of horses and cattle, all those things! Work to build for yourself a property, starting small. Maybe a ranch. You work. You build it bigger. If you need money, you know who to ask? You ask Ludwig — Chico — Sterner. You see if you get it! You find a nice girl and get married and have a good family and build something for them in this country and be citizen."

"You learned a lot, Chico, while I was in Mexico. You learned more than I did. You know more than I do."

"*Ach*, we know different things. Some things we know together. For example, you are good man." Embarrassed, Ludwig picked up Martin's battered hat from the bunk, and turning it in his hands, examined it. "The hat we sold you, before you went to Mexico. The hatband is fine. Something new."

"Sergeant Sutton made it for me. He give it to me for New Year's."

"Black and white woven. You were scout for soldiers bringing back their commander — "

Wakefield's big voice called out from the office door, "What you scoundrels chewing the rag about? Why don't you come in here by the stove?"

"You cold, Chico?" Martin put on his hat. "Shall we go on in the office?"

"Buster Sterner," Wakefield said. " 'Buster' don't seem quite right with that beard. But I'm sot in my ways."

"It's my first Puerto name, Mr. Wakefield. Then 'Chico,' " Ludwig grinned.

"How is it going, over in Del Norte?"

"For business, very good."

"Mart, this morning I saw Gates Davis, the new Customs Collector. He gets most of the news from the south, and he tells me Governor Castro has organized a kind of state police responsible only to the governor himself. You heard anything about them?"

"No," Martin said.

"These new outfits go armed to the teeth and ride like vaqueros carrying a jackleg judge right along horseback to hold court anytime at the side of the road! They use lots of rope damn quick, and Chihuahua is getting peaceful as hell. What about that, Buster, is it a fact?"

"You mean *Rurales*, Mr. Wakefield."

"That's them. Are they doing a job?"

"Chihuahua — has strong government." Ludwig glanced carefully at Martin.

"Your old boss Castro has took things by the big iron handle, ain't he, Mart?" Wakefield was suddenly uncomfortable with his own words. "No matter who runs it, it's a sneaking damn sorry country."

"The Castros will run it, for a long time," Ludwig said.

"Buster, if my Mex ever shows up so we can leave the place, Mart and me are going out to eat. You're invited. How about it? We're going to make a try at that new place on McBee Street. With a name like Sprando's Delmonico Café, by God, we're expecting celery and oysters."

"Ah, thank you! Another time, I hope. Today I have dinner with my uncle, and I go now. I came only to greet you. I wish you both *good* New Year!"

Wakefield tapped Ludwig's shoulder. "Same to you!"

"Chico," Martin said, "I'm glad you came."

"And I am glad." Ludwig went out the door.

The handyman Seguro, red-eyed, ravaged with celebration, appeared shortly after noon. He took charge of the corral, and Martin went with Wakefield for dinner.

Sprando's Delmonico Café never heard of celery or oysters. When Martin and Wakefield had eaten fried pork chops and applesauce and cornbread and custard pie with coffee, and paid Mr. Sprando fifty cents, and put toothpicks in their mouths, they walked out again on McBee Street. Past spattering tin rainspouts

and loafers leaning against walls in the welcome sun, across Puerto
Street, through a muddy-footed shambling crowd, and saddle
ponies, and the sound of piano music from the Fashion Saloon, and
the smells of stale beer, and urine in sunless places, around a
jammed corner, Martin suddenly saw John Rucker, tall and
straight.

"Cap!" said Wakefield, putting out his hand, "when'd you git
in?"

"Last evening on the San Antonio Mail."

"New Year's with your family," Wakefield grinned. "All well
at your house?"

"Fine, thank you, Joe! — Hello, Brady." Martin shook the captain's offered hand. A smile showed in the captain's black beard —
Martin noticed the beard was touched with gray. The captain's
pale eyes, the remembered pale quiet eyes, looked in Martin's face.
"I saw your name in the Austin papers," the captain said. "The
dispatch from Jefflin, when the troop brought Colton back. A
credit to you, Brady. I congratulate you."

"Captain Rucker, I was not sure whether you would speak to
me. After what I done that night I left your house I — "

"Never mind that." The smile was gone. "You been in any
scrapes since?"

"No sir."

"Good."

Wakefield laughed. "Cap, what's the news from Austin? We
going to keep our ranger force?"

"The legislature got around to passing the appropriation, finally!
Company E will be around for a while. I talked to the governor
and Major Jones both. At this point, old Fuego is my main
business. Brady, did you see that brute down in Mexico?"

"No sir."

The smile showed abruptly. "Funny thing, to meet you two
together. Brady, I believe you were acquainted with one Abrán
Rascón. Joe, you remember the man that robbed your mail — "

"You caught him!"

"No. I thought you'd like to know Abrán Rascón has been
unmistakably identified as the assassin of the ex-governor Salcido
in San Antonio."

Martin swallowed, trying to hold his face immobile.

Wakefield spit in the mud. "And he got away."

"Got away. Traced to the river. I expect the rascal is right popular with Governor Castro," Rucker said, looking at Martin. "Brady, how do you stand with Castro? Eh?"

Martin faced the pale eyes. "I quit Castro last summer, and left Chihuahua. I'm through down there. For good."

"What are you doing now?"

"Working for Wakefield."

"Are you going to come around and see me?"

"If you say so."

"What's the matter? You changed your mind?"

"No sir. I thought maybe — you changed yours."

"I haven't," Rucker said. He turned to Wakefield. "Last spring I asked Brady if he wanted to enlist in my company."

"He told me about it, before he come to work."

"Could you spare him, Joe? Are you shorthanded?"

"Hell. There ain't much excitement shoveling horseshit and selling oats. Go on, Mart. Catch that bastard Rascón and kill Fuego for me."

The smile showed again. "You come see me, Brady."

Martin stood remembering the sound of the words in the rain, the cold rain of the sierra, "a man has to decide." Maybe a man didn't decide. Maybe a man couldn't decide, himself. Maybe something else decided. But a man had to decide —

"I have to tell you something," Martin said. "When I shook loose from Castro — he — I wouldn't be much good to you, in Chihuahua! They don't like me down there, Castro's bunch don't — "

"We're not so fond of them either, are we? Company E lives on the north side of the river, Brady. If you haven't got cold feet, if you want to enlist, maybe Joe Wakefield will write you a reference to go with your application."

Martin glanced around at Wakefield.

"Mart, ain't you the vice president and assistant proprietor of the Star Livery Stable?"

"Come see me, Brady."

"I will be there, Captain."

A package waited at the Star Livery Stable. The handyman Seguro had put it on Martin's bunk in the buggy shed. Inside the wrapping was a fine, broad-brimmed Philadelphia hat, stiffly new, clean, uncreased. Tucked in it was a folded piece of ledger paper. Martin unfolded it. He looked at the flourished penmanship.

MARTIN BRADY:

Here is a new hat for the hatband. And for ranching.

From LUDWIG (CHICO) STERNER

CHAPTER XXIV

WIDE AWAKE
suddenly in the quiet, Martin opened his eyes. His cot creaked as
he stirred turning to lie on his back, and wait. It was too early yet,
but he listened. On the other cot in the room, Print Ruebush
shifted and sighed, then settled again to the long-drawn breathing
of his sleep.

Martin lay watching the augury of day grow outside the open
door of the black room. A flaw of wind came with the paleness, as
if the faint dawn fretted at the sleeping earth; the windsound
carried the distant crowing of a cock, and died to silence. Above
the vague line of the patio's wall, stars lost their fire in the lighting
sky.

Suppose she don't hear it, Martin thought, suppose she sleeps right through it. She is bound to hear it, if they come. They better come.

Then he heard it.

It came easing, delicately, through the dim morning light. It came with the fiddle lilt melting sweet with guitars in a strum and tinkle above the beat of the throaty bull fiddle. A cornet slipped its brass voice mellow along the plink of the strings, and Martin smiled. It was all right. The handyman Seguro had done it all right.

They are standing like I told them in the archway at the gate. She must be awake by now, she must be. I wonder what she thinks!

> *Despierta, mi bien, despierta,*
> *Mira que amaneció,*
> *Ya los pajarillos cantan,*
> *La luna ya se metió.*

That's *las mañanitas* for your birthday morning, Miss Louisa, they are playing it for you.

"Hey Brady — " Print Ruebush called from his cot.

"I hear it."

"Who's gitting that?"

"I don't know."

"First time this place ever did git a serenade."

"Some grateful Mexican friend giving a *gallo* for the captain, maybe," Martin said. "That might be it."

> *— Ya los pajarillos cantan,*
> *La luna ya se metió.*

"Brady. They make a fiddle cry."

"Sounds pretty good, waking up with music. Let's rise. It's good daylight."

"Sleeping on this bed again without no rocks in my back, I git a town feeling for forty winks."

The musicians were gone and the blackbirds were chattering in the peach tree by the time the rangers had pulled on their boots and walked out into the patio, into the day. At roll call and at breakfast in the mess room, there were comments about the early music.

"The captain don't know who it was for," Sergeant Grif Miles said. "They just played, and bowed, and left."

That Seguro, Martin thought, he did it all right.

"I got it figured," Print Ruebush announced. "The kin of that Canutilla horse thief was so glad to git shut of him, they come this morning to play me and Brady a little tune!"

"It sounded to me — " the words came slow and Grif Miles squinted an eye — "like courtin' music — Ruebush. — You scoundrel!"

"Godamighty!" The genuinely pained look on Print Ruebush's face changed to an abrupt grin. "Gives me an idy. But, hey — Brady! You done it! Brady, you bought that fiddling this morning sure as God made curly hair! Come on, shell down the corn! You done it!"

"Why Print!"

"My new bunky. Beating my time!"

"How in the world you — "

"Print," said Grif Miles, "you never had no time to beat! You been damn near satisfactory since you give up that gone look and quit trying to shave every day — " Rangers at the mess table were hooting. "Brady, you have been around for a couple of months: you must have noticed. There is some kind of moony epizoodic takes holt of Company E! Every man gits it, and every man gits over it. While he's got it, it seems to put a peculiar hitch in his gait and kind of walls his eyes." Grif Miles looked down the table.

"Just to think," a ranger named Henry Lavelle said, "nobody never thought of hiring a Mexkin band before!"

"Don't you know old Brady give the señoriters fits down there?" Print Ruebush said.

Martin's ears felt hot. He poured more sorghum on his cornbread. "I never seen any female fits," Martin said, "anywhere."

"Just one more thing," Grif Miles said. "About these gone fawnskin sinking spells. It don't fit big old hamhanded burrheaded boys earning just thirty dollars a month from the State of Texas for apparhending criminals and pursuing Indian hostiles. It ain't like roughhousing with a bear or a haybag. But you all know that. It's a real silly disease." Grif Miles squinted at the far wall, grinning. "Lucky it's harmless and don't last long."

"Grif," Print Ruebush said, "you mean a poor damn ranger can't even dream?"

"Dream away," Grif Miles said. "The guard list for the day will now dream in the corral." The sergeant stood up. "Come on, boys. Zoeller, don't forget to see about fixing that gate."

Martin was not on the guard list. "Sergeant," he said. "Permission requested for one hour absence in town this morning."

"Permission granted," Grif Miles said. "You got enough to pay those musicos?"

"Sergeant, I don't know what you mean!"

The Ruckers' kitchen window opened as Martin rode from the corral gate and along the wall toward the corner. Moving past the window, he heard his name called; the captain's wife looked out at him. "Mr. Brady, are you going down town?"

"Yes mam, Mrs. Rucker!" Martin swept off his hat and reined so that Lágrimas reared wheeling and came down stopped still, neck arched, facing the window. "Can I do something for you?"

"Land!" Kate Rucker said, smiling. "Mr. Brady. I declare I'm out of vanilla. Would it trouble you to bring me a bottle on your way back? No hurry. Anytime this morning. It's for a cake. This is Louisa's birthday."

"Yes mam. Barney was telling me. Yesterday when I got in from the bosky. I will sure bring vanilla."

"Did you hear that pretty music early this morning?"

"Yes mam."

"We can't think who would serenade us, and on Louisa's birthday. It was lovely. About that vanilla, you just go by old Mr. Sterner's and tell him I want exactly the kind I got before and put it on the bill."

"Uh — yes mam!"

That is what she said, just go by old Mr. Sterner's. For vanilla. It will be quite a surprise to old Mr. Sterner.

Lágrimas paced briskly in the bright morning sunshine, across town to the Star Livery Stable. Martin rapped on the back gate without dismounting, and called. The gate finally opened; Seguro grinned up at him.

"How was it?" Seguro asked.

"Very good. All very very good!"

"I brought them from down by the river. Not too drunk. Not too sober."

"Just right, my friend. Was the five dollars agreeable?"

"Agreeable. I deducted the sotol."

"I came to thank you." Martin pulled a *tostón* from his pocket and reached down to Seguro's hand. "Buy yourself a cigar."

Seguro's eyebrows arched, looking up. "And the campaign? It advances?"

"No campaign, Seguro. A dream only."

"*Vah!* Do not tell me!"

"How is the *patrón* Don José Wakefield this morning?"

"In Ramblazo buying hay."

"Salute him. Tell him I will be in Puerto for some days now, I think. Tell him I will buy him a dinner."

"Very well. They tell me you brought in that *picarón* Chucho Pino from the Canutillo. I knew him."

"You won't see him for a long time. He wears bracelets on his ankles. — I'm going, Seguro. Thank the musicians, eh?"

"Until I see you, my Police Chief Martín!"

He tied Lágrimas at the new rack near the cottonwood tree, and walked toward the sign ISAAC STERNER GENL MDSE. It had been repainted, in larger letters. But the feel of the door handle, the very squeak, seemed familiar. Martin stepped in. The smell, the look, had not changed. Isaac Sterner glanced up from waiting on a customer. He glanced again, startled. When the customer had gone, Martin stepped to the counter. Isaac Sterner backed a step.

"Mr. Sterner," Martin said. "I would like a bottle of vanilla."

"What? What?"

"A bottle of vanilla. Exactly the kind Mrs. Rucker bought last time."

"Vanilla." Without taking his eyes from Martin, Isaac Sterner got the bottle from the shelf. He put it on the counter. "You want it wrapped?"

"Wrap it up real good, Mr. Sterner. And charge it to the captain. By the way, have I got an unpaid bill here? If I have, I want to settle with you."

"Nothing to settle! Nothing!"

"I thought I owed you for those .44 cartridges that Gil brought me last May."

"You owe me nothing." Sterner's hand seemed unsteady, breaking off the string.

"I think I do."

"The cartridges were with my compliments!"

"I still owe you. Just about a year ago — they carried me through that door. You were good to me, while I got well. I remember that. Mr. Sterner, I want to tell you I don't recall anything else about it."

Isaac Sterner stood stiffly behind his counter, with his eyes fastened on the armed figure before him.

"I thought you would like to know," Martin said. He held out his hand, over the counter.

Isaac Sterner hesitated. He gave the hand a single quick shake, and let it go.

"You ever believe anybody, Mr. Sterner?"

"Sometimes."

"You believe me?"

"Well — "

"Well, start believing." Martin half smiled. "How you been, all this time?"

"All right."

"Take care of yourself. Whenever you see Chico, give him my regards." Martin picked up the little wrapped bottle, stuffed it in his jacket, and walked out.

Stopping at the rack before he untied Lágrimas, he glanced up at the cottonwood. A birdnest hung tattered and empty on a bare branch. The old tree looked tired, not so high, dusty in the dusty street. Beyond it, the plank-bridged *acequia* was gone, filled in, smoothed for traffic, leaving no trace. He looked at the wagons, the buggies, the people walking, the buildings lining Puerto Street almost to the river. Above the corner where once a tumbleweed had blown, workmen were fastening a high tin cornice on the new two-story Puerto Hotel. Martin stood reading the signs, DEMO-CRAT PRESS JOB PRINTING, SHOE REPAIR, RADEMACHER CARPENTER AND BUILDER, PURITY DRUGS AND STATIONERY. A big sign said

FURNITURE, CROCKERY, COFFINS where Peeble's barbershop had been.

"Howdy, Brady. *Qué tal*," the hoarse voice said. Tod Hogan's black coat looked rusty. His puffed jowls needed shaving.

"Morning, Mr. Hogan."

Around the corner northward, beyond the walls, a train whistle sounded and an engine chuffed slowing in the Puerto yards. Martin and Tod Hogan both glanced toward the sound. A murky puff of black smoke arose beyond Isaac Sterner's roof and drifted thinning across the face of Mount Jefflin.

"It's a sight," Tod Hogan said. "That was a high-heel do, when the first cars arrived."

"I didn't get to see it. I was on scout."

"You missed one, feller," Hogan said. "It was one for old Travis, and he missed it too — " Hogan put his hands in his pockets and looked down Puerto Street. "Hell. I come here in '56. The place got away from me."

Martin untied Lágrimas.

"Come along," Hogan said. "I'll set you to a drink."

"Thanks, Mr. Hogan. I've quit."

Tod Hogan eyed him. "You like the rangers?"

"Yes sir."

"I never did get to see that black stud horse run. Sorry you won't take a drink."

Martin swung into the saddle. "I'm obliged to you."

Hogan dodged a hack with brass lanterns and went down the street.

Martin rode feeling well, feeling the sun in the bright windless sky. Along the front of the Heffridge house, birds were singing in the chinaberry trees.

Ya los pajarillos cantan —

There were green buds swelling.

Mrs. Rucker was no longer at her kitchen window. Matt Zoeller was not working on the corral gate. Martin opened it and led Lágrimas in — and saw no rangers. The four mules belonging to the first and second messes of the company stood with packsaddles thrown on their backs. Martin hurried through the passageway from the corral into the patio. Nearly two dozen rangers stood gathered there, listening to their captain's quiet voice.

"This time," Martin heard John Rucker say, "we stand a chance to nail him." The captain glanced at Martin as he walked to the edge of the crowd. "The governor of Chihuahua has communicated the information to Major Stoker. This is the big try. Stoker will be taking, he says, one colored troop and a whole company of Chiricahua scouts he has brought in from Arizona, and he will cross here at Del Norte. The Mexican volunteers from the little towns along the river will assemble down at Juan Ocampo's ranch, and our friend Don Juan has invited Company E to join the party. We will cross this side of Owl Spring and move with the *rancheros* and work sign I presume toward the Apache stronghold in the Sierra del Lobo. Stoker's force will be converging on our right. In the meantime, some kind of Mexican troops, in force, will be fanning up from the south to cut the Indians off.

"Now, except for this company, I can't count on anybody showing real fight. But if nigger cavalry and Chiricahua trailers and Mexican soldiers can just make Fuego hold still until this outfit gets to him, boys, here's your chance to make some good Indians —

"The Mexican has already started back to Ocampo telling him we will be at the ranch tonight. That's better than fifty miles. I want to see this outfit ready to move in one hour. Sergeant Miles will issue each man ten days' rations and three hundred rounds apiece. The day's guard list will pack the four mules. Corporal Fleming will set the advance, flankers, and rear of the guard, when necessary. That's all, boys. Git!"

In the hubbub toward the storeroom, Martin stepped to John Rucker's side. "Captain, I didn't hear the first of it. Are we all going?"

Rucker stopped and looked at Martin. "Where were you?"

"Over in town."

"Messes number one and two are going. And Sergeant Miles. I'm leaving Second Corporal Billings here, instead of Miles, in charge of quarters and number three mess."

Martin was in number three mess.

"Captain Rucker. Let me go with you to Mexico."

"There is duty assigned here."

"Captain — let me volunteer out of my mess. Let me go. I got to go! I got to show you — that I'm good for something — let me go with you — "

"It seems to me you once hinted there was quite a crowd that might not be pleased to meet you, down there. I'm just saving my company of rangers from what might be an incident."

"Yes sir."

Men carrying ammunition were jostling from the issue counter. Martin stood still, looking at the ground by his boot toe. The captain started away.

He turned back suddenly.

"Brady! By George, this is the first time in my life I ever let Mexicans bluff me! I was about to let them do it! I want you on this scout, you and that black horse both! There is no Mexican alive that is going to bluff me! Come on."

Martin looked in Rucker's face. "Captain. I will tell you the truth," Martin said. "That is the closest I ever was, to having my heart broke." Crowding to the counter in the storeroom, the captain slapped Martin on the back.

The vanilla bottle fell out of his jacket as he stooped to pack his saddlebags. He picked it up and put it in his breeches pocket where it made a bulge he could remember, and he went on packing. When the blanket was tied behind the cantle, and the *cabrestante* was neatly coiled, and Lágrimas stood ready, most of the rangers were in their saddles, waiting. Martin started through the passageway, toward the patio and the Ruckers' kitchen door, with the vanilla in his hand.

He met the captain on the way. He had been with his family in the house. "Where you headed, Brady? We are ready!"

Martin held up the package. "I brought Mrs. Rucker this vanilla from town this morning."

"Vanilla?"

"She asked me to bring it."

"Well leave it in the kitchen and come on!"

"Yes sir."

There was no one in the kitchen when he rapped on the door. He went in, and put the bottle on a zinc-topped table.

As he stepped again across the patio, he heard a door slam, and looked around. Louisa Rucker came toward him. He pulled his hat off.

"Mr. Brady," she called. She stopped by the peach tree, a little out of breath. "Mother just told father good-by and she — " Martin saw that Louisa Rucker had dried tears of her own — "she asked me to thank you for the errand. She is sorry that she bothered you, and made you late — "

"No, Miss Louisa, and it wasn't no bother! I — I wish you happy birthday."

The lids shut suddenly, hiding her eyes. He saw the alarming two wet rolling tears. "Oh!" she said, "I hate crying. With everyone gone, it will be a — just a — different kind of a birthday."

Martin stood distressed, holding his hat with both hands, looking at the little woven horsehair checkers in his hatband. "I wish you a happy birthday anyway," was all he could think of to say. He glanced up, to see if the tears were still there. They were not!

"It was a lovely birthday, so early this morning," Louisa Rucker said. "It was the very loveliest thing anyone ever did — "

"Hey Brady for — " Grif Miles bellowed from the passageway. "Oh — excuse me — "

"Good-by, Miss Louisa, they are waiting."

"Good-by — " she said.

His knees felt rubbery as he hurried, jamming on his hat, not looking back.

"For Christ sake," Grif Miles mumbled, while the rangers all watched Martin mount.

When the armed horsemen and loaded mules moved out around the corner by the shade of the long wall, Louisa and her mother stood together by the gate in the archway.

The captain spoke to them. "Tell Barney I'm sorry he was in school and couldn't see us off to Mexico — "

Kate Rucker said, "Oh, he would be wanting to go!" She was waving. "The Lord watch over you all — "

Louisa waved too.

Riding by, the rangers took their hats off to the ladies.

CHAPTER XXV

Don Juan
Ocampo and Captain John Rucker dismounted at the head of the
halted column and walked forward to where the advance guard
stood examining the ground.

Martin sat his saddle watching, with a pale chunk of goat cheese
in his hand. The *ranchero* who had shared the cheese from his

saddlebag reached over and touched Martin's arm. "What was that the sergeant said?"

"He says we have something, up there."

The mounted men waited. Martin had finished the cheese and wiped his gun hand dry on his breeches when Grif Miles and a Mexican came walking back to the column.

"Fleming," Grif Miles said, "you and Ruebush and Brady ride up there to the captain. He wants to see you." The Mexican called out the names of three *rancheros*, with the same instructions, in Spanish.

Smiling with such prominence, the six horsemen broke from the files and trotted to where Ocampo and Rucker stood.

"Explain it, Don Juan," Rucker said. "Brady will interpret for my boys." The horsemen dismounted, to hear.

"The fire is not four hours old," Ocampo said, pointing and spitting. "And you see over there — " A bloody dead mule lay on the ground behind a mesquite. "They sliced meat off the poor beast while it yet lived." Martin saw that neither Print Ruebush nor Jasper Fleming needed any translations. Ocampo pointed and spit again. "Apache moccasins." They looked at the tracks. "The guard has backtracked, to count. They make from the tracks eight or nine horses and five or six mules." Ocampo's swarthy face twisted to a smile as he pointed to the dim shape of mountain fifty miles west across the sunny emptiness. "These brutes are returning to their chief Fuego in that Sierra del Lobo! They would scatter like quail if this whole crowd went raising a dust after them — and going too slow. So the Señor Captain and I have each chosen three men who have the fastest horses. You. There are eight hours of sun yet today. Find those Apaches! Stop them! Pin them until this force moves up to finish them! We will be following you as fast as we can move." Ocampo's eyes went to his three *rancheros*. "The Ranger Corporal Fleming has much experience, and is very wise with reading sign. He will command you in all things. He is in charge — is that clear?"

Rucker looked at Fleming and Ruebush. "You get all that? Tell them, Brady."

"Tickled plumb in my boots, Cap!" Fleming said when Martin had explained.

Ocampo was talking earnestly with his *rancheros*.

"I wish I was going with you," Rucker said, "but I can't. Grif Miles is chewing his mustache off — but he hasn't got enough horse for this job. You make those Indians take a stand. Move out around them. Hold them, just hold them till we get there! And you better start. They have three or four hours on you. They will be in that sierra tomorrow if you don't get them today!"

They swung into their saddles and followed Jasper Fleming, waving. Martin looked out across the flat, feeling his mouth opened grinning, feeling sweat in the palms of his hands.

The six men rode together at a long fast steady trot, reading the trail as plain as a line of letters on a page. At noon they crossed a dry wash and moved up a wide incline toward the crest of a gentle divide ridging for miles along the breadth of the plain.

"Traveling right smart," Corporal Fleming finally said. "If they ain't stopped someplace for more mule chittlins and a snooze, I figure we got another two-three hours to come up to them — " he looked around. "Best save the wind in these animals till we need it. When we make that rise out there, we'll stop and have us a big look — " he reined suddenly — "*whoa*, Muffin!"

Fleming jumped from his saddle and walked to the horse droppings. He bent down, looked at them, touched one with his finger, walked back to his stirrup, and climbed on.

"Ain't more than a hour old," Fleming said. "We are warmer than I thought. — Como lee goosta?" he asked the Mexicans.

They smiled.

"Leesto?"

"*Muy listos, Señor Cabo!*"

"Brady, tell them we are about to cut off a side of hog in the off house."

"Whee!" Print Ruebush added.

They came up the almost imperceptible tilt of the divide; at the top quite suddenly, they saw over, along the slant westward into an immense shallow dish where, on its other side, the plain broke into a line of hills toward the foot of the Sierra del Lobo.

They stopped to look, with their horses breathing hard. A wind moved along the ridge stirring the spindly stalks of candlewood, bending the gray bunch grass. The riders squinted toward the sun.

"They usually see you before you see them."

"They won't be much for fighting six men armed in the open. When they see us, they will make for the breaks and lay up in the rocks."

"Or scatter and git away — "

"*Ahí están!*" The Mexican named Enrique was excited, pointing.

"Where, man?"

"There!"

"How far?"

"The other side of those thick dots of *amole*, in the low place! Maybe a league. Look exactly below the second knob from the right of Sierra del Lobo — there! Again. There they are!"

"Damn my eyes!" Ruebush said.

"There!" Martin pointed. He saw the faint dots move.

"Goddam," Fleming said. "All right, bubbies! We don't want any paintfaces cutting back around us. Look sharp both sides of the trail!" He spurred. "Stay together — till we see their mind!"

None of the hoofmarks cut away from the trail. For ten minutes Fleming led the horsemen at a run. Then he held up his hand and they slowed to a walk.

"Take a breather. They probably seen dust by now. Time to spread some! Brady, you and a *ranchero* pull out to the right. Print, two of you go left. Me and the other boy will stick this trail. See can we worry them to a stand! Keep in the saddle and keep working up around them — and by God keep your hair!"

Martin turned to Enrique. "*Vámonos!*"

Edging rightward from where Fleming followed the sign, they had hurried more than a mile and were climbing the side of a shallow dip when Martin located the dust hanging over the brush ahead. A bullet whirred from his left and he swerved, hearing the pop of a rifle. He pulled his carbine from its scabbard. There were two more shots, and he yelled to Enrique, "The gang in front — " he pointed to the dust — "come on!" Enrique came, waving his rifle. The horses jumped, stretching into racing stride. They swept wide out, hearing shots crackle from far at their backs where Ruebush and Fleming and the two *rancheros* rode.

Turning along an open space heading into the sun, Martin saw Apaches. They were running away. In the dust and joggle they were hard to count. Narrowing his eyes into the light, Martin understood suddenly that not all the animals bore riders; there were only four horseback Apaches. The others — four — five — six — were loaded pack mules.

The rest of the Indians, Martin thought, the other four sets of horse tracks on that trail — they have dropped back to fight. While these get away. These Apaches running bunched. The way Apaches don't run. Driving pack mules —

"I go to turn them!" he shouted to Enrique. "Keep them in sight! Shoot them when you can! Remember: I wear a hat!" He bent forward giving Lágrimas the spurs.

"*Aiiii —* " Martin talked to the black ears.

He felt the power, with the *ramal* high, with the carbine gripped, with the ground blurred beneath him. "*Aiiii —* " it melted with the gather and stretch of the springing sinewed legs; his eyes glassed in the wind, watching the black forelock fly bringing the wild riders, the galloping whipped mules closer, closer yet.

Horse, I never asked you out like this before — that's enough! Save some.

Don't use it all. You don't need to use it all. Just run now they know you. You taught them and they're turning, they're turning for cover of that rise and we will beat them there. He is going to shoot and he won't hit us! He never could hit us. The Apache is not made that could hit us.

Forty varas short, the dirt puff jumped; the spent ball sank faintly.

Something about those mules, Martin thought, we will shoot us a mule, we will see if —

He moved in, loosing the *ramal* to the pommel, raising the carbine. He cocked the hammer and aimed and shot from his running horse. And missed. An Apache bullet whinged as he slid the carbine lever. "Hu — " he pulled the lever back, aiming. The shot banged and he sucked air through his teeth, seeing the mule's hindquarters wrench and sag. The mule fell.

For a moment of indecision, the four Apaches and the remaining five mules ran on. Then three of the Apaches jerked around as if by command. Martin saw them come for him, shooting. A bullet knocked dirt behind him and Lágrimas sprang frightened. Two shots whistled high. The Apaches ran reloading, spreading out to work him.

"*Our chances, Horse!*"

He turned straight at his nearest enemy and dug a spur. Lágrimas plunged closing; the startled Apache veered exposing his side. Martin fired. The Apache pitched from the horse and hit the ground rolling, done.

Swinging to judge the angle, Martin felt the quick slap and whine at his ear: the ball raked a hole in his hatbrim. He loosed the *ramal* to aim. Another ball whined. He brought the gun up fast in a snap shot that missed as the Apache broke away reloading. Martin slid the lever and shot again. Dust sprayed beyond his target, and he spurred in a turn. When the faster of the two Apaches pointed to fire, Martin jerked low, with his chin at the black mane, swerving. In the instant of the whirr and sharp pop of the shot, he rocked back to check Lágrimas skidding.

"*Hu!*" he barked, raising his gun.

Stopped still, he aimed; the banging flash spurted. Coupled queerly with his sight of the writhing body fallen to the ground, Martin felt the jolting whack at his groin, a stinging daze whish in his face. He opened his batted eyes seeing the splintered groove plowed along the top of his saddle's pommel, seeing the last Apache running, looking back, beating full tilt along the backtrail — away from where the pack mules had been driven.

Martin jumped from his trembling horse. He threw the lever and knelt down, bracing. He squeezed the trigger. The hammer clicked, at the empty chamber.

"*Fool!*" he cried out. Anguished he fumbled at his belt for a load.

He saw the Apache's horse drop sprawling before he heard the shot. There were two more shots. He stood tranced, reloading, hearing the clicks of the sliding brass, hearing the blood pound in his head, hearing his horse's racked breath. Then he saw Enrique's hat, Enrique in the saddle, trotting from the brush. He came carrying in his hand a black tangle of hair held together red at its dangling end.

Enrique bared his teeth, and held up the hair. "Never saw me! Twenty varas away — he was looking back!"

Martin jerked his thumb. "Finish that one on the ground!" His voice croaked. He patted Lágrimas, hearing Enrique's shot. With the reloaded carbine in his hand, he stepped into the stirrup and whirled toward where Enrique stooped.

"You coming?"

Enrique gave his knife a fast wipe, stuffed the two scalps in his saddlebag, climbed on his horse, and caught up with Martin. They found the trail and broke into a run.

A league nearer the Sierra del Lobo, the dots moved in the low brush on the open flat. Against slanting sunlight the dots raised a wisp of shining dust.

"Ahí!" Enrique pointed. "Six!"

Martin pulled his hat tighter, touching at the torn hole in the brim, and let Lágrimas into a rocking gallop.

With the distance closing, the dots grew. Peering into the shine, Martin watched the tallest dot moving at the backs of the other dots. The tallest dot zigzagged driving at the other dots as if to urge them. The tallest dot became a man on a horse. The other dots became mules with packs bobbling. The mules threw their legs in a tired run with the dark lumps on their backs. The man on the horse had something in his hand. He waved it, driving at the mules.

Then the man on the horse had a head on his dark shoulders. He had an Apache head. He had a gun in his hand. He turned his Apache head and he looked back gripping his gun. When he had looked back he struck his horse's flanks with his heels and rode at the mules poking their laggard docks with his gun's barrel.

I am going to kill that Apache, Martin thought. He heard the thought with the wind humming, with the hooves pounding. He knows I am going to kill him.

The Apache whirled suddenly lifting his gun. A puff came from the end of it. Martin heard the whang and crack as he cut in, bent low, gripping with his knees, rushing the Apache who aimed and shot again.

At the split grain of time when the lined sights moving caught the image they sought, Martin Brady crooked his right forefinger an eighth inch more. The gun kicked hurtling its slug through a short yellow spurt of flame. He heard his throat rasp a grunt as the slug struck. The image tumbled. He bore down upon the image, bending a finger around the *ramal*, grabbing the gun into his left hand, drawing the pistol with his right to fire at the stumbling Apache by the fallen horse. He saw the hit thud. He saw the Apache jerk and twist dropping. He fired again. Reining twenty feet from the thrashing Apache head, he sent a shot knocking through its skull.

In the silence, Enrique shouted.

Martin looked up. "Bring the mules!" He motioned. Enrique turned after them.

Martin licked his teeth, tasting gunsmoke. He looked down again, at the strangely boneless lump lying still, at the wet red splotch in the small of its back, at the sprawled brown naked legs soiled with gray scuff, at the glistering ooze from the black mat of hair on the head face down in the dirt. He looked at it stirred with the intent curiosity a man feels for the alien world and life and way of an enemy in the field. The greasy green headband was still around the hair, awry. He looked over at the horse with its neck stretched thin, with red running from its yellow teeth. He looked at the Sharps rifle with its breech flung open on the ground.

He was suddenly sick sweating at the eyes; he put his guns away and slipped from the saddle. Standing shaky with his chin on the saddle seat, with both his hands around the splintered pommel, he leaned against Lágrimas hearing the quick squeak of the leathers moving with the labored rise and fall of the horse's winded breath. Then Martin retched, dry. He shook his head swallowing the sour burn in his gullet, and his hands shook as he turned again to his horse to pat the hot sweated hide.

An instinct for an uncaught sound, an uncaught motion, brought him alert. In the same instant he saw the riders, he saw they wore hats and he saw there were only three. Then he saw there were two men, two hats, bobbling on one horse, on Print Ruebush's horse. When he could see their faces, he could see them grinning, Ruebush and Fleming on the same horse, and the two Mexicans. One of the Mexicans carried a saddle and bridle bundled across his pommel.

Print Ruebush shouted. "You git them all?"

Martin nodded and turned to look into the sun, for Enrique. He saw him, herding the five mules.

The riders got down with their spurs clinking. Martin walked to them. He found himself shaking hands with them, as if they had been away a long time.

"Meet the walking committee," Ruebush said.

Fleming grinned, putting down his saddle and bridle and rifle by a soapweed. "Shot old Muffin right out from under! And you can call me Sugar if that long-legged Indian son of a bitch didn't look like business when he jumped with that butcher knife! Brady, Print Ruebush saved my little goozle. Thank ye, Print!"

"Jasper you are always welcome!"

Martin looked at the two grinning *rancheros*. "How did it go?"

"It went like a combat, *eeho!* A combat authentic enough! And you?"

"Like a stake race, *eeho!* With mules."

Fleming stood scratching his seat. "Rucker put the valuation paper at a hundred and sixty dollars for old Muffin. Goddam I hope I don't have to go to the Supreme Court and Cumpt-roller of Texas — "

"Just a nice walk from here to the Supreme — "

"Walk, my ass! I'll climb me one of them skimshanked Apache jinnies. Say Brady what are them mules carrying?"

"I don't know. I left one dead back there, but I didn't have time to look."

"We seen it. We didn't look neither. We seen three dead paint-faces too. And this one here makes four. And added to our god-dam four makes goddam eight!"

"Brady," Print said, "I seen you and the other feller light out like blacktail bucks right at the start. You come a good six miles fogging!"

"I had to use my horse pretty hard. I hated to."

"You done the job, Brady," Fleming said, "you done just right! I will say this: they run, but they was the least skulking Indians I ever heard of. They was goddam pecky people! Brady, holler to that cowboy to flip his rope on one of those mules. Let's look in them packsacks."

"Brady, listen to him try to git somebody to rope him a mount — "

"Shit. I want to see what them Indians were so crazy about. Them mules, they look just about peetered."

"Enrique! Rope one! To see what he carries!"

The mule submitted with a weary lack of interest. When the two heavy rawhide *alforjas* were lifted from the crosses of the pack saddle and lowered to the ground, Fleming pulled the dirty wadding from the top of one of them, and looked inside.

"I'll be dipped in dung!"

It was an unopened wooden thousand-round box plainly stenciled .45 CAL. U.S. SPRINGFIELD (.45–70). The other *alforja* held a tow sack of loose .52 rimfires for Spencer repeaters.

"You don't reckon, do you — unload them all, bubbies! Let's look!"

One of the *rancheros* touched Martin on the arm. "*Ahí vienen!*" He pointed up the backtrail.

"Here they all come!" Martin said, seeing the dust. He went to tie Lágrimas to a bush. The horse's ears pointed at the crowd of riders.

You all right? Martin patted at the black neck. Did you catch your wind?

"Wait till Rucker sees this!" Fleming whooped. "All cattridges!"

Rucker and Ocampo came loping, side by side.

"Boys — " the smile showed in the captain's beard — "you didn't save me a shot!"

"Captain, we told them to wait and they wouldn't — "

"Cap!" Fleming bellowed from the line of *alforjas*. "Looka here! Goddam we got old Fuego's whole ammunition train!"

Rucker and Ocampo jumped from their horses. Enrique and the other two *rancheros* were all talking to Ocampo at once.

"Well sir!" Rucker said.

"Cap, it looks like twelve or fourteen thousand rounds!"

"More! That dead mule back there," Rucker said, "we picked up about twenty-five hundred rounds of .40s and .50s. I thought that was the lot! But look at this — Don Juan — "

"*Un triunfo, mi Capitán!*"

The rangers and *rancheros* from the column were off their horses, crowding around.

"Now we know," Rucker said, "why Fuego has been holed up in the Sierra del Lobo — by George, that old Indian has been waiting for something! We have drawn his teeth, we have drawn his teeth!"

"It took a sight of dirty work to get all this together, Captain!"

"It has come from somewhere down the river. I would like to meet the degenerates that trade with Apaches. But never mind. We got it now. Boys, I believe we are going to get Fuego! If he's still in that sierra tomorrow, we are going to get him. Fleming, did you let any Indians get away to carry word?"

"Eight horse tracks: eight dead Apaches. Six mule tracks: one dead mule and five alive."

"I saw your horse, Fleming, back there."

"Hundred and sixty dollars, Captain!"

"I'll see you get it. Who headed off these mules?"

"I believe Brady spent a little time at the 2:40 gait."

Martin felt the pale eyes. "What's the matter with your hat, Brady?" The smile was showing.

"It got a hole in it."

"Everybody else all right?"

"All but old Muffin," Fleming said. "And the paintfaces. They are in poor shape."

"Let's look at this one over here."

"He might be the boss," Martin said. "The way he did."

"Let's look at him."

Rucker reached down and rolled the body over, exposing the face.

"Ugly, ain't he — "

"*Magues!*" said Don Juan Ocampo, "*hijo de la chingada, Magues!*"

Martin looked down at Magues.

"Tell the captain!" Ocampo said, "I know this face! I saw it at Potrero! At the Laguna Elena!"

Martin heard Grif Miles' calm voice saying. "That's Magues. I know him from the reservation at Stafford. That is him for sure. And I didn't get to do it! Brady, I am going to buy you a cigar anyway."

"Did you scalp him too, Brady?"

Martin looked around, at Enrique.

"In my saddlebag," Enrique smiled.

"Listen," Ocampo was beaming, "we do not bother ourselves with just hair! We take the head! The head of Magues and all these cartridges — *tck* — what an enchantment for the authorities tomorrow at Ojo del Lobo! Enrique, the knife is sharp?"

"Eh Don Juan, first we find a sack — "

Martin saw that John Rucker understood a good deal of Spanish. "Grif," the captain called, "mount the outfit — let's prepare to march. We ought to move along. You better have some of the boys reload the loot on the mules and fix something for Fleming to ride. Brady, ask Don Juan what he has in mind now for camp — the sun is not an hour high."

"Don Juan says there is a spring by some little white oaks the other side of those hills — " Martin saw Enrique coming with the sack. "Captain, I believe I will go and get ready to move."

Wind blew the dust the many hooves churned along the shadows as the riders moved toward the hills. The wind was cold. The sun went down behind the Sierra del Lobo.

Martin rode tired, thirsty. He rode a tired and thirsty horse. He rode wordless in the trotting jog of the column feeling pieces of his life lock with the image of a tall dot driving dots too slow on a lonely flat while a black horse came. The tall dot Magues. Magues, and Santiago Santos and Bavinuchi. Magues, and Starke Colton and the troop. Magues, and Martin Brady and — he pulled his pistol from its holster, to look. He had not reloaded. Working the ejector rod, he watched the empties falling past his stirrup and dropping in the dirt. There was blue paint mixed with blood above the eyes, red paint mixed with sand grains on the chin pushed out like brown rock under the mouth slit, yellow paint in a line smeared across the cheekbones, across the blunt nose. It looked down the many rifle barrels, it turned the many knives in flesh, it hung a meat hook into screaming soft nakedness. It bobbled dead in a stinking sack on a mule. Magues. Martin turned the cylinder sliding cartridges into the empty holes and slipped the gun into its leather.

At a fold of hill by scrub oaks the riders made camp in cold and windy dark. When the messes had filled their buckets at the springhead and the men had drunk, the horses were led to the meagre water. Lágrimas drank long, while fires sprang flickering. By a tree where dry grass rustled, Martin tethered the stallion away from the horse camp. He unbridled and unsaddled and rubbed down the sweat-caked back. He hung the *morral* of corn with the cord behind the black ears. He listened for a while to the steady muffled munching before he took the tortillas and dried goat meat and coffee cup in the sack from his saddlebag and moved to the fire.

"My bunky," Print Ruebush said. "With Mexkin eats."

"I traded for it. I guess I like it better than soft bread and that bacon when I ride." He pierced the meat on a stick he found, and held it to the fire.

"My idy of a ration tonight would be a side of calf ribs and a can of tomatoes. Anyway, we got coffee. You beat as I am?"

"I could sleep standing up."

Gusts of wind blew sparks from the fire as they chewed meat and drank scalding coffee.

"I got some corn-shuck smokes here," Print said. "You want one before we take to the blanket?"

John Rucker came out of the darkness to their fire while they squatted smoking.

"Captain, how about a cup of coffee grounds with us?"

"Thank you, no. I just wanted to see everybody before turning in. We are going to be on the move two hours before sun and be at that meeting place by noon tomorrow."

"Captain, who all are we meeting?"

"Stoker for sure. And whatever Mexicans show up. Boys, I guess you know I'm proud. It may well be that in denying Fuego his ammunition you have put his back to the wall! Brady, I have been thinking how your horse paid off this afternoon for all the extra trouble that stud puts on you. It has reminded me: I forgot to give you a message from Doctor Stovall. I saw him the evening before we left. He wanted me to tell you that his mare foaled."

"She did?"

"A dandy bay filly like the dam."

"Oh."

"I forgot to tell you about it. Well. Get some rest for tomorrow. We might see Fuego!" The captain walked away.

Martin threw the corn-shuck butt in the coals and rose to his feet. "Goodnight, Print."

"Sleep tight."

He walked out into the dark, and took the *morral* off Lágrimas' nose.

You sired a bay mare, Horse. I wish it had been like you.

He arranged his saddle and guns, and lay down in his blanket and took off his hat. He had to anchor it with a rock. Hearing the wind, hearing the horse move grazing in the brittle grass, he closed his eyes. In the thoughtless deep of his weariness, sleep found him.

He awoke feeling the turn of the stars toward morning and got to his numbed feet shivering, stretching to ease the stiffness from his legs, his back, standing with the blanket flapping from his shoulders, with the sweatband of his hat cold on his forehead, with grit in his eyes. He went to the mess bucket for a drink, hearing the jing of his spurs.

In the coldest time of the darkest hour before the morning star, Grif Miles called "Rise and shine and ready to ride!" The camp stirred with the sound of awakening, the voices, the coughs, the moving hooves, as the last guard rode in. The rangers stood by their humpy horses answering roll call in the dark, hearing the *rancheros* preparing to march. The column moved, hungry, sleepy on the cold leather of the saddle seats. The van, the flankers, the rear guard, fanned out.

A ghost of daybreak brushed at their backs. Its glow carved the shape of Sierra del Lobo against the sky. The light brightening cast suddenly from the east a red of day like a blood of battle on the stones. The riders moved toward the mountain with their long shadows before them.

"He is up there somewhere, boys."

"Or running for Sonora."

"He is up there. He is waiting for Magues and the mules. He is anxious."

"Too windy for signal smokes."

"*Y la plaza fuerte?*"

"It is on the other side of the highest point," Martin heard the *ranchero* say. "I was there. Last November when we went with Don Juan, after the butchery of the party from Potrero. The Apaches were not there. They were gone, and we made camp. The summit of the world! You can see the pass at Del Norte and east to the Río Bravo, west to Sonora, south to the Sierra Mojina at Carmen! Up there a water pours from high rocks into a pool — enough for hundreds of animals, for all the Indians that live! We found rawhide pony shoes and rotten moccasins and saddles and two broken Winchestays rusted and a mountain of bones, of mule, of horse, the *cabrones* had eaten!"

Shadows shortened, swinging sideward from the dusty hooves as the hours moved and the column turned north along the breaks around the end of Sierra del Lobo.

"You see the notch? There it is!"

It looked pale, high, without substance, against a sky gone colorless with dust.

Martin saw the *ranchero* of the vanguard come riding in with the stranger. It was a stranger with a big gray hat, a red chin string, a Remington, a long knife, a horse that bore upon its hip the brand of Valdepeñas. Martin did not know the stranger's face; he watched it. The column halted. The stranger tipped the gray hat to the riders leading the column, and spoke to them. Too far back, Martin could not hear the words. He saw Rucker turn and talk to Grif Miles. Then the captain and Ocampo and the stranger spurred. They loped out of sight over a ridge. The column resumed its march.

"What's going on, Grif?"

"That was an outpost from the bunch we are meeting. The captain and Don Juan have gone ahead to meet some highup general."

"He say anything about Fuego, up there?"

"I don't know."

And I don't know, Martin thought, I don't know. How it is going to be.

Beyond a swathe of tangled tracks, the column came out upon a road. It led along winding wheelmarks and hoofprints over a hill to the meeting place.

Huddled in the windy glare on the bank of a gravel wash, facing the loom of the sierra, Ojo del Lobo was a desolate adobe square and big corral, a dirt tank of water, and salt cedars with gray-leafed plumes swaying in the wind. Men and horses moved by the walls, by the unhitched carts and wagons, by the livestock in the leeward corners of the corral. At the other side of the water stood a separate camp, with a picket line and a single tent. Above it a red and white swallowtail banner, the guidon of a troop of United States cavalry, whipped out straight and small in the wind.

A trooper with a black face trotted out to the column as it neared the walls.

"Rangers!" the trooper called, holding up his arm. "Your captain sent me. You is to make your camp there beyond the troop!" The rangers halted, gathering around; Ocampo's *rancheros* moved on, toward the building by the corral.

"Camp?" Grif Miles said to the trooper. "I thought we were scouting for Fuego."

"Yassuh. We waiting. They got Fuego up there in them rocks, surrounded."

"Surrounded by who?"

"Mexkins."

"They couldn't surround a pile of corn shucks with a blanket."

"*Ffff!* Anyway, that's the claim. Major and your captain and our interpreter the packer name of Luna, is talking with the Mexkin muckymucks over there in that house."

"When did you get here?"

"Lass night."

"You run any sign on the way down?"

"Just marched. You all see anything?"

"We killed eight. Including Magues."

"Huh? Ma — You mean old Magoosh?"

"Fuego's right bower."

"Lord God, that's the one tangled with L Troop and Major Colton! You really kill him?"

"His head is in that sack over there."

"*Naw!* Too bad L Troop ain't here to see that! Ho! Is you giving me the taffy, Mr. Ranger?"

"Go on over and look. Go on!"

"No thank you no thank you!"

"What troop is this?"

"K Troop suh."

"You didn't bring along Sergeant Sutton?"

"Old Tobe probly laying in barracks about now. Eating commissary ham and pink butter and canned peaches."

"I see you got Apache Scouts in camp."

"Fifty-six Cheericows! The Mexkins don't like it. Major is having a little go with the muckymucks about Cheericows. I'll tell you something — the Mexkins might be right! Cheericows looks to me just like the kind we shoots at — "

"*All right, boys!*" John Rucker came riding, motioning with his arm. "This way!"

When they had watered at the tank and tied their horses by the trees tossing in the wind, the captain called his men together.

"There is a general here named Castro, the brother of the governor." Rucker's voice sounded dry. His mouth was a thin straight line in his beard. "Castro has a force of about four hundred men, cavalry and infantry, spread out up there on the mountain. He says Fuego is cut off from escape. Castro is waiting for a report on the envelopment, and when he gets it he intends to go up that mountain and join his men in the assault. He says Fuego's whole band is trapped, maybe a hundred fighting bucks and twice as many squaws and children. It sounds like the thing we have been trying to come at ever since Company E took station at Puerto!" Rucker looked at his men.

"The general cracked about a forty cent smile, and shook Don Juan's hand, and mine, over the capture of the ammunition and the killing of Magues. Right now, we are invited to draw a ration of fresh beef — the general has had cattle driven up here from his ranch at Carmen. We'll all have that breakfast we missed this morning, while we wait on the general's orders." Rucker's eyes went to Martin's face, and paused there. "Remember. We are not on our own ground. Stay to yourselves and avoid trouble. We are here by courtesy of the Mexican authorities and we conduct ourselves accordingly."

Martin walked with half a dozen rangers past the rickety wagons to the wall of the beef corral. At the sagging scaffold where butchered meat hung on a long and crooked crosspiece, there were no gray hats nor red chin strings in sight. Ragged teamsters, ox drivers, vaqueros, lounged in corners away from the wind; Ocampo's *rancheros* were crowding at the scaffold, cutting their rations. As Martin waited his turn, Enrique came by.

"Good, eh?"

"Very good."

"We eat, and then we move!" Enrique indicated the Sierra del Lobo with a sweep of his arm. "This time, *Apaches!*"

"What do they say of the troops up there?"

"Plenty! Cavalry with the commander Verdugo! Infantry of Castro Indians that carry a gun and a knife and a bag of *pinole* and fight like devils! There are even some of the governor's new *Rurales*. I saw one that I knew — he was leaving with a message from the general to El Verdugo on the sierra. That *Rural* is a rare type, they call him Green Eyes. I once sold him a horse. He speaks your English well — "

"Come on, Brady — cut your meat!"

"Here's Ruebush's ribs he was talking about."

"It has been some time since they was calf's ribs."

"Come with plenty of covering don't it, bubbies?"

"That's just flavoring."

"Goddam I'll fight the country but I hate to eat it."

"This sand will give you a little grit for a mountain climb, Jasper."

As Martin turned with meat in his hand, he saw a brown face under a crimped straw hat with a frayed brim. It was a familiar face.

"*Qué hubo!*" said the mouth in the brown face.

"El Carmen!" Martin said. "How does it go?"

"Well enough. A little dust this morning."

"You drove a haycart. For a sergeant of forage named Casas — "

The brown face grinned. "Your twin. He once gave me sotol — "

"Is Casas up there?"

"No señor. We have now a sergeant of forage who is pure coyote."

"What happened to Casas?"

"They say he returned to Valdepeñas. His father died — "

"Hey, Brady, quit the hymolligating — let's go! Them's orders!"

Old Mateo, not blind any more. Diego gone back. Rascón on the sierra. That is a pair, Rascón and Verdugo. But old Mateo, old Mateo. The sorrow of my Mexico. I have seen it. My son, pour me one cup —

"What's the matter, bunky?"

"Nothing. Nothing's the matter."

The ranger messes broiled and ate their gritty beef in the wind. They sat by their line of horses, drinking coffee in the gritty shade of thin salt cedars, waiting.

Old Mateo, Martin kept thinking, watching the wind whip ashes from the fire. Old Mateo. The last night at Valdepeñas listening to the music. And I hear it. With meat in my mouth, smelling the smoke —

A black trooper walked into camp.

"Is they a Mr. Brady?"

"Right here."

"Major Stoker's compliments. Him and your captain wants to see you. If you will come with me, over at the troop."

Martin looked at Grif Miles.

"Go ahead. Sounds like Rucker wants you."

He walked with the trooper in the blowing sand. Past the horses on the neat picket line, through clusters of black men with black hats pulled tight against the wind, he saw the Chiricahuas with their Springfields propped against the brush. The wind blew their long Apache hair as they eyed him. They wore dirty wool army blouses, number tags around their necks, issue cartridge belts with brass buckles shining US big on their bellies. Some of them wore troopers' gauntlets and pistols. All of them woke peak-toed moccasins and greasy wraps of rawhide leggins half way to their knees. The queer hang of white man's trappings gave the Apache bodies, the wild Apache faces, a strange savagery.

The stained tent shook and billowed with wind as Martin walked to its opened flap.

"Here is Mr. Brady," said the trooper.

"Come in!"

In the luminous half light under the canvas, Martin saw the

lean face and hawk eyes, the dark mustaches and pointed goatee, the thick swag of dark hair across the forehead, the rough shirt with the shoulder straps dulled dusty, the faded yellow stripes on the breeches, the worn black boots, the small spurs. He saw the hand extended. It was a hard hand.

"It took a good long time to meet you, Brady," Stoker said. "Glad to know you! Sit down on that saddle over there. Have a smoke?"

John Rucker sat on a patched camp stool by the major. "We were talking, sitting, waiting for that Mexican general," Rucker said. "Major mentioned he never had got to meet you. So I sent for you."

"I wanted to meet you ever since you came in with L Troop and Colton," Stoker said. "Captain Rucker tells me now that you killed Magues!"

"I didn't know it was him when I did it," Martin said. "He is sure dead — "

Stoker smiled. "Big Tobe Sutton told me how you helped L Troop, how you took care of Colton. I know what you did."

"Major, I didn't do much."

"At the Academy, we called him Mule. Mule Colton. He was all right. And he was spared a damned sorry mess when he got home to Jefflin. — Enough of that!" Stoker puffed on his raveled stogie. The wind rumbled at the tent canvas and grabbed the tobacco smoke whirling. "If we can just get at the old he-wolf up there on the Wolf Mountain this afternoon — "

"Brady," Rucker said. "Did you see anybody you knew when you went to draw your ration?"

"I recognized an ox driver from El Carmen."

"You used to work for that general, didn't you?"

"I worked for his brother."

"The general is not the pleasantest man I ever met."

"I better tell you while I have a chance that Abrán Rascón is up there on that mountain. He is one of the governor's *Rurales*. I may have trouble with — "

A trooper came to the tent flap. "Major! Here is — "

Martin saw the gray hat. He heard the words in Spanish.

"What does he say, Brady?"

"He says General Castro wishes to see Major Stoker and Captain Rucker."

Stoker was on his feet. "*That's* what we're waiting for! Call that packer Luna! Tell Lieutenant Heath! Captain, let's go!"

"Report to camp, Brady," Rucker said. "I'll be there directly. Tell the boys to be ready to move up that hill!"

As Martin came around the end of the cavalry picket line he almost bumped Grif Miles. "Brady — " Miles talked through his teeth — "coming to find you! Where's captain?"

"Gone with Stoker to see about orders — what's the matter?"

"A bunch of fancy-dans in gray rigs had the gall to come into camp just now, to take your horse. — Don't worry, the horse is there. What I could understand, they claimed that horse was stolen. I told the nervy bastards to get out before they got cut in two. I've got the boys ready and waiting for a new Mexican War. But I'd like to know. What in hell is this? Huh?"

"I'll tell you what in hell is this — " Martin swallowed. "At one time I carried a pistol for the man who is now governor of Chihuahua. I worked for him. He gave me that black horse. I don't deserve any good for what I done in those days. I don't claim any. I never did like it, but I did it. To eat. Last spring I went to Puerto. Rucker talked to me. Since then I have been trying to do right. Last summer when the governor of Chihuahua tried to get me to do a piece of his dirty work, I didn't do it. I left the country. He is gunning for me ever since, making up charges, any charges, to get me. I guess he says now I stole the horse. Look here. The way things have been with me — it seems like I — spend my time asking people if they believe me. Now is a goddamned good time to tell me what you believe! If you and the boys mistrust me I got no business in the outfit! I will ride right now, if you say. That's what in hell I — "

"Cool down and listen to me — I never had reasonable doubt of anything you ever told." Grif Miles squinted one eye. "Except that little Mexican music." The blowing dust had caught in his eyebrows and mustache like pale fur. "Listen. I don't sit in any judgment seat. You suit me fine. You suit Company E fine. You did live too long across the river. But you don't any more! Now get your big old country ass up there with the boys and be ready to kill the next saddle-colored son of a bitch that tries to touch your horse."

The rangers stood by the horses and the wind-tossed gray trees, with their rifles ready in their hands. They came grinning toward Martin.

"We pretty near splattered some sour chili, Brady!"

"I wish I had been here. I would of — "

"Look yonder!" Jasper Fleming pointed. "Look! Wouldn't you swear it was Brady's?"

A company of horsemen trotted across the gravel of the wash, toward Sierra del Lobo. Their leader rode a black horse. Sunlight glinted from the gold on the horse's saddle, the gold on the leader's hat, his thighs. He led his company into the brush, into the dust toward the mountain.

"General Castro's horse," Martin said. "And General Castro."

A big hat came galloping from beyond the trees. Martin's hand touched at his gun as he jumped for Lágrimas. The big hat was Don Juan Ocampo's hat. Don Juan shouted as he came into camp.

"What's he saying?"

"He's asking for captain — "

"A moment, Don Juan — " In the confusion, Martin saw John Rucker coming. As the captain approached, Ocampo took off his hat. He leaned from his saddle, offering his hand. "*Mi capitán!*" Ocampo said. He turned to Martin and spoke. "You tell my captain he deserves better! Tell him he deserves to share the victory on that mountain! Tell him it is without justice, and I know it! Tell him I have no remedy. Tell him I am sorry. Tell him I am grateful for all he has done. Tell him I am always at his orders!" Ocampo saluted. He spurred away to his column of *rancheros* riding toward the mountain.

"Captain, what — "

The rangers looked up, at John Rucker's rigid face. Only the black beard and the horse's mane and tail moved, blowing in the wind.

"The last time I used an oath was at Chickamauga when my right folded," Rucker said. "Stoker and I have been ordered off Mexican soil. We won't get our chance at a showdown scrap with Fuego. You have come a long way for that chance. I'm sorry that you won't get it, that I won't get it. As near as I can recall the words of the interpreter, this is what General Castro told Major Stoker and me a few moments ago: the Apaches are now entirely contained by the Mexican forces and will be quickly destroyed; the general could not and would not be responsible for the safety of the Chiricahua Scouts whom he and his people viewed with distrust as treacherous Apaches; it was inadvisable to lead United States forces any deeper into the sovereign State of Chihuahua; in the circumstances, he officially requested the immediate withdrawal of American units to their own territory. With his thanks."

"*Cap!* Let's go cut that gold-plated son of a bitch to size!"

The smile almost showed in the beard. "This is Mexico, Corporal. They have every right to order us out. Boys, there is nothing for us to do but obey orders, pack up, and vamoose. Set your guard for the march. We will head for the stage road, north to the Tinajas fork, then make for the river. Stoker is going his own way."

"The sooner I git the dirt of this place out of my teeth, the better."

"That ain't dirt. That's gristle."

"We come a long way, for a beef ration."

"Captain," Martin said, "while I was at the tent, Castro sent men to see if they could bluff us out of my horse. They come claiming I stoled that horse. You know I didn't. But you know that I did make a mistake coming here. Just being here, it was me that ruined things for you. It's my fault — "

"No, Brady — the ill-feeling is a good deal bigger than any one man. You might as well cheer up. I am glad that I brought you. As far as missing a chance at Fuego is concerned — we may see him yet! He isn't caught yet, not yet. As far as Castro is concerned, I have you to thank for a pleasing last word with that — fine gentleman. After the general had spoken his piece and just before he climbed on his horse, he looked at me and said there was a man in my company wanted for robbery and murder in Mexico. I looked at him and said there was a scoundrel in his company wanted for robbery and murder in the United States and did he wish to discuss that. He didn't."

CHAPTER XXVI

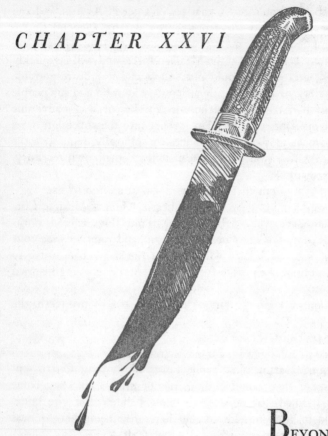

Beyond the seep of the brackish water at Lucero, past the high and windy fork of the road at the Tinajas and the defile between the broken mesas of the Soledad, the dry slope of the world bent down along bare ridges of sand and winding draws through a gray dust north to the valley of the river, to the shape of the pass, to another country. Moving toward them Martin Brady rode his guard alone in the emptiness, in the quietness.

As he came climbing a rise in sight of the jogging horseback rangers and the mules a quarter of a mile to his left, he saw the riders of the rear guard closing. Wondering why, wondering what word, what warning they brought to the captain at the head of the file, Martin watched. He saw the file halt and break, gathering, dismounting, around the riders from the rear. He heard the three quick shots, the signal recalling all outriders. It was peculiar. He reined leftward, spurring to a run, turning his eyes for sign of dust and movement on the backtrail, seeing only the sun-glare, the afternoon shadow, silent, unmoving. When he neared the gathered rangers, he heard Print Ruebush yell, "*A man from Ocampo —* " The other outriders were loping in, asking.

Ocampo's *ranchero* stood with John Rucker looking at a piece of paper. Martin jumped down from his saddle. The captain glanced toward him.

"Brady, will you read this exactly, please?"

"*Bredi!*" the *ranchero* said. "*Ya los indios son completamente reducidos, hombre!*"

"*No me dígas, hombre!*" Martin looked at the spidery penciling on the roughly torn, wrinkled piece of paper. It was hard to read. It was signed with a large elaborate rubric. He studied it. "Captain," Martin said, "listen. Written in the stronghold of the Sierra del Lobo on the field of battle. The twenty-first of March. Now the head of Fuego is in the same most excellent condition as the head of Magues. It will be a — something — on a pole in the Plaza of Chihuahua. Complete triumph. Not a brute Apache remains alive. The women and children captured will be paraded in chains to the Capital. The bearer of this, Narciso Chávez — "

"*Su seguro servidor —* " the *ranchero* smiled.

"Narciso Chávez," Martin went on, "will supply details. He carries the news with all haste to our people along the Río Bravo. A new — it says *epoca*, Captain, it means a new time — "

"Epoch, a new epoch," Rucker said. "Go on."

"A new — *epoca* now for both our countries. I am, my captain, with all gratitude for your help in the final victory, your always attentive and faithful servant Juan Ocampo."

Narciso Chávez stood grinning while the rangers looked at each other in the silence.

"Captain — " a ranger said, finally. "You believe it?"

"Yes. I am feeling it sink in. I believe it. I had come to believe Castro wouldn't do it, that he couldn't do it. Now by George he did it!"

Martin handed the paper to Rucker.

"The gold embroidery fooled me," Rucker said. "The general fooled me. He fooled Stoker. He used us both as beaters for his game. When he got the bear in the trap, he did his own killing and skinning and made right certain who got the meat!"

Grif Miles spit in the dirt. "The bear was a hell of a ways from a trap until he lost his fifteen thousand rounds of ammunition. And I didn't get a shot. Not one shot." He spit again.

In the babble of voices, Narciso Chávez spoke to Martin. "I do not understand these people. They do not rejoice!"

"Brady," Rucker said, "get some of those details."

"Señor Chávez," Martin said, "these people wanted to fight. Tell us about the battle."

"It was like this. We made the assault at the hour of dawn. Without horses. The infantry of Castro moved first. We followed. The Apaches fired very little. Then, near the summit there was heavy fire, very heavy! When we came into the high place, and we shot from the cover of the rocks, the Apaches moved behind a ledge. The commander Verdugo led a charge. Blood! Fuego fell with the knife in his hand. His people, all enclosed, had panic. They ran. In one more hour it was done, with women and children screaming in a cave. We took a hundred of them alive. All the rest?" Narciso Chávez crooked his brown trigger finger. "*Dead!*"

"And you? You lost many?"

"Not a volunteer! A few cavalry. Many Castro Indians of infantry — "

"El Verdugo?"

"A hero very alive!"

"You don't know how many Castro lost?"

"No, señor. When it was quiet, Don Juan wrote the express, and sent me north!"

"How did you find us?"

"I passed the black cavalry on the stage road. They told me you took the Tinajas fork, and I rode!"

"Will you join us now? Our camp is yours."

"Thank you. I ride straight for my ranch at Rosario. With a fresh horse I will take the news north, up the river, to Del Norte."

They watched Narciso Chávez, the bearer of tidings, move east, away from the sun.

"Shall we have some coffee, boys?"

The last of the brackish water from Lucero boiled with the last of the coffee from the mess sacks. In the bright light slanting from the west, the fire licked pale around the two blackened pots; a fragrance smoked from the dented spouts. The rangers squatted holding battered cups from dust-caked saddlebags. The horses and mules stood quiet in the greasewood brush, pulling mouthfuls of dry grass. A sigh of wind moved across the silence, bending the flames, the gray rag of smoke from the fire.

"Seems different, someway," a ranger said. "With old Fuego a good Indian."

"Kind of quiet."

"Don Juan was right," John Rucker said, "about that *epoca* business. The Apaches gone. The railroads here. It will be different, all right enough. Different for us all. It will be a different country — " he sipped his coffee, looking at the spent fire.

"Captain," Print Ruebush said, "you remember when little Barney took the old rooster Rebel Red and sneaked him across the river to the rooster fights at the Guadalupey fiesta? And how your friend the Heffy Politico of Del Norte come bringing Barney home by the ear, and the rooster without a scratch, without a fight? Damn if I don't feel like Barney, or the rooster, one. The wind kind of missing from my sails. Coming home from Mexico without a scrap — "

"Print," the captain said, "at least you won't get a whaling with my razor strap — " He tossed the grounds from his cup, and wiped his beard. "We ought to make the river before midnight, boys. I suppose this may be our last fire in the *republica*. Our last scout in Mexico. Our scouts in Mexico will probably be to the city hall in Del Norte, with extradition papers for cow thieves and bunko men. Let's move! Fuego's gone, but we'll move with our guard posted just the same in our marching order. Since we came through that Soledad gap I have been seeing deer sign. You outriders keep your eyes peeled. See if you can't bring in something for that breakfast we have on the other side of the river — "

Far out on the flank, Martin rode alone with Lágrimas. The quietness was huge, huge as the land outspread to the rim of the sky. The four black hooves beat a quiet cadence in the quietness, muffled along the soft sand, clacking over rocky screes, rustling dusty brush. Shadow grew long and blue through the quietness. Dim in the north Mount Jefflin stood touched with a late light like burnished silver.

Last scout in Mexico, Lágrimas, last scout where we rode like this so long, you and me alone. We are leaving it. The only reason we feel bad about it is because it is gone. We wouldn't want it back, would we? Ah black horse there is something about Mexico! It was more than half our life. The music old Mateo —

It came fast as the flash of the powder at the Arroyo Varas, the bullet's *thwack*, the sickening give, the sound of the shot, the headlong hurl with the scream of the struck horse, the smash on the ground. Dazed for a spinning quick instant, knocked flat Martin saw light, saw blood splashing from the horse's black mouth.

A remembered wild image pierced through the rage along the living flash in Martin's skull, along the unthought grip of his hand on the gun at his hip: don't move like Magues moved you lie still lie still you play dead wait wait *wait*.

Hearing the hooves come *wait wait wait* watching where they came, he gathered himself. *Now:* he whipped ready — it brought a slashing whap and flat crack of sound. Belly to the dirt with the upright stub of the sight notched black on the high shape rattling at him in the flapping curtain of his rage he felt the bang kick solid in his two braced hands. He saw the high shape topple; the horse reared, swerving from it.

He raised up sending the solid bang again. Then he jumped. He jumped hot at the shape on the ground. He jumped to kick, grapple, rend; he heard the hack of his own breath, the beat of his own feet. The shape twitched and went stiff in the quiet. The green eyes were round and wide, staring up at him. The puckered great scar was pale along the jaw, up the cheek.

He poked his gun to its holster and yanked the knife from his belt. Clenching hair to hold the head firm to the ground, he plunged the knife into the flesh of the throat. He twisted the blade to rip the gash wide, feeling the steel point scrape turning on the hard bone deep in the soft welling pour of red. When it was done, he wiped the knife with a cleansing jab into the dirt.

Then he sheathed the knife and walked the blurred world to the black horse. He found Lágrimas dead with a blurred gout of blood soaking to the ground from the blurred hole crimson by the cinch strap.

"*Brady!*" Print Ruebush slipped from his saddle and jumped to Martin Brady's side. "God, good God — " John Rucker and Grif Miles both came running.

The three men saw Martin Brady's face, and they looked away. They walked away. They left him.

They came back to him standing by his horse. He looked at them, and looked again at the horse, and wiped at the blur with his sleeve. In the quiet Print Ruebush had a look on his face as if a young eagle could cry; he put his hand on Martin Brady's shoulder, and patted it.

John Rucker cleared his throat. "I see you got Rascón," the captain said.

"Yes sir."

"A damn poor trade," Grif Miles said, "for the black horse — "

"Grif," the captain said, "bring up Rascón's horse. For Brady to ride. Print, get Brady's saddle off for him."

"Let it go," Martin Brady said.

"What?"

"I'll walk. I won't ride that other horse. Never. Let it go. Let it go back, let it go tell them — "

"You ain't walking, Brady. We will see to that."

"Print. Leave the saddle. It belongs to my horse. If I could, I would dig a grave. I would bury that horse and his saddle. Leave everything with him. It's his. Everything I had in Mexico. Leave it with him. The saddlebags too. Everything."

"Everything but the saddle gun. You have to take that."

Good-by Lágrimas.

"Brady. Here. Git up behind me."

"Let's move toward the river, Brady."

You know I will be afoot now. You know that. Leaving you I will be afoot for the rest of my life.

A wind came growing in the dark, pelting grit along the ridges. It cried down in gusts from great space, from beyond the pass.

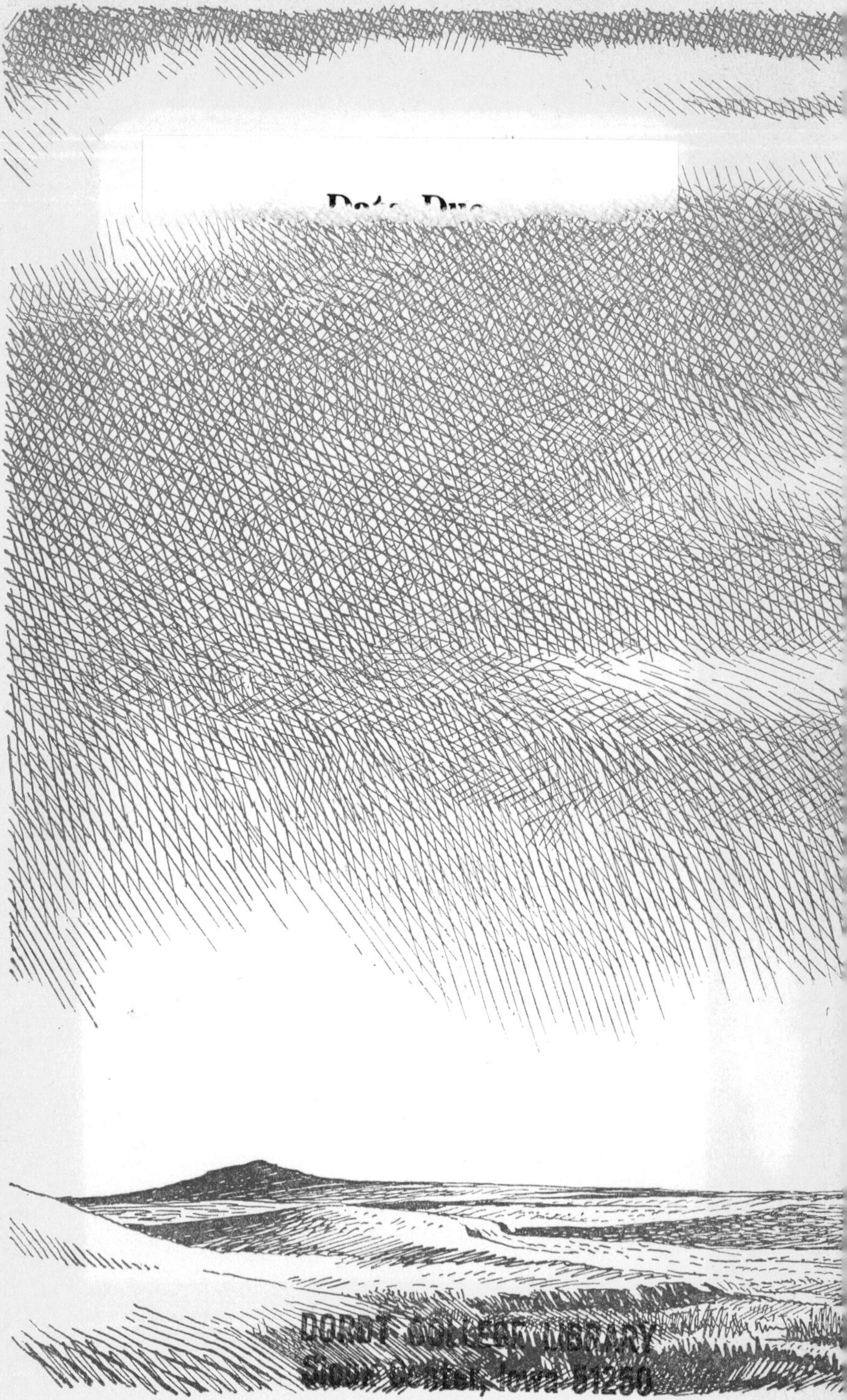